Praise for #1 *New York Times* bestselling author

NORA ROBERTS

"America's favorite writer."

—*The New Yorker*

"When Roberts puts her expert fingers on the pulse of romance, legions of fans feel the heartbeat."

—*Publishers Weekly*

"Roberts' bestselling novels are some of the best in the romance genre."

—*USA TODAY*

"Roberts' style has a fresh, contemporary snap."

—*Kirkus Reviews*

"Nora Roberts is among the best."

—*The Washington Post Book World*

"You can't bottle wish fulfillment, but Nora Roberts certainly knows how to put it on the page."

—*The New York Times*

Also available from Silhouette Books and Harlequin Books by

NORA ROBERTS

AT SUNRISE
A whirlwind summer romance...

A MOTHER'S LOVE
It's never too late for romance...

ONCE AGAIN
You can't turn your back on love...

GETAWAY
Some risks are worth taking...

WHEN WE MEET
One magical moment can change everything...

THE CHRISTMAS WISH
'Tis the season for love...

* * *

Be sure to look for more Nora Roberts titles
at your local stores, or contact our
Harlequin Reader Service Center:
USA: 3010 Walden Avenue
PO Box 1325, Buffalo, NY 14269
Canada: PO Box 609, Fort Erie, Ontario L2A 5X3

Visit Silhouette Books at www.Harlequin.com

NORA ROBERTS

ENDLESS SUMMER

Silhouette® Books
Published by Silhouette Books
America's Publisher of Contemporary Romance

SILHOUETTE BOOKS

Recycling programs for this product may not exist in your area.

Endless Summer

ISBN-13: 978-1-335-91188-9

This edition published by arrangement with Harlequin Books S.A.

For questions and comments about the quality of this book, please contact us at CustomerService@Harlequin.com.

Visit Silhouette Books at www.Harlequin.com

Printed in U.S.A.

CONTENTS

ONE SUMMER

Chapter 1

The room was dark. Pitch-dark. But the man named Shade was used to the dark. Sometimes he preferred it. It wasn't always necessary to see with your eyes. His fingers were both clever and competent, his inner eye as keen as a knife blade.

There were times, even when he wasn't working, when he'd sit in a dark room and simply let images form in his mind. Shapes, textures, colors. Sometimes they came clearer when you shut your eyes and just let your thoughts flow. He courted darkness, shadows, just as relentlessly as he courted the light. It was all part of life, and life—its images—was his profession.

He didn't always see life as others did. At times it was harsher, colder, than the naked eye could see—or wanted to. Other times it was softer, more lovely, than the busy world imagined. Shade observed it, grouped the elements, manipulated time and shape, then recorded it his way. Always his way.

Now, with the room dark and the sound of recorded jazz coming quiet and disembodied from the corner, he worked with his hands and his mind. Care and timing. He used them both in every aspect of his work. Slowly, smoothly, he opened the capsule and transferred the undeveloped film onto the reel. When the light-tight lid was on the developing tank, he set the timer with his free hand, then pulled the chain that added the amber light to the room.

Shade enjoyed developing the negative and making the print as much as, sometimes more than, he enjoyed taking the photograph. Darkroom work required precision and accuracy. He needed both in his life. Making the print allowed for creativity and experimentation. He needed those as well. What he saw, what he felt about what he saw, could be translated exactly or left as an enigma. Above all, he needed the satisfaction of creating something himself, alone. He always worked alone.

Now, as he went through each precise step of developing—temperature, chemicals, agitation, timing—the amber light cast his face into shadows. If Shade had been looking to create the image of photographer at work, he'd never have found a clearer statement than himself.

His eyes were dark, intense now as he added the stop bath to the tank. His hair was dark as well, too long for the convention he cared nothing about. It brushed over his ears, the back of his T-shirt, and fell over his forehead nearly to his eyebrows. He never gave much thought to style. His was cool, almost cold, and rough around the edges.

His face was deeply tanned, lean and hard, with strong bones dominating. His mouth was taut as he concentrated. There were lines spreading out finely from his eyes, etched there by what he'd seen and what he'd felt about it. Some would say there'd already been too much of both.

The nose was out of alignment, a result of a professional hazard. Not everyone liked to have his picture taken. The Cambodian soldier had broken Shade's nose, but Shade had gotten a telling picture of the city's devastation, of the waste. He still considered it an even exchange.

In the amber light, his movements were brisk. He had a rangy, athletic body, the result of years in the field—often a foreign, unfriendly field—miles of legwork and missed meals.

Even now, years after his last staff assignment for *International View,* Shade remained lean and agile. His work wasn't as grueling as it had been in his early years in Lebanon, Laos, Central America, but his pattern hadn't changed. He worked long hours, sometimes waiting endlessly for just the right shot, sometimes using a roll of film within minutes. If his style and manner were aggressive, it could be said that they'd kept him alive and whole during the wars he'd recorded.

The awards he'd won, the fee he now commanded, remained secondary to the picture. If no one had paid him or recognized his work, Shade would still have been in the darkroom, developing his film. He was respected, successful and rich. Yet he had no assistant and continued to work out of the same darkroom he'd set up ten years before.

When Shade hung his negatives up to dry, he already had an idea which ones he'd print. Still, he barely glanced at them, leaving them hanging as he unlocked the darkroom door and stepped out. Tomorrow his outlook would be fresher. Waiting was an advantage he hadn't always had. Right now he wanted a beer. He had some thinking to do.

He headed straight for the kitchen and grabbed a cold bottle. Popping off the lid, he tossed it into the can his once-a-week housekeeper lined with plastic. The room was clean, not particularly cheerful with the hard whites and blacks, but then it wasn't dull.

After he tilted the bottle back, he chugged the beer down, draining half. He lit a cigarette, then took the beer to the kitchen table where he leaned back in a chair and propped his feet on the scrubbed wood surface.

The view out the kitchen window was of a not-so-glamorous L.A. It was a little seamy, rough, sturdy and tough. The early-evening light couldn't make it pretty. He could've moved to a glossier part of town, or out to the hills, where the lights of the city at night looked like a fairy tale. Shade preferred the small apartment that looked out over the unpampered streets of a city known for glitz. He didn't have much patience with glitz.

Bryan Mitchell. She specialized in it.

He couldn't deny that her portraits of the rich, famous and beautiful were well done—even excellent ones of their kind. There was compassion in her photographs, humor and a smooth sensuality. He wouldn't even deny that there was a place for her kind of work in the field. It just wasn't his angle. She reflected culture, he went straight for life.

Her work for *Celebrity* magazine had been professional, slick and often searing in its way. The larger-than-life people she'd photographed had often been cut down to size in a way that made them human and approachable. Since she'd decided to freelance, the stars, near-stars and starmakers she'd photographed for the glossy came to her. Over the years, she'd developed a reputation and style that had made her one of them, part of the inner, select circle.

It could happen to a photographer, he knew. They could come to resemble their own themes, their own studies. Sometimes what they tried to project became a part of them. Too much a part. No, he didn't begrudge Bryan Mitchell her state of the art. Shade simply had doubts about working with her.

He didn't care for partnerships.

Yet those were the terms. When he'd been approached by *Life-style* to do a pictorial study of America, he'd been intrigued. Photo essays could make a strong, lasting statement that could rock and jar or soothe and amuse. As a photographer, he had sought to do that. *Life-style* wanted him, wanted the strong, sometimes concise, sometimes ambiguous emotions his pictures could portray. But they also wanted a counterbalance. A woman's view.

He wasn't so stubborn that he didn't see the point and the possibilities. Yet it irked him to think that the assignment hinged on his willingness to share the summer, his van and the credit with a celebrity photographer. And with a woman at that. Three months on the road with a female who spent her time perfecting snapshots of rock stars and personalities. For a man who'd cut his professional teeth in war-torn Lebanon, it didn't sound like a picnic.

But he wanted to do it. He wanted the chance to capture an American summer from L.A. to New York, showing the joy, the pathos, the sweat, the cheers and disappointments. He wanted to show the heart, even while he stripped it to the bone.

All he had to do was say yes, and share the summer with Bryan Mitchell.

* * *

"Don't think about the camera, Maria. Dance." Bryan lined up the forty-year-old ballet superstar in her viewfinder. She liked what she saw. Age? Touches of it, but years meant nothing. Grit, style, elegance. Endurance—most of all, endurance. Bryan knew how to catch them all and meld them.

Maria Natravidova had been photographed countless times over her phenomenal twenty-five-year career. But never with sweat running down her arms and dampening her leotard. Never with the strain showing. Bryan wasn't looking for the illusions dancers live with, but the exhaustion, the aches that were the price of triumph.

She caught Maria in a leap, legs stretched parallel to the floor, arms flung wide in perfect alignment. Drops of moisture danced from her face and shoulders; muscles bunched and held. Bryan pressed the shutter, then moved the camera slightly to blur the motion.

That would be the one. She knew it even as she finished off the roll of film.

"You make me work," the dancer complained as she slid into a chair, blotting her streaming face with a towel.

Bryan took two more shots, then lowered her camera. "I could've dressed you in costume, backlit you and had you hold an arabesque. That would show that you're beautiful, graceful. Instead I'm going to show that you're a strong woman."

"And you're a clever one." Maria sighed as she let the towel drop. "Why else do I come to you for the pictures for my book?"

"Because I'm the best." Bryan crossed the studio and disappeared into a back room. Maria systematically worked a cramp out of her calf. "Because I understand you, admire you. And—" she brought out a tray, two glasses and a pitcher clinking with ice "—because I squeeze oranges for you."

"Darling." With a laugh, Maria reached for the first glass. For a moment, she held it to her high forehead, then drank deeply. Her dark hair was pulled back severely in a style only good bones and flawless skin could tolerate. Stretching out her long, thin body in the chair, she studied Bryan over the rim of her glass.

Maria had known Bryan for seven years, since the photographer had started at *Celebrity* with the assignment to take pictures of the dancer backstage. The dancer had been a star, but Bryan hadn't shown awe. Maria could still remember the young woman with the thick honey-colored braid and bib overalls. The elegant prima ballerina had found herself confronted with candid eyes the color of pewter, an elegant face with slanting cheekbones and a full mouth. The tall, athletic body had nearly been lost inside the baggy clothes. She'd worn ragged sneakers and long, dangling earrings.

Maria glanced down at the dingy Nikes Bryan wore. Some things didn't change. At first glance, you'd categorize the tall, tanned blonde in sneakers and shorts as typically California. Looks could be deceiving. There was nothing typical about Bryan Mitchell.

Bryan accepted the stare as she drank. "What do you see, Maria?" It interested her to know. Conceptions and preconceptions were part of her trade.

"A strong, smart woman with talent and ambition." Maria smiled as she leaned back in the chair. "Myself, nearly."

Bryan smiled. "A tremendous compliment."

Maria acknowledged this with a sweeping gesture. "There aren't many women I like. Myself I like, and so, you. I hear rumors, my love, about you and that pretty young actor."

"Matt Perkins." Bryan didn't believe in evading or pretending. She lived, by choice, in a town fueled by rumors, fed by gossip. "I took his picture, had a few dinners."

"Nothing serious?"

"As you said, he's pretty." Bryan smiled and chewed on a piece of ice. "But there's barely room enough for his ego and mine in his Mercedes."

"Men." Maria leaned forward to pour herself a second glass.

"Now you're going to be profound."

"Who better?" Maria countered. "Men." She said the word again, savoring it. "I find them tedious, childish, foolish and indispensable. Being loved…sexually, you understand?"

Bryan managed to keep her lips from curving. "I understand."

"Being loved is exhilarating, exhausting. Like Christmas. Sometimes I feel like the child who doesn't understand why Christmas ends. But it does. And you wait for the next time."

It always fascinated Bryan how people felt about love, how they dealt with it, groped for it and avoided it. "Is that why you never married, Maria? You're waiting for the next time?"

"I married dance. To marry a man, I would have to divorce dance. There's no room for two for a woman like me. And you?"

Bryan stared into her drink, no longer amused. She understood the words too well. "No room for two," she murmured. "But I don't wait for the next time."

"You're young. If you could have Christmas every day, would you turn away from it?"

Bryan moved her shoulders. "I'm too lazy for Christmas every day."

"Still, it's a pretty fantasy." Maria rose and stretched. "You've made me work long enough. I have to shower and change. Dinner with my choreographer."

Alone, Bryan absently ran a finger over the back of her camera. She didn't often think about love and marriage. She'd been there already. Once a fantasy was exposed to reality, it faded, like a photo improperly fixed. Permanent relationships rarely worked, and still more rarely worked well.

She thought of Lee Radcliffe, married to Hunter Brown for nearly a year, helping to raise his daughter and pregnant with her first child. Lee was happy, but then she'd found an extraordinary man, one who wanted her to be what she was, even encouraged her to explore herself. Bryan's own experience had taught her that what's said and what's felt can be two opposing things.

Your career's as important to me as it is to you. How many times had Rob said that *before* they'd been married? *Get your degree. Go for it.*

So they'd gotten married, young, eager, idealistic. Within six months he'd been unhappy with the time she'd put into her classes and her job at a local studio. He'd wanted his dinner hot and his socks washed. Not so much to ask, Bryan mused. To be fair, she had to say that Rob had asked for little of her. Just too much at the time.

They'd cared for each other, and both had tried to make adjustments. Both had discovered they'd wanted different things for themselves—different things from each other, things neither could be, neither could give.

It would've been called an amicable divorce—no fury, no bitterness. No passion. A signature on a legal document, and the dream had been over. It had hurt more than anything Bryan had ever known. The taint of failure had stayed with her a long, long time.

She knew Rob had remarried. He was living in the suburbs with his wife and their two children. He'd gotten what he'd wanted.

And so, Bryan told herself as she looked around her studio, had she. She didn't just want to be a photographer. She was a photographer. The hours she spent in the field, in her studio, in the darkroom, were as essential to her as sleep. And what she'd done in the six years since the end of her marriage, she'd done on her own. She didn't have to share it. She didn't have to share her time. Perhaps she was a great deal like Maria. She was a woman who ran her own life, made her own decisions, personally and professionally. Some people weren't made for partnerships.

Shade Colby. Bryan propped her feet on Maria's chair. She might just have to make a concession there. She admired his work. So much so, in fact, that she'd plunked down a heady amount for his print of an L.A. street scene at a time when money had been a large concern. She'd studied it, trying to analyze and guess at the techniques he'd used for setting the shot and making the print. It was a moody piece, so much gray, so little light. And yet, Bryan had sensed a certain grit in it, not hopelessness, but ruthlessness. Still, admiring his work and working with him were two different things.

They were based in the same town, but they moved in different circles. For the most part, Shade Colby didn't move in any circles. He kept to himself. She'd seen him at a handful of photography functions, but they'd never met.

He'd be an interesting subject, she reflected. Given enough time, she could capture that air of aloofness and earthiness on film. Perhaps if they agreed to take the assignment she'd have the chance.

Three months of travel. There was so much of the country she hadn't seen, so many pictures she hadn't taken. Thoughtfully, she pulled a candy bar out of her back pocket and unwrapped it. She liked the idea of taking a slice of America, a season, and pulling the images together. So much could be said.

Bryan enjoyed doing her portraits. Taking a face, a personality, especially a well-known one, and finding out what lay behind it was fascinating. Some might find it limited, but she found it endlessly varied. She could take the tough female rock star and show her vulnerabilities, or pull the humor from the cool, regal megastar. Capturing the unexpected, the fresh—that was the purpose of photography to her.

Now she was being offered the opportunity to do the same thing with a country. The people, she thought. So many people.

She wanted to do it. If it meant sharing the work, the discoveries, the fun, with Shade Colby, she still wanted to do it. She bit into the chocolate. So what if he had a reputation for being cranky and remote? She could get along with anyone for three months.

"Chocolate makes you fat and ugly."

Bryan glanced up as Maria swirled back into the room. The sweat was gone. She looked now as people expected a prima ballerina to look. Draped in silk, studded with diamonds. Cool, composed, beautiful.

"It makes me happy," Bryan countered. "You look fantastic, Maria."

"Yes." Maria brushed a hand down the draping silk at her hip. "But then it's my job to do so. Will you work late?"

"I want to develop the film. I'll send you some test proofs tomorrow."

"And that's your dinner?"

"Just a start." Bryan took a huge bite of chocolate. "I'm sending out for pizza."

"With pepperoni?"

Bryan grinned. "With everything."

Maria pressed a hand to her stomach. "And I eat with my choreographer, the tyrant, which means I eat next to nothing."

"And I'll have a soda instead of a glass of Taittinger. We all have our price to pay."

"If I like your proofs, I'll send you a case."

"Of Taittinger?"

"Of soda." With a laugh, Maria swept out.

An hour later, Bryan hung her negatives up to dry. She'd need to make the proofs to be certain, but out of more than forty shots, she'd probably print no more than five.

When her stomach rumbled, she checked her watch. She'd ordered the pizza for seven-thirty. Well timed, she decided as she left the darkroom. She'd eat and go over the prints of Matt she'd shot for a layout in a glossy. Then she could work on the one she chose until the negatives of Maria were dry. She began rummaging through the two dozen folders on her desk—her personal method of filing—when someone knocked at the studio door.

"Pizza," she breathed, greedy. "Come on in. I'm

starving." Plopping her enormous canvas bag on the desk, Bryan began to hunt for her wallet. "This is great timing. Another five minutes and I might've just faded away. Shouldn't miss lunch." She dropped a fat, ragged notebook, a clear plastic bag filled with cosmetics, a key ring and five candy bars on the desk. "Just set it down anywhere, I'll find the money in a minute." She dug deeper into the bag. "How much do you need?"

"As much as I can get."

"Don't we all." Bryan pulled out a worn man's billfold. "And I'm desperate enough to clean out the safe for you, but…" She trailed off as she looked up and saw Shade Colby.

He gave her face a quick glance, then concentrated on her eyes. "What would you like to pay me for?"

"Pizza." Bryan dropped the wallet onto the desk with half the contents of her purse. "A case of starvation and mistaken identity. Shade Colby." She held out her hand, curious and, to her surprise, nervous. He looked more formidable when he wasn't in a crowd. "I recognize you," she continued, "but I don't think we've met."

"No, we haven't." He took her hand and held it while he studied her face a second time. Stronger than he'd expected. He always looked for the strength first, then the weaknesses. And younger. Though he knew she was only twenty-eight, Shade had expected her to look harder, more aggressive, glossier. Instead, she looked like someone who'd just come in from the beach.

Her T-shirt was snug, but she was slim enough to warrant it. The braid came nearly to her waist and made him speculate on how her hair would look loose and free. Her eyes interested him—gray edging toward silver, and almond-shaped. They were eyes he'd like to photograph with the rest of her face in shadow. She might carry a bag of cosmetics, but it didn't look as if she used any of them.

Not vain about her appearance, he decided. That would make things simpler if he decided to work with her. He didn't have the patience to wait while a woman painted and groomed and fussed. This one wouldn't. And she was assessing him even as he assessed her. Shade accepted that. A photographer, like any artist, looked for angles.

"Am I interrupting your work?"

"No, I was just taking a break. Sit down."

They were both cautious. He'd come on impulse. She wasn't certain how to handle him. Each decided to bide their time before they went beyond the polite, impersonal stage. Bryan remained behind her desk. Her turf, his move, she decided.

Shade didn't sit immediately. Instead, he tucked his hands in his pockets and looked around her studio. It was wide, well lit from the ribbon of windows. There were baby spots and a blue backdrop still set up from an earlier session in one section. Reflectors and umbrellas stood in another, with a camera still on a tripod. He didn't have to look closely to see that the equipment was first-class. But then, first-class equipment didn't make a first-class photographer.

She liked the way he stood, not quite at ease, but ready, remote. If she had to choose now, she'd have photographed him in shadows, alone. But Bryan insisted on knowing the person before she made a portrait.

How old was he? she wondered. Thirty-three, thirty-five. He'd already been nominated for a Pulitzer when she'd still been in college. It didn't occur to her to be intimidated.

"Nice place," he commented before he dropped into the chair opposite the desk.

"Thanks." She tilted her chair so that she could study him from another angle. "You don't use a studio of your own, do you?"

"I work in the field." He drew out a cigarette. "On the rare occasion I need a studio, I can borrow or rent one easily enough."

Automatically she hunted for an ashtray under the chaos on her desk. "You make all your own prints?"

"That's right."

Bryan nodded. On the few occasions at *Celebrity* when she'd been forced to entrust her film to someone else, she hadn't been satisfied. That had been one of the major reasons she'd decided to open her own business. "I love darkroom work."

She smiled for the first time, causing him to narrow his eyes and focus on her face. What kind of power was that? he wondered. A curving of lips, easy and relaxed. It packed one hell of a punch.

Bryan sprang up at the knock on the door. "At last."

Shade watched her cross the room. He hadn't known she was so tall. Five-ten, he estimated, and most of it leg. Long, slender, bronzed leg. It wasn't easy to ignore the smile, but it was next to impossible to ignore those legs.

Nor had he noticed her scent until she moved by him. Lazy sex. He couldn't think of another way to describe it. It wasn't floral, it wasn't sophisticated. It was basic. Shade drew on his cigarette and watched her laugh with the delivery boy.

Photographers were known for their preconceptions; it was part of the trade. He'd expected her to be sleek and cool. That was what he'd nearly resigned himself to working with. Now it was a matter of rearranging his thinking. Did he want to work with a woman who smelled like twilight and looked like a beach bunny?

Turning away from her, Shade opened a folder at random. He recognized the subject—a box-office queen with two Oscars and three husbands under her belt. Bryan had dressed her in glitters and sparkles. Royal trappings for royalty. But she hadn't shot the traditional picture.

The actress was sitting at a table jumbled with pots and tubes of lotions and creams, looking at her own reflection in a mirror and laughing. Not the poised, careful smile that didn't make wrinkles, but a full, robust laugh that could nearly be heard. It was up to the viewer to speculate whether she laughed at her reflection or an image she'd created over the years.

"Like it?" Carrying the cardboard box, Bryan stopped beside him.

"Yeah. Did she?"

Too hungry for formalities, Bryan opened the lid and dug out the first piece. "She ordered a sixteen-by-twenty-four for her fiancé. Want a piece?"

Shade looked inside the box. "They miss putting anything on here?"

"Nope." Bryan searched in a drawer of her desk for napkins and came up with a box of tissues. "I'm a firm believer in overindulgence. So…" With the box opened on the desk between them, Bryan leaned back in her chair and propped up her feet. It was time, she decided, to get beyond the fencing stage. "You want to talk about the assignment?"

Shade took a piece of pizza and a handful of tissues. "Got a beer?"

"Soda—diet or regular." Bryan took a huge, satisfying bite. "I don't keep liquor in the studio. You end up having buzzed clients."

"We'll skip it for now." They ate in silence a moment, still weighing each other. "I've been giving a lot of thought to doing this photo essay."

"It'd be a change for you." When he only lifted a brow, Bryan wadded a tissue and tossed it into the trash can. "Your stuff overseas—it hit hard. There was sensitivity and compassion, but for the most part, it was grim."

"It was a grim time. Everything I shoot doesn't have to be pretty."

This time she lifted a brow. Obviously he didn't think much of the path she'd taken in her career. "Everything I shoot doesn't have to be raw. There's room for fun in art."

He acknowledged this with a shrug. "We'd see different things if we looked through the same lens."

"That's what makes each picture unique." Bryan leaned forward and took another piece.

"I like working alone."

She ate thoughtfully. If he was trying to annoy her, he was right on target. If it was just an overflow of his personality, it still wouldn't make things any easier. Either way, she wanted the assignment, and he was part of it. "I prefer it that way myself," she said slowly. "Sometimes there has to be compromise. You've heard of compromise, Shade. You give, I give. We meet somewhere close to the middle."

She wasn't as laid-back as she looked. Good. The last thing he needed was to go on the road with someone so mellow she threatened to mold. Three months, he thought again. Maybe. Once the ground rules were set. "I map out the route," he began briskly. "We start here in L.A. in two weeks. Each of us is responsible for their own equipment. Once we're on the road, each of us goes our own way. You shoot your pictures, I shoot mine. No questions."

Bryan licked sauce from her finger. "Anyone ever question you, Colby?"

"It's more to the point whether I answer." It was said simply, as it was meant. "The publisher wants both views, so he'll have them. We'll be stopping off and on to rent a darkroom. I'll look over your negatives."

Bryan wadded more tissues. "No, you won't." Lazily, she crossed one ankle over the other. Her eyes had gone to slate, the only outward show of a steadily growing anger.

"I'm not interested in having my name attached to a series of pop-culture shots."

To keep herself in control, Bryan continued to eat. There were things, so many clear, concise things, she'd like to say to him. Temper took a great deal of energy, she reminded herself. It usually accomplished nothing. "The first thing I'll want written into the contract is that each of our pictures carries our own bylines. That way neither of us will be embarrassed by the other's work. I'm not interested in having the public think I have no sense of humor. Want another piece?"

"No." She wasn't soft. The skin on the inside of her elbow might look soft as butter, but the lady wasn't. It might annoy him to be so casually insulted, but he preferred it to spineless agreement. "We'll be gone from June fifteenth until after Labor Day." He watched her scoop up a third piece of pizza. "Since I've seen you eat, we'll each keep track of our own expenses."

"Fine. Now, in case you have any odd ideas, I don't cook and I won't pick up after you. I'll drive my share, but I won't drive with you if you've been drinking. When we rent a darkroom, we trade off as to who uses it first. From June fifteenth to after Labor Day, we're partners. Fifty-fifty. If you have any problems with that, we'll hash it out now, before we sign on the dotted line."

He thought about it. She had a good voice, smooth, quiet, nearly soothing. They might handle the close quarters well enough—as long as she didn't smile at him too often and he kept his mind off her legs. At the moment, he considered that the least of his problems. The assignment came first, and what he wanted for it, and from it.

"Do you have a lover?"

Bryan managed not to choke on her pizza. "If that's an offer," she began smoothly, "I'll have to decline. Rude, brooding men just aren't my type."

Inwardly he acknowledged another hit; outwardly his face remained expressionless. "We're going to be living in each other's pockets for three months." She'd challenged him, whether she realized it or not. Whether he realized it or not, Shade had accepted. He leaned closer. "I don't want to hassle with a jealous lover chasing along after us or constantly calling while I'm trying to work."

Just who did he think she was? Some bimbo who couldn't handle her personal life? She made herself pause a moment. Perhaps he'd had some uncomfortable experiences in his relationships. His problem, Bryan decided.

"I'll worry about my lovers, Shade." Bryan bit into her crust with a vengeance. "You worry about yours." She wiped her fingers on the last of the tissues and smiled. "Sorry to break up the party, but I've got to get back to work."

He rose, letting his gaze skim up her legs before he

met her eyes. He was going to take the assignment. And he'd have three months to figure out just how he felt about Bryan Mitchell. "I'll be in touch."

"Do that."

Bryan waited until he'd crossed the room and shut the studio door behind him. With uncommon energy, and a speed she usually reserved for work, she jumped up and tossed the empty cardboard box at the door.

It promised to be a long three months.

Chapter 2

She knew exactly what she wanted. Bryan might've been a bit ahead of the scheduled starting date for the American Summer project for *Life-style*, but she enjoyed the idea of being a step ahead of Shade Colby. Petty, perhaps, but she did enjoy it.

In any case, she doubted a man like him would appreciate the timeless joy of the last day of school. When else did summer really start, but with that one wild burst of freedom?

She chose an elementary school because she wanted innocence. She chose an inner-city school because she wanted realism. Children who would step out the door and into a limo weren't the image she wanted to project. This school could've been in any city across the country. The kids who'd bolt out the door would be all kids. People who looked at the photograph, no matter what their age, would see something of themselves.

Bryan gave herself plenty of time to set up, choosing and rejecting half a dozen vantage points before she settled on one. It wasn't possible or even advisable to stage the shoot. Only random shots would give her what she wanted—the spontaneity and the rush.

When the bell rang and the doors burst open, she got exactly that. It was well worth nearly being trampled under flying sneakers. With shouts and yells and whistles, kids poured out into the sunshine.

Stampede. That was the thought that went through her mind. Crouching quickly, Bryan shot up, catching the first rush of children at an angle that would convey speed, mass and total confusion.

Let's go, let's go! It's summer and every day's Saturday. September was years away. She could read it on the face of every child.

Turning, she shot the next group of children head-on. In the finished spot, they'd appear to be charging right out of the page of the magazine. On impulse, she shifted her camera for a vertical shot. And she got it. A boy of eight or nine leaped down the flight of steps, hands flung high, a grin splitting his face. Bryan shot him in midair while he hung head and shoulders above the scattering children. She'd captured the boy filled with the triumph of that magic, golden road of freedom spreading out in all directions.

Though she was dead sure which shot she'd print for the assignment, Bryan continued to work. Within ten minutes, it was over.

Satisfied, she changed lenses and angles. The school was empty now, and she wanted to record it that way. She didn't want the feel of bright sunlight here, she decided as she added a low-contrast filter. When she developed the print, Bryan would "dodge" the light in the sky by holding something over that section of the paper to keep it from being overexposed. She wanted the sense of emptiness, of waiting, as a contrast to the life and energy that had just poured out of the building. She'd exhausted a roll of film before she straightened and let the camera hang by its strap.

School's out, she thought with a grin. She felt that charismatic pull of freedom herself. Summer was just beginning.

Since resigning from the staff of *Celebrity*, Bryan had found her work load hadn't eased. If anything, she'd found herself to be a tougher employer than the magazine. She loved her work and was likely to give it all of her day and most of her evenings. Her ex-husband had once accused her of being obsessed not with her camera, but by it. It was something she'd neither been able to deny nor defend. After two days of working with Shade, Bryan had discovered she wasn't alone.

She'd always considered herself a meticulous craftsman. Compared to Shade, she was lackadaisical. He had a patience in his work that she admired even as it set her teeth on edge. They worked from entirely different perspectives. Bryan shot a scene and conveyed her personal viewpoint—her emotions, her feelings about the image. Shade deliberately courted ambiguity. While his photographs might spark off a dozen varied reactions, his personal view almost always remained his secret. Just as everything about him remained half shadowed.

He didn't chat, but Bryan didn't mind working in silence. It was nearly like working alone. His long, quiet looks could be unnerving, however. She didn't care to be dissected as though she were in a viewfinder.

They'd met twice since their first encounter in her

studio, both times to argue out their basic route and the themes for the assignment. She hadn't found him any easier, but she had found him sharp. The project meant enough to both of them to make it possible for them to do as she'd suggested—meet somewhere in the middle.

After her initial annoyance with him had worn off, Bryan had decided they could become friends over the next months—professional friends, in any case. Then, after two days of working with him, she'd known it would never happen. Shade didn't induce simple emotions like friendship. He'd either dazzle or infuriate. She didn't choose to be dazzled.

Bryan had researched him thoroughly, telling herself her reason was routine. You didn't go on the road with a man you knew virtually nothing about. Yet the more she'd found out—rather, the more she hadn't found out—the deeper her curiosity had become.

He'd been married and divorced in his early twenties. That was it—no anecdotes, no gossip, no right and wrong. He covered his tracks well. As a photographer for *International View,* Shade had spent a total of five years overseas. Not in pretty Paris, London and Madrid, but in Laos, Lebanon, Cambodia. His work there had earned him a Pulitzer nomination and the Overseas Press Club Award.

His photographs were available for study and dissection, but his personal life remained obscure. He socialized rarely. What friends he had were unswervingly loyal and frustratingly closedmouthed. If she wanted to learn more about him, Bryan would have to do it on the job.

Bryan considered the fact that they'd agreed to spend their last day in L.A. working at the beach a good sign. They'd decided on the location without any argument.

Beach scenes would be an ongoing theme throughout the essay—California to Cape Cod.

At first they walked along the sand together, like friends or lovers, not touching but in step with each other. They didn't talk, but Bryan had already learned that Shade didn't make idle conversation unless he was in the mood.

It was barely ten, but the sun was bright and hot. Because it was a weekday morning, most of the sun- and water-seekers were the young or the old. When Bryan stopped, Shade kept walking without either of them saying a word.

It was the contrast that had caught her eye. The old woman was bundled in a wide, floppy sun hat, a long beach dress and a crocheted shawl. She sat under an umbrella and watched her granddaughter—dressed only in frilly pink panties—dig a hole in the sand beside her. Sun poured over the little girl. Shadow blanketed the old woman.

She'd need the woman to sign a release form. Invariably, asking someone if you could take her picture stiffened her up, and Bryan avoided it whenever it was possible. In this case it wasn't, so she was patient enough to chat and wait until the woman had relaxed again.

Her name was Sadie, and so was her granddaughter's. Before she'd clicked the shutter the first time, Bryan knew she'd title the print *Two Sadies*. All she had to do was get that dreamy, faraway look back in the woman's eyes.

It took twenty minutes. Bryan forgot she was uncomfortably warm as she listened, thought and reasoned out the angles. She knew what she wanted. The old woman's careful self-preservation, the little girl's total lack of it, and the bond between them that came with blood and time.

Lost in reminiscence, Sadie forgot about the camera, not noticing when Bryan began to release the shutter. She wanted the poignancy—that's what she'd seen. When she printed it, Bryan would be merciless with the lines and creases in the grandmother's face, just as she'd highlight the flawlessness of the toddler's skin.

Grateful, Bryan chatted a few more minutes, then noted the woman's address with the promise of a print. She walked on, waiting for the next scene to unfold.

Shade had his first subject as well, but he didn't chat. The man lay facedown on a faded beach towel. He was red, flabby and anonymous. A businessman taking the morning off, a salesman from Iowa—it didn't matter. Unlike Bryan, he wasn't looking for personality, but for the sameness of those who grilled their bodies under the sun. There was a plastic bottle of tanning lotion stuck in the sand beside him and a pair of rubber beach thongs.

Shade chose two angles and shot six times without exchanging a word with the snoring sunbather. Satisfied, he scanned the beach. Three yards away, Bryan was casually stripping out of her shorts and shirt. The sleek red maillot rose tantalizing high at the thighs. Her profile was to him as she stepped out of her shorts. It was sharp, well defined, like something sculpted with a meticulous hand.

Shade didn't hesitate. He focused her in his viewfinder, set the aperture, adjusted the angle no more than a fraction and waited. At the moment when she reached down for the hem of her T-shirt, he began to shoot.

She was so easy, so unaffected. He'd forgotten anyone could be so totally unselfconscious in a world where self-absorption had become a religion. Her body was one long lean line, with more and more exposed as she drew the shirt over her head. For a moment, she tilted her face up to the sun, inviting the heat. Something crawled into his stomach and began to twist, slowly.

Desire. He recognized it. He didn't care for it.

It was, he could tell himself, what was known in the trade as a decisive moment. The photographer thinks, then shoots, while watching the unfolding scene. When the visual and the emotional elements come together—as they had in this case, with a punch—there was success. There were no replays here, no reshooting. Decisive moment meant exactly that, all or nothing. If he'd been shaken for an instant, it only proved he'd been successful in capturing that easy, lazy sexuality.

Years before, he'd trained himself not to become overly emotional about his subjects. They could eat you alive. Bryan Mitchell might not look as though she'd take a bite out of a man, but Shade didn't take chances. He turned away from her and forgot her. Almost.

It was more than four hours later before their paths crossed again. Bryan sat in the sun near a concession stand, eating a hot dog buried under mounds of mustard and relish. On one side of her she'd set her camera bag, on the other a can of soda. Her narrow red sunglasses shot his reflection back at him.

"How'd it go?" she asked with her mouth full.

"All right. Is there a hot dog under that?"

"Mmm." She swallowed and gestured toward the stand. "Terrific."

"I'll pass." Reaching down, Shade picked up her warming soda and took a long pull. It was orange and sweet. "How the hell do you drink this stuff?"

"I need a lot of sugar. I got some shots I'm pretty

pleased with." She held out a hand for the can. "I want to make prints before we leave tomorrow."

"As long as you're ready at seven."

Bryan wrinkled her nose as she finished off her hot dog. She'd rather work until 7:00 a.m. than get up that early. One of the first things they'd have to iron out on the road was the difference in their biological schedules. She understood the beauty and power of a sunrise shot. She just happened to prefer the mystery and color of sunset.

"I'll be ready." Rising, she brushed sand off her bottom, then pulled her T-shirt over her suit. Shade could've told her she was more modest without it. The way the hem skimmed along her thighs and drew the eyes to them was nearly criminal. "As long as you drive the first shift," she continued. "By ten I'll be functional."

He didn't know why he did it. Shade was a man who analyzed each movement, every texture, shape, color. He cut everything into patterns, then reassembled them. That was his way. Impulse wasn't. Yet he reached out and curled his fingers around her braid without thinking of the act or the consequences. He just wanted to touch.

She was surprised, he could see. But she didn't pull away. Nor did she give him that small half smile women used when a man couldn't resist touching what attracted him.

Her hair was soft; his eyes had told him that, but now his fingers confirmed it. Still, it was frustrating not to feel it loose and free, not to be able to let it play between his fingers.

He didn't understand her. Yet. She made her living recording the elite, the glamorous, the ostentatious, yet she seemed to have no pretensions. Her only jewelry was a thin gold chain that fell to her breasts. On the end was a tiny ankh. Again, she wore no makeup, but her scent was there to tantalize. She could, with a few basic female touches, have turned herself into something breathtaking, but she seemed to ignore the possibilities and rely on simplicity. That in itself was stunning.

Hours before, Bryan had decided she didn't want to be dazzled. Shade was deciding at that moment that he didn't care to be stunned. Without a word, he let her braid fall back to her shoulder.

"Do you want me to take you back to your apartment or your studio?"

So that was it? He'd managed to tie her up in knots in a matter of seconds, and now he only wanted to know where to dump her off. "The studio." Bryan reached down and picked up her camera bag. Her throat was dry, but she tossed the half-full can of soda into the trash. She wasn't certain she could swallow. Before they'd reached Shade's car, she was certain she'd explode if she didn't say something.

"Do you enjoy that cool, remote image you've perfected, Shade?"

He didn't look at her, but he nearly smiled. "It's comfortable."

"Except for the people who get within five feet of you." Damned if she wouldn't get a rise out of him. "Maybe you take your own press too seriously," she suggested. "Shade Colby, as mysterious and intriguing as his name, as dangerous and as compelling as his photographs."

This time he did smile, surprising her. Abruptly he looked like someone she'd want to link hands with, laugh with. "Where in hell did you read that?"

"*Celebrity*," she muttered. "April, five years ago. They did an article on the photo sales in New York. One of your prints sold for seventy-five hundred at Sotheby's."

"Did it?" His gaze slid over her profile. "You've a better memory than I."

Stopping, she turned to face him. "Damn it, I bought it. It's a moody, depressing, fascinating street scene that I wouldn't have given ten cents for if I'd met you first. And if I wasn't so hooked on it, I'd pitch it out the minute I get home. As it is, I'll probably have to turn it to face the wall for six months until I forget that the artist behind it is a jerk."

Shade watched her soberly, then nodded. "You make quite a speech once you're rolling."

With one short, rude word, Bryan turned and started toward the car again. As she reached the passenger side and yanked open the door, Shade stopped her. "Since we're essentially going to be living together for the next three months, you might want to get the rest of it out now."

Though she tried to speak casually, it came out between her teeth. "The rest of what?"

"Whatever griping you have to do."

She took a deep breath first. She hated to be angry. Invariably it exhausted her. Resigned to it, Bryan curled her hands around the top of the door and leaned toward him. "I don't like you. I'd say it's just that simple, but I can't think of anyone else I don't like."

"No one?"

"No one."

For some reason, he believed her. He nodded, then dropped his hands over hers on top of the door. "I'd rather not be lumped in a group in any case. Why should we have to like each other?"

"It'd make the assignment easier."

He considered this while holding her hands beneath his. The tops of hers were soft, the palms of his hard. He liked the contrast, perhaps too much. "You like things easy?"

He made it sound like an insult, and she straightened. Her eyes were on a level with his mouth, and she shifted slightly. "Yes. Complications are just that. They get in the way and muck things up. I'd rather shovel them aside and deal with what's important."

"We've had a major complication before we started."

She might've concentrated on keeping her eyes on his, but that didn't prevent her from feeling the light, firm pressure of his hands. It didn't prevent her from understanding his meaning. Since it was something they'd meticulously avoided mentioning from the beginning, Bryan lunged at it, straight on.

"You're a man and I'm a woman."

He couldn't help but enjoy the way she snarled it at him. "Exactly. We can say we're both photographers and that's a sexless term." He gave her the barest hint of a smile. "It's also bullshit."

"That may be," she said evenly. "But I intend to handle it, because the assignment comes first. It helps a great deal that I don't like you."

"Liking doesn't have anything to do with chemistry."

She gave him an easy smile because her pulse was beginning to pound. "Is that a polite word for lust?"

She wasn't one to dance around an issue once she'd opened it up. Fair enough, he decided. "Whatever you call it, it goes right back to your complication. We'd better take a good look at it, then shove it aside."

When his fingers tightened on hers, she dropped

her gaze to them. She understood his meaning, but not his reason.

"Wondering what it would be like's going to distract both of us," Shade continued. She looked up again, wary. He could feel her pulse throb where his fingers brushed her wrist, yet she'd made no move to pull back. If she had… There was no use speculating; it was better to move ahead. "We'll find out. Then we'll file it, forget it and get on with our job."

It sounded logical. Bryan had a basic distrust of anything that sounded quite so logical. Still, he'd been right on target when he'd said that wondering would be distracting. She'd been wondering for days. His mouth seemed to be the softest thing about him, yet even that looked hard, firm and unyielding. How would it feel? How would it taste?

She let her gaze wander back to it, and the lips curved. She wasn't certain if it was amusement or sarcasm, but it made up her mind.

"All right." How intimate could a kiss be when a car door separated them?

They leaned toward each other slowly, as if each waited for the other to draw back at the last moment. Their lips met lightly, passionlessly. It could've ended then, with each of them shrugging the other off in disinterest. It was the basic definition of a kiss. Two pairs of lips meeting. Nothing more.

Neither one would be able to say who changed it, whether it was calculated or accidental. They were both curious people, and curiosity might have been the factor. Or it might have been inevitable. The texture of the kiss changed so slowly that it wasn't possible to stop it until it was too late for regrets.

Lips opened, invited, accepted. Their fingers clung.

His head tilted, and hers, so that the kiss deepened. Bryan found herself pressing against the hard, unyielding door, searching for more, demanding it, as her teeth nipped at his bottom lip. She'd been right. His mouth was the softest thing about him. Impossibly soft, unreasonably luxurious as it heated on hers.

She wasn't used to wild swings of mood. She'd never experienced anything like it. It wasn't possible to lie back and enjoy. Wasn't that what kisses were for? Up to now, she'd believed so. This one demanded all her strength, all her energy. Even as it went on, she knew when it ended she'd be drained. Wonderfully, totally drained. While she reveled in the excitement, she could anticipate the glory of the aftermath.

He should've known. Damn it, he should've known she wasn't as easy and uncomplicated as she looked. Hadn't he looked at her and ached? Tasting her wasn't going to alleviate any of it, only heighten it. She could undermine his control, and control was essential to his art, his life, his sanity. He'd developed and perfected it over years of sweat, fear and expectations. Shade had learned that the same calculated control he used in the darkroom, the same careful logic he used to set up a shot, could be applied to a woman successfully. Painlessly. One taste of Bryan and he realized just how tenuous control could be.

To prove to himself, perhaps to her, that he could deal with it, he allowed the kiss to deepen, grow darker, moister. Danger hovered, and perhaps he courted it.

He might lose himself in the kiss, but when it was over, it would be over, and nothing would be changed.

She tasted hot, sweet, strong. She made him burn. He had to hold back, or the burn would leave a scar. He had enough of them. Life wasn't as lovely as a first kiss on a hot afternoon. He knew better than most.

Shade drew away, satisfying himself that his control was still in place. Perhaps his pulse wasn't steady, his mind not perfectly clear, but he had control.

Bryan was reeling. If he'd asked her a question, any question, she'd have had no answer. Bracing herself against the car door, she waited for her equilibrium to return. She'd known the kiss would drain her. Even now, she could feel her energy flag.

He saw the look in her eyes, the soft look any man would have to struggle to resist. Shade turned away from it. "I'll drop you at the studio."

As he walked around the car to his side, Bryan dropped down on the seat. File it and forget it, she thought. Fat chance.

She tried. Bryan put so much effort into forgetting what Shade had made her feel that she worked until 3:00 a.m. By the time she'd dragged herself back to her apartment, she'd developed the film from the school and the beach, chosen the negatives she wanted to print and perfected two of them into what she considered some of her best work.

Now she had four hours to eat, pack and sleep. After building herself an enormous sandwich, Bryan took out the one suitcase she'd been allotted for the trip and tossed in the essentials. Groggy with fatigue, she washed down bread, meat and cheese with a great gulp of milk. None of it felt too steady on her stomach, so she left her partially eaten dinner on the bedside table and went back to her packing.

She rummaged in the top of her closet for the box with the prim man-tailored pajamas her mother had given her for Christmas. Definitely essential, she decided as she dropped them on the disordered pile of lingerie and jeans. They were sexless, Bryan mused. She could only hope she felt sexless in them. That afternoon she'd been forcibly reminded that she was a woman, and a woman had some vulnerabilities that couldn't always be defended.

She didn't want to feel like a woman around Shade again. It was too perilous, and she avoided perilous situations. Since she wasn't the type to make a point of her femininity, there should be no problem.

She told herself.

Once they were started on the assignment, they'd be so wound up in it that they wouldn't notice if the other had two heads and four thumbs.

She told herself.

What had happened that afternoon was simply one of those fleeting moments the photographer sometimes came across when the moment dictated the scene. It wouldn't happen again, because the circumstances would never be the same.

She told herself.

And then she was finished thinking of Shade Colby. It was nearly four, and the next three hours were all hers, the last she had left to herself for a long time. She'd spend them the way she liked best. Asleep. Stripping, Bryan let her clothes fall in a heap, then crawled into bed without remembering to turn off the light.

Across town, Shade lay in the dark. He hadn't slept, although he'd been packed for hours. His bag and his equipment were neatly stacked at the door. He was organized, prepared and wide-awake.

He'd lost sleep before. The fact didn't concern him,

but the reason did. Bryan Mitchell. Though he'd managed to push her to the side, to the back, to the corner of his mind throughout the evening, he couldn't quite get her out.

He could dissect what had happened between them that afternoon point by point, but it didn't change one essential thing. He'd been vulnerable. Perhaps only for an instant, only a heartbeat, but he'd been vulnerable. That was something he couldn't afford. It was something he wouldn't allow to happen a second time.

Bryan Mitchell was one of the complications she claimed she liked to avoid. He, on the other hand, was used to them. He'd never had any problem dealing with complications. She'd be no different.

He told himself.

For the next three months, they'd be deep into a project that should totally involve all their time and energy. When he worked, he was well able to channel his concentration on one point and ignore everything else. That was no problem.

He told himself.

What had happened had happened. He still believed it was best done away with before they started out—best that they did away with the speculation and the tension it could cause. They'd eliminated the tension.

He told himself.

But he couldn't sleep. The ache in his stomach had nothing to do with the dinner that had grown cold on his plate, untouched.

He had three hours to himself, then he'd have three months of Bryan. Closing his eyes, Shade did what he was always capable of doing under stress. He willed himself to sleep.

Chapter 3

Bryan was up and dressed by seven, but she wasn't ready to talk to anyone. She had her suitcase and tripod in one hand, with two camera bags and her purse slung crosswise over her shoulders. As Shade pulled up to the curb, she was walking down the stairs and onto the sidewalk. She believed in being prompt, but not necessarily cheerful.

She grunted to Shade; it was as close to a greeting as she could manage at that hour. In silence, she loaded her gear into his van, then kicked back in the passenger seat, stretched out her legs and closed her eyes.

Shade looked at what he could see of her face behind round, amber-lensed sunglasses and under a battered straw hat. "Rough night?" he asked, but she was already asleep. Shaking his head, he released the brake and pulled out into the street. They were on their way.

Shade didn't mind long drives. They gave him a

chance to think or not think, as he chose. In less than an hour, he was out of L.A. traffic and heading northeast on the interstate. He liked riding into the rising sun with a clear road ahead. Light bounced off the chrome on the van, shimmered on the hood and sliced down on the road signs.

He planned to cover five or six hundred miles that day, leading up toward Utah, unless something interesting caught his eye and they stopped for a shoot. After this first day, he saw no reason for them to be mileage-crazy. It would hamper the point of the assignment. They'd drive as they needed to, working toward and around the definite destinations they'd ultimately agreed on.

He had a route that could easily be altered, and no itinerary. Their only time frame was to be on the East Coast by Labor Day. He turned the radio on low and found some gritty country music as he drove at a steady, mile-eating pace. Beside him, Bryan slept.

If this was her routine, he mused, they wouldn't have any problems. As long as she was asleep, they couldn't grate on each other's nerves. Or stir each other's passion. Even now he wondered why thoughts of her had kept him restless throughout the night. What was it about her that had worried him? He didn't know, and that was a worry in itself.

Shade liked to be able to put his finger on things and pick a problem apart until the pieces were small enough to rearrange to his preference. Even though she was quiet, almost unobtrusive, at the moment, he didn't believe he'd be able to do that with Bryan Mitchell.

After his decision to take the assignment, he'd made it his business to find out more about her. Shade might guard his personal life and snarl over his privacy, but he wasn't at a loss for contacts. He'd known of her work for

Celebrity, and her more inventive and personalized work for magazines like *Vanity* and *In Touch.* She'd developed into something of a cult artist over the years with her offbeat, often radical photographs of the famous.

What he hadn't known was that she was the daughter of a painter and a poet, both eccentric and semisuccessful residents of Carmel. She'd been married to an accountant before she was twenty, and divorced him three years later. She dated with an almost studied casualness, and she had vague plans about buying a beach house at Malibu. She was well liked, respected and, by all accounts, dependable. She was often slow in doing things—a combination of her need for perfection and her belief that rushing was a waste of energy.

He'd found nothing surprising in his research, and no clue as to his attraction to her. But a photographer, a successful one, was patient. Sometimes it was necessary to come back to a subject again and again until you understood your own emotion toward it.

As they crossed the border into Nevada, Shade lit a cigarette and rolled down his window. Bryan stirred, grumbled, then groped for her bag.

"Morning." Shade sent her a brief, sidelong look.

"Mmm-hmm." Bryan rooted through the bag, then gripped the chocolate bar in relief. With two quick rips, she unwrapped it and tossed the trash in her purse. She usually cleaned it out before it overflowed.

"You always eat candy for breakfast?"

"Caffeine." She took a huge bite and sighed. "I prefer mine this way." Slowly, she stretched, torso, shoulders, arms, in one long, sinuous move that was completely unplanned. It was, Shade thought ironically, one definitive clue as to the attraction. "So where are we?"

"Nevada." He blew out a stream of smoke that whipped out the open window. "Just."

Bryan folded her legs under her as she nibbled on the candy bar. "It must be about my shift."

"I'll let you know."

"Okay." She was content to ride as long as he was content to drive. She did, however, give a meaningful glance at the radio. Country music wasn't her style. "Driver picks the tunes."

He shrugged his acceptance. "If you want to wash that candy down with something, there's some juice in a jug in the back."

"Yeah?" Always interested in putting something into her stomach, Bryan unfolded herself and worked her way into the back of the van.

She hadn't paid any attention to the van that morning, except for a bleary scan that told her it was black and well cared-for. There were padded benches along each side that could, if you weren't too choosy, be suitable for beds. Bryan thought the pewter carpet might be the better choice.

Shade's equipment was neatly secured, and hers was loaded haphazardly into a corner. Above, glossy ebony cabinets held some essentials. Coffee, a hot plate, a small teakettle. They'd come in handy, she thought, if they stopped in any campgrounds with electric hookups. In the meantime, she settled for the insulated jug of juice.

"Want some?"

He glanced in the rearview mirror to see her standing, legs spread for balance, one hand resting on the cabinet. "Yeah."

Bryan took two jumbo plastic cups and the jug back to her seat. "All the comforts of home," she commented with a jerk of her head toward the back. "Do you travel in this much?"

"When it's necessary." He heard the ice thump against the cup and held out his hand. "I don't like to fly. You lose any chance you'd have at getting a shot at something on the way." After flipping his cigarette out the window, he drank his juice. "If it's an assignment within five hundred miles or so, I drive."

"I hate to fly." Bryan propped herself in the V between the seat and the door. "It seems I'm forever having to fly to New York to photograph someone who can't or won't come to me. I take a bottle of Dramamine, a supply of chocolate bars, a rabbit's foot and a socially significant, educational book. It covers all the bases."

"The Dramamine and the rabbit's foot, maybe."

"The chocolate's for my nerves. I like to eat when I'm tense. The book's a bargaining point." She shook her cup so the ice clinked. "I feel like I'm saying—see, I'm doing something worthwhile here. Let's not mess it up by crashing the plane. Then, too, the book usually puts me to sleep within twenty minutes."

The corner of Shade's mouth lifted, something Bryan took as a hopeful sign for the several thousand miles they had to go. "That explains it."

"I have a phobia about flying at thirty thousand feet in a heavy tube of metal with two hundred strangers, many of whom like to tell the intimate details of their lives to the person next to them." Propping her feet on the dash, she grinned. "I'd rather drive across country with one cranky photographer who makes it a point to tell me as little as possible."

Shade sent her a sidelong look and decided there was no harm in playing the game as long as they both knew the rules. "You haven't asked me anything."

"Okay, we'll start with something basic. Where'd Shade come from? The name, I mean."

He slowed down, veering off toward a rest stop. "Shadrach."

Her eyes widened in appreciation. "As in Meshach and Abednego in the Book of Daniel?"

"That's right. My mother decided to give each of her offspring a name that would roll around a bit. I've a sister named Cassiopeia. Why Bryan?"

"My parents wanted to show they weren't sexist."

The minute the van stopped in a parking space, Bryan hopped out, bent from the waist and touched her palms to the asphalt—much to the interest of the man climbing into the Pontiac next to her. With the view fuddling his concentration, it took him a full thirty seconds to fit his key in the ignition.

"God, I get so stiff!" She stretched up, standing on her toes, then dropped down again. "Look, there's a snack bar over there. I'm going to get some fries. Want some?"

"It's ten o'clock in the morning."

"Almost ten-thirty," she corrected. "Besides, people eat hash browns for breakfast. What's the difference?"

He was certain there was one, but didn't feel like a debate. "You go ahead. I want to buy a paper."

"Fine." As an afterthought, Bryan climbed back inside and grabbed her camera. "I'll meet you back here in ten minutes."

Her intentions were good, but she took nearly twenty. Even as she approached the snack bar, the formation of the line of people waiting for fast food caught her imagination. There were perhaps ten people wound out like a snake in front of a sign that read Eat Qwik.

They were dressed in baggy Bermudas, wrinkled

sundresses and cotton pants. A curvy teenager had on a pair of leather shorts that looked as though they'd been painted on. A woman six back from the stand fanned herself with a wide-brimmed hat banded with a floaty ribbon.

They were all going somewhere, all waiting to get there, and none of them paid any attention to anyone else. Bryan couldn't resist. She walked up the line one way, down it another, until she found her angle.

She shot them from the back so that the line seemed elongated and disjointed and the sign loomed promisingly. The man behind the counter serving food was nothing more than a vague shadow that might or might not have been there. She'd taken more than her allotted ten minutes before she joined the line herself.

Shade was leaning against the van reading the paper when she returned. He'd already taken three calculated shots of the parking lot, focusing on a line of cars with license plates from five different states. When he glanced up, Bryan had her camera slung over her shoulder, a giant chocolate shake in one hand and a jumbo order of fries smothered in ketchup in the other.

"Sorry." She dipped into the box of fries as she walked. "I got a couple of good shots of the line at the snack bar. Half of summer's hurry up and wait, isn't it?"

"Can you drive with all that?"

"Sure." She swung into the driver's side. "I'm used to it." She balanced the shake between her thighs, settled the fries just ahead of it and reached out a hand for the keys.

Shade glanced down at the breakfast snuggled between very smooth, very brown legs. "Still willing to share?"

Bryan turned her head to check the rearview as she

backed out. "Nope." She gave the wheel a quick turn and headed toward the exit. "You had your chance." With one competent hand steering, she dug into the fries again.

"You eat like that, you should have acne down to your navel."

"Myths," she announced, and zoomed past a slower-moving sedan. With a few quick adjustments, she had an old Simon and Garfunkel tune pouring out of the radio. "That's music," she told him. "I like songs that give me a visual. Country music's usually about hurting and cheating and drinking."

"And life."

Bryan picked up her shake and drew on the straw. "Maybe. I guess I get tired of too much reality. Your work depends on it."

"And yours often skirts around it."

Her brows knit, then she deliberately relaxed. In his way, he was right. "Mine gives options. Why'd you take this assignment, Shade?" she asked suddenly. "Summer in America exemplifies fun. That's not your style."

"It also equals sweat, crops dying from too much sun and frazzled nerves." He lit another cigarette. "More my style?"

"You said it, I didn't." She swirled the chocolate in her mouth. "You smoke like that, you're going to die."

"Sooner or later." Shade opened the paper again and ended the conversation.

Who the hell was he? Bryan asked herself as she leveled the speed at sixty. What factors in his life had brought out the cynicism as well as the genius? There was humor in him—she'd seen it once or twice. But he seemed to allow himself only a certain degree and no more.

Passion? She could attest firsthand that there was a powder keg inside him. What might set it off? If she was certain of one thing about Shade Colby, it was that he held himself in rigid control. The passion, the power, the fury—whatever label you gave it—escaped into his work, but not, she was certain, into his personal life. Not often, in any case.

She knew she should be careful and distant; it would be the smartest way to come out of this long-term assignment without scars. Yet she wanted to dig into his character, and she knew she'd have to give in to the temptation. She'd have to press the buttons and watch the results, probably because she didn't like him and was attracted to him at the same time.

She'd told him the truth when she'd said that she couldn't think of anyone else she didn't like. It went hand in hand with her approach to her art—she looked into a person and found qualities, not all of them admirable, not all of them likable, but something, always something, that she could understand. She needed to do that with Shade, for herself. And because, though she'd bide her time telling him, she wanted very badly to photograph him.

"Shade, I want to ask you something else."

He didn't glance up from the paper. "Hmm?"

"What's your favorite movie?"

Half annoyed at the interruption, half puzzled at the question, he looked up and found himself wondering yet again what her hair would look like out of that thick, untidy braid. "What?"

"Your favorite movie," she repeated. "I need a clue, a starting point."

"For what?"

"To find out why I find you interesting, attractive and unlikable."

"You're an odd woman, Bryan."

"No, not really, though I have every right to be." She stopped speaking a moment as she switched lanes. "Come on, Shade, it's going to be a long trip. Let's humor each other on the small points. Give me a movie."

"*To Have and Have Not.*"

"Bogart and Bacall's first together." It made her smile at him in the way he'd already decided was dangerous. "Good. If you'd named some obscure French film, I'd have had to find something else. Why that one?"

He set the paper aside. So she wanted to play games. It was harmless, he decided. And they still had a long day ahead of them. "On-screen chemistry, tight plotting and camera work that made Bogart look like the consummate hero and Bacall the only woman who could stand up to him."

She nodded, pleased. He wasn't above enjoying heroes, fantasies and bubbling relationships. It might've been a small point, but she could like him for it. "Movies fascinate me, and the people who make them. I suppose that was one of the reasons I jumped at the chance to work for *Celebrity*. I've lost count of the number of actors I've shot, but when I see them up on the screen, I'm still fascinated."

He knew it was dangerous to ask questions, not because of the answers, but because of the questions you'd be asked in return. Still, he wanted to know. "Is that why you photograph the beautiful people? Because you want to get close to the glamour?"

Because she considered it a fair question, Bryan decided not to be annoyed. Besides, it made her think about something that had simply seemed to evolve, almost unplanned. "I might've started out with something like that in mind. Before long, you come to see them as ordinary people with extraordinary jobs. I like finding that spark that's made them the chosen few."

"Yet for the next three months you're going to be photographing the everyday. Why?"

"Because there's a spark in all of us. I'd like to find it in a farmer in Iowa, too."

So he had his answer. "You're an idealist, Bryan."

"Yes." She gave him a frankly interested look. "Should I be ashamed of it?"

He didn't like the way the calm, reasonable question affected him. He'd had ideals of his own once, and he knew how much it hurt to have them rudely taken away. "Not ashamed," he said after a moment. "Careful."

They drove for hours. In midafternoon, they switched positions and Bryan skimmed through Shade's discarded paper. By mutual consent, they left the freeway and began to travel over back roads. The pattern became sporadic conversations and long silences. It was early evening when they crossed the border into Idaho.

"Skiing and potatoes," Bryan commented. "That's all I can think of when I think of Idaho." With a shiver, she rolled up her window. Summer came slower in the north, especially when the sun was low. She gazed out the glass at the deepening twilight.

Sheep, hundreds of them, in what seemed like miles of gray or white bundles, were grazing lazily on the tough grass that bordered the road. She was a woman of the city, of freeways and office buildings. It might've surprised Shade to know she'd never been this far north, nor this far east except by plane.

The acres of placid sheep fascinated her. She was

reaching for her camera when Shade swore and hit the brakes. Bryan landed on the floor with a plop.

"What was that for?"

He saw at a glance that she wasn't hurt, not even annoyed, but simply curious. He didn't bother to apologize. "Damn sheep in the road."

Bryan hauled herself up and looked out the windshield. There were three of them lined unconcernedly across the road, nearly head to tail. One of them turned its head and glanced up at the van, then looked away again.

"They look like they're waiting for a bus," she decided, then grabbed Shade's wrist before he could lean on the horn. "No, wait a minute. I've never touched one."

Before Shade could comment, she was out of the van and walking toward them. One of them shied a few inches away as she approached, but for the most part, the sheep couldn't have cared less. Shade's annoyance began to fade as she leaned over and touched one. He thought another woman might look the same as she stroked a sable at a furrier. Pleased, tentative and oddly sexual. And the light was good. Taking his camera, he selected a filter.

"How do they feel?"

"Soft—not as soft as I'd thought. Alive. Nothing like a lamb's-wool coat." Still bent over, one hand on the sheep, Bryan looked up. It surprised her to be facing a camera. "What's that for?"

"Discovery." He'd already taken two shots, but he wanted more. "Discovery has a lot to do with summer. How do they smell?"

Intrigued, Bryan leaned closer to the sheep. He framed her when her face was all but buried in the wool. "Like sheep," she said with a laugh, and straightened. "Want to play with the sheep and I'll take your picture?"

"Maybe next time."

She looked as if she belonged there, on the long deserted road surrounded by stretches of empty land, and it puzzled him. He'd thought she set well in L.A., in the center of the glitz and illusions.

"Something wrong?" She knew he was thinking of her, only of her, when he looked at her like that. She wished she could've taken it a step further, yet was oddly relieved that she couldn't.

"You acclimate well."

Her smile was hesitant. "It's simpler that way. I told you I don't like complications."

He turned back to the truck, deciding he was thinking about her too much. "Let's see if we can get these sheep to move."

"But, Shade, you can't just leave them on the side of the road." She jogged back to the van. "They'll wander right back out. They might get run over."

He gave her a look that said he clearly wasn't interested. "What do you expect me to do? Round 'em up?"

"The least we can do is get them back over the fence." As if he'd agreed wholeheartedly, Bryan turned around and started back to the sheep. As he watched, she reached down, hauled one up and nearly toppled over. The other two bleated and scattered.

"Heavier than they look," she managed, and began to stagger toward the fence strung along the shoulder of the road while the sheep she carried bleated, kicked and struggled. It wasn't easy, but after a test of wills and brute strength, she dropped the sheep over the fence. With one hand, she swiped at the sweat on her forehead as she turned to scowl at Shade. "Well, are you going to help or not?"

He'd enjoyed the show, but he didn't smile as he

leaned against the van. “They’ll probably find the hole in the fence again and be back on the road in ten minutes.”

“Maybe they will,” Bryan said between her teeth as she headed for the second sheep. “But I’ll have done what should be done.”

“Idealist,” he said again.

With her hands on her hips, she whirled around. “Cynic.”

“As long as we understand each other.” Shade straightened. “I’ll give you a hand.”

The others weren’t as easily duped as the first. It took Shade several exhausting minutes to catch number two, with Bryan running herd. Twice he lost his concentration and his quarry because her sudden husky laughter distracted him.

“Two down and one to go,” he announced as he set the sheep free in the pasture.

“But this one looks stubborn.” From opposite sides of the road, the rescuers and the rescuee studied each other. “Shifty eyes,” Bryan murmured. “I think he’s the leader.”

“She.”

“Whatever. Look, just be nonchalant. You walk around that side, I’ll walk around this side. When we have her in the middle, wham!”

Shade sent her a cautious look. “Wham?”

“Just follow my lead.” Tucking her thumbs in her back pockets, she strolled across the road, whistling.

“Bryan, you’re trying to outthink a sheep.”

She sent him a bland look over her shoulder. “Maybe between the two of us we can manage to.”

He wasn’t at all sure she was joking. His first urge was to simply get back in the van and wait until she’d finished making a fool of herself. Then again, they’d already wasted enough time. Shade circled around to the left as Bryan moved to the right. The sheep eyed them both, swiveling her head from side to side.

"Now!" Bryan shouted, and dived.

Without giving himself the chance to consider the absurdity, Shade lunged from the other side. The sheep danced delicately away. Momentum carrying them both, Shade and Bryan collided, then rolled together onto the soft shoulder of the road. Shade felt the rush of air as they slammed into each other, and the soft give of her body as they tumbled together.

With the breath knocked out of her, Bryan lay on her back, half under Shade. His body was very hard and very male. She might not have had her wind, but Bryan had her wit. She knew if they stayed like this, things were going to get complicated. Drawing in air, she stared up into his face just above her.

His look was contemplative, considering and not altogether friendly. He wouldn't be a friendly lover, that she knew instinctively. It was in his eyes—those dark, deepset eyes. He was definitely a man to avoid having a personal involvement with. He'd overwhelm quickly, completely, and there'd be no turning back. She had to remind herself that she preferred easy relationships, as her heart started a strong, steady rhythm.

"Missed," she managed to say, but didn't try to move away.

"Yeah." She had a stunning face, all sharp angles and soft skin. Shade could nearly convince himself that his interest in it was purely professional. She'd photograph wonderfully from any angle, in any light. He could make her look like a queen or a peasant, but she'd always look like a woman a man would want. The lazy sexuality he could sense in her would come across in the photograph.

Just looking at her, he could plot half a dozen settings he'd like to shoot her in. And he could think of dozens of ways he'd like to make love to her. Here was first, on the cool grass along the roadside with the sun setting behind them and no sound.

She saw the decision in his eyes, saw it in time to avoid the outcome. But she didn't. She had only to shift away, only to protest with one word or a negative movement. But she didn't. Her mind told her to, arguing with an urge that was unarguably physical. Later, Bryan would wonder why she hadn't listened. Now, with the air growing cool and the sky darkening, she wanted the experience. She couldn't admit that she wanted him.

When he lowered his mouth to hers, there wasn't any of the light experimentation of the first time. Now he knew her and wanted the full impact of her passion. Their mouths met greedily, as if each one were racing the other to delirium.

Her body heated so quickly that the grass seemed to shimmer like ice beneath her. She wondered it didn't melt. It was a jolt that left her bewildered. With a small sound in her throat, Bryan reached for more. His fingers were in her hair, tangled in the restriction of her braid as if he didn't choose, or didn't dare, to touch her yet. She moved under him, not in retreat but in advance. Hold me, she seemed to demand. Give me more. But he continued to make love only to her mouth. Devastatingly.

She could hear the breeze; it tickled through the grass beside her ear and taunted her. He'd give sparingly of himself. She could feel it in the tenseness of his body. He'd hold back. While his mouth stripped away her defenses, one by one, he held himself apart. Frustrated, Bryan ran her hands up his back. She'd seduce.

Shade wasn't used to the pressure to give, to the

desire to. She drew from him a need for merging he'd thought he'd beaten down years before. There seemed to be no pretenses in her—her mouth was warm and eager, tasting of generosity. Her body was soft and agile, tempting. Her scent drifted around him, sexual, uncomplicated. When she said his name, there seemed to be no hidden meaning. For the first time in too long for him to remember, he wanted to give, unheedingly, boundlessly.

He held himself back. Pretenses, he knew, could be well hidden. But he was losing to her. Even though Shade was fully aware of it, he couldn't stop it. She drew and drew from him, with a simplicity that couldn't be blocked. He might've sworn against it, cursed her, cursed himself, but his mind was beginning to swim. His body was throbbing.

They both felt the ground tremble, but it didn't occur to either of them that it was anything but their own passion. They heard the noise, the rumble, growing louder and louder, and each thought it was inside his or her own head. Then the wind rocketed by them and the truck driver gave one long, rude blast of the horn. It was enough to jolt them back to sanity. Feeling real panic for the first time, Bryan scrambled to her feet.

"We'd better take care of that sheep and get going." She swore at the breathiness of her own voice and wrapped her arms protectively around herself. There was a chill in the air, she thought desperately. That was all. "It's nearly dark."

Shade hadn't realized how deep the twilight had become. He'd lost track of his surroundings—something he never allowed to happen. He'd forgotten that they were on the side of the road, rolling in the grass like a couple of brainless teenagers. He felt the lick of anger, but stemmed it. He'd nearly lost control once. He wouldn't lose it now.

She caught the sheep on the other side of the road, where it grazed, certain that both humans had lost interest. It bleated in surprised protest as she scooped it up. Swearing under his breath, Shade stalked over and grabbed the sheep from her before Bryan could take another tumble. He dumped it unceremoniously in the pasture.

"Satisfied now?" he demanded.

She could see the anger in him, no matter how tightly he reined it in. Her own bubbled. She'd had her share of frustrations as well. Her body was pulsing, her legs were unsteady. Temper helped her to forget them.

"No," she tossed back. "And neither are you. It seems to me that should prove to both of us that we'd better keep a nice, clean distance."

He grabbed her arm as she started to swing past. "I didn't force you into anything, Bryan."

"Nor I you," she reminded him. "I'm responsible for my own actions, Shade." She glanced down at the hand that was curled around her arm. "And my own mistakes. If you like to shift blame, it's your prerogative."

His fingers tightened on her arm, briefly, but long enough for her eyes to widen in surprise at the strength and the depth of his anger. No, she wasn't used to wild swings of mood in herself or to causing them in others.

Slowly, and with obvious effort, Shade loosened his grip. She'd hit it right on the mark. He couldn't argue with honesty.

"No," he said a great deal more calmly. "I'll take my share, Bryan. It'll be easier on both of us if we agree to that nice, clean distance."

She nodded, steadier. Her lips curved into a slight

smile. "Okay." Lighten up, she warned herself, for everyone's sake. "It'd have been easier from the beginning if you'd been fat and ugly."

He'd grinned before he'd realized it. "You, too."

"Well, since I don't suppose either of us is willing to do anything about that particular problem, we just have to work around it. Agreed?" She held out her hand.

"Agreed."

Their hands joined. A mistake. Neither of them had recovered from the jolt to their systems. The contact, however casual, only served to accentuate it. Bryan linked her hands behind her back. Shade dipped his into his pockets.

"Well..." Bryan began, with no idea where to go.

"Let's find a diner before we head into camp. Tomorrow's going to start early."

She wrinkled her nose at that but started toward her side of the truck. "I'm starving," she announced, and pretended she was in control by propping her feet on the dash. "Think we'll find something decent to eat soon, or should I fortify myself with a candy bar?"

"There's a town about ten miles down this road." Shade turned on the ignition. His hand was steady, he told himself. Or nearly. "Bound to be a restaurant of some kind. Probably serve great lamb chops."

Bryan looked at the sheep grazing beside them, then sent Shade a narrowed-eyed glance. "That's disgusting."

"Yeah, and it'll keep your mind off your stomach until we eat."

They bumped back onto the road and drove in silence. They'd made it over a hump, but each of them knew there'd be mountains yet to struggle over. Steep, rocky mountains.

Chapter 4

Bryan recorded vacationers floating like corks in the Great Salt Lake. When the shot called for it, she used a long or a wide-angle lens to bring in some unusual part of the landscape. But for the most part, Bryan concentrated on the people.

In the salt flats to the west, Shade framed race car enthusiasts. He angled for the speed, the dust, the grit. More often than not, the people included in his pictures would be anonymous, blurred, shadowy. He wanted only the essence.

Trips to large cities and through tidy suburbs used up rolls of film. There were summer gardens, hot, sweaty traffic jams, young girls in thin dresses, shirtless men, and babies in strollers being pushed along sidewalks and in shopping malls.

Their route through Idaho and Utah had been winding, but steady. Neither was displeased with the pace or the subjects. For a time, after the turbulent detour on the country road in Idaho, Bryan and Shade worked side by side in relative harmony. They concentrated on their own subjects, but they did little as a team.

They'd already taken hundreds of pictures, a fraction of which would be printed and still a smaller fraction published. Once it occurred to Bryan that the pictures they'd taken far outnumbered the words they'd spoken to each other.

They drove together up to eight hours a day, stopping along the way whenever it was necessary or desirable to work. And they worked as much as they drove. Out of each twenty-four hours, they were together an average of twenty. But they grew no closer. It was something either of them might have accomplished with the ease of a friendly gesture or a few casual words. It was something both of them avoided.

Bryan learned it was possible to keep an almost obsessive emotional distance from someone while sharing a limited space. She also learned a limited space made it very difficult to ignore what Shade had once termed chemistry. To balance the two, Bryan kept her conversations light and brief and almost exclusively centered on the assignment. She asked no more questions. Shade volunteered no more information.

By the time they crossed the border into Arizona, at the end of the first week, she was already finding it an uncomfortable way to work.

It was hot. The sun was merciless. The van's air-conditioning helped, but just looking out at the endless desert and faded sage made the mouth dry. Bryan had an enormous paper cup filled with soda and ice. Shade drank bottled iced tea as he drove.

She estimated that they hadn't exchanged a word

for fifty-seven miles. Nor had they spoken much that morning when they'd set up to shoot, each in separate territory, at Glen Canyon in Utah. Bryan might be pleased with the study she'd done of the cars lined up at the park's entrance, but she was growing weary of their unspoken agreement of segregation.

The magazine had hired them as a team, she reminded herself. Each of them would take individual pictures, naturally, but there had to be some communication if the photo essay were to have any cohesion. There had to be some blending if the final result was the success both of them wanted. Compromise, she remembered with a sigh. They'd forgotten the operative word.

Bryan thought she knew Shade well enough at this point to be certain he'd never make the first move. He was perfectly capable of driving thousands of miles around the country without saying her name more than once a day. As in, Pass the salt, Bryan.

She could be stubborn. Bryan thought about it as she brooded out the window at the wide stretches of Arizona. She could be just as aloof as he. And, she admitted with a grimace, she could bore herself to death within another twenty-four hours.

Contact, she decided. She simply couldn't survive without some kind of contact. Even if it was with a hard-edged, casually rude cynic. Her only choice was to swallow her pride and make the first move herself. She gritted her teeth, gnawed on ice and thought about it for another ten minutes.

"Ever been to Arizona?"

Shade tossed his empty bottle into the plastic can they used for trash. "No."

Bryan pried off one sneaker with the toe of the other. If at first you don't succeed, she told herself. "They filmed

Outcast in Sedona. Now that was a tough, thinking-man's Western," she mused, and received no response. "I spent three days there covering the filming for *Celebrity.*" After adjusting her sun visor, she sat back again. "I was lucky enough to miss my plane and get another day. I spent it in Oak Creek Canyon. I've never forgotten it—the colors, the rock formations."

It was the longest speech she'd made in days. Shade negotiated the van around a curve and waited for the rest.

Okay, she thought, she'd get more than one word out of him if she had to use a crowbar. "A friend of mine settled there. Lee used to work for *Celebrity.* Now she's a novelist with her first book due out in the fall. She married Hunter Brown last year."

"The writer?"

Two words, she thought, smug. "Yes, have you read his stuff?"

This time Shade merely nodded and pulled a cigarette out of his pocket. Bryan began to sympathize with dentists who had to coax a patient to open wide.

"I've read everything he's written, then I hate myself for letting his books give me nightmares."

"Good horror fiction's supposed to make you wake up at 3:00 a.m. and wonder if you've locked your doors."

This time she grinned. "That sounds like something Hunter would say. You'll like him."

Shade merely moved his shoulders. He'd agreed to the stop in Sedona already, but he wasn't interested in taking flattering, commercial pictures of the occult king and his family. It would, however, give Shade the break he needed. If he could dump Bryan off for a day or two with her friends, he could take the time to get his system back to normal.

He hadn't had an easy moment since the day they'd started out of L.A. Every day that went by only tightened his nerves and played havoc with his libido. He'd tried, but it wasn't possible to forget she was there within arm's reach at night, separated from him only by the width of the van and the dark.

Yes, he could use a day away from her, and that natural, easy sexuality she didn't even seem aware of.

"You haven't seen them for a while?" he asked her.

"Not in months." Bryan relaxed, more at ease now that they'd actually begun a two-way conversation. "Lee's a good friend. I've missed her. She'll have a baby about the same time her book comes out."

The change in her voice had him glancing over. There was something softer about her now. Almost wistful.

"A year ago, we were both still with *Celebrity*, and now..." She turned to him, but the shaded glasses hid her eyes. "It's odd thinking of Lee settled down with a family. She was always more ambitious than me. It used to drive her crazy that I took everything with such a lack of intensity."

"Do you?"

"Just about everything," she murmured. Not you, she thought to herself. I don't seem to be able to take you easily. "It's simpler to relax and live," she went on, "than to worry about how you'll be living next month."

"Some people have to worry *if* they'll be living next month."

"Do you think the fact they worry about it changes things?" Bryan forgot her plan to make contact, forgot the fact that she'd been groping for some sort of compromise from him. He'd seen more than she'd seen of the world, of life. She had to admit that he'd seen more than she wanted to see. But how did he feel about it?

"Being aware can change things. Looking out for yourself's a priority some of us haven't a choice about."

Some of us. She noted the phrase but decided not to pounce on it. If he had scars, he was entitled to keep them covered until they'd faded a bit more.

"Everyone worries from time to time," she decided. "I'm just not very good at it. I suppose it comes from my parents. They're…" She trailed off and laughed. It occurred to him he hadn't heard her laugh in days, and that he'd missed it. "I guess they're what's termed bohemians. We lived in this little house in Carmel that was always in varying states of disrepair. My father would get a notion to take out a wall or put in a window, then in the middle of the project, he'd get an inspiration, go back to his canvases and leave the mess where it lay."

She settled back, no longer aware that she was doing all the talking and Shade all the listening. "My mother liked to cook. Trouble was, you'd never know what mood she'd be in. You might have grilled rattlesnake one day, cheeseburgers the next. Then, when you least expected it, there'd be gooseneck stew."

"Gooseneck stew?"

"I ate at the neighbors' a lot." The memory brought on her appetite. Taking out two candy bars, she offered one to Shade. "How about your parents?"

He unwrapped the candy absently while he paced his speed to the state police car in the next lane. "They retired to Florida. My father fishes and my mother runs a craft shop. Not as colorful as yours, I'm afraid."

"Colorful." She thought about it, and approved. "I never knew they were unusual until I'd gone away to college and realized that most kids' parents were grown-up and sensible. I guess I never realized how much I'd been influenced by them until Rob pointed out things like most people preferring to eat dinner at six, rather than scrounging for popcorn or peanut butter at ten o'clock at night."

"Rob?"

She glanced over quickly, then straight ahead. Shade listened too well, she decided. It made it too easy to say more than you intended. "My ex-husband." She knew she shouldn't still see the "ex" as a stigma; these days it was nearly a status symbol. For Bryan, it was the symbol that proved she hadn't done what was necessary to keep a promise.

"Still sore?" He'd asked before he could stop himself. She made him want to offer comfort, when he'd schooled himself not to become involved in anyone's life, anyone's problem.

"No, it was years ago." After a quick shrug, she nibbled on her candy bar. Sore? she thought again. No, not sore, but perhaps she'd always be just a little tender. "Just sorry it didn't work out, I suppose."

"Regrets are more a waste of time than worrying."

"Maybe. You were married once, too."

"That's right." His tone couldn't have been more dismissive. Bryan gave him a long, steady look.

"Sacred territory?"

"I don't believe in rehashing the past."

This wound was covered with scar tissue, she mused. She wondered if it troubled him much, or if he'd truly filed it away. In either case, it wasn't her business, nor was it the way to keep the ball rolling between them.

"When did you decide to become a photographer?" That was a safe topic, she reflected. There shouldn't be any tender points.

"When I was five and got my hands on my father's new thirty-five-millimeter. When he had the film developed, he discovered three close-ups of the family dog. I'm told he didn't know whether to congratulate me or give me solitary confinement when they turned out to be better than any of his shots."

Bryan grinned. "What'd he do?"

"He bought me a camera of my own."

"You were way ahead of me," she commented. "I didn't have any interest in cameras until high school. Just sort of fell into it. Up until then, I'd wanted to be a star."

"An actress?"

"No." She grinned again. "A star. Any kind of a star, as long as I had a Rolls, a gold lamé dress and a big tacky diamond."

He had to grin. She seemed to have the talent for forcing it out of him. "An unassuming child."

"No, materialistic." She offered him her drink, but he shook his head. "That stage coincided with my parents' return-to-the-earth period. I guess it was my way of rebelling against people who were almost impossible to rebel against."

He glanced down at her ringless hands and her faded jeans. "Guess you got over it."

"I wasn't made to be a star. Anyway, they needed someone to take pictures of the football team." Bryan finished off the candy bar and wondered how soon they could stop for lunch. "I volunteered because I had a crush on one of the players." Draining her soda, she dumped the cup in with Shade's bottle. "After the first day, I fell in love with the camera and forgot all about the defensive lineman."

"His loss."

Bryan glanced over, surprised by the offhand compliment. “That was a nice thing to say, Colby. I didn’t think you had it in you.”

He didn’t quite defeat the smile. “Don’t get used to it.”

“Heaven forbid.” But she was a great deal more pleased than his casual words warranted. “Anyway, my parents were thrilled when I became an obsessive photographer. They’d lived with this deadly fear that I had no creative drives and would end up being a smashing business success instead of an artist.”

“So now you’re both.”

She thought about it a moment. Odd how easy it was to forget about one aspect of her work when she concentrated so hard on the other. “I suppose you’re right. Just don’t mention it to Mom and Dad.”

“They won’t hear it from me.”

They both saw the construction sign at the same time. Whether either of them realized it, their minds followed the same path. Bryan was already reaching for her camera when Shade slowed and eased off the road. Ahead of them, a road crew patched, graded and sweated under the high Arizona sun.

Shade walked off to consider the angle that would show the team and machinery battling against the erosion of the road. A battle that would be waged on roads across the country each summer as long as roads existed. Bryan homed in on one man.

He was bald and had a yellow bandanna tied around his head to protect the vulnerable dome of his scalp. His face and neck were reddened and damp, his belly sagging over the belt of his work pants. He wore a plain white T-shirt, pristine compared to the colorful ones slashed with sayings and pictures the workmen around him had chosen.

To get in close she had to talk to him and deal with the comments and grins from the rest of the crew. She did so with an aplomb and charm that would've caused a public relations expert to rub his hands together. Bryan was a firm believer that the relationship between the photographer and the subject showed through in the final print. So first, in her own way, she had to develop one.

Shade kept his distance. He saw the men as a team—the sunburned, faceless team that worked roads across the country and had done so for decades. He wanted no relationship with any of them, nothing that would color the way he saw them as they stood, bent and dug.

He took a telling shot of the grime, dust and sweat. Bryan learned that the foreman's name was Al and he'd worked for the road commission for twenty-two years.

It took her a while to ease her way around his self-consciousness, but once she got him talking about what the miserable winter had done to his road, everything clicked. Sweat dribbled down his temple. When he reached up with one beefy arm to swipe at it, Bryan had her picture.

The impulsive detour took them thirty minutes. By the time they piled back in the van, they were sweating as freely as the laborers.

"Are you always so personal with strangers?" Shade asked her as he switched on the engine and the air-conditioning.

"When I want their picture, sure." Bryan opened the cooler and pulled out one of the cold cans she'd stocked, and another bottle of iced tea for Shade. "You get what you wanted?"

"Yeah."

He'd watched her at work. Normally they separated, but this time he'd been close enough to see just how she went about her job. She'd treated the road man with more respect and good humor than many photographers showed their hundred-dollar-an-hour models. And she hadn't done it just for the picture, though Shade wasn't sure she realized it. She'd been interested in the man—who he was, what he was and why.

Once, a long time before, Shade had had that kind of curiosity. Now he strapped it down. Knowing involved you. But it wasn't easy, he was discovering, to strap down his curiosity about Bryan. Already she'd told him more than he'd have asked. Not more than he wanted to know, but more than he'd have asked. It still wasn't enough.

For nearly a week he'd backed off from her—just as far as it was possible under the circumstances. He hadn't stopped wanting her. He might not like to rehash the past, but it wasn't possible to forget that last molten encounter on the roadside.

He'd closed himself off, but now she was opening him up again. He wondered if it was foolish to try to fight it, and the attraction they had for each other. It might be better, simpler, more logical, to just let things progress to the only possible conclusion.

They'd sleep together, burn the passion out and get back to the assignment.

Cold? Calculated? Perhaps, but he'd do nothing except follow the already routed course. He knew it was important to keep the emotions cool and the mind sharp.

He'd let his emotions fuddle his logic and his perception before. In Cambodia, a sweet face and a generous smile had blinded him to treachery. Shade's fingers tightened on the wheel without his realizing it. He'd learned a lesson about trust then—it was only the flip side of betrayal.

"Where've you gone?" Bryan asked quietly. A look had come into his eyes that she didn't understand, and wasn't certain she wanted to understand.

He turned his head. For an instant she was caught in the turmoil, in the dark place he remembered too well and she knew nothing about. Then it was over. His eyes were remote and calm. His fingers eased on the wheel.

"We'll stop in Page," he said briefly. "Get some shots of the boats and tourists on Lake Powell before we go down to the canyon."

"All right."

He hadn't been thinking of her. Bryan could comfort herself with that. She hoped the look that had come into his eyes would never be applied to her. Even so, she was determined that sooner or later she'd discover the reason for it.

She could've gotten some good technical shots of the dam. But as they passed through the tiny town of Page, heading for the lake, Bryan saw the high golden arches shimmering behind waves of heat. It made her grin. Cheeseburgers and fries weren't just summer pastimes. They'd become a way of life. Food for all seasons. But she couldn't resist the sight of the familiar building settled low below the town, almost isolated, like a mirage in the middle of the desert.

She rolled down her window and waited for the right angle. "Gotta eat," she said as she framed the building. "Just gotta." She clicked the shutter.

Resigned, Shade pulled into the lot. "Get it to go,"

he ordered as Bryan started to hop out. "I want to get to the marina."

Swinging her purse over her shoulder, she disappeared inside. Shade didn't have the chance to become impatient before she bounded back out again with two white bags. "Cheap, fast and wonderful," she told him as she slid back into her seat. "I don't know how I'd make it through life if I couldn't get a cheeseburger on demand."

She pulled out a wrapped burger and handed it to him.

"I got extra salt," she said over her first taste of fries. "Mmm, I'm starving."

"You wouldn't be if you'd eat something besides a candy bar for breakfast."

"I'd rather be awake when I eat," she mumbled, involved in unwrapping her burger.

Shade unwrapped his own. He hadn't asked her to bring him anything. He'd already learned it was typical of her to be carelessly considerate. Perhaps the better word was *naturally.* But it wasn't typical of him to be moved by the simple offer of a piece of meat in a bun. He reached in a bag and brought out a paper napkin. "You're going to need this."

Bryan grinned, took it, folded her legs under her and dug in. Amused, Shade drove leisurely to the marina.

They rented a boat, what Bryan termed a putt-putt. It was narrow, open and about the size of a canoe. It would, however, carry them, and what equipment they chose, out on the lake.

She liked the little marina, with its food stands and general stores with displays of suntan oil and bathing suits. The season was in full swing; people strolled by dressed in shorts and cover-ups, in hats and sunglasses.

She spotted a teenage couple, brown and gleaming, on a bench, licking at dripping ice-cream cones. Because they were so involved with each other, Bryan was able to take some candid shots before the paperwork on the rental was completed.

Ice cream and suntans. It was a simple, cheerful way to look at summer. Satisfied, she secured her camera in its bag and went back to Shade.

"Do you know how to drive a boat?"

He sent her a mild look as they walked down the dock. "I'll manage."

A woman in a neat white shirt and shorts gave them a rundown, pointing out the life jackets and explaining the engine before she handed them a glossy map of the lake. Bryan settled herself in the bow and prepared to enjoy herself.

"The nice thing about this," she called over the engine, "is it's so unexpected." She swept one arm out to indicate the wide expanse of blue.

Red-hued mesas and sheer rock walls rose up steeply to cradle the lake, settled placidly where man had put it. The combination was fascinating to her. Another time, she might've done a study on the harmony and power that could result in a working relationship between human imagination and nature.

It wasn't necessary to know all the technical details of the dam, of the labor force that built it. It was enough that it was, that they were here—cutting through water that had once been desert, sending up a spray that had once been sand.

Shade spotted a tidy cabin cruiser and veered in its direction. For the moment, he'd navigate and leave the camera work to Bryan. It'd been a long time since he'd spent a hot afternoon on the water. His muscles began to relax even as his perception sharpened.

Before he was done, he'd have to take some pictures of the rocks. The texture in them was incredible, even in their reflection on the water. Their colors, slashed against the blue lake, made them look surreal. He'd make the prints sharp and crisp to accent the incongruity. He edged a bit closer to the cabin cruiser as he planned the shot for later.

Bryan took out her camera without any definite plan. She hoped there'd be a party of people, perhaps greased up against the sun. Children maybe, giddy with the wind and water. As Shade steered, she glanced toward the stern and lifted the camera quickly. It was too good to be true.

Poised at the stern of the cruiser was a hound—Bryan couldn't think of any other description for the floppy dog. His big ears were blowing back, and his tongue was lolling as he stared down at the water. Over his chestnut fur was a bright orange life vest.

"Go around again!" she yelled to Shade.

She waited impatiently for the angle to come to her again. There were people on the boat, at least five of them, but they no longer interested her. Just the dog, she thought, as she gnawed on her lip and waited. She wanted nothing but the dog in the life jacket leaning out and staring down at the water.

There were towering mesas just behind the boat. Bryan had to decide quickly whether to work them in or frame them out. If she'd had more time to think… She opted against the drama and settled on the fun. Shade had circled the trim little cruiser three times before she was satisfied.

"Wonderful!" With a laugh, Bryan lowered her camera. "That one print's going to be worth the whole trip."

He veered off to the right. "Why don't we see what else we can dig up, anyway?"

They worked for two hours, shifting positions after the first. Stripped to the waist as defense against the heat, Shade knelt at the bow and focused in on a tour boat. The rock wall rose in the background, the water shimmered cool and blue. Along the rail the people were no more than a blur of color. That's what he wanted. The anonymity of tours, and the power of what drew the masses to them.

While Shade worked, Bryan kept the speed low and looked at everything. She'd decided after one glimpse of his lean, tanned torso that it'd be wiser for her to concentrate on the scenery. If she hadn't, she might've missed the cove and the rock island that curved over it.

"Look." Without hesitating, she steered toward it, then cut the engines until the boat drifted in its own wake. "Come on, let's take a swim." Before he could comment, she'd hopped out in the ankle-deep water and was securing the lines with rocks.

Wearing a snug tank top and drawstring shorts, Bryan dashed down to the cove and sank in over her head. When she surfaced, laughing, Shade was standing on the island above her. "Fabulous," she called out. "Come on, Shade, we haven't taken an hour to play since we started."

She was right about that. He'd seen to it. Not that he hadn't needed to relax, but he'd thought it best not to around her. He knew, even as he watched her smoothly treading in the rock-shadowed water, that it was a mistake. Yet he'd told himself it was logical to stop fighting what would happen between them. Following the logic, he walked down to the water.

"It's like opening a present," she decided, shifting onto her back to float briefly. "I had no idea I was being slowly boiled until I stepped in here." With a sigh, she dipped under the water and rose again so that it flowed from her face. "There was a pond a few miles away from home when I was a kid. I practically lived there in the summer."

The water was seductive, almost painfully so. As Shade lowered himself into it, he felt the heat drain, but not the tension. Sooner or later, he knew, he'd have to find an outlet for it.

"We did a lot better here than I expected to." Lazily she let the water play through her fingers. "I can't wait to get to Sedona and start developing." She tossed her dripping braid behind her back. "And sleep in a real bed."

"You don't seem to have any trouble sleeping." One of the first things he'd noticed was that she could fall asleep anywhere, anytime, and within seconds of shutting her eyes.

"Oh, it's not the sleeping, it's the waking up." And waking up only a few feet away from him, morning after morning—seeing his face shadowed by a night's growth of beard, dangerously attractive, seeing his muscles ripple as he stretched, dangerously strong. No, she couldn't deny that the accommodations occasionally gave her a few twinges.

"You know," she began casually, "the budget could handle a couple of motel rooms every week or so—nothing outrageous. A real mattress and a private shower, you know. Some of those campgrounds we've stopped in advertise hot water with their tongues in their cheeks."

He had to smile. It hadn't given him much pleasure to settle for tepid water after a long day on the road. But there was no reason to make it too easy on her. "Can't handle roughing it, Bryan?"

She stretched out on her back again, deliberately kicking water up and over him. "Oh, I don't mind roughing it," she said blandly. "I just like to do it on my own time. And I'm not ashamed to say I'd rather spend the weekend at the Beverly Wilshire than rubbing two sticks together in the wilderness." She closed her eyes and let her body drift. "Wouldn't you?"

"Yeah." With the admission, he reached out, grabbed her braid and tugged her head under.

The move surprised her, but it pleased her as well, even as she came up sputtering. So he was capable of a frivolous move from time to time. It was something else she could like him for.

"I'm an expert on water games," she warned him as she began to tread again.

"Water suits you." When had he relaxed? He couldn't pinpoint the moment when the tension began to ease from him. There was something about her—laziness? No, that wasn't true. She worked every bit as hard as he, though in her own fashion. *Easiness* was a better word, he decided. She was an easy woman, comfortable with herself and whatever surroundings she found herself in.

"It looks pretty good on you, too." Narrowing her eyes, Bryan focused on him—something she'd avoided for several days. If she didn't allow herself a clear look, it helped bank down on the feelings he brought out in her. Many of them weren't comfortable, and Shade had been right. She was a woman who liked to be comfortable. But now, with the water lapping cool around her and the only sound that of boats putting in the distance, she wanted to enjoy him.

His hair was damp and tangled around his face, which was as relaxed as she'd ever seen it. There didn't seem to be any secrets in his eyes just now. He was nearly too lean, but there were muscles in his forearms, in his back. She already knew just how strong his hands were. She smiled at him because she wasn't sure just how many quiet moments they'd share.

"You don't let up on yourself enough, Shade."

"No?"

"No. You know…" She floated again, because treading took too much effort. "I think deep down, really deep down, there's a nice person in you."

"No, there isn't."

But she heard the humor in his voice. "Oh, it's buried in there somewhere. If you let me do your portrait, I'd find it."

He liked the way she floated in the water; there was absolutely no energy expended. She lay there, trusting buoyancy. He was nearly certain that if she lay quietly for five minutes, she'd be asleep. "Would you?" he murmured. "I think we can both do without that."

She opened her eyes again, but had to squint against the sun to see him. It was at his back, glaring. "Maybe you can, but I've already decided to do it—once I know you better."

He circled her ankle with his finger, lightly. "You have to have my cooperation to do both."

"I'll get it." The contact was more potent than she could handle. She'd tensed before she could stop it. And so, she realized after a long ten seconds, had he. Casually, she let her legs drop. "The water's getting cold."

She swam toward the boat with smooth strokes and a racing heart.

Shade waited a moment. No matter what direction he took with her, he always ended up in the same place. He wanted her, but wasn't certain he could handle the consequences of acting on that desire. Worse now, she was perilously close to becoming his friend. That wouldn't make things any easier on either of them.

Slowly, he swam out of the cove and toward the boat, but she wasn't there. Puzzled, he looked around and started to call, but then he saw her perched high on the rock.

She'd unbraided her hair and was brushing it dry in the sun. Her legs were folded under her, her face tilted up. The thin summer clothes she wore were drenched and clung to every curve. She obviously didn't care. It was the sun she sought, the heat, just as she'd sought the cool water only moments before.

Shade reached in his camera bag and attached his long lens. He wanted her to fill the viewfinder. He focused and framed her. For the second time, her careless sexuality gave him a staggering roundhouse punch. He was a professional, Shade reminded himself as he set the depth of field. He was shooting a subject, that was all.

But when she turned her head and her eyes met his through the lens, he felt the passion sizzle—from himself and from her. They held each other there a moment, separated, yet irrevocably joined. He took the picture, and as he did, Shade knew he was recording a great deal more than a subject.

A bit steadier, Bryan rose and worked her way down the curve of the rock. She had to remind herself to play it lightly—something that had always come easily to her. "You didn't get a release form, Colby," she reminded him as she dropped her brush into her oversize bag.

Reaching out, he touched her hair. It was damp, hanging rich and heavy to her waist. His fingers curled into it, his eyes locked on hers. "I want you."

She felt her legs liquefy, and heat started somewhere in the pit of her stomach and spread out to her fingertips. He was a hard man, Bryan reminded herself. He wouldn't give, but take. In the end, she'd need him to do both.

"That's not good enough for me," she said steadily. "People want all the time—a new car, a color TV. I have to have more than that."

She stepped around him and into the boat. Without a word, Shade joined her and they drifted away from the cove. As the boat picked up speed, both of them wondered if Shade could give any more than what he'd offered.

Chapter 5

Bryan had romanticized Oak Creek Canyon over the years since she'd been there. When she saw it again, she wasn't disappointed. It had all the rich strength, all the colors, she'd remembered.

Campers would be pocketed through it, she knew. They'd be worth some time and some film. Amateur and serious fishermen by the creek, she mused, with their intense expressions and colorful lures. Evening campfires with roasting marshmallows. Coffee in tin cups. Yes, it would be well worth the stop.

They planned to stay for three days, working, developing and printing. Bryan was itching to begin. But before they drove into town to handle the details, they'd agreed to stop in the canyon where Bryan could see Lee and her family.

"According to the directions, there should be a little dirt road leading off to the right just beyond a trading post."

Shade watched for it. He, too, was anxious to begin. Some of the shots he'd taken were pulling at him to bring them to life. He needed the concentration and quiet of a darkroom, the solitude of it. He needed to let his creativity flow, and hold in his hands the results.

The picture of Bryan sitting on the island of rock. He didn't like to dwell on that one, but he knew it would be the first roll he developed.

The important thing was that he'd have the time and the distance he'd promised himself. Once he dropped her at her friends'—and he was certain they'd want her to stay with them—he could go into Sedona, rent a darkroom and a motel room for himself. After living with her for twenty-four hours a day, he was counting on a few days apart to steady his system.

They'd each work on whatever they chose—the town, the canyon, the landscape. That gave him room. He'd work out a schedule for the darkroom. With luck, they wouldn't so much as see each other for the next three days.

"There it is," Bryan told him, though he'd already seen the narrow road and slowed for it. She looked at the steep, tree-lined road and shook her head. "God, I'd never have pictured Lee here. It's so wild and rough and she's...well, elegant."

He'd known a few elegant women in his life. He'd lived with one. Shade glanced at the terrain. "What's she doing here, then?"

"She fell in love," Bryan said simply, and leaned forward. "There's the house. Fabulous."

Glass and style. That's what she thought of it. It wasn't the distinguished town house she would have imagined for Lee, but Bryan could see how it would suit her friend. There were flowers blooming, bright red-orange blossoms she couldn't identify. The grass was thick, the trees leafy.

In the driveway were two vehicles, a dusty late-model Jeep and a shiny cream-colored sedan. As they pulled up behind the Jeep, a huge silver-gray form bounded around the side of the house. Shade swore in sheer astonishment.

"That must be Santanas." Bryan laughed, but gave the dog a wary once-over with her door firmly closed.

Fascinated, Shade watched the muscles bunch as the dog moved. But the tail was wagging, the tongue lolling. Some pet, he decided. "It looks like a wolf."

"Yeah." She continued to look out the window as the dog paced up and down the side of the van. "Lee tells me he's friendly."

"Fine. You go first."

Bryan shot him a look that he returned with a casual smile. Letting out a deep breath, Bryan opened the door. "Nice dog," she told him as she stepped out, keeping one hand on the handle of the door. "Nice Santanas."

"I read somewhere that Brown raised wolves," Shade said carelessly as he stepped out of the opposite side.

"Cute," Bryan mumbled, and cautiously offered her hand for the dog to sniff.

He did so, and obviously liked her, because he knocked her to the ground in one bounding leap. Shade was around the van before Bryan had a chance to draw a breath. Fear and fury had carried him, but whatever he might've done was stopped by the sound of a high whistle.

"Santanas!" A young girl darted around the house, braids flying. "Cut it out right now. You're not supposed to knock people down."

Caught in the act, the huge dog plopped down on his

belly and somehow managed to look innocent. “He’s sorry.” The girl looked at the tense man looming over the dog and the breathless woman sprawled beside him. “He just gets excited when company comes. Are you Bryan?”

Bryan managed a nod as the dog dropped his head on her arm and looked up at her.

“It’s a funny name. I thought you’d look funny, too, but you don’t. I’m Sarah.”

“Hello, Sarah.” Catching her wind, Bryan looked up at Shade. “This is Shade Colby.”

“Is that a real name?” Sarah demanded.

“Yeah.” Shade looked down as the girl frowned up at him. He wanted to scold her for not handling her dog, but found he couldn’t. She had dark, serious eyes that made him want to crouch down and look into them from her level. A heartbreaker, he decided. Give her ten years, and she’ll break them all.

“Sounds like something from one of my dad’s books. I guess it’s okay.” She grinned down at Bryan and shuffled her sneakers in the dirt. Both she and her dog looked embarrassed. “I’m really sorry Santanas knocked you down. You’re not hurt or anything, are you?”

Since it was the first time anyone had bothered to ask, Bryan thought about it. “No.”

“Well, maybe you won’t say anything to my dad.” Sarah flashed a quick smile and showed her braces. “He gets mad when Santanas forgets his manners.”

Santanas swiped an enormous pink tongue over Bryan’s shoulder.

“No harm done,” she decided.

“Great. We’ll go tell them you’re here.” She was off

in a bound. The dog clambered up and raced after her without giving Bryan a backward look.

"Well, it doesn't look like Lee's settled for a dull life," Bryan commented.

Shade reached down and hauled her to her feet. He'd been frightened, he realized. Seriously frightened for the first time in years, and all because a little girl's pet had knocked down his partner.

"You okay?"

"Yeah." With quick swipes, she began to brush the dirt off her jeans. Shade ran his hands up her arms, stopping her cold.

"Sure?"

"Yes, I…" She trailed off as her thoughts twisted into something incoherent. He wasn't supposed to look at her like that, she thought. As though he really cared. She wished he'd look at her like that again, and again. His fingers were barely touching her arms. She wished he'd touch her like that again. And again.

"I'm fine," she managed finally. But it was hardly more than a whisper, and her eyes never left his.

He kept his hands on her arms. "That dog had to weigh a hundred and twenty."

"He didn't mean any harm." Why, she wondered vaguely, were they talking about a dog, when there really wasn't anything important but him and her?

"I'm sorry." His thumb skimmed over the inside of her elbow, where the skin was as soft as he'd once imagined. Her pulse beat like an engine. "I should've gotten out first instead of playing around." If she'd been hurt… He wanted to kiss her now, right now, when he was thinking only of her and not the reasons that he shouldn't.

"It doesn't matter," she murmured, and found that her

hands were resting on his shoulders. Their bodies were close, just brushing. Who had moved? "It doesn't matter," she said again, half to herself, as she leaned closer. Their lips hovered, hesitated, then barely touched. From the house came the deep, frantic sound of barking. They drew back from each other with something close to a jerk.

"Bryan!" Lee let the door slam behind her as she came onto the porch. It wasn't until she'd already called out that she noticed how intent the two people in her driveway were on each other.

With a quick shudder, Bryan took another step back before she turned. Too many feelings, was all she could think. Too many feelings, too quickly.

"Lee." She ran over, or ran away—she wasn't certain. All she knew was, at that moment she needed someone. Grateful, she felt herself closed in Lee's arms. "Oh, God, it's so good to see you."

The greeting was just a little desperate. Lee took a long look over Bryan's shoulder at the man who remained several paces back. Her first impression was that he wanted to stay that way. Separate. What had Bryan gotten herself into? she wondered, and gave her friend a fierce hug.

"I've got to look at you," Bryan insisted, laughing now as the tension drained. The elegant face, the carefully styled hair—they were the same. But the woman wasn't. Bryan could feel it before she glanced down to the rounded swell beneath Lee's crisp summer dress.

"You're happy." Bryan gripped Lee's hands. "It shows. No regrets?"

"No regrets." Lee took a long, hard study. Bryan looked the same, she decided. Healthy, easy, lovely in a way that seemed exclusively her own. The same, she thought, but for the slightest hint of trouble in her eyes. "And you?"

"Things are good. I've missed you, but I feel better about it after seeing you here."

With a laugh, Lee slipped her arm around Bryan's waist. If there was trouble, she'd find the source. Bryan was hopeless at hiding anything for long. "Come inside. Sarah and Hunter are making iced tea." She sent a significant look in Shade's direction and felt Bryan tense. Just a little, but Lee felt it and knew she'd already found the source.

Bryan cleared her throat. "Shade."

He moved forward, Lee thought, like a man who was used to testing the way.

"Lee Radcliffe—Lee Radcliffe Brown," Bryan corrected, and relaxed a bit. "Shade Colby. You remember when I spent the money I'd saved for a new car on one of his prints."

"Yes, I told you you were crazy." Lee extended her hand and smiled, but her voice was cool. "It's nice to meet you. Bryan's always admired your work."

"But you haven't," he returned, with more interest and respect than he'd intended to feel.

"I often find it harsh, but always compelling," Lee said simply. "Bryan's the expert, not me."

"Then she'd tell you that we don't take pictures for experts."

Lee nodded. His handshake had been firm—not gentle, but far from cruel. His eyes were precisely the same. She'd have to reserve judgment for now. "Come inside, Mr. Colby."

He'd intended to simply drop Bryan off and move along, but he found himself accepting. It wouldn't hurt, he rationalized, to cool off a bit before he drove into town. He followed the women inside.

"Dad, if you don't put more sugar in it, it tastes terrible."

As they walked into the kitchen, they saw Sarah with her hands on her hips, watching her father mop up around a pitcher of tea.

"Not everyone wants to pour sugar into their system the way you do."

"I do." Bryan grinned when Hunter turned. She thought his work brilliant—often cursing him for it in the middle of the night, when it kept her awake. She thought he looked like a man one of the Brontë sisters would have written about—strong, dark, brooding. But more, he was the man who loved her closest friend. Bryan opened her arms to him.

"It's good to see you again." Hunter held her close, chuckling when he felt her reach behind him to the plate of cookies Sarah had set out. "Why don't you gain weight?"

"I keep trying," Bryan claimed, and bit into the chocolate chip cookie. "Mmm, still warm. Hunter, this is Shade Colby."

Hunter put down his dishcloth. "I've followed your work," he told Shade as they shook hands. "It's powerful."

"That's the word I'd use to describe yours."

"Your latest had me too paranoid to go down to the basement laundry room for weeks," Bryan accused Hunter. "I nearly ran out of clothes."

Hunter grinned, pleased. "Thanks."

She glanced around the sunlit kitchen. "I guess I expected your house to have cobwebs and creaking boards."

"Disappointed?" Lee asked.

"Relieved."

With a laugh, Lee settled at the kitchen table with Sarah on her left and Bryan across from her. "So how's the project going?"

"Good." But Lee noticed she didn't look at Shade as she spoke. "Maybe terrific. We'll know more once we develop the film. We've made arrangements with one of the local papers for the use of a darkroom. All we have to do is drive into Sedona, check in and get a couple of rooms. Tomorrow, we work."

"Rooms?" Lee set down the glass Hunter handed her. "But you're staying here."

"Lee." Bryan gave Hunter a quick smile as he offered the plate of cookies. "I wanted to see you, not drop in bag and baggage. I know both you and Hunter are working on new books. Shade and I'll be up to our ears in developing fluid."

"How are we supposed to visit if you're in Sedona?" Lee countered. "Damn it, Bryan, I've missed you. You're staying here." She laid a hand on her rounded stomach. "Pregnant women have to be pampered."

"You should stay," Shade put in before Bryan could comment. "It might be the last chance for quite a while for a little free time."

"We've a lot of work to do," Bryan reminded him.

"It's a short drive into town from here. That won't make any difference. We're going to need to rent a car, in any case, so we can both be mobile."

Hunter studied the man across the room. Tense, he thought. Intense. Not the sort of man he'd have picked for the free-rolling, slow-moving Bryan, but it wasn't his place to judge. It was his place, and his talent, to observe. What was between them was obvious to see. Their reluctance to accept it was just as obvious. Calmly, he picked up his tea and drank.

"The invitation applies to both of you."

Shade glanced over with an automatic polite refusal on the tip of his tongue. His eyes met Hunter's. They were both intense, internalized men. Perhaps that's why they understood each other so quickly.

I've been there before, Hunter seemed to say to him with a hint of a smile. *You can run fast but only so far.*

Shade sensed something of the understanding, and something of the challenge. He glanced down to see Bryan giving him a long, cool look.

"I'd love to stay," he heard himself say. Shade crossed to the table and sat.

Lee looked over the prints in her precise, deliberate way. Bryan paced up and down the terrace, ready to explode.

"Well?" she demanded. "What do you think?"

"I haven't finished looking through them yet."

Bryan opened her mouth, then shut it again. It wasn't like her to be nervous over her work. She knew the prints were good. Hadn't she put her sweat and her heart into each of them?

More than good, she told herself as she yanked a chocolate bar out of her pocket. These prints ranked with her best work. It might've been the competition with Shade that had pushed her to produce them. It might've been the need to feel a bit smug after some of the comments he'd made on her particular style of work. Bryan didn't like to think she was base enough to resort to petty rivalry, but she had to admit that now she was. And she wanted to win.

She and Shade had lived in the same house, worked

in the same darkroom for days, but had managed to see almost nothing of each other. A neat trick, Bryan thought ruefully. Perhaps it had worked so well because they'd both played the same game. Hide and don't seek. Tomorrow they'd be back on the road.

Bryan found that she was anxious to go even while she dreaded it. And she wasn't a contrary person, Bryan reminded herself almost fiercely. She was basically straightforward and…well, yes, she was amiable. It was simply her nature to be. So why wasn't she with Shade?

"Well."

Bryan whirled around as Lee spoke. "Well?" she echoed, waiting.

"I've always admired your work, Bryan. You know that." In her tidy way, Lee folded her hands on the wrought-iron table.

"But?" Bryan prompted.

"But these are the best." Lee smiled. "The very best you've ever done."

Bryan let out the breath she'd been holding and crossed to the table. Nerves? Yes, she had them. She didn't care for them. "Why?"

"I'm sure there're a lot of technical reasons—the light and the shading, the cropping."

Impatiently, Bryan shook her head. "Why?"

Understanding, Lee chose a print. "This one of the old woman and the little girl on the beach. Maybe it's my condition," she said slowly as she studied it again, "but it makes me think of the child I'll have. It also makes me remember I'll grow old, but not too old to dream. This picture's powerful because it's so basically simple, so straightforward and so incredibly full of emotion. And this one…"

She shuffled the prints until she came to the one of

the road worker. "Sweat, determination, honesty. You know when you look at this face that the man believes in hard work and paying his bills on time. And here, these teenagers. I see youth just before those inevitable changes of adulthood. And this dog." Lee laughed as she looked at it. "The first time I looked, it just struck me as cute and funny, but he looks so proud, so, well, human. You could almost believe the boat was his."

While Bryan remained silent, Lee tidied the prints again. "I could go over each one of them with you, but the point is, each one of them tells a story. It's only one scene, one instant of time, yet the story's there. The feelings are there. Isn't that the purpose?"

"Yes." Bryan smiled as her shoulders relaxed. "That's the purpose."

"If Shade's pictures are half as good, you'll have a wonderful essay."

"They will be," Bryan murmured. "I saw some of his negatives in the darkroom. They're incredible."

Lee lifted a brow and watched Bryan devour chocolate. "Does that bother you?"

"What? Oh, no, no, of course not. His work is his work—and in this case it'll be part of mine. I'd never have agreed to work with him if I hadn't admired him."

"But?" This time Lee prompted with a raised brow and half smile.

"I don't know, Lee, he's just so—so perfect."

"Really?"

"He never fumbles," Bryan complained. "He always knows exactly what he wants. When he wakes up in the morning, he's perfectly coherent, he never misses a turn on the road. He even makes decent coffee."

"Anyone would detest him for that," Lee said dryly.

"It's frustrating, that's all."

"Love often is. You are in love with him, aren't you?"

"No." Genuinely surprised, Bryan stared over at Lee. "Good God, I hope I've more sense than that. I have to work hard at even liking him."

"Bryan, you're my friend. Otherwise what I'm calling concern would be called prying."

"Which means you're going to pry," Bryan put in.

"Exactly. I've seen the way the two of you tiptoe around each other as if you're terrified that if you happened to brush up against each other there'd be spontaneous combustion."

"Something like that."

Lee reached out and touched her hand. "Bryan, tell me."

Evasions weren't possible. Bryan looked down at the joined hands and sighed. "I'm attracted," she admitted slowly. "He's different from anyone I've known, mostly because he's just not the type of man I'd normally socialize with. He's very remote, very serious. I like to have fun. Just fun."

"Relationships have to be made up of more than just fun."

"I'm not looking for a relationship." On this point she was perfectly clear. "I date so I can go dancing, go to a party, listen to music or see a movie. That's it. The last thing I want is all the tension and work that goes into a relationship."

"If someone didn't know you, they'd say that was a pretty shallow sentiment."

"Maybe it is," Bryan tossed back. "Maybe I am."

Lee said nothing, just tapped a finger on the prints.

"That's my work," Bryan began, then gave up. A lot of people might take what she said at face value, not Lee. "I don't want a relationship," she repeated, but in a quieter tone. "Lee, I've been there before, and I'm lousy at it."

"Relationship equals two," Lee pointed out. "Are you still taking the blame?"

"Most of the blame was mine. I was no good at being a wife."

"At being a certain kind of wife," Lee corrected.

"I imagine there's only a handful of definitions in the dictionary."

Lee only raised a brow. "Sarah has a friend whose mother is wonderful. She keeps not just a clean house, but an interesting one. She makes jelly, takes the minutes at the P.T.A. and runs a Girl Scout troop. The woman can take colored paper and some glue and create a work of art. She's lovely and helps herself stay that way with exercise classes three times a week. I admire her a great deal, but if Hunter had wanted those things from me, I wouldn't have his ring on my finger."

"Hunter's special," Bryan murmured.

"I can't argue with that. And you know why I nearly ruined it with him—because I was afraid I'd fail at building and maintaining a relationship."

"It's not a matter of being afraid." Bryan shrugged her shoulders. "It's more a matter of not having the energy for it."

"Remember who you're talking to," Lee said mildly.

With a half laugh, Bryan shook her head. "All right, maybe it's a matter of being cautious. *Relationship*'s a very weighty word. *Affair*'s lighter," she said consideringly. "But an affair with a man like Shade's bound to have tremendous repercussions."

That sounded so cool, Bryan mused. When had she started to think in such logical terms? "He's not an easy man, Lee. He has his own demons and his own way of dealing with them. I don't know whether he'd share them with me, or if I'd want him to."

"He works at being cold," Lee commented. "But I've seen him with Sarah. I admit the basic kindness in him surprised me, but it's there."

"It's there," Bryan agreed. "It's just hard to get to."

"Dinner's ready!" Sarah yanked open the screen door and let it hit the wall with a bang. "Shade and I made spaghetti, and it's terrific."

It was. During the meal, Bryan watched Shade. Like Lee, she'd noticed his easy relationship with Sarah. It was more than tolerance, she decided as she watched him laugh with the girl. It was affection. It hadn't occurred to her that Shade could give his affection so quickly or with so few restrictions.

Maybe I should be a twelve-year-old with braces, she decided, then shook her head at her own thought pattern. She didn't want Shade's affection. His respect, yes.

It wasn't until after dinner that she realized she was wrong. She wanted a great deal more.

It was the last leisurely evening before the group separated. On the front porch they watched the first stars come out and listened to the first night sounds begin. By that time the next evening, Shade and Bryan would be in Colorado.

Lee and Hunter sat on the porch swing with Sarah nestled between them. Shade stretched out in a chair just to the side, relaxed, a little tired, and mentally satisfied after his long hours in the darkroom. Still, as he sat talking easily to the Browns, he realized that he'd needed this visit as much as, perhaps more than, Bryan.

He'd had a simple childhood. Until these past days, he'd nearly forgotten just how simple, and just how solid. The things that had happened to him as an adult had blocked a great deal of it out. Now, without consciously realizing it, Shade was drawing some of it back.

Bryan sat on the first step, leaning back against a post. She joined in the conversation or distanced herself from it as she chose. There was nothing important being said, and the easiness of the conversation made the scene that much more appealing. A moth battered itself against the porch light, crickets called, and the breeze rippled through the full leaves of the surrounding trees. The sounds made a soothing conversation of their own.

She liked the way Hunter had his arm across the back of the swing. Though he spoke to Shade, his fingers ran lightly over his wife's hair. His daughter's head rested against his chest, but once in a while, she'd reach a hand over to Lee's stomach as if to test for movement. Though she hadn't been consciously setting the scene, it grew in front of her eyes. Unable to resist, Bryan slipped inside.

When she returned a few moments later, she had her camera, tripod and light stand.

"Oh, boy." Sarah took one look and straightened primly. "Bryan's going to take our picture."

"No posing," Bryan told her with a grin. "Just keep talking," she continued before anyone could protest. "Pretend I'm not even here. It's so perfect," she began to mutter to herself as she set up. "I don't know why I didn't see it before."

"Let me give you a hand."

Bryan glanced up at Shade in surprise, and nearly refused before she stopped the words. It was the first time he'd made any attempt to work with her. Whether it was a gesture to her or to the affection he'd come to feel for her friends, she wouldn't toss it back at him. Instead, she smiled and handed him her light meter.

"Give me a reading, will you?"

They worked together as though they'd been doing so for years. Another surprise, for both of them. She adjusted her light, already calculating her exposure as Shade gave her the readings. Satisfied, Bryan checked the angle and framing through the viewfinder, then stepped back and let Shade take her place.

"Perfect." If she was looking for a lazy summer evening and a family content with it and one another, she could've done no better. Stepping back, Shade leaned against the wall of the house. Without thinking about it, he continued to help by distracting the trio on the swing.

"What do you want, Sarah?" he began as Bryan moved behind the camera again. "A baby brother or a sister?"

As she considered, Sarah forgot her enchantment with being photographed. "Well..." Her hand moved to Lee's stomach again. Lee's hand closed over it spontaneously. Bryan clicked the shutter. "Maybe a brother," she decided. "My cousin says a little sister can be a real pain."

As Sarah spoke Lee leaned her head back, just slightly, until it rested on Hunter's arm. His fingers brushed her hair again. Bryan felt the emotion well up in her and blur her vision. She took the next shot blindly.

Had she always wanted that? she wondered as she continued to shoot. The closeness, the contentment that came with commitment and intimacy? Why had it waited to slam into her now, when her feelings toward Shade were already tangled and much too complicated? She blinked her eyes clear and opened the shutter just as Lee turned her head to laugh at something Hunter said.

Relationship, she thought as the longing rose up in her. Not the easy, careless friendships she'd permitted herself, but a solid, demanding, sharing relationship. That was what she saw through the viewfinder. That was what she discovered she needed for herself. When she straightened from the camera, Shade was beside her.

"Something wrong?"

She shook her head and reached over to switch off the light. "Perfect," she announced with a casualness that cost her. She gave the family on the swing a smile. "I'll send you a print as soon as we stop and develop again."

She was trembling. Shade was close enough to see it. He turned and dealt with the camera and tripod himself. "I'll take this up for you."

She turned to tell him no, but he was already carrying it inside. "I'd better pack my gear," she said to Hunter and Lee. "Shade likes to leave at uncivilized hours."

When she went inside, Lee leaned her head against Hunter's arm again. "They'll be fine," he told her. "She'll be fine."

Lee glanced toward the doorway. "Maybe."

Shade carried Bryan's equipment up to the bedroom she'd been using and waited. The moment she came in with the light, he turned to her. "What's wrong?"

Bryan opened the case and packed her stand and light. "Nothing. Why?"

"You were trembling." Impatient, Shade took her arm and turned her around. "You're still trembling."

"I'm tired." In its way, it was true. She was tired of having her emotions sneak up on her.

"Don't play games with me, Bryan. I'm better at it than you."

God, could he have any idea just how much she wanted to be held at that moment? Would he have any way of understanding how much she'd give if only he'd hold her now? "Don't push it, Shade."

She should've known he wouldn't listen. With one hand, he cupped her chin and held her face steady. The eyes that saw a great deal more than he was entitled to looked into hers. "Tell me."

"No." She said it quietly. If she'd been angry, insulted, cold, he'd have dug until he'd had it all. He couldn't fight her this way.

"All right." He backed off, dipping his hands into his pockets. He'd felt something out on the porch, something that had pulled at him, offered itself to him. If she'd made one move, the slightest move, he might have given her more at that moment than either of them could imagine. "Maybe you should get some sleep. We'll leave at seven."

"Okay." Deliberately she turned away to pack up the rest of her gear. "I'll be ready."

He was at the door before he felt compelled to turn around again. "Bryan, I saw your prints. They're exceptional."

She felt the first tears stream down her face and was appalled. Since when did she cry because someone acknowledged her talent? Since when did she tremble because a picture she was taking spoke to her personally?

She pressed her lips together for a moment and continued to pack without turning around. "Thanks."

Shade didn't linger any longer. He closed the door soundlessly on his way out.

Chapter 6

By the time they'd passed through New Mexico and into Colorado, Bryan felt more in tune with herself. In part, she thought that the break in Oak Creek Canyon had given her too much time for introspection. Though she often relied heavily on just that in her work, there were times when it could be self-defeating.

At least that's what she'd been able to convince herself of after she and Shade had picked up the routine of drive and shoot and drive some more.

They weren't looking for cities and major events on this leg. They sought out small, unrecognizable towns and struggling ranches. Families that worked with the land and one another to make ends meet. For them, summer was a time of hard, endless work to prepare for the rigors of winter. It wasn't all fun, all games, all sun and sand. It was migrant workers waiting to pick

August peaches, and gardens being weeded and tended to offset the expense of winter vegetables.

They didn't consider Denver, but chose instead places like Antonito. They didn't go after the big, sprawling cattle spreads, but the smaller, more personal operations.

Bryan had her first contact with a cattle branding on a dusty little ranch called the Bar T. Her preconception of sweaty, loose-limbed cowboys rounding 'em up and heading 'em out wasn't completely wrong. It just didn't include the more basic aspects of branding—such as the smell of burned flesh and the splash of blood as potential bulls were turned into little steers.

She was, she discovered as her stomach heaved, a city girl at heart.

But they got their pictures. Cowboys with bandannas over their faces and spurs on their boots. Some of them laughed, some of them swore. All of them worked.

She learned the true meaning of *workhorse* as she watched the men push their mounts through their paces. The sweat of a horse was a heavy, rich smell. It hung thickly in the air with the sweat of men.

Bryan considered her best shot a near-classic study of a man taking hold of his leisure time with both hands. The young cowboy was rangy and ruddy, which made him perfect for what she was after. His chambray shirt was dark with patches of sweat down the front, down the back and spreading from under the arms. More sweat mixed with dust ran down his face. His work boots were creased and caked with grime. The back pocket of his jeans was worn from the constant rub against a round can of chewing tobacco. With his hat tilted back and his bandanna tied loosely around his throat, he straddled the fence and lifted an icy can of beer to his lips.

Bryan thought when the picture was printed you'd almost be able to see his Adam's apple move as he swallowed. And every woman who looked at it, she was certain, would be half in love. He was the mystic, the swashbuckler, the last of the knights. Having that picture in her camera nearly made up for almost losing her lunch over the branding.

She'd seen Shade home right in on it and known his pictures would be gritty, hard and detailed. Yet she'd also seen him focusing in on a young boy of eleven or twelve as he'd ridden in his first roundup with all the joy and innocence peculiar to a boy of that age. His choice had surprised her, because he rarely went for the lighter touch. It was also, unfortunately for her state of mind, something else she could like him for. There were others.

He hadn't made any comment when she'd turned green and distanced herself for a time from what was going on in the small enclosed corral where calves bawled for their mothers and let out long, surprised wails when knife and iron were applied. He hadn't said a word when she'd sat down in the shade until she was certain her stomach would stay calm. Nor had he said a word when he'd handed her a cold drink. Neither had she.

That night they camped on Bar T land. Shade had given her space since they'd left Arizona, because she suddenly seemed to need it. Oddly, he found he didn't. In the beginning, it had always been Bryan who'd all but forced him into conversations when he'd have been content to drive in silence for hours. Now he wanted to talk to her, to hear her laugh, to watch the way her hands moved when she became enthusiastic about a certain point. Or to watch the way she stretched, easily, degree by inching degree, as her voice slowed.

Something undefinable had shifted in both of them during their time in Oak Creek. Bryan had become remote, when she'd always been almost too open for his comfort. He found he wanted her company, when he'd always been solitary. He wanted, though he didn't fully comprehend why, her friendship. It was a shift he wasn't certain he cared for, or even understood. In any case, because the opposing shifts had happened in both of them simultaneously, it brought them no closer.

Shade had chosen the open space near a fast-running creek for a campsite for no reason other than that it appealed to him. Bryan immediately saw other possibilities.

"Look, I'm going down to wash off." She was as dusty as the cowboys she'd focused on all afternoon. It occurred to her, not altogether pleasantly, that she might smell a bit too much like the horses she'd watched. "It's probably freezing, so I'll make it fast and you can have a turn."

Shade pried the top off a beer. Perhaps they hadn't rounded up cattle, but they'd been on their feet and in the sun for almost eight hours. "Take your time."

Bryan grabbed a towel and a cake of soap and dashed off. The sun was steadily dropping behind the mountains to the west. She knew enough of camping by now to know how quickly the air would cool once the sun went down. She didn't want to be wet and naked when it did.

She didn't bother to glance around before she stripped off her shirt. They were far enough away from the ranch house that none of the men would wander out that way at sunset. Shade and she had already established the sanctity of privacy without exchanging a word on the subject.

Right now, she thought as she wiggled out of her jeans, the cowboys they'd come to shoot were probably sitting down to an enormous meal—red meat and potatoes, she mused. Hot biscuits with plenty of butter. Lord knows they deserved it, after the day they'd put in. And me, too, she decided, though she and Shade were making do with cold sandwiches and a bag of chips.

Slim, tall and naked, Bryan took a deep breath of the pine-scented air. Even a city girl, she thought as she paused a moment to watch the sunset, could appreciate all this.

Gingerly she stepped into the cold knee-high water and began to rinse off the dust. Strange, she didn't mind the chill as much as she once had. The drive across America was bound to leave its mark. She was glad of it.

No one really wanted to stay exactly the same throughout life. If her outlook changed and shifted as they traveled, she was fortunate. The assignment was giving her more than the chance for professional exposure and creative expression. It was giving her experiences. Why else had she become a photographer, but to see things and understand them?

Yet she didn't understand Shade any better now than when they'd started out. Had she tried? In some ways, she thought, as she glided the soap over her arms. Until what she saw and understood began to affect her too deeply and too personally. Then she'd backed off fast.

She didn't like to admit it. Bryan shivered and began to wash more swiftly. The sun was nearly set. Self-preservation, she reminded herself. Perhaps her image was one of take what comes and make the best of it, but she had her phobias as well. And she was entitled to them.

It had been a long time since she'd been hurt, and that was because of her own deceptively simple maneuvering. If she stood at a crossroads and had two routes, one smooth, the other rocky, with a few pits, she'd take the smooth one. Maybe it was less admirable, but she'd always felt you ended up in the same place with less energy expended. Shade Colby was a rocky road.

In any case, it wasn't just a matter of her choice. They could have an affair—a physically satisfying, emotionally shallow affair. It worked well for a great many people. But…

He didn't want to be involved with her any more than she did with him. He was attracted, just as she was, but he wasn't offering her any more than that. If he ever did… She dropped that line of thought like a stone. Speculation wasn't always healthy.

The important thing was that she felt more like herself again. She was pleased with the work she'd done since they'd left Arizona, and was looking forward to crossing over into Kansas the next day. The assignment, as they'd both agreed from the outset, was the first priority.

Wheat fields and tornadoes, she thought with a grin. Follow the yellow brick road. That was what Kansas brought to her mind. She knew better now, and looked forward to finding the reality. Bryan was beginning to enjoy having her preconceptions both confirmed and blown to bits.

That was for tomorrow. Right now it was dusk and she was freezing.

Agile, she scrambled up the small bank and reached for the towel. Shade could wash up while she stuffed herself with whatever was handy in the cupboards. She pulled on a long-sleeved oversize shirt and reached up to button it. That's when she saw the eyes.

For a moment she only stared with her hands poised at the top button. Then she saw there was more to it than a pair of narrow yellow eyes peering out of the lowering light. There was a sleek, muscled body and a set of sharp, white teeth only a narrow creek bed away.

Bryan took two steps back, tripped over her own tangled jeans and let out a scream that might've been heard in the next county.

Shade was stretched out in a folding chair beside the small campfire he'd built on impulse. He'd enjoyed himself that day—the rough-and-ready atmosphere, the baking sun and cold beer. He'd always admired the camaraderie that went hand in hand with people who work outdoors.

He needed the city—it was in his blood. For the most part, he preferred the impersonal aspects of people rushing to their own places, in their own time. But it helped to touch base with other aspects of life from time to time.

He could see now, even after only a few weeks on the road, that he'd been getting stale. He hadn't had the challenge of his early years. That get-the-shot-and-stay-alive sort of challenge. He didn't want it. But he'd let himself become too complacent with what he'd been doing.

This assignment had given him the chance to explore himself as well as his country. He thought of his partner with varying degrees of puzzlement and interest. She wasn't nearly as simple or laid-back as he'd originally believed. Still, she was nearly 180 degrees removed from him. He was beginning to understand her. Slowly, but he was beginning to.

She was sensitive, emotional and inherently kind. He was rarely kind, because he was careful not to be. She was comfortable with herself, easily amused and candid. He'd learned long ago that candor can jump back on you with teeth.

But he wanted her—because she was different or in spite of it, he wanted her. Forcing himself to keep his hands off her in all the days and nights that had passed since that light, interrupted kiss in Hunter Brown's driveway was beginning to wear on him. He had his control to thank for the fact that he'd been able to, the control that he honed so well that it was nearly a prison.

Shade tossed his cigarette into the fire and leaned back. He wouldn't lose that control, or break out of that prison, but that didn't mean that sooner or later he and Bryan wouldn't be lovers. He meant it to happen. He would simply bide his time until it happened his way. As long as he was holding the reins, he wouldn't steer himself into the mire.

When he heard her scream, a dozen agonizing images rushed into his head, images that he'd seen and lived through, images that only someone who had could conjure up. He was out of the chair and running before he'd fully realized they were only memories.

When he got to her, Bryan was scrambling up from the tumble she'd taken. The last thing she expected was to be hauled up and crushed against Shade. The last thing she expected was exactly what she needed. Gasping for air, she clung to him.

"What happened?" Her own panic muffled her ears to the thread of panic in his voice. "Bryan, are you hurt?"

"No, no. It scared me, but it ran away." She pushed her face against his shoulder and just breathed. "Oh, God, Shade."

"What?" Gripping her by the elbows, he pulled her back far enough to see her face. "What scared you?"

"A cat."

He wasn't amused. His fear turned to fury, tangibly enough that Bryan could see the latter even before he cursed her. "Damn it! What kind of fool are you?" he demanded. "Letting out a scream like that over a cat."

She drew air in and out, in and out, and concentrated on her anger—genuine fear was something she didn't care for. "Not a house cat," she snapped. She was still shaken, but not enough to sit back and be called a fool. "It was one of those… I don't know." She lifted a hand to push at her hair and dropped it again when it trembled. "I have to sit down." She did so with a plop on the grass.

"A bobcat?" Calmer, Shade crouched down beside her.

"I don't know. Bobcat, cougar—I wouldn't know the difference. It was a hell of a lot bigger than any tabby." She lowered her head to her knees. Maybe she'd been frightened before in her life, but she couldn't remember anything to compare with this. "He just stood over there, staring at me. I thought—I thought he was going to jump over the creek. His teeth…" She shuddered and shut her eyes. "Big," she managed, no longer caring if she sounded like a simpleminded fool. "Real big."

"He's gone now." His fury turned inward. He should've known she wasn't the kind of woman who jumped at shadows. He knew what it was to be afraid and to feel helpless with it. This time he cursed himself as he slipped an arm around her. "The way you screamed, he's ten miles away and still running."

Bryan nodded but kept her face buried against her knees. "I guess he wasn't that big, but they look different out of the zoo. I just need a minute to pull myself together."

"Take your time."

He found he didn't mind offering comfort, though it was something he hadn't done in a long time. The air was cool, the night still. He could hear the sound of the water rushing by in the creek. For a moment he had a quick flash of the Browns' porch, of the easy family portrait on the swing. He felt a touch of the same contentment here, with his arm around Bryan and night closing in.

Overhead a hawk screeched, out for its first flight of the night. Bryan jolted.

"Easy," Shade murmured. He didn't laugh at her reaction, or even smile. He soothed.

"I guess I'm a little jumpy." With a nervous laugh, she lifted her hand to push at her hair again. It wasn't until then that Shade realized she was naked beneath the open, billowing shirt.

The sight of her slim, supple body beneath the thin, fluttering material sent the contentment he'd felt skyrocketing into need. A need, he discovered only in that instant, that was somehow exclusively for her—not just for a woman with a lovely face, a desirable body, but for Bryan.

"Maybe we should get back and…" She turned her head and found her eyes only inches from his. In his, she saw everything he felt. When she started to speak again, he shook his head.

No words. No words now. Only needs, only feelings.

He wanted that with her. As his mouth closed over hers, he gave her no choice but to want it as well.

Sweetness? Where had it come from and how could she possibly turn away from it? They'd been together nearly a month, but she'd never suspected he had sweetness in him. Nor had she known just how badly she'd needed to find it there.

His mouth demanded, but so slowly, so subtly, that she was giving before she was aware of it. Once she'd given, she couldn't take away again. She felt his hand, warm and firm on her bare skin, but she sighed in pleasure, not in protest. She'd wanted him to touch her, had waited for it, had denied her waiting. Now she leaned closer. There'd be no denying.

He'd known she'd feel like this—slim, strong, smooth. A hundred times, he'd imagined it. He hadn't forgotten that she'd taste like this—warm, tempting, generous. A hundred times, he'd tried not to remember.

This time she smelled of the creek, fresh and cool. He could bury his face in her throat and smell the summer night on her. He kissed her slowly, leaving her lips for her throat, her throat for her shoulder. As he lingered there, he gave himself the pleasure of discovering her body with his fingertips.

It was torture. Exquisite. Agonizing. Irresistible. Bryan wanted it to go on, and on and on. She drew him closer, loving the hard, lean feel of his body against hers, the brush of his clothes against her skin, the whisper of his breath across it. And through it all, the quick, steady beat of his heart near hers.

She could smell the work of the day on him, the faint tang of healthy sweat, the traces of dust he hadn't yet washed off. It excited her with memories of the way his muscles had bunched beneath his shirt when he'd climbed onto a fence for a better angle. She could remember exactly how he'd looked then, though she'd pretended to herself that she hadn't seen, hadn't needed to.

She wanted his strength. Not the muscles, but the inner strength she'd sensed in him from the start. The strength that had carried him through what he'd seen, what he'd lived with.

Yet wasn't it that strength that helped to harden him, to separate him emotionally from the people around him? With her mind whirling, her body pulsing, she struggled to find the answer she needed.

Wants weren't enough. Hadn't she told him so herself? God, she wanted him. Her bones were melting from the desire for him. But it wasn't enough. She only wished she knew what was.

"Shade..." Even when she tried to speak, he cut her off with another long, draining kiss.

She wanted him to drain her. Mind, body, soul. If he did, there'd be no question and no need for answers. But the questions were there. Even as she held him to her, they were there.

"Shade," she began again.

"I want to make love with you." He lifted his head, and his eyes were so dark, so intense, it was almost impossible to believe his hands were so gentle. "I want to feel your skin under my hand, feel your heart race, watch your eyes."

The words were quiet, incredibly calm when his eyes were so passionate. More than the passion and demand in his eyes, the words frightened her.

"I'm not ready for this." She barely managed the words as she drew away from him.

He felt the needs rise and the anger begin. It took

all his skill to control both. "Are you saying you don't want me?"

"No." She shook her head as she drew her shirt together. When had it become so cold? she wondered. "No, lying's foolish."

"So's backing away from something we both want to happen."

"I'm not sure I do. I can't be logical about this, Shade." She gathered her clothes quickly and hugged them against her as she stood. "I can't think something like this through step-by-step the way you do. If I could, it'd be different, but I can only go with my feelings, my instincts."

There was a deadly calm around him when he rose. The control he'd nearly forfeited to her was back in place. Once more he accepted the prison he'd built for himself. "And?"

She shivered without knowing if it was from the cold without or the cold within. "And my feelings tell me I need more time." When she looked up at him again, her face was honest, her eyes were eloquent. "Maybe I do want this to happen. Maybe I'm just a little afraid of how much I want you."

He didn't like her use of the word *afraid.* She made him feel responsible, obliged. Defensive. "I've no intention of hurting you."

She gave herself a moment. Her breathing was easier, even if her pulse was still unsteady. Whether he knew it or not, Shade had already given her the distance she needed to resist him. Now she could look at him, calmer. Now she could think more clearly.

"No, I don't think you do, but you could, and I have a basic fear of bruises. Maybe I'm an emotional coward. It's not a pretty thought, but it might be true." With a sigh, she lifted both hands to her hair and pushed it back. "Shade, we've a bit more than two months left on the road. I can't afford to spend it being torn up inside because of you. My instincts tell me you could very easily do that to me, whether you planned on it or not."

She knew how to back a man into a corner, he thought in frustration. He could press, relieve the knot she'd tightened in his stomach. And by doing so, he'd run the risk of having her words echo back at him for a long time to come. It'd only taken a few words from her to remind him what it felt like to be responsible for someone else.

"Go back to the van," he told her, turning away to strip off his shirt. "I have to clean up."

She started to speak, then realized there was nothing more she could say. Instead, she left him to follow the thin, moonlit trail back to the van.

Chapter 7

Wheat fields. Bryan's preconception wasn't slashed as they drove through the Midwest, but reinforced. Kansas was wheat fields.

Whatever else Bryan saw as they crossed the state, it was the endless, rippling gold grass that captivated her, first and last. Color, texture, shape, form. Emotion. There were towns, of course, cities with modern buildings and plush homes, but in seeing basic Americana, grain against sky, Bryan saw it all.

Some might have found the continuous spread of sun-ripened grain waving, acre after acre, monotonous. Not Bryan. This was a new experience for a woman of the city. There were no jutting mountains, no glossy towering buildings, no looping freeways, to break the lines. Here was space, just as awesome as the terrain of Arizona, but lusher, and somehow calmer. She could look at it and wonder.

In the fields of wheat and acres of corn, Bryan saw the heart and the sweat of the country. It wasn't always an idyllic scene. There were insects, dirt, grimy machinery. People worked here with their hands, with their backs.

In the cities, she saw the pace and energy. On the farms, she saw a schedule that would have made a corporate executive wilt. Year after year, the farmer gave himself to the land and waited for the land to give back.

With the right angle, the proper light, she could photograph a wheat field and make it seem endless, powerful. With evening shadows, she could give a sense of serenity and continuity. It was only grass, after all, only stalks growing to be cut down, processed, used. But the grain had a life and a beauty of its own. She wanted to show it as she saw it.

Shade saw the tenuous, inescapable dependence of man on nature. The planter, keeper and harvester of the wheat, was irrevocably tied to the land. It was both his freedom and his prison. The man riding the tractor in the Kansas sunlight, damp with healthy sweat, lean from years of labor, was as dependent on the land as the land was on him. Without man, the wheat might grow wild, it might flourish, but then it would wither and die. It was the tie Shade sensed, and the tie he meant to record.

Still, perhaps for the first time since they'd left L.A., he and Bryan weren't shooting as separate entities. They might not have realized it yet, but their feelings, perceptions and needs were drawing them closer to the same mark.

They made each other think. How did she see this scene? How did he feel about this setting? Where before each of them had considered their photographs separately, now subtly, unconsciously, they began to do two things that would improve the final result: compete and consult.

They'd spent a day and a night in Dodge City for the Fourth of July celebrations in what had once been a Wild West town. Bryan thought of Wyatt Earp, of Doc Holliday and the desperadoes who had once ridden through town, but she'd been drawn to the street parade that might've been in Anytown, U.S.A.

It was here, caught up in the pageantry and the flavor, that she'd asked Shade his opinion of the right angle for shooting a horse and rider, and he in turn had taken her advice on capturing a tiny, bespangled majorette.

The step they'd taken had been lost in the moment to both of them. But they'd stood side by side on the curb as the parade had passed, music blaring, batons flying. Their pictures had been different—Shade had looked for the overview of holiday parades while Bryan had wanted individual reactions. But they'd stood side by side.

Bryan's feelings for Shade had become more complex, more personal. When the change had begun or how, she couldn't say. But because her work was most often a direct result of her emotions, the pictures she took began to reflect both the complexity and the intimacy. Their view of the same wheat field might be radically different, but Bryan was determined that when their prints were set side by side, hers would have equal impact.

She'd never been an aggressive person. It just wasn't her style. But Shade had tapped a need in her to compete—as a photographer, and as a woman. If she had to travel in close quarters for weeks with a man who ruffled her professional feathers and stirred her feminine needs, she had to deal with him directly—on both counts. Directly, she decided, but in her own fashion and her own time. As the days went on, Bryan wondered if it would be possible to have both success and Shade without losing something vital.

She was so damn calm! It drove him crazy. Every day, every hour, they spent together pushed Shade closer to the edge. He wasn't used to wanting anyone so badly. He didn't enjoy finding out he could, and that there was nothing he could do about it. Bryan put him in the position of needing, then having to deny himself. There were times he nearly believed she did so purposely. But he'd never known anyone less likely to scheme than Bryan. She wouldn't think of it—and if she did, she'd consider it too much bother.

Even now, as they drove through the Kansas twilight, she was stretched out in the seat beside him, sound asleep. It was one of the rare times she'd left her hair loose. Full, wavy and lush, it was muted to a dull gold in the lowering light. The sun had given her skin all the color it needed. Her body was relaxed, loose like her hair. Shade wondered if he'd ever had the capability to let his mind and body go so enviably limp. Was it that that tempted him, that drove at him? Was he simply pushed to find that spark of energy she could turn on and off at will? He wanted to set it to life. For himself.

Temptation. The longer he held himself back, the more intense it became. To have her. To explore her. To absorb her. When he did—he no longer used the word *if*—what cost would there be? Nothing was free.

Once, he thought as she sighed in sleep. Just once. His way. Perhaps the cost would be high, but he wouldn't be the one to pay it. His emotions were trained and disciplined. They wouldn't be touched. There wasn't a woman alive who could make him hurt.

His body and his mind tensed as Bryan slowly woke. Groggy and content to be so, she yawned. The scent of smoke and tobacco stung the air. On the radio was low, mellow jazz. The windows were half open, so that when she shifted, the slap of wind woke her more quickly than she'd have liked.

It was fully dark now. Surprised, Bryan stretched and stared out the window at a moon half covered by clouds. "It's late," she said on another yawn. The first thing she remembered as her mind cleared of sleep was that they hadn't eaten. She pressed a hand to her stomach. "Dinner?"

He glanced at her just long enough to see her shake back her hair. It rippled off her shoulders and down her back. As he watched, he had to fight back the urge to touch it. "I want to get over the border tonight."

She heard it in his voice—the tension, the annoyance. Bryan didn't know what had prompted it, nor at the moment did she want to. Instead, she lifted a brow. If he was in a hurry to get to Oklahoma and was willing to drive into the night to get there, it was his business. She'd stocked a cabinet in the back of the van with a few essentials just for moments like this. Bryan started to haul herself out of her seat when she heard the long blare of a horn and the rev of an engine.

The scarred old Pontiac had a hole in the muffler you could've tossed a baseball through. The sound of the engine clattered like a badly tuned plane. It swerved around the van at a dangerous speed, fishtailed, then bolted ahead, radio blaring. As Shade swore, Bryan got a glimpse that revealed the dilapidated car was packed with kids.

"Saturday night in July," she commented.

"Idiots," he said between his teeth as he watched the taillights weave.

"Yeah." She frowned as she watched the car barrel ahead, smoke streaming. "They were just kids, I hope they don't..."

Even as she thought it, it happened. The driver decided to press his luck by passing another car over the double yellow lines. The truck coming toward him laid on the horn and swerved. Bryan felt her blood freeze.

Shade was already hitting the brakes as the Pontiac screeched back into its own lane. But it was out of control. Skidding sideways, the Pontiac kissed the fender of the car it had tried to pass, then flipped into a telephone pole.

The sound of screaming tires, breaking glass and smashing metal whirled in her head. Bryan was up and out of the van before Shade had brought it to a complete stop. She could hear a girl screaming, others weeping. Even as the sounds shuddered through her, she told herself it meant they were alive.

The door on the passenger's side was crushed against the telephone pole. Bryan rushed to the driver's side and wrenched at the handle. She smelled the blood before she saw it. "Good God," she whispered as she managed to yank the door open on the second try. Then Shade was beside her, shoving her aside.

"Get some blankets out of the van," he ordered without looking at her. It had only taken him one glance at the driver to tell him it wasn't going to be pretty. He shifted enough to block Bryan's view, then reached in to check the pulse in the driver's throat as he heard her run back to the van. Alive, he thought, then blocked out everything but what had to be done. He worked quickly.

The driver was unconscious. The gash on his head was serious, but it didn't worry Shade as much as the probability of internal injuries. And nothing worried him as much as the smell of gas that was beginning to sweeten the air. Under other circumstances, Shade would've been reluctant to move the boy. Now there was no choice. Locking his arms under the boy's arms, Shade hauled him out. Even as Shade began to drag him, the driver of the truck ran over and took the boy's legs.

"Got a CB in the truck," he told Shade breathlessly. "Called for an ambulance."

With a nod, Shade laid the boy down. Bryan was already there with the first blanket.

"Stay here. The car's going to go up." He said it calmly. Without a backward glance, he went back to the crippled Pontiac.

Terror jolted through her. Within seconds, Bryan was at the car beside him, helping to pull the others out of the wreck.

"Get back to the van!" Shade shouted at her as Bryan half carried a sobbing girl. "Stay there!"

Bryan spoke soothingly, covered the girl with a blanket, then rushed back to the car. The last passenger was also unconscious. A boy, Bryan saw, of no more than sixteen. She had to half crawl into the car to reach him. By the time she'd dragged him to the open door, she was drenched and exhausted. Both Shade and the truck driver carried the other injured passengers. Shade had just set a young girl on the grass when he turned and saw Bryan struggling with the last victim.

Fear was instant and staggering. Even as he started to run, his imagination worked on him. In his mind, Shade could see the flash of the explosion, hear the sound of bursting metal and shattering, flying glass. He knew exactly what it would smell like the moment the gas ignited. When he reached Bryan, Shade scooped up the unconscious boy as though he were weightless.

"Run!" he shouted at her. Together, they raced away from the Pontiac.

Bryan didn't see the explosion. She heard it, but more, she felt it. The whoosh of hot air slammed into her back and sent her sprawling onto the grassy shoulder of the road. There was a whistle of metal as something hot and twisted and lethal flew overhead. One of the teenagers screamed and buried her face in her hands.

Stunned, Bryan lay prone a moment, waiting to catch her breath. Over the sound of fire, she could hear the whine of sirens.

"Are you hurt?" Shade half dragged her up to her knees. He'd seen the flying slice of metal whiz by her head. Hands that had been rock steady moments before trembled as they gripped her.

"No." Bryan shook her head and, finding her balance, turned to the whimpering girl beside her. A broken arm, she realized as she tucked the blanket under the girl's chin. And the cut on her temple would need stitches. "Take it easy," Bryan murmured, pulling out a piece of gauze from the first-aid box she'd brought from the van. "You're going to be fine. The ambulance is coming. Can you hear it?"

As she spoke, she pressed the gauze against the wound to stop the bleeding. Her voice was calm, but her fingers trembled.

"Bobby." Tears ran down the girl's face as she clung to Bryan. "Is Bobby all right? He was driving."

Bryan glanced over and looked directly at Shade before she lowered her gaze to the unconscious boy. "He's going to be fine," she said, and felt helpless.

Six young, careless children, she thought as she scanned those sitting or lying on the grass. The driver of the other car sat dazedly across from them, holding a rag to the cut on his own head. For a moment, a long, still moment, the night was quiet—warm, almost balmy. Stars were brilliant overhead. Moonlight was strong and lovely. Thirty feet away, what was left of the Pontiac crackled with flame. Bryan slipped her arm around the shoulders of the girl and watched the lights of the ambulance speed up the road.

As the paramedics began to work, another ambulance and the fire department were called. For twenty minutes, Bryan sat by the young girl, talking to her, holding her hand while her injuries were examined and tended to.

Her name was Robin. She was seventeen. Of the six teenagers in the car, her boyfriend, Bobby, was the oldest at nineteen. They'd only been celebrating summer vacation.

As Bryan listened and soothed, she glanced up to see Shade calmly setting his camera. Astonished, she watched as he carefully focused and framed in the injured. Dispassionately, he recorded the scene of the accident, the victims and what was left of the car. As astonishment faded, Bryan felt the fury bubble inside her. When Robin was carried to the second ambulance, Bryan sprang up.

"What the hell are you doing?" She grabbed his shoulder, spoiling a shot. Still calm, Shade turned to her and gave her one quick study.

She was pale. Her eyes showed both strain and fury. And, he thought, a dull sheen of shock. For the first time since he'd known her, Shade saw how tense her body could be. "I'm doing my job," he said simply, and lifted the camera again.

"Those kids are bleeding!" Bryan grabbed his shoulder again, swinging herself around until she was face-to-face with him. "They've got broken bones. They're hurt and they're frightened. Since when is your job taking pictures of their pain?"

"Since I picked up a camera for pay." Shade let the camera swing by its strap. He'd gotten enough, in any case. He didn't like the feeling in his own stomach, the tension behind his eyes. Most of all, he didn't like the look in Bryan's as she stared at him. Disgust. He shrugged it off.

"You're only willing to take pictures of fun in the sun for this assignment, Bryan. You saw the car, those kids. That's part of it, too. Part of life. If you can't handle it, you'd better stick to your celebrity shots and leave the real world alone."

He'd taken two steps toward the van when Bryan was on him again. She might avoid confrontations as a matter of habit, take the line of least resistance as often as possible, but there were times when she'd fight. When she did, she used everything.

"I can handle it." She wasn't pale any longer; her face glowed with anger. Her eyes gleamed with it. "What I can't handle are the vultures who love picking at bones, making a profit off misery in the name of art. There were six people in that car. *People,*" she repeated, hissing at him. "Maybe they were foolish, maybe they deserved what happened, but I'll be damned if I'm going to judge. Do you think it makes you a better photographer, a better artist, because you're cold enough, you're *professional* enough, to freeze their pain on printing paper? Is this the way you look for another Pulitzer nomination?"

She was crying now, too angry, too churned up by what she'd seen, to be aware of the tears streaming down her cheeks. Yet somehow the tears made her look stronger. They thickened her voice and gave it impact. "I'll tell you what it makes you," she went on when Shade remained silent. "It makes you empty. Whatever compassion you were born with died somewhere along the way, Shade. I'm sorry for you."

She left him standing in the middle of the road by the shell of the car.

It was nearly 3:00 a.m. Shade had learned that the mind was at its most helpless in those early hours of the morning. The van was dark and quiet, parked in a small campground just over the Oklahoma border. He and Bryan hadn't exchanged a word since the accident. Each had prepared for bed in silence, and though both of them had lain awake for some time, neither had spoken. Now they slept, but only Bryan slept dreamlessly.

There'd been a time, during the first months after his return from Cambodia, that Shade had had the dream regularly. Over the years it had come to him less and less. Often he could force himself awake and fight the dream off before it really took hold. But now, in the tiny Oklahoma campground, he was powerless.

He knew he was dreaming. The moment the figures and shapes began to form in his mind, Shade understood it wasn't real—that it wasn't real any longer. It didn't stop the panic or the pain. The Shade Colby in the dream would go through the same motions he'd gone through all those years ago, leading to the same end. And in the dream there were no soft lines, no mists to lessen the impact. He saw it as it had happened, in strong sunlight.

Shade came out of the hotel and onto the street with Dave, his assistant. Between them, they carried all their luggage and equipment. They were going home. After four months of hard, often dangerous work in a city torn, ravaged and smoldering, they were going home. It had occurred to Shade that they were calling it close—but he'd called it close before. Every day they stayed on added to the risk of getting out at all. But there'd always been one more picture to take, one more statement to make. And there'd been Sung Lee.

She'd been so young, so eager, so wise. As a contact in the city, she'd been invaluable. She'd been just as invaluable to Shade personally. After a bumpy, unpleasant divorce from a wife who'd wanted more glamour and less reality, Shade had needed the long, demanding assignment. And he'd needed Sung Lee.

She was devoted, sweet, undemanding. When he'd taken her to bed, Shade had finally been able to block out the rest of the world and relax. His only regret in going back home was that she wouldn't leave her country.

As they'd stepped out on the street, Shade had been thinking of her. They'd said their goodbyes the night before, but he was thinking of her. Perhaps if he hadn't been, he'd have sensed something. He'd asked himself that hundreds of times in the months that followed.

The city was quiet, but it wasn't peaceful. The tension in the air could erupt at any time. Those who were getting out were doing so in a hurry. Tomorrow, the next day, the doors might be closed. Shade took one last look around as they started toward their car. One last picture, he'd thought, of the calm before the storm.

A few careless words to Dave and he was alone, standing on the curb pulling his camera out of its case. He laughed as Dave swore and struggled with the luggage on his way to the car. Just one last picture. The next time he lifted his camera to shoot, it would be on American soil.

"Hey, Colby!" Young, grinning, Dave stood beside the car. He looked like a college student on spring break. "How about taking one of a future award-winning photographer on his way out of Cambodia?"

With a laugh, Shade lifted his camera and framed in his assistant. He remembered exactly the way he'd looked. Blond, tanned, a bit gangly, with a crooked front tooth and a faded USC T-shirt.

He took the shot. Dave turned the key in the lock.

"Let's go home," his assistant yelled the instant before the car exploded.

"Shade. Shade!" Heart pounding, Bryan shook him. "Shade, wake up, it's a dream." He grabbed her hard enough to make bruises, but she kept talking. "It's Bryan, Shade. You're having a dream. Just a dream. We're in Oklahoma, in your van. Shade." She took his face in her hands and felt the skin cold and damp. "Just a dream," she said quietly. "Try to relax. I'm right here."

He was breathing too quickly. Shade felt himself straining for air and forced himself to calm. God, he was cold. He felt the warmth of Bryan's skin under his hands, heard her voice, calm, low, soothing. With an oath, he dropped back down again and waited for the shuddering to stop.

"I'll get you some water."

"Scotch."

"All right." The moonlight was bright enough. She found the plastic cup and the bottle and poured. Behind her, she heard the flare of his lighter and the hiss as it caught paper and tobacco. When Bryan turned, he was sitting up on the bunk, resting back against the side of the van. She had no experience with whatever trauma haunted Shade, but she did know how to soothe nerves. She handed him the drink, then, without asking, sat beside him. She waited until he'd taken the first sip.

"Better?"

He took another sip, a deeper one. "Yeah."

She touched his arm lightly, but the contact was made. "Tell me."

He didn't want to speak of it, not to anyone, not to her. Even as the refusal formed on his lips, she increased the grip on his arm.

"We'll both feel better if you do. Shade…" She had to wait again, this time for him to turn and look at her. Her heartbeat was steadier now, and so, as her fingers lay over his wrist, was his. But there was still a thin sheen of sweat drying on his skin. "Nothing gets better and goes away if you hold it in."

He'd held it in for years. It'd never gone away. Perhaps it never would. Maybe it was the quiet understanding in her voice, or the late hour, but he found himself talking.

He told her of Cambodia, and though his voice was flat, she could see it as he had. Ripe for explosion, crumbling, angry. Long, monotonous days punctuated by moments of terror. He told her how he'd reluctantly taken on an assistant and then learned to appreciate and enjoy the young man fresh out of college. And Sung Lee.

"We ran across her in a bar where most of the journalists hung out. It wasn't until a long time later that I put together just how convenient the meeting was. She was twenty, beautiful, sad. For nearly three months, she gave us leads she supposedly learned from a cousin who worked at the embassy."

"Were you in love with her?"

"No." He drew on his cigarette until there was nothing left but filter. "But I cared. I wanted to help her. And I trusted her."

He dropped his cigarette into an ashtray and concentrated on his drink. The panic was gone. He'd never realized he could talk about it calmly, think about it calmly. "Things were heating up, and the magazine decided to pull its people out. We were going home. We were coming out of the hotel, and I stopped to take a couple of shots. Like a tourist." He swore and drained the rest of the Scotch. "Dave got to the car first. It'd been booby-trapped."

"Oh, my God." Without realizing it, she moved closer to him.

"He was twenty-three. Carried a picture of the girl he was going to marry."

"I'm sorry." She laid her head against his shoulder, wound her arm around him. "I'm so sorry."

He braced himself against the flood of sympathy. He wasn't ready for it. "I tried to find Sung Lee. She was gone; her apartment was empty. It turned out that I'd been her assignment. The group she'd worked for had let things leak through so I'd relax and trust her. They'd intended to make a statement by blowing away an important American reporter. They'd missed me. An assistant photographer on his first overseas assignment didn't make any impact. The kid died for nothing."

And he'd watched the car explode, she thought. Just as he'd watched the car explode tonight. What had it done to him—then and now? Was that why, she wondered, he'd coolly taken out his camera and recorded it all? He was so determined not to feel.

"You blame yourself," she murmured. "You can't."

"He was a kid. I should've looked out for him."

"How?" She shifted so that they were face-to-face again. His eyes were dark, full of cold anger and frustration. She'd never forget just how they looked at that moment. "How?" she repeated. "If you hadn't stopped to take those pictures, you'd have gotten into the car with him. He'd still be dead."

"Yeah." Suddenly weary, Shade ran his hands over his face. The tension was gone, but not the bitterness. Perhaps that's what he was weary of.

"Shade, after the accident—"

"Forget it."

"No." This time she had his hand caught in hers. "You were doing what you had to, for your own reasons. I said I wouldn't judge those kids, but I was judging you. I'm sorry."

He didn't want her apology, but she gave it. He didn't want her to cleanse him, but she was washing away the guilt. He'd seen so much—too much—of the dark side of human nature. She was offering him the light. It tempted him and it terrified him.

"I'll never see things as you do," he murmured. After a moment's hesitation, he laced his fingers with hers. "I'll never be as tolerant."

Puzzled, she frowned as they stared at each other. "No, I don't think you will. I don't think you have to."

"You were right earlier when you said my compassion was dead. I haven't any." She started to speak, but he shook his head. "I haven't any patience, very little sympathy."

Did he look at his own pictures? she wondered.

Didn't he see the carefully harnessed emotion in them? But she said nothing, letting him make whatever point he needed to.

"I stopped believing in intimacy, genuine intimacy, permanency, between two people a long time ago. But I do believe in honesty."

She might've drawn away from him. There was something in his voice that warned her, but she stayed where she was. Their bodies were close. She could feel his heartbeat steady as hers began to race. "I think permanency works for some people." Was that her voice? she wondered, so calm, so practical. "I stopped looking for it for myself."

Isn't that what he'd wanted to hear? Shade looked down at their joined hands and wondered why her words left him dissatisfied. "Then it's understood that neither of us wants or needs promises."

Bryan opened her mouth, amazed that she wanted to object. She swallowed. "No promises," she managed. She had to think, had to have the distance to manage it. Deliberately she smiled. "I think we both could use some sleep, though."

He tightened his grip on her hand as she started to move. Honesty, he'd said. Though the words weren't easy for him, he'd say what he meant. He looked at her a long time. What was left of the moonlight showered her face and shadowed her eyes. Caught in his, her hand was steady. Her pulse wasn't.

"I need you, Bryan."

There were so many things he could have said, and to any of them she'd have had an answer. Wants—no, wants weren't enough. She'd already told him. Demands could be refused or shrugged off.

Needs. Needs were deeper, warmer, stronger. A need was enough.

He didn't move. He waited. Watching him, Bryan knew he'd let her take the step toward or away. Choices. He was a man who demanded them for himself, yet he was also capable of giving them. How could he know she'd had none the moment he'd spoken?

Slowly, she drew her hand from his. Just as slowly, she lifted both hands to his face and brought her mouth to his. With their eyes open, they shared a long, quiet kiss. It was a move that both offered and took.

She offered, with her hands light on his skin. She took, with her mouth warm and certain. He accepted. He gave. And then in the same instant, they both forgot the rules.

Her lashes fluttered down, her lips parted. Mindlessly he pulled her against him until their bodies were crushed close. She didn't resist, but went with him as they slid from the bunk and onto the rug.

She'd wanted this—the triumph and the weakness of being touched by him. She'd wanted the glory of letting herself go, of allowing her longings freedom. With his mouth hungry on hers, there was no need to think, no need to hold back what she'd wanted so desperately to give him. Only to him.

Take more. Her mind was reeling from the demands of her body. Take all. She could feel him tug at the wide neck of her sleep shirt until her shoulder was bare and vulnerable to his mouth. Still more. She skimmed her hands up his back, naked and warm from the night breeze flowing in the windows.

He wasn't easy as a lover. Hadn't she known it? There was no patience in him. Hadn't he told her? She'd known it before, but she was already aware that she'd never know relaxation with Shade. He drove her quickly, thoroughly. While she experienced all, she had no time to luxuriate in separate sensations. Masses of them swirled around, inside her.

Tastes…his lips, his skin—dark flavor. Scents… flowers, flesh—sweet and pungent. Textures…the nap of the rug rubbing against her legs, the hard brush of his palm, the soft warmth of his mouth. Sounds…her heartbeat pounding in her head, the murmur of her name in his whisper. She could see shadows, moonlight, the gleam of his eyes before his mouth took hers again. Everything merged and mixed together until they were one overpowering sensation. Passion.

He pulled the shirt lower until her arms were pinned. For a moment, she was helpless as he trailed his lips down her breast, pausing to taste, taste thoroughly, with lips, tongue, teeth. Some women would've found him merciless.

Perhaps it was the sound of her moan that made him linger when he was driven to hurry on. She was so slender, so smooth. The moonlight filtered in so that he could see where her tan gave way to paler, more vulnerable skin. Once he'd have turned away from vulnerability, knowing the dangers of it. Now it drew him—the softness of it. Her scent was there, clinging to the underside of her breast where he could taste as well as smell it. Sexy, tempting, subtle. It was as she was, and he was lost.

He felt his control slip, skid away from him. Ruthlessly, he brought it back. They would make love once—a hundred times that night—but he'd stay in control. As he was now, he thought as she arched under him. As he'd promised himself he would be, always. He would drive her, but he would not, could not, be driven by her.

Pulling the material down, he explored every inch of her mercilessly. He would show no mercy to either of them. Already she was beyond thought and he knew it. Her skin was hot, and somehow softer with the heat; her scent intensified with it. He could run those hungry, openmouthed kisses wherever he chose.

Her hands were free. Energy and passion raced together inside her. She tumbled over the first peak, breathless and strong. Now she could touch, now she could enrage him, entice him, weaken him. She moved quickly, demanding when he'd expected surrender. It was too sudden, too frantic, to allow him to brace himself against it. Even as she raced to the next peak, she felt the change in him.

He couldn't stop it. She wouldn't permit him to take without giving. His mind swam. Though he tried to clear it, fought to hold himself back, she seduced. Not his body, he'd have given that freely. She seduced his mind until it reeled with her. Emotion raged through him. Clean, hot, strong.

Tangled together, body and mind, they drove each other higher. They took each other over.

Chapter 8

They were both very careful. Neither Bryan nor Shade wanted to say anything the other could misunderstand. They'd made love, and for each of them it had been more intense, more vital, than anything they'd ever experienced. They'd set rules, and for each of them the need to abide by them was paramount.

What had happened between them had left them both more than a little stunned, and more wary than ever.

For a woman like Bryan, who was used to saying what she wanted, doing as she pleased, it wasn't easy to walk on eggshells twenty-four hours a day. But they'd made themselves clear before making love, she reminded herself. No complications, no commitments. No promises. They'd both failed once at the most important of relationships, marriage. Why should either of them risk failure again?

They traveled in Oklahoma, giving an entire day to

a small-town rodeo. Bryan hadn't enjoyed anything as much since the Fourth of July celebrations they'd seen in Kansas. She enjoyed watching the heat of competition, the pitting of man against animal and man against man and the clock. Every man who'd lowered himself onto a bronc or a bull had been determined to make it to the bell.

Some had been young, others had been seasoned, but all had had one goal. To win, and then to go on to the next round. She'd liked seeing that a game could be turned into a way of life.

Unable to resist, she bought a pair of boots with fancy stitching and a stubby heel. Since the van was too small to permit indiscriminate souvenir buying, she'd restrained herself this far. But there wasn't any point in being a martyr about it. The boots made her happy, but she resisted buying a leather belt with an oversize silver buckle for Shade. It was just the sort of gesture he might misunderstand. No, they wouldn't give each other flowers or trinkets or pretty words.

She drove south toward Texas while Shade read the paper in the seat beside her. On the radio was a raspy Tina Turner number that was unapologetically sexy.

Summer had reached the point when the heat began to simmer. Bryan didn't need the radio announcer to tell her it was ninety-seven and climbing, but both she and Shade had agreed to use the air-conditioning sparingly on the long trips. On the open highway, the breeze was almost enough. In defense, she was wearing a skimpy tank top and shorts while she drove in her bare feet. She thought of Dallas and an air-conditioned hotel room with cool sheets on a soft mattress.

"I've never been to Texas," she said idly. "I can't imagine any place that has cities fifty and sixty miles across. A cab ride across town could cost you a week's pay."

The paper crackled as he flipped the page. "You live in Dallas or Houston, you own a car."

It was like him to give a brief practical answer, and she'd come to accept it. "I'm glad we're taking a couple of days in Dallas to print. Ever spent any time there?"

"A little." He shrugged as he turned the next section of the paper. "Dallas, Houston—those cities are Texas. Big, sprawling, wealthy. Plenty of Tex-Mex restaurants, luxury hotels and a freeway system that leaves the out-of-towner reeling. That's why I routed in San Antonio as well. It's something apart from the rest of Texas. It's elegant, serene, more European."

She nodded, glancing out at the road signs. "Did you have an assignment in Texas?"

"I tried living in Dallas for a couple of years in between the overseas work."

It surprised her. She just couldn't picture him anywhere but L.A. "How'd you like it?"

"Not my style," he said simply. "My ex-wife stayed on and married oil."

It was the first time he'd made any sort of reference to his marriage. Bryan wiped her damp hands on her shorts and wondered how to handle it. "You don't mind going back?"

"No."

"Does it…" She trailed off, wondering if she was getting in deeper than she should.

Shade tossed the paper aside. "What?"

"Well, does it bother you that she's remarried and settled? Don't you ever think back and try to figure out what messed things up?"

"I know what messed things up. There's no use

dwelling on it. After you admit you've made a mistake, you've got to go on."

"I know." She pushed at her sunglasses. "I just sometimes wonder why some people can be so happy together, and others so miserable."

"Some people don't belong with each other."

"And yet it often seems like they do before they walk up the aisle."

"Marriage doesn't work for certain kinds of people."

Like us? Bryan wondered. After all, they'd both failed at it. Perhaps he was right, and it was as simple as that. "I made a mess out of mine," she commented.

"All by yourself?"

"Seems that way."

"Then you screwed up and married Mr. Perfect."

"Well, I..." She glanced over and saw him looking at her, one brow raised and a bland look of anticipation on his face. She'd forgotten he could make her laugh as well as ache. "Mr. Nearly Perfect, anyway." She grinned. "I'd have been smarter to look for someone with flaws."

After lighting a cigarette, he rested his feet on the dash as Bryan was prone to do. "Why didn't you?"

"I was too young to realize flaws were easier to deal with. And I loved him." She hadn't realized it would be so painless to say it, to put it in the past tense. "I really did," she murmured. "In a naive, rose-tinted way. At the time I didn't realize I'd have to make a choice between his conception of marriage and my work."

He understood exactly. His wife hadn't been cruel, she hadn't been vindictive. She'd simply wanted things he couldn't give. "So you married Mr. Nearly Perfect and I married Ms. Socially Ambitious. I wanted to take important pictures, and she wanted to join the country club. Nothing wrong with either goal—they just don't mesh."

"But sometimes don't you regret that you couldn't make it fit?"

"Yeah." It came out unexpectedly, surprising him a great deal more than it surprised her. He hadn't realized he had regrets. He hadn't allowed himself to. "You're getting low on gas," he said abruptly. "We'll stop in the next town and fill up."

Bryan had heard of one-horse towns, but nothing fitted the phrase more perfectly than the huddle of houses just over the Oklahoma-Texas border. Everything seemed to be dusty and faded by the heat. Even the buildings looked tired. Perhaps the state was enriched by oil and growth, but this little corner had slept through it.

As a matter of habit, Bryan took her camera as she stepped from the van to stretch her legs. As she walked around the side of the van, the skinny young attendant goggled at her. Shade saw the boy gape and Bryan smile before he walked into the little fan-cooled store behind the pumps.

Bryan found a small, fenced yard just across the street. A woman in a cotton housedress and a faded apron watered the one colorful spot—a splash of pansies along the edge of the house. The grass was yellow, burned by the sun, but the flowers were lush and thriving. Perhaps they were all the woman needed to keep her content. The fence needed painting badly and the screen door to the house had several small holes, but the flowers were a bright, cheerful slash. The woman smiled as she watered them.

Grateful she'd picked up the camera she'd loaded with color film, Bryan tried several angles. She wanted to catch the tired, sun-faded wood of the house and the parched lawn, both a contrast to that bouquet of hope.

Dissatisfied, she shifted again. The light was good, the colors perfect, but the picture was wrong. Why? Stepping back, she took it all in again and asked herself the all-important question. What do I feel?

Then she had it. The woman wasn't necessary, just the illusion of her. Her hand holding the watering can, no more. She could be any woman, anywhere, who needed flowers to complete her home. It was the flowers and the hope they symbolized that were important, and that was what Bryan finally recorded.

Shade came out of the store with a paper bag. He saw Bryan across the street, experimenting with angles. Content to wait, he set the bag in the van, drawing out the first cold can before he turned to pay the attendant for the gas. The attendant, Shade noticed, who was so busy watching Bryan he could hardly screw on the gas cap.

"Nice van," he commented, but Shade didn't think he'd even looked at it.

"Thanks." He allowed his own gaze to follow the boy's until it rested on Bryan's. He had to smile. She was a very distracting sight in the swatch of material she called shorts. Those legs, he mused. They seemed to start at the waist and just kept going. Now he knew just how sensitive they could be—on the inside of the knee, just above the ankle, on the warm, smooth skin high on the thigh.

"You and your wife going far?"

"Hmm?" Shade lost track of the attendant as he became just as fascinated by Bryan.

"You and the missus," the boy repeated, sighing a little as he counted out Shade's change. "Going far?"

"Dallas," he murmured. "She's not…" He started to correct the boy's mistake about their relationship, then found himself stopping. The *missus.* It was a quaint word, and somehow appealing. It hardly mattered if a boy in a border town thought Bryan belonged to him. "Thanks," he said absently and, stuffing the change in his pocket, walked to her.

"Good timing," she told him as she crossed toward him. They met in the middle of the road.

"Find something?"

"Flowers." She smiled, forgetting the unmerciful sun. If she breathed deeply enough, she could just smell them over the dust. "Flowers where they didn't belong. I think it's…" She felt the rest of the words slide back down her throat as he reached out and touched her hair.

He never touched her, not in the most casual of ways. Unless they were making love, and then it was never casual. There was never any easy brush of hands, no gentle squeeze. Nothing. Until now, in the center of the road, between a parched yard and a grimy gas station.

"You're beautiful. Sometimes it stuns me."

What could she say? He never spoke soft words. Now they flowed over her as his fingers trailed to her cheek. His eyes were so dark. She had no idea what he saw when he looked at her, what he felt. She'd never have asked. Perhaps for the first time, he was giving her the opportunity, but she couldn't speak, only stare.

He might have told her that he saw honesty, kindness, strength. He might have told her he felt needs that were growing far beyond the borders he'd set up between him and the rest of the world. If she'd asked, he might have told her that she was making a difference in his life he hadn't foreseen but could no longer prevent.

For the first time, he bent toward her and kissed

her, with an uncharacteristic gentleness. The moment demanded it, though he wasn't sure why. The sun was hot and hard, the road dusty, and the smell of gasoline was strong. But the moment demanded tenderness from him. He gave it, surprised that it was in him to offer.

"I'll drive," he murmured as he slipped her hand into his. "It's a long way to Dallas."

His feelings had changed. Not for the city they drove into, but for the woman beside him. Dallas had changed since he'd lived there, but Shade knew from experience that it seemed to change constantly. Even though he'd only lived there briefly, it had seemed as though a new building would grow up overnight. Hotels, office buildings, popped up wherever they could find room, and there seemed to be an endless supply of room in Dallas. The architecture leaned toward the futuristic—glass, spirals, pinnacles. But you never had to look far to find that unique southwestern flavor. Men wore cowboy hats as easily as they wore three-piece suits.

They'd agreed on a midtown hotel because it was within walking distance of the darkroom they'd rented for two days. While one worked in the field, the other would have use of the equipment to develop and print. Then they'd switch.

Bryan looked up at the hotel with something like reverence as they pulled up in front of it. Hot running water, feather pillows. Room service. Stepping out, she began to unload her share of the luggage and gear.

"I can't wait," she said as she hauled out another case and felt sweat bead down her back. "I'm going to wallow in the bathtub. I might even sleep there."

Shade pulled out his tripod, then hers. "Do you want your own?"

"My own?" She swung the first camera bag strap over her shoulder.

"Tub."

She looked up and met his calm, questioning glance. He wouldn't assume, she realized, that they'd share a hotel room as they shared the van. They might be lovers, but the lack of strings was still very, very clear. Yes, they'd agreed there'd be no promises, but maybe it was time she took the first step. Tilting her head, she smiled.

"That depends."

"On?"

"Whether you agree to wash my back."

He gave her one of his rare spontaneous smiles as he lifted the rest of the luggage. "Sounds reasonable."

Fifteen minutes later, Bryan dropped her cases inside their hotel room. With equal negligence, she tossed down her shoes. She didn't bother to go to the window and check out the view. There'd be time for that later. There was one vital aspect of the room that demanded immediate attention. She flopped lengthwise on the bed.

"Heaven," she decided, and closed her eyes on a sigh. "Absolute heaven."

"Something wrong with your bunk in the van?" Shade stacked his gear in a corner before pulling open the drapes.

"Not a thing. But there's a world of difference between bunk and bed." Rolling onto her back, she stretched across the spread diagonally. "See? It's just not possible to do this on a bunk."

He gave her a mild look as he opened his suitcase. "You won't be able to do that on a bed, either, when you're sharing it with me."

True enough, she thought as she watched him methodically unpack. She gave her own suitcase an absent glance. It could wait. With the same enthusiasm as she'd had when she'd plopped down, Bryan sprang up. "Hot bath," she said, and disappeared into the bathroom.

Shade dropped his shaving kit onto the dresser as he heard the water begin to run. He stopped for a moment, listening. Already, Bryan was beginning to hum. The combination of sounds was oddly intimate—a woman's low voice, the splash of water. Strange that something so simple could make him burn.

Perhaps it'd been a mistake to take only one room in the hotel. It wasn't quite like sharing the van in a campground. Here, they'd had a choice, a chance for privacy and distance. Before the day was over, he mused, her things would be spread around the room, tossed here, flung there. It wasn't like him to freely invite disorder. And yet he had.

Glancing up, he saw himself in the mirror, a dark man with a lean body and a lean face. Eyes a bit too hard, mouth a bit too sensitive. He was too used to his own reflection to wonder what Bryan saw when she looked at him. He saw a man who looked a bit weary and needed a shave. And he didn't want to wonder, though he stared at himself as an artist stares at his subject, if he saw a man who'd already taken one irrevocable step toward change.

Shade looked at his face, reflected against the hotel room behind him. Just inside the door were Bryan's cases and the shoes she'd carried into the room. Fleetingly, he wondered if he took his camera and set the shot to take in his reflection, and that of the room and cases behind, just what kind of picture he'd have. He wondered if he'd be able to understand it. Shaking off the mood, he crossed the room and walked into the bath.

Her head moved, but that was all. Though her breath

caught when he strolled into the room, Bryan kept her body still and submerged. This kind of intimacy was new and left her vulnerable. Foolishly, she wished she'd poured in a layer of bubbles so that she'd have some mystique.

Shade leaned against the sink and watched her. If she had plans to wash, she was taking her time about it. The little cake of soap sat wrapped in its dish while she lay naked in the tub. It struck him that it was the first time he'd seen her, really seen her, in the light. Her body was one long, alluring line. The room was small and steamy. He wanted her. Shade wondered if a man could die from wanting.

"How's the water?" he asked her.

"Hot." Bryan told herself to relax, be natural. The water that had soothed her now began to arouse.

"Good." Calmly, he began to strip.

Bryan opened her mouth, but shut it again. She'd never seen him undress. Always they'd held to their own unspoken, strict code of ethics. When they camped, each of them changed in the showers. Since they'd become lovers, they'd fallen into a sense of urgency at the end of the day, undressing themselves and each other in the dark van while they made love. Now, for the first time, she could watch her lover casually reveal his body to her.

She knew how it looked. Her hands had shown her. But it was a far different experience to see the slopes, the contours. Athletic, she thought, in the way of a runner or a hurdler. She supposed it was apt enough. Shade would always expect the next hurdle and be prepared to leap over it.

He left his clothes on the sink but made no comment when he had to step over hers where she'd dropped them.

"You said something about washing your back," he commented as he eased in behind her. Then he swore lightly at the temperature of the water. "You like to take off a couple layers of skin when you bathe?"

She laughed, relaxed and shifted to accommodate him. When his body rubbed and slid against hers, she decided there was something to be said for small tubs. Content, she snuggled back against him, a move that at first surprised him, then pleased.

"We're both a little long," she said as she adjusted her legs. "But it helps that we're on the slim side."

"Keep eating." He gave in to the urge to kiss the top of her head. "It's bound to stick sooner or later."

"Never has." She ran her hand along his thigh, trailing from the knee. It was a light, casual stroke that made his insides churn. "I like to believe I burn up calories just thinking. But you…"

"Me?"

On a quiet sigh, Bryan closed her eyes. He was so complex, so…driven. How could she explain it? She knew so little of what he'd seen and been through. Just one isolated incident, she thought. Just one scar. She didn't have to be told there were others.

"You're very physical," she said at length. "Even your thought pattern has a kind of physical force to it. You don't relax. It's like—" She hesitated for another moment, then plunged. "It's like you're a boxer in the ring. Even between rounds you're tensed and waiting for the bell to ring."

"That's life, isn't it?" But he found himself tracing the line of her neck with his finger. "One long match. A quick breather, then you're up and dancing."

"I've never looked at it that way. It's an adventure," she said slowly. "Sometimes I don't have the energy for it, so I can sit back and watch everyone else go through the moves. Maybe that's why I wanted to be a photographer, so I could pull in little pieces of life and keep them. Think of it, Shade."

Shifting slightly, she turned her head so that she could look at him. "Think of the people we've met, the places we've been and seen. And we're only halfway done. Those rodeo cowboys," she began, eyes brightening. "All they wanted was a plug of tobacco, a bad-tempered horse and a handful of sky. The farmer in Kansas, riding his tractor in the heat of the day, sweating and aching and looking out over acres of his own land. Children playing hopscotch, old men weeding kitchen gardens or playing checkers in the park. That's what life is. It's women with babies on their hips, young girls sunning at the beach and kids splashing in little rubber swimming pools in the side yard."

He touched her cheek. "Do you believe that?"

Did she? It sounded so simplistic.... Idealistic? She wondered. Frowning, she watched the steam rise from the water. "I believe that you have to take what good there is, what beauty there is, and go with it. The rest has to be dealt with, but not every minute of every day. That woman today..."

Bryan settled back again, not sure why it was so important for her to tell him. "The one in the house just across from where we stopped for gas. Her yard was burning up in the sun, the paint was peeling on the fence. I saw arthritis in her hands. But she was watering her pansies. Maybe she's lived in that tiny little house all her life. Maybe she'll never know what it's like to sit in a new car and smell the leather or fly first-class or shop at Saks. But she was watering her pansies. She'd planted, weeded and tended them because they gave her pleasure. Something of value, one bright foolish spot she can look at, smile at. Maybe it's enough."

"Flowers can't grow everywhere."

"Yes, they can. You only have to want them to."

It sounded true when she said it. It sounded like something he'd like to believe. Unconsciously, he rested his cheek against her hair. It was damp from the steam, warm, soft. She made him relax. Just being with her, listening to her, uncurled something in him. But he remembered the rules, those they'd both agreed on. Keep it easy, he reminded himself. Keep it light.

"Do you always have philosophical discussions in the tub?"

Her lips curved. It was so rare and so rewarding to hear that touch of humor in his voice. "I figure if you're going to have one, you might as well be comfortable. Now, about my back..."

Shade picked up the soap and unwrapped it. "Do you want the first shift in the darkroom tomorrow?"

"Mmm." She leaned forward, stretching as he rubbed the dampened soap over her back. Tomorrow was too far away to worry about. "Okay."

"You can have it from eight to twelve."

She started to object to the early hour, then subsided. Some things didn't change. "What're you..." The question trailed off into a sigh as he skimmed the soap around her waist and up to her throat. "I like being pampered."

Her voice was sleepy, but he traced a soapy finger over her nipple and felt the quick shudder. He ran the soap over her in steady circles, lower, still lower, until all thought of relaxation was over. Abruptly, she twisted until he was trapped beneath her, her mouth fixed on his. Her hands raced over him, taking him to the edge before he had a chance to brace himself.

"Bryan—"

"I love to touch you." She slid down until her mouth could skim over his chest, tasting flesh and water. She nibbled, listening to the thunder of his heart, then rubbed her cheek against his damp flesh just to feel, just to experience. She felt him tremble and lie still a moment. When was the last time he'd let himself be made love to? she wondered. Perhaps this time she'd give him no choice.

"Shade." She let her hands roam where they pleased. "Come to bed with me." Before he could answer, she rose. While the water streamed from her, she smiled down at him and slowly pulled the pins from her hair. As it fell, she shook it back, then reached for a towel. It seemed they were through with words.

She waited until he stepped from the tub, then took another towel and rubbed it over him herself. He made no objection, but she could sense him building up the emotional defense. Not this time, she thought. This time it would be different.

As she dried him, she watched his eyes. She couldn't read his thoughts, she couldn't see beneath the desire. For now, it was enough. Taking his hand, she walked toward the bed.

She would love him this time. No matter how strong, how urgent, the need, she would show him what he made her feel. Slowly, her arms already around him, she lowered herself to the bed. As the mattress gave, her mouth found his.

The need was no less. It tore through him. But this time, Shade found himself unable to demand, unable to pull her to his pace. She was satiating him with the luxury of being enjoyed. Her lips took him deep, deeper, but lazily. He learned that with her, passion could be built, layer by finite layer, until there was nothing else. They smelled of the bath they'd shared, of the soap that had rubbed from his skin to hers. She seemed content to breathe it in, to breathe it out, while slowly driving him mad.

It was pleasure enough to see him in the late-afternoon sunlight. No darkness now, no shadows. To make love in the light, freely and without barriers, was something she hadn't even known she craved. His shoulders were still damp. She could see the sheen of water on them, taste it. When their mouths met, she could watch his eyes and see the desire there that echoed what pulsed inside her. In this they were the same, she told herself. In this, if nothing else, they understood each other.

And when he touched her, when she saw his gaze follow the trail of his hand, she trembled. Needs, his and hers, collided, shuddered, then merged together.

There was more here than they'd allowed themselves or each other before. At last this was intimacy, shared knowledge, shared pleasure. No one led, no one held back. For the first time, Shade dropped all pretenses of keeping that thin emotional barrier between them. She filled him, completed him. This time he wanted her—all of her—more than he'd ever wanted anything. He wanted the fun of her, the joy, the kindness. He wanted to believe it could make a difference.

The sun slanted in across the deep, vivid gray of her eyes, highlighting them as he'd once imagined. Her mouth was soft, yielding. Above him, her hair flowed down, wild, free. The lowering sun seemed trapped in her skin, making it gleam gold. She might have been something he'd only imagined—woman, lean, agile and primitive, woman without restraints, accepting her own passions. If he photographed her this way, would he recognize her? Would he be able to recapture the emotions she could push into him?

Then she tossed back her head and she was young, vibrant, reachable. This woman he'd know, this feeling he'd recognize, if he went away alone for decades. He'd need no photograph to remind him of that one astonishing instant of give and take.

Shade drew her closer, needing her. You, he thought dizzily as their bodies merged and their thoughts twined. Only you. He watched her eyes slowly close as she gave herself to him.

Chapter 9

"I could get used to this."

With her camera settled comfortably in her lap, Bryan stretched back in the pirogue, the trim little dugout canoe they'd borrowed from a family who lived on the bayou. A few miles away was the bustling city of Lafayette, Louisiana, but here was a more slumberous view of summer.

Bees humming, shade spreading, birds trilling. Dragonflies. One whisked by, too fast for her camera, but slow enough to appreciate. Spanish moss hung overhead, shading and dipping toward the river as the water moved slowly. Why hurry? It was summer, fish were there for catching, flowers were there for picking. Cypress trees thrust their way out of the water, and an occasional frog stirred himself enough to plop from his pad and take a swim.

Why hurry, indeed? Life was there to be enjoyed.

As Shade had once pointed out, Bryan was adaptable. In the rush of Dallas, she'd worked long hours in the darkroom and on the street. All business. When the moment called for it, she could be efficient, quick and energetic. But here, where the air was heavy and the living slow, she was content to lie back, cross her ankles and wait for whatever came.

"We're supposed to be working," he pointed out.

She smiled. "Aren't we?" While she swung one foot in lazy circles, she wished they'd thought to borrow a fishing pole as well. What did it feel like to catch a catfish? "We took dozens of pictures before we got in the boat," she reminded him.

It'd been her idea to detour into the bayou, though she was all but certain Shade had topped her with his pictures of the family who'd welcomed them. She might've charmed them into the use of their boat, but Shade had won hands down with camera work.

"The one you took of Mrs. Bienville shelling beans has to be fabulous. Her hands." Bryan shook her head and relaxed. "I've never seen such hands on a woman. I imagine she could make the most elegant of soufflés right before she went out and cut down a tree."

"Cajuns have their own way of life, their own rules."

She tilted her head as she studied him. "You like that."

"Yeah." He rowed, not because they needed to get anywhere, but because it felt so good. It warmed his muscles and relaxed his mind. He nearly smiled, thinking that being with Bryan accomplished almost the same thing. "I like the independence and the fact that it works."

Bryan lay back, listening to the buzz and hum of insects, the sounds of the river. They'd walked along another river in San Antonio, but the sounds had been different there. Soft Spanish music from musicians, the clink of silver on china from the outdoor cafés. It had been fabulous at night, she remembered. The lights had glowed on the water, the water had rippled from the river taxis, the taxis had been full of people content with the Texas version of a gondola. She'd taken a picture of two young lovers, newlyweds perhaps, huddled together on one of the arched stone bridges above the water.

When they'd driven into Galveston, she'd seen yet another kind of Texas, one with white sand beaches, ferries and bicycle surreys. It'd been easier to talk Shade into renting one than she'd imagined. With a smile, she thought of just how far they'd come, and not only in miles. They were working together, and when he could be distracted, they played.

In Malibu, they'd gone their separate ways on the beach. In Galveston, after two hours of work, they'd walked hand in hand along the shore. A small thing for many people, Bryan mused, but not for either of them.

Each time they made love, there seemed to be something more. She didn't know what it was, but she didn't question it. It was Shade she wanted to be with, laugh with, talk with. Every day she discovered something new, something different, about the country and the people. She discovered it with Shade. Perhaps that was all the answer she needed.

What was it about him? Whether she chose to or not, there were times she wondered. What was it about Shade Colby that made her happy? He wasn't always patient. One moment he might be generous and something close to sweet, and the next he could be as cool and aloof as a stranger. Being with him wasn't without its frustrations for a woman accustomed to less fluctuating moods. But being with him was exactly what she wanted.

At the moment, he was relaxed. He wasn't often, she knew, but the mood of the river seemed to have seeped into him. Still, he was watching. Someone else might have floated down the river, glancing at the scenery, appreciating the overall effect. Shade dissected it.

This she understood, because it was her way as well. A tree might be studied for the texture of its leaves, the grain in the wood, the pattern of shade and light it allowed to fall on the ground. A layman might take a perfectly competent picture of the tree, but it would be only that. When Bryan took the picture, she wanted it to pull feelings out of the viewer.

She specialized in people, Bryan remembered as she watched Shade draw the oars through the water. Landscapes, still lifes, she considered a change of pace. It was the human element that fascinated her, and always would. If she wanted to understand her feelings about Shade, maybe it was time to treat him as she would any other subject.

Under half-lowered lashes, she studied and dissected. He had very dominating physical looks, she mused. Being dominated was definitely not her ambition in life. Perhaps that was why she was so often drawn to his mouth, because it was sensitive, vulnerable.

She knew his image—cool, distant, pragmatic. Part of it was true, she thought, but part of it was illusion. Once she'd thought to photograph him in shadows. Now she wondered what sort of study she'd get if she photographed him in quiet sunlight. Without giving herself a chance to think, she lifted her camera, framed him in and shot.

"Just testing," she said lightly when he arched a brow. "And after all, you've already taken a couple of me."

"So I have." He remembered the picture he'd taken of her brushing her hair on the rock in Arizona. He hadn't told her that he'd sent the print back to the magazine, even though he had no doubt it would be used in the final essay. Nor had he told her it was a print he intended to keep in his private collection.

"Hold it a minute." With brisk, professional movements, she changed her lens, adjusted for distance and depth and focused on a heron perched on top of a cypress knee. "A place like this," she murmured as she took two more insurance shots, "makes you think summer just goes on and on."

"Maybe we should take another three months traveling back and do autumn."

"It's tempting." She stretched back again. "Very tempting. A study on all seasons."

"Your clients might get testy."

"Unfortunately true. Still…" She let her fingers dip into the water. "We miss the seasons in L.A. I'd like to see spring in Virginia and winter in Montana." Tossing her braid back, she sat up. "Have you ever thought of chucking it, Shade? Just packing up and moving to, oh, say, Nebraska, and setting up a little studio. Wedding and graduation pictures, you know."

He gave her a long steady look. "No."

With a laugh, she flopped back. "Me either."

"You wouldn't find many megastars in Nebraska."

She narrowed her eyes but spoke mildly. "Is that another subtle shot at my work?"

"Your work," he began as he gently turned the boat back, "is uniformly excellent. Otherwise, we wouldn't be working together."

"Thank you very much. I think."

"And because of the quality of your work," he continued, "I wonder why you limit yourself to the pretty people."

"It's my specialty." She saw a clump of wildflowers on the mossy, muddy edge of the river. Carefully she adjusted her camera again. "And a great many of my subjects are far from pretty—physically or emotionally. They interest me," she said before he could comment. "I like to find out what's under the image and give a glimpse of it."

And she was well skilled at it, he decided. In truth, he'd discovered he admired her for it—not only for her skill, but for her perception. He simply couldn't rationalize her following the glitz trail. "Culture art?"

If he'd meant it as an insult, however mild, it missed its mark. "Yes. And if you asked, I'd say Shakespeare wrote culture art. Are you hungry?"

"No." Fascinating woman, he thought, as reluctant as ever to be fascinated. He craved her, it was true. Her body, her company. But he couldn't resolve the constant fascination she held for him, mind to mind. "You had a bowl of shrimp and rice big enough to feed a family of four before we started out."

"That was hours ago."

"Two, to be exact."

"Picky," she mumbled, and stared up at the sky. So peaceful, she mused. So simple. Moments like this were meant to be savored. Lowering her gaze, she smiled at him. "Ever made love in a pirogue?"

He had to grin. She made it impossible to do otherwise. "No, but I don't think we should ever refuse a new experience."

Bryan touched her tongue to her top lip. "Come here."

* * *

They left the lazy, insect-humming air of the bayou behind and landed in bustling, raucous New Orleans. Sweating trumpet players on Bourbon Street, merchants fanning themselves in the Farmers Market, artists and tourists around Jackson Square—it was a taste of the South, they both agreed, that was as far apart from the South as San Antonio had been apart from Texas.

From there, they traveled north to Mississippi for a touch of July in the Deep South. Heat and humidity. Tall, cool drinks and precious shade. Life was different here. In the cities, men sweated in white shirts and loosened ties. In the rural districts, farmers worked under the sweltering sun. But they moved more slowly than their counterparts to the north and west. Perhaps temperatures soaring to a hundred and more caused it, or perhaps it was just a way of life.

Children exercised the privilege of youth and wore next to nothing. Their bodies were browned and damp and dusty. In a city park, Bryan took a close-up of a grinning boy with mahogany skin cooling himself in a fountain.

The camera didn't intimidate him. As she homed in, he laughed at her, squealing as the water cascaded over him, white and cool, until he looked encased in glass.

In a small town just northwest of Jackson, they stumbled across a Little League game. It wasn't much of a field, and the bleachers looked as if they'd object to more than fifty people at a time, but they pulled off and parked between a pickup and a rusted-out sedan.

"This is great." Bryan grabbed her camera bag.

"You just smell hot dogs."

"That, too," she agreed easily. "But this *is* summer. We might get to a Yankee game in New York, but we'll get better pictures here today." She hooked her arm through his before he could get too far away. "I'll reserve judgment on the hot dogs."

Shade took a long, sweeping view. The crowd was spread out, on the grass, in folding chairs, on the bleachers. They cheered, complained, gossiped and gulped iced drinks. He was all but certain everyone there knew one another by name or by sight. He watched an old man in a baseball cap casually spit out a plug of tobacco before he berated the umpire.

"I'm going to wander around a bit," he decided, considering a seat on the bleachers too limiting for the moment.

"Okay." Bryan had taken her own scan and considered the bleachers the focal point for what she wanted.

They separated, Shade moving toward the old man who'd already captured his attention. Bryan walked to the bleachers, where she and the onlookers would have a solid view of the game.

The players wore white pants, already grass-stained and dusty, with bright red or blue shirts emblazoned with team names. A good many of them were too small for the uniforms, and the mitts looked enormous on the ends of gangling arms. Some wore spikes, some wore sneakers. A few had batting gloves hung professionally from their back pocket.

It was the hats, she decided, that told of the individual's personality. One might wear it snug or tipped back, another tilted rakishly over the eyes. She wanted an action shot, something that would bring the color and the personalities together with the sport itself. Until something formed for her, Bryan contented herself with taking a shot of the second baseman, who passed the time until the batter stepped into the box by kicking his spikes against the bag and blowing bubbles with his wad of gum.

Scooting up another step, she tried her long lens. Better, she decided, and was pleased to see that her second baseman had a face full of freckles. Above her, someone snapped gum and whistled when the umpire called a strike.

Bryan lowered her camera and allowed herself to become involved in the game. If she wanted to portray the atmosphere, she had to let herself feel it. It was more than the game, she thought, it was the feeling of community. As the batters came up, people in the crowd called them by name, tossing out casual remarks that indicated a personal knowledge. But the sides were definitely drawn.

Parents had come to the game from work, grandparents had pushed away from an early dinner, and neighbors had chosen the game against an evening by the TV. They had their favorites, and they weren't shy about rooting for them.

The next batter interested Bryan mainly because she was a strikingly pretty girl of about twelve. At a glance, Bryan would've set her more easily at a ballet bar than home plate. But when she watched the way the girl gripped the bat and bent into her stance, Bryan lifted her camera. This was one to watch.

Bryan caught her in the first swing on a strike. Though the crowd moaned, Bryan was thrilled with the flow of movement. She might be shooting a Little League game in a half-forgotten town in Mississippi, but she thought of her studio work with the prima ballerina. The batter poised for the pitch, and Bryan poised for the next shot. She had to wait, growing impatient, through two balls.

"Low and outside," she heard someone mumble beside her. All she could think was, if the girl walked, she'd lose the picture she wanted.

Then it came over, too fast for Bryan to judge the placement of the ball, but the girl connected with a solid swing. The batter took off, and using the motor drive, Bryan followed her around the bases. When she rounded second, Bryan homed in on her face. Yes, Maria would understand that look, Bryan thought. Strain, determination and just plain guts. Bryan had her as she slid into third with a storm of dust and a swing of body.

"Wonderful!" She lowered the camera, so thrilled that she didn't even realize she'd spoken out loud. "Just wonderful!"

"That's our girl."

Distracted, Bryan glanced over to the couple beside her. The woman was her own age, perhaps a year or two older. She was beaming. The man beside her was grinning over a wad of gum.

Perhaps she hadn't heard properly. They were so young. "She's your daughter?"

"Our oldest." The woman slipped a hand into her husband's. Bryan saw the plain twin wedding bands. "We've got three others running around here, but they're more interested in the concession stand than the game."

"Not our Carey." The father looked out to where his daughter took a short lead on third. "She's all business."

"I hope you don't mind my taking her picture."

"No." The woman smiled again. "Do you live in town?"

It was a polite way to find out who she was. Bryan hadn't a doubt the woman knew everyone within ten miles. "No, I'm traveling." She paused as the next batter blooped to right field and brought Carey home. "Actually, I'm a freelance photographer on assignment for *Life-style*. Perhaps you've heard of it."

"Sure." The man jerked a head at his wife as he kept his eyes on the game. "She picks it up every month."

Pulling a release form out of her bag, she explained her interest in using Carey's picture. Though she kept it short and her voice low, word spread throughout the bleachers. Bryan found herself answering questions and dealing with curiosity. In order to handle it all in the simplest fashion, she climbed down from the bleachers, changed to a wide-angle lens and took a group shot. Not a bad study, she decided, but she didn't want to spend the next hour having people pose for her. To give the baseball fans time to shift their attention back to the game, she wandered to the concession stand.

"Any luck?"

She swiveled her head around to see Shade fall into step beside her. "Yeah. You?"

He nodded, then leaned on the counter of the stand. There was no relief from the heat, though the sun was lowering. It promised to be as sweltering a night as it had a day. He ordered two large drinks and two hot dogs.

"Know what I'd love?" she asked as she began to bury her hot dog under relish.

"A shovel?"

Ignoring him, she piled on mustard. "A long, cool dip in an enormous pool, followed closely by an iced margarita."

"For now you'll have to settle for the driver's seat of the van. It's your turn."

She shrugged. A job was a job. "Did you see the girl who hit the triple?" They walked over the uneven grass toward the van.

"Kid that ran like a bullet?"

"Yes. I sat next to her parents in the stands. They have four kids."

"So?"

"Four kids," she repeated. "And I'd swear she wasn't more than thirty. How do people do it?"

"Ask me later and I'll show you."

With a laugh, she jabbed him with her elbow. "That's not what I meant—though I like the idea. What I mean is, here's this couple—young, attractive. You could tell they even liked each other."

"Amazing."

"Don't be cynical," she ordered as she pulled open the door to the van. "A great many couples don't, especially when they've got four kids, a mortgage and ten or twelve years of marriage under their belts."

"Now who's being cynical?"

She started to speak and frowned instead. "I guess I am," she mused as she turned on the engine. "Maybe I've picked a world that's tilted my outlook, but when I see a happily married couple with a track record, I'm impressed."

"It is impressive." Carefully, he stored his camera bag under the dash before he sat back. "When it really works."

"Yeah."

She fell silent, remembering the jolt of envy and longing she'd felt when she'd framed the Browns in her viewfinder. Now, weeks and miles later, it was another jolt for Bryan to realize she hadn't brushed off that peculiar feeling. She had managed to put it aside, somewhere to the back of her mind, but it popped out again now as she thought of the couple in the bleachers of a small-town park.

Family, cohesion. Bonding. Did some people just keep promises better than others? she wondered. Or were some people simply unable to blend their lives with someone else's, make those adjustments, the compromises?

When she looked back, she believed both she and Rob had tried, but in their own ways. There'd been no meeting of the minds, but two separate thought patterns making decisions that never melded with each other. Did that mean that a successful marriage depended on the mating of two people who thought along the same lines?

With a sigh, she turned onto the highway that would lead them into Tennessee. If it was true, she decided, she was much better off single. Though she'd met a great many people she liked and could have fun with, she'd never met anyone who thought the way she did. Especially the man seated next to her with his nose already buried in the newspaper. There alone they were radically different.

He'd read that paper and every paper in every town they stopped in from cover to cover, devouring the words. She'd skim the headlines, glance over the style or society pages and go straight for the comics. If she wanted news, she'd rather have it in spurts on the radio or blurbs on televisions. Reading was for relaxation, and relaxation was not an analysis of détente.

Relationships. She thought back on the discussion she'd had with Lee just weeks before. No, she simply wasn't cut out for relationships on a long-term basis. Shade himself had pointed out that some people just weren't capable of permanency. She'd agreed, hadn't she? Why should the truth suddenly depress her?

Whatever her feelings were for Shade, and she'd

yet to define them satisfactorily, she wasn't going to start smelling orange blossoms. Maybe she had a few twinges when she saw couples together who seemed to complete each other rather than compete, but that was only natural. After all, she didn't want to start making adjustments in her lifestyle to accommodate someone else at this stage. She was perfectly content the way things were.

If she was in love… Bryan felt the twinge again and ignored it. *If* she was, it would complicate things. The fact was, she was very happy with a successful career, her freedom and an attractive, interesting lover. She'd be crazy if she wasn't happy. She'd be insane to change one single thing.

"And it doesn't have anything to do with being afraid," she said aloud.

"What?"

She turned to Shade and, to his astonishment and hers, blushed. "Nothing," she muttered. "Thinking out loud."

He gave her a long, quiet look. Her expression came very close to a baffled sort of pout. Giving in to the urge, he leaned over and touched a hand to her cheek. "You're not eating your hot dog."

She could have wept. For some absurd reason, she wanted to stop the van, drop her head on the steering wheel and drown herself in hot, violent tears. "Not hungry," she managed.

"Bryan." He watched her snatch her sunglasses from the dash and push them on, though the sun was riding low. "Are you all right?"

"Fine." She took a deep breath and kept her eyes straight ahead. "I'm fine."

No, she wasn't. Though strain in her voice was rare,

he recognized it. Only a few weeks before, he'd have shrugged and turned back to his reading. Deliberately, he dropped the paper on the floor at his feet. "What is it?"

"Nothing." She cursed herself and turned up the radio. Shade simply switched it off.

"Pull over."

"What for?"

"Just pull over."

With more violence than necessary, Bryan swung the van toward the shoulder, slowed and stopped. "We won't make very good time if we stop ten minutes after we start."

"We won't be making any time at all until you tell me what's wrong."

"Nothing's wrong!" Then she gritted her teeth and sat back. It wasn't any use saying nothing was wrong if you snarled at the same time. "I don't know," she evaded. "I'm edgy, that's all."

"You?"

She turned on him with a vengeance. "I've a right to foul moods, Colby. You don't have a patent on them."

"You certainly have," he said mildly. "Since it's the first one I've witnessed, I'm interested."

"Don't be so damn patronizing."

"Wanna fight?"

She stared through the windshield. "Maybe."

"Okay." Willing to oblige, he made himself comfortable. "About anything in particular?"

She swung her head around, ready to pounce on anything. "Do you have to bury your face in a paper every time I get behind the wheel?"

He smiled maddeningly. "Yes, dear."

A low sound came from her throat as she stared through the windshield again. "Never mind."

"I could point out that you have a habit of falling asleep when you sit in this seat."

"I said never mind." She reached for the key. "Just never mind. You make me sound like a fool."

He put his hand over hers before she could turn the key. "You sound foolish skirting around whatever's bothering you." He wanted to reach her. Without being aware when, he'd passed the point where he could tell himself not to get involved and follow the advice. Whether he wanted it or not, whether she accepted it or not, he was involved. Slowly, he lifted her hand to his lips. "Bryan, I care."

She sat there stunned that a simple statement could spin through her with such force. *I care*. He'd used the same word when he'd spoken about the woman who'd caused his nightmare. Along with the pleasure his words brought her came an inescapable sense of responsibility. He wouldn't allow himself to care indiscriminately. Glancing up, she met his eyes, patient, puzzled, as they studied her face.

"I care, too," she said quietly. She twined her fingers with his, only briefly, but it unsettled them both.

Shade took the next step carefully, not certain of her, or himself. "Is that what's bothering you?"

She let out a long breath, as wary as he now. "Some. I'm not used to it…not like this."

"Neither am I."

She nodded, watching the cars breeze by. "I guess we'd both better take it easy then."

"Sounds logical." And next to impossible, he thought. Right now he wanted to gather her close, forget where they were. Just hold her, he realized. It was all he wanted to do. With an effort, he drew back. "No complications?"

She managed to smile. Rule number one was the most important, after all. "No complications," she agreed. Again she reached for the key. "Read your paper, Colby," she said lightly. "I'll drive until dark."

Chapter 10

They took a slice out of Tennessee—Nashville, Chattanooga—caught the eastern corner of Arkansas—mountains and legends—and headed up through Twain's Missouri to Kentucky. There they found tobacco leaves, mountain laurel, Fort Knox and Mammoth Cave, but when Bryan thought of Kentucky, she thought of horses. Kentucky was sleek, glossy Thoroughbreds grazing on rich grass. It made her think of long-legged foals running in wide pastures and wide-chested colts pounding the track at Churchill Downs.

As they crossed the state toward Louisville, she saw much more. Tidy suburban homes bordered the larger cities and smaller towns as they did in every state across the country. Farms spread acre after acre—tobacco, horses, grain. Cities rose with their busy office buildings and harried streets. So much was the same as it had been to the west and to the south, and yet so much was different.

"Daniel Boone and the Cherokees," Bryan murmured as they traveled down another long, monotonous highway.

"What?" Shade glanced up from the map he'd been checking. When Bryan was driving, it didn't hurt to keep an eye on the navigation.

"Daniel Boone and the Cherokees," Bryan repeated. She increased the speed to pass a camper loaded down with bikes on the back bumper and fishing poles on the front. And where were they going? she wondered. Where had they come from? "I was thinking maybe it's the history of a place that makes it different from another. Maybe it's the climate, the topography."

Shade glanced back down at the map, idly figuring the time and mileage. He didn't give the camper rolling along behind them more than a passing thought. "Yes."

Bryan shot him an exasperated smile. One and one always added up to two for Shade. "But people are basically the same, don't you think? I imagine if you took a cross section of the country and polled, you'd find out that most people want the same things. A roof over their heads, a good job, a couple weeks off a year to play."

"Flowers in the garden?"

"All right, yes." She gave a careless little shrug and refused to believe it sounded foolish. "I think most people's wants are fairly simple. Italian shoes and a trip to Barbados might add in, but it's the basic things that touch everyone. Healthy children, a nest egg, a steak on the grill."

"You've a way of simplifying things, Bryan."

"Maybe, but I don't see any reason to complicate them."

Interested, he set down the map and turned to her. Perhaps he'd avoided digging too deeply into her, leery of what he might find. But now, behind his sunglasses, his eyes were direct. So was his question. "What do you want?"

"I..." She faltered a moment, frowning as she took the van around a long curve. "I don't know what you mean."

He thought she did, but they always seemed to end up fencing. "A roof over your head, a good job? Are those the most important things to you?"

Two months before, she might've shrugged and agreed. Her job came first, and gave her whatever she needed. That was the way she'd planned it, the way she'd wanted it. She wasn't sure any longer. Since she'd left L.A., she'd seen too much, felt too much. "I have those things," she said evasively. "Of course I want them."

"And?"

Uncomfortable, she shifted. She hadn't meant to have her idle speculation turned back on her. "I wouldn't turn down a trip to Barbados."

He didn't smile as she'd hoped he would, but continued to watch her from behind the protection of tinted glasses. "You're still simplifying."

"I'm a simple person."

Her hands were light and competent on the wheel, and her hair was scooped back in its habitual braid. She wore no makeup, a pair of faded cut-offs and a T-shirt two sizes too large for her. "No," he decided after a moment, "you're not. You only pretend to be."

Abruptly wary, she shook her head. Since her outburst in Mississippi, Bryan had managed to keep herself level, and to keep herself, she admitted, from thinking too deeply. "You're a complicated person, Shade, and you see complications where there aren't any."

She wished she could see his eyes. She wished she could see the thoughts behind them.

"I know what I see when I look at you, and it isn't simple."

She shrugged carelessly, but her body had begun to tense. "I'm easily read."

He corrected her with a short, concise word calmly spoken. Bryan blinked once, then gave her attention to the road. "Well, I'm certainly not full of mysteries."

Wasn't she? Shade watched the thin gold loops sway at her ears. "I wonder what you're thinking when you lie beside me after we've made love—in those minutes after passion and before sleep. I often wonder."

She wondered, too. "After we've made love," she said in a tolerably steady voice, "I have a hard time thinking at all."

This time he did smile. "You're always soft and sleepy," he murmured, making her tremble. "And I wonder what you might say, what I might hear if you spoke your thoughts aloud."

That I might be falling in love with you. That every day we have together takes us a day closer to the end. That I can't imagine what my life will be like when I don't have you there to touch, to talk to. Those were her thoughts, but she said nothing.

She had her secrets, Shade thought. Just as he did. "One day, before we're finished, you'll tell me."

He was easing her into a corner; Bryan felt it, but she didn't know why. "Haven't I told you enough already?"

"No." Giving in to the urge that came over him more and more often, he touched her cheek. "Not nearly."

She tried to smile, but she had to clear her throat to

speak. "This is a dangerous conversation to have when I'm driving on an interstate at sixty miles an hour."

"It's a dangerous conversation in any case." Slowly, he drew his hand away. "I want you, Bryan. I can't look at you and not want you."

She fell silent, not because he was saying things she didn't want to hear, but because she no longer knew how to deal with them, and with him. If she spoke, she might say too much and break whatever bond had begun to form. She couldn't tell him so, but it was a bond she wanted.

He waited for her to speak, needing her to say something after he'd all but crossed over the line they'd drawn in the beginning. Risk. He'd taken one. Couldn't she see it? Needs. He needed her. Couldn't she feel it? But she remained silent, and the step forward became a step back.

"Your exit's coming up," he told her. Picking up the map, he folded it carefully. Bryan switched lanes, slowed down and left the highway.

Kentucky had made her think of horses; horses led them to Louisville, and Louisville to Churchill Downs. The Derby was long over, but there were races and there were crowds. If they were going to include in their glimpse of summer those who spent an afternoon watching races and betting, where else would they go?

The moment Bryan saw it, she thought of a dozen angles. There were cathedrallike domes and clean white buildings that gave a quiet elegance to the frenzy. The track was the focal point, a long oval of packed dirt. Stands rose around it. Bryan walked about, wondering just what kind of person would come there, or to any track, to plop down two dollars—or two hundred—on a race that would take only minutes. Again, she saw the variety.

There was the man with reddened arms and a sweaty T-shirt who pored over a racing form, and another in casually elegant slacks who sipped something long and cool. She saw women in quietly expensive dresses holding field glasses and families treating their children to the sport of kings. There was a man in a gray hat with tattoos snaking up both arms and a boy laughing on top of his father's shoulders.

They'd been to baseball games, tennis matches, drag races across the country. Always she saw faces in the crowd that seemed to have nothing in common except the game. The games had been invented, Bryan mused, and turned into industries. It was an interesting aspect of human nature. But people kept the games alive; they wanted to be amused, they wanted to compete.

She spotted one man leaning against the rail, watching a race as though his life depended on the outcome. His body was coiled, his face damp. She caught him in profile.

A quick scan showed her a woman in a pale rose dress and summer hat. She watched the race idly, distanced from it the way an empress might've been from a contest in a coliseum. Bryan framed her as the crowd roared the horses down the stretch.

Shade rested a hip on the rail and shot the horses in varying positions around the track, ending with the final lunge across the finish line. Before, he'd framed in the odds board, where numbers flashed and tempted. Now he waited until the results were posted and focused on it again.

Before the races were over, Shade saw Bryan standing at the two-dollar window. With her camera hanging around her neck and her ticket in her hand, she walked back toward the stands.

"Haven't you got any willpower?" he asked her.

"No." She'd found a vending machine, and she offered Shade a candy bar that was already softening in the heat. "Besides, there's a horse in the next race called Made in the Shade." When his eyebrow lifted up, she grinned. "How could I resist?"

He wanted to tell her she was foolish. He wanted to tell her she was unbearably sweet. Instead, he drew her sunglasses down her nose until he could see her eyes. "What's his number?"

"Seven."

Shade glanced over at the odds board and shook his head. "Thirty-five to one. How'd you bet?"

"To win, of course."

Taking her arm, he led her down to the rail again. "You can kiss your two bucks goodbye, hotshot."

"Or I can win seventy." Bryan pushed her glasses back in place. "Then I'll take you out to dinner. If I lose," she continued as the horses were led to the starting gate, "I've always got plastic. I can still take you out to dinner."

"Deal," Shade told her as the bell rang.

Bryan watched the horses lunge forward. They were nearly to the first turn before she managed to find number 7, third from the back. She glanced up to see Shade shake his head.

"Don't give up on him yet."

"When you bet on a long shot, love, you've got to be ready to lose."

A bit flustered by his absent use of the endearment, she turned back to the race. Shade rarely called her by name, much less one of those sweetly intimate terms. A long shot, she agreed silently. But she wasn't altogether sure she was as prepared to lose as she might've been.

"He's moving up," she said quickly as number 7 passed three horses with long, hard-driving strides. Forgetting herself, she leaned on the rail and laughed. "Look at him! He's moving up." Lifting her camera, she used the telephoto lens like a field glass. "God, he's beautiful," she murmured. "I didn't know he was so beautiful."

Watching the horse, she forgot the race, the competition. He was beautiful. She could see the jockey riding low in a blur of color that had a style of its own, but it was the horse, muscles bunching, legs pounding, that held her fascinated. He wanted to win; she could feel it. No matter how many races he'd lost, how many times he'd been led back to the stables sweating, he wanted to win.

Hope. She sensed it, but she no longer heard the call of the crowd around her. The horse straining to overtake the leaders hadn't lost hope. He believed he could win, and if you believed hard enough… With a last burst of speed, he nipped by the leader and crossed the wire like a champion.

"I'll be damned," Shade murmured. He found he had his arm around Bryan's shoulders as they watched the winner take his victory lap in long, steady strides.

"Beautiful." Her voice was low and thick.

"Hey." Shade tipped up her chin when he heard the tears. "It was only a two-dollar bet."

She shook her head. "He did it. He wanted to win, and he just didn't give up until he did."

Shade ran a finger down her nose. "Ever hear of luck?"

"Yeah." More composed, she took his hand in hers. "And this had nothing to do with it."

For a moment, he studied her. Then, with a shake of his head, he lowered his mouth to hers lightly, sweetly. "And this from a woman who claims to be simple."

And happy, she thought as her fingers laced with his. Ridiculously happy. "Let's go collect my winnings."

"There was a rumor," he began as they worked their way through the stands, "about you buying dinner."

"Yeah. I heard something about it myself."

She was a woman of her word. That evening, as the sky flashed with lightning and echoed with the thunder of a summer storm, they stepped into a quiet, low-lighted restaurant.

"Linen napkins," Bryan murmured to Shade as they were led to a table.

He laughed in her ear as he pulled out her chair. "You're easily impressed."

"True enough," she agreed, "but I haven't seen a linen napkin since June." Picking it off her plate, she ran it through her hands. It was smooth and rich. "There isn't a vinyl seat or a plastic light in this place. There won't be any little plastic containers of ketchup either." With a wink, she knocked a finger against a plate and let it ring. "Try that with paper and all you get is a thump."

Shade watched her experiment with the water glass next. "All this from the queen of fast food?"

"A steady diet of hamburgers is all right, but I like a change of pace. Let's have champagne," she decided as their waiter came over. She glanced at the list, made her choice and turned back to Shade again.

"You just blew your winnings on a bottle of wine."

"Easy come, easy go." Cupping her chin on her

hands, she smiled at him. "Did I mention you look wonderful by candlelight?"

"No." Amused, he leaned forward as well. "Shouldn't that be my line?"

"Maybe, but you didn't seem in a rush to come out with it. Besides, I'm buying. However..." She sent him a slow, simmering look. "If you'd like to say something flattering, I wouldn't be offended."

Lazily, she ran a finger along the back of his hand, making him wonder why any man would object to the benefits of women's liberation. It wasn't a hardship to be wined and dined. Nor would it be a hardship to relax and be seduced. All the same, Shade decided as he lifted her hand to his lips, there was something to be said for partnership.

"I might say that you always look lovely, but tonight..." He let his gaze wander over her face. "Tonight, you take my breath away."

Momentarily flustered, she allowed her hand to stay in his. How was it he could say such things so calmly, so unexpectedly? And how could she, when she was used to casual, inconsequential compliments from men, deal with one that seemed so serious? Carefully, she warned herself. Very carefully.

"In that case I'll have to remember to use lipstick more often."

With a quick smile, he kissed her fingers again. "You forgot to put any on."

"Oh." Stuck, Bryan stared at him.

"Madame?" The wine steward held out the bottle of champagne, label up.

"Yes." She let out a quiet breath. "Yes, that's fine."

Still watching Shade, she heard the cork give in to pressure and the wine bubble into her glass. She sipped, closing her eyes to enjoy it. Then, with a nod, she waited until the steward filled both glasses. Steadier, Bryan lifted her glass and smiled at Shade.

"To?"

"One summer," he said, and touched his rim to hers. "One fascinating summer."

It made her lips curve again, so that her eyes reflected the smile as she sipped. "I expected you to be a terrible bore to work with."

"Really." Shade let the champagne rest on his tongue a moment. Like Bryan, it was smooth and quiet, with energy bubbling underneath. "I expected you to be a pain in the—"

"However," she interrupted dryly. "I've been pleased that my preconception didn't hold true." She waited a moment. "And yours?"

"Did," he said easily, then laughed when she narrowed her eyes at him. "But I wouldn't have enjoyed you nearly as much if it'd been otherwise."

"I liked your other compliment better," she mumbled, and picked up her menu. "But I suppose since you're stingy with them, I have to take what I get."

"I only say what I mean."

"I know." She pushed back her hair as she skimmed the menu. "But I— Oh look, they've got chocolate mousse."

"Most people start at the appetizers."

"I'd rather work backward, then I can gauge how much I want to eat and still have room for dessert."

"I can't imagine you turning down anything chocolate."

"Right you are."

"What I can't understand is how you can shovel it in the way you do and not be fat."

"Just lucky, I guess." With the menu open over her plate, she smiled at him. "Don't you have any weaknesses, Shade?"

"Yeah." He looked at her until she was baffled and flustered again. "A few." And one of them, he thought as he watched her eyes, was becoming more and more acute.

"Are you ready to order?"

Distracted, Bryan looked up at the well-mannered waiter. "What?"

"Are you ready to order?" he repeated. "Or would you like more time?"

"The lady'll have the chocolate mousse," Shade said smoothly.

"Yes, sir." Unflappable, the waiter marked it down. "Will that be all?"

"Not by a long shot," Shade told him, and picked up his wine again.

With a laugh, Bryan worked her way through the menu.

"Stuffed," Bryan decided over an hour later, as they drove through a hard, driving rain. "Absolutely stuffed."

Shade cruised through an amber light. "Watching you eat is an amazing way to pass the time."

"We're here to entertain," she said lightly. Snuggled back in her seat with champagne swimming in her head and thunder grumbling in a bad-tempered sky, she was content to ride along wherever he chose to go. "It was sweet of you to let me have a bite of your cheesecake."

"Half," Shade corrected her. Deliberately he turned away from the campground they'd decided on that afternoon. The wipers made quick swishing sounds against the windshield. "But you're welcome."

"It was lovely." She let out a sigh, quiet and sleepy. "I like being pampered. Tonight should get me through another month of fast-food chains and diners with stale doughnuts." Content, she glanced around at the dark, wet streets, the puddles at the curbs. She liked the rain, especially at night, when it made everything glisten. Watching it, she fell to dreaming, rousing herself only when he turned into the lot of a small motel.

"No campground tonight," he said before she could question. "Wait here while I get a room."

She didn't have time to comment before he was out of the van and dashing through the rain. No campground, she thought, looking over her shoulder at the narrow twin bunks on either side of the van. No skinny, make-shift beds and trickling showers.

With a grin, she jumped up and began to gather his equipment and hers. She never gave the suitcases a thought.

"Champagne, linen napkins and now a bed." She laughed as he climbed back into the van, soaking wet. "I'm going to get spoiled."

He wanted to spoil her. There was no logic to it, only fact. Tonight, if only for tonight, he wanted to spoil her. "Room's around the back." When Bryan dragged the equipment forward, he drove slowly around, checking numbers on the lines of doors. "Here." He strapped camera bags over his shoulder. "Wait a minute." She'd grabbed another bag and her purse by the time he'd pulled open her door from the outside. To her astonishment, she found herself lifted into his arms.

"Shade!" But the rain slapped into her face, making her gasp as he dashed across the lot to an outside door.

"Least I could do after you sprang for dinner," he told her as he maneuvered the oversize key into the lock.

Bryan was laughing as he struggled to open the door holding her, the camera bags and tripods.

Kicking the door closed with his foot, he fastened his mouth on hers. Still laughing, Bryan clung to him.

"Now we're both wet," she murmured, running a hand through his hair.

"We'll dry off in bed." Before she knew his intention, Bryan was falling through the air and landing with two bounces full-length onto the mattress.

"So romantic," she said dryly, but her body stayed limp. She lay there, smiling, because he'd made a rare frivolous gesture and she intended to enjoy it.

Her dress clung to her, her hair fanned out. He'd seen her change for dinner and knew she wore a thin teddy cut high at the thigh, low over her breasts, and sheer, sheer stockings. He could love her now, love her for hours. It wouldn't be enough. He knew how relaxed, how pliant, her body could be. How full of fire, strength, vibrancy. He could want all of it, have all of it. It wouldn't be enough.

He was an expert at capturing the moment, the emotions, the message. Letting his own feelings hum, he reached for his camera bag.

"What're you doing?"

When she started to sit up, Shade turned back. "Stay there a minute."

Intrigued and wary, she watched him set his camera. "I don't—"

"Just lie back like you were," he interrupted. "Relaxed and rather pleased with yourself."

His intention was obvious enough now. Bryan lifted a brow. An obsession, she thought, amused. The camera was an obsession for both of them. "Shade, I'm a photographer, not a model."

"Humor me." Gently, he pushed her back on the bed.

"I've too much champagne in my system to argue with you." She smiled up at him as he held the camera over his face. "You can play if you like, or take serious pictures if you must. As long as I don't have to do anything."

She did nothing but smile, and he began to throb. So often he'd used the camera as a barrier between himself and his subject, other times as a conductor for his emotion, emotion he refused to let loose any other way. Now, it was neither. The emotion was already in him, and barriers weren't possible.

He framed her quickly and shot, but was unsatisfied.

"That's not what I want." He was so businesslike that Bryan didn't see it as a defense, only as his manner. But when he came over, pulled her into a sitting position and unzipped her dress, her mouth fell open.

"Shade!"

"It's that lazy sex," he murmured as he slipped the dress down over one shoulder. "Those incredible waves of sensuality that take no effort at all, but just are. It's the way your eyes look." But when his came back to hers, she forgot the joke she'd been about to make. "The way they look when I touch you—like this." Slowly, he ran a hand over her naked shoulder. "The way they look just after I kiss you—like this." He kissed her, lingering over it while her mind emptied of thought and her body filled with sensation.

"Like this," he whispered, more determined than ever to capture that moment, make it tangible so that he could hold it in his hands and see it. "Just like this," he said again, backing off one step, then two. "The way you look just before we make love. The way you look just after."

Helplessly aroused, Bryan stared into the lens of the camera as he lifted it. He caught her there, like a quarry in the crosshairs of a scope, empty of thoughts, jumbled with feeling. At the same time, he caught himself.

For an instant her heart was in her eyes. The shutter opened, closed and captured it. When he printed the photograph, he thought as he carefully set down his camera, would he see what she felt? Would he be certain of his own feelings?

Now she sat on the bed, her dress disarrayed, her hair tumbled, her eyes clouded. Secrets, Shade thought again. They both had them. Was it possible he'd locked a share of each of their secrets on film inside his camera?

When he looked at her now, he saw a woman aroused, a woman who aroused. He could see passion and pliancy and acceptance. He could see a woman whom he'd come to know better than anyone else. Yet he saw a woman he'd yet to reach—one he'd avoided reaching.

He went to her in silence. Her skin was damp but warm, as he'd known it would be. Raindrops clung to her hair. He touched one, then it was gone. Her arms lifted.

While the storm raged outside, he took her and himself where there was no need for answers.

Chapter 11

If they had more time…

As August began to slip by, that was the thought that continued to run through Bryan's mind. With more time, they could have stayed longer at each stop. With more time, they might have passed through more states, more towns, more communities. There was so much to see, so much to record, but time was running out.

In less than a month, the school she'd photographed empty and waiting in the afternoon light would be filled again. Leaves that were full and green would take on those vibrant colors before they fell. She would be back in L.A., back in her studio, back to the routine she'd established. For the first time in years, the word *alone* had a hollow ring.

How had it happened? Shade Colby had become her partner, her lover, her friend. He'd become, though it was frightening to admit, the most important person in her life. Somehow she'd become dependent on him, for his opinion, his company, for the nights they spent involved only with each other.

She could imagine how it would be when they returned to L.A. and went their separate ways. Separate parts of the city, she thought, separate lives, separate outlooks.

The closeness that had so slowly, almost painfully, developed between them would dissolve. Wasn't that what they'd both intended from the start? They'd made a bargain with each other, just as they'd made the bargain to work together. If her feelings had changed, she was responsible for them, for dealing with them. As the odometer turned over on the next mile, as the next state was left behind, she wondered how to begin.

Shade had his own thoughts to deal with. When they'd crossed into Maryland, they'd crossed into the East. The Atlantic was close, as close as the end of summer. It was the end that disturbed him. The word no longer seemed to mean finished, but over. He began to realize he was far from ready to draw that last line. There were ways to rationalize it. He tried them all.

They'd missed too much. If they took their time driving back, rather than sticking to their plan of going straight across the country, they could detour into so many places they'd eliminated on the way out. It made sense. They could stay in New England a week, two weeks after Labor Day. After long days in the van and the intense work they'd both put in, they deserved some time off. It was reasonable.

They should work their way back, rather than rush. If they weren't preoccupied with making time, making miles, how many pictures would come out of it?

If one of them was special, it would be worth it. That was professional.

When they returned to L.A., perhaps Bryan could move in with him, share his apartment as they'd shared the van. It was impossible. Wasn't it?

She didn't want to complicate their relationship. Hadn't she said so? He didn't want the responsibility of committing himself to one person. Hadn't he made himself clear? Perhaps he'd come to need her companionship on some level. And it was true he'd learned to appreciate the way she could look at anything and see the fun and the beauty of it. That didn't equal promises, commitments or complications.

With a little time, a little distance, the need was bound to fade. The only thing he was sure of was that he wanted to put off that point for as long as possible.

Bryan spotted a convertible—red, flashy. Its driver had one arm thrown over the white leather seat while her short blond hair flew in the wind. Grabbing her camera, Bryan leaned out the open window. Half kneeling, half crouching, on the seat, she adjusted for depth.

She wanted to catch it from the rear, elongating the car into a blur of color. But she didn't want to lose the arrogant angle of the driver's arm, or the negligent way her hair streamed back. Already she knew she would dodge the plain gray highway and the other cars in the darkroom. Just the red convertible, she thought as she set her camera.

"Try to keep just this distance," she called to Shade. She took one shot and, dissatisfied, leaned out farther for the next. Though Shade swore at her, Bryan got her shot before she laughed and flopped back on her seat.

He was guilty of the same thing, he knew. Once the camera was in place, you tended to think of it as a shield.

Nothing could happen to you—you simply weren't part of what was happening. Though he'd known better, it had happened to him often enough, even after his first stint overseas. Perhaps it was the understanding that made his voice mild, though he was annoyed.

"Don't you have more sense than to climb out the window of a moving car?"

"Couldn't resist. There's nothing like a convertible on an open highway in August. I'm always toying with the idea of getting one myself."

"Why don't you?"

"Buying a new car is hard work." She looked at the green-and-white road signs as she'd looked at so many others that summer. There were cities, roads and routes she'd never heard of. "I can hardly believe we're in Maryland. We've come so far and yet, I don't know, it doesn't seem like two months."

"Two years?"

She laughed. "Sometimes. Other times it seems like days. Not enough time," she said, half to herself. "Never enough."

Shade didn't give himself the chance to think before he took the opening. "We've had to leave out a lot."

"I know."

"We went through Kansas, but not Nebraska, Mississippi, and not the Carolinas. We didn't go to Michigan or Wisconsin."

"Or Florida, Washington State, the Dakotas." She shrugged, trying not to think of what was left behind. Just today, Bryan told herself. Just take today.

"I've been thinking about tying them in on the way back."

"On the way back?" Bryan turned to him as he reached for a cigarette.

"We'd be on our own time." The van's lighter glowed red against the tip. "But I think we could both take a month or so and finish the job."

More time. Bryan felt the quick surge of hope, then ruthlessly toned it down. He wanted to finish the job his way. It was his way, she reminded herself, to do things thoroughly. But did the reason really matter? They'd have more time. Yes, she realized as she stared out the side window. The reason mattered a great deal too much.

"The job's finished in New England," she said lightly. "Summer's over, and it's back to business. My work at the studio will be backed up for a month. Still…" She felt herself weakening, though he said nothing, did nothing, to persuade her. "I wouldn't mind a few detours on the trip back."

Shade kept his hands easy on the wheel, his voice casual. "We'll think about it," he said, and let the subject they both wanted to pursue drop.

Weary of the highway, they took to the back roads. Bryan took her pictures of kids squirting each other with garden hoses, of laundry drying in the breeze, of an elderly couple sitting on a porch glider. Shade took his of sweating construction workers spreading tar on roofs, of laborers harvesting peaches and, surprisingly, of two ten-year-old businessmen hawking lemonade in their front yard.

Touched, Bryan accepted the paper cup Shade handed her. "That was sweet."

"You haven't tasted it yet," he commented, and climbed into the passenger's seat. "To keep down the overhead, they used a light hand on the sugar."

"I meant you." On impulse, she leaned over and

kissed him, lightly, comfortably. "You can be a very sweet man."

As always, she moved him, and he couldn't stop it. "I can give you a list of people who'd disagree."

"What do they know?" With a smile, she touched her lips to his again. She drove down the neat, shady street appreciating the trim lawns, flower gardens and dogs barking in the yards. "I like the suburbs," she said idly. "To look at, anyway. I've never lived in one. They're so orderly." With a sigh, she turned right at the corner. "If I had a house here, I'd probably forget to fertilize the lawn and end up with crab grass and dandelions. My neighbors would take up a petition. I'd end up selling my house and moving into a condo."

"So ends Bryan Mitchell's career as a suburbanite."

She made a face at him. "Some people aren't cut out for picket fences."

"True enough."

She waited, but he said nothing that made her feel inadequate—nothing that made her feel as though she should be. She laughed delightedly, then grabbed his hand and squeezed. "You're good for me, Shade. You really are."

He didn't want to let her hand go, and released it reluctantly. Good for her. She said it so easily, laughing. Because she did, he knew she had no idea just what it meant to him to hear it. Maybe it was time he told her. "Bryan—"

"What's that?" she said abruptly, and swung toward the curb. Excited, she inched the car forward until she could read the colorful cardboard poster tacked to a telephone pole. "Nightingale's Traveling Carnival." Pulling on the brake, she nearly climbed over Shade to see it more clearly. "Voltara, the Electric Woman." With a half whoop, she nudged closer to Shade. "Terrific, just terrific. Sampson, the Dancing Elephant. Madame Zoltar, Mystic. Shade, look, it's their last night in town. We can't miss it. What's summer without a carny? Thrilling rides, games of skill and chance."

"And Dr. Wren, the Fire Eater."

It was easy to ignore the dry tone. "Fate." She scrambled back to her own seat. "It has to be fate that we turned down this road. Otherwise, we might've missed it."

Shade glanced back at the sign as Bryan pulled away from the curb. "Think of it," he murmured. "We might've gotten all the way to the coast without seeing a dancing elephant."

A half hour later, Shade leaned back in his seat, calmly smoking, his feet on the dash. Frazzled, Bryan swung the van around the next turn.

"I'm not lost."

Shade blew out a lazy stream of smoke. "I didn't say a word."

"I know what you're thinking."

"That's Madame Zoltar's line."

"And you can stop looking so smug."

"Was I?"

"You always look smug when I get lost."

"You said you weren't."

Bryan gritted her teeth and sent him a killing look. "Why don't you just pick up that map and tell me where we are?"

"I started to pick it up ten minutes ago and you snarled at me."

Bryan let out a long breath. "It was the *way* you picked it up. You were smirking, and I could hear you thinking—"

"You're stepping into Madame Zoltar's territory again."

"Damn it, Shade." But she had to choke back a laugh as she drove down the long, unlit country road. "I don't mind making a fool of myself, but I hate it when someone lifts an eyebrow over it."

"Did I?"

"You know you did. Now, if you'd just—"

Then she caught the first glimmer of red, blue, green lights flickering. A Ferris wheel, she thought. It had to be. The sound of tinny music came faintly through the summer dusk. A calliope. This time it was Bryan who looked smug. "I knew I'd find it."

"I never had a doubt."

She might've had something withering to say to that, but the lights glowing in the early-evening dusk, and the foolish piping music held her attention. "It's been years," she murmured. "Just years since I've seen anything like this. I've got to watch the fire eater."

"And your wallet."

She shook her head as she turned off the road onto the bumpy field where cars were parked. "Cynic."

"Realist." He waited until she maneuvered the van next to a late-model pickup. "Lock the van." Shade gathered his bag and waited outside the van until Bryan had hers. "Where first?"

She thought of pink cotton candy but restrained herself. "Why don't we just wander around a bit? We might want some shots now, but at night they'd have more punch."

Without the dark, without the bright glow of colored lights, the carnival looked too much like what it was—a little weary, more than a little tawdry. Its illusions were too easily unmasked now, and that wasn't why Bryan had come. Carnivals, like Santa Claus, had a right to their mystique. In another hour, when the sun had completely set behind those rolling, blue-tinted hills to the west, the carnival would come into its own. Peeling paint wouldn't be noticed.

"Look, there's Voltara." Bryan grabbed Shade's arm and swung him around to see a life-size poster that gave her lavish curves and scant cover as she was being strapped into what looked like a homemade electric chair.

Shade looked at the painted spangles over generous cleavage. "Might be worth watching, after all."

With a quick snort, Bryan pulled him toward the Ferris wheel. "Let's take a ride. From the top we'll be able to see the whole layout."

Shade pulled a bill out of his wallet. "That's the only reason you want to ride."

"Don't be ridiculous." They walked over, waiting while the attendant let a couple off. "It's a good way of covering ground and sitting down at the same time," she began as she took the vacated seat. "It's sure to be an excellent angle for some aerial pictures, and…" She slipped a hand into his as they started the slow swing up. "It's the very best place to neck at a carnival."

When he laughed, she wrapped her arms around him and silenced his lips with hers. They reached the top where the evening breeze flowed clean and hung there one moment—two—aware only of each other. On the descent, the speed picked up and the drop had her stomach shivering, her mind swimming. It was no different from the sensation of being held by him, loved by him. They held tight and close through two revolutions.

Gathering her against his shoulder, Shade watched the carnival rush up toward them. It'd been years since he'd held someone soft and feminine on a Ferris wheel. High school? he wondered. He could hardly remember. Now he realized he'd let his youth slip by him because so many other things had seemed important at the time. He'd let it go freely, and though he wouldn't, couldn't, ask for the whole of it back, perhaps Bryan was showing him how to recapture pieces of it.

"I love the way this feels," she murmured. She could watch the sun go down in a last splashy explosion of arrogance, hear the music, the voices, ebb and fade as the wheel spun around. She could look down and be just removed enough from the scene to enjoy it, just separate enough to understand it. "A ride on a Ferris wheel should be required once a year, like a routine physical."

With her head against Shade's shoulder, she examined the scene below, the midway, the concessions, the booths set up for games of skill. She wanted to see it all, close up. She could smell popcorn, grilling meat, sweat, the heavy-handed after-shave of the attendant as their car swung by him. It gave her the overall view. This was life, a sidelong glance at it. This was the little corner of life where children could see wonders and adults could pretend for just a little while.

Taking her camera, she angled down through the cars and wires to focus in on the attendant. He looked a bit bored as he lifted the safety bar for one couple and lowered it for the next. A job for him, Bryan thought, a small thrill for the rest. She sat back, content to ride.

When it was dark, they went to work. There were people gathered around the wheel of fortune, plopping down a dollar for a chance at more. Teenagers showed off for their girls or their peers by hurling softballs at stacked bottles. Toddlers hung over the rope and tossed Ping-Pong balls at fishbowls, hoping to win a goldfish whose life expectancy was short at best. Young girls squealed on the fast-spinning Octopus, while young boys goggled at the posters along the midway.

Bryan took one telling shot of a woman carrying a baby on one hip while a three-year-old dragged her mercilessly along. Shade took another of a trio of boys in muscle shirts standing apart and doing their best to look tough and aloof.

They ate slices of pizza with rubber crusts as they watched with the rest of the crowd as Dr. Wren, Fire Eater, came out of his tent to give a quick, teasing demonstration of his art. Like the ten-year-old boy who watched beside her, Bryan was sold.

With an agreement to meet back at the entrance to the midway in thirty minutes, they separated. Caught up, Bryan wandered. She wasn't able to resist Voltara, and slipped into part of the show to see the somewhat weary, glossy-faced woman strapped into a chair that promised to zap her with two thousand volts.

She pulled it off well enough, Bryan thought, closing her eyes and giving a regal nod before the lever was pulled. The special effects weren't top-notch, but they worked. Blue light shimmered up the chair and around Voltara's head. It turned her skin to the color of summer lightning. At fifty cents a shot, Bryan decided as she stepped back out, the audience got their money's worth.

Intrigued, she wandered around in back of the midway to where the carnival workers parked their trailers. No colorful lights here, she mused as she glanced over the small caravan. No pretty illusions. Tonight, they'd pack up the equipment, take down the posters and drive on.

The moonlight hit the metal of a trailer and showed the scratches and dents. The shades were drawn at the little windows, but there was faded lettering on the side. Nightingale's.

Bryan found it touching and crouched to shoot.

"Lost, little lady?"

Surprised, Bryan sprang up and nearly collided with a short, husky man in T-shirt and work pants. If he worked for the carnival, Bryan thought quickly, he'd been taking a long break. If he'd come to watch, the lights and sideshows hadn't held his interest. The smell of beer, warm and stale, clung to him.

"No." She gave him a careful smile and kept a careful distance. Fear hadn't entered into it. The move had been automatic and mild. There were lights and people only a few yards away. And she thought he might give her another angle for her photographs. "Do you work here?"

"Woman shouldn't wander around in the dark alone. 'Less she's looking for something."

No, fear hadn't been her first reaction, nor did it come now. Annoyance did. It was that that showed in her eyes before she turned away. "Excuse me."

Then he had her arm, and it occurred to her that the lights were a great deal farther away than she'd have liked. Brazen it out, she told herself. "Look, I've people waiting for me."

"You're a tall one, ain't you?" His fingers were very firm, if his stance wasn't. He weaved slightly as he looked Bryan over. "Don't mind looking eye to eye with a woman. Let's have a drink."

"Some other time." Bryan put her hand on his arm to push it away and found it solid as a concrete block. That's when the fear began. "I came back here to take some pictures," she said as calmly as she could. "My partner's waiting for me." She pushed at his arm again. "You're hurting me."

"Got some more beer in my truck," he mumbled as he began to drag her farther away from the lights.

"No." Her voice rose on the first wave of panic. "I don't want any beer."

He stopped a moment, swaying. As Bryan took a good look in his eyes, she realized he was as drunk as a man could get and still stand. Fear bubbled hot in her throat. "Maybe you want something else." He skimmed down her thin summer top and brief shorts. "Woman usually wants something when she wanders around half naked."

Her fear ebbed as cold fury rushed in. Bryan glared. He grinned.

"You ignorant ass," she hissed just before she brought her knee up, hard. His breath came out in a whoosh as he dropped his hand. Bryan didn't wait to see him crouch over. She ran.

She was still running when she rammed straight into Shade.

"You're ten minutes late," he began, "but I've never seen you move that fast."

"I was just— I had to…" She trailed off, breathless, and leaned against him. Solid, dependable, safe. She could have stayed just like that until the sun rose again.

"What is it?" He could feel the tension before he drew her away and saw it on her face. "What happened?"

"Nothing really." Disgusted with herself, Bryan dragged her hair back from her face. "I just ran into some jerk who wanted to buy me a drink whether I was thirsty or not."

His fingers tightened on her arms, and she winced as they covered the same area that was already tender. "Where?"

"It was nothing," she said again, furious with herself that she hadn't taken the time to regain her composure before she ran into him. "I went around back to get a look at the trailers."

"Alone?" He shook her once, quickly. "What kind of idiot are you? Don't you know carnivals aren't just cotton candy and colored lights? Did he hurt you?"

It wasn't concern she heard in his voice, but anger. Her spine straightened. "No, but you are."

Ignoring her, Shade began to drag her through the crowds toward the parking section. "If you'd stop looking at everything through rose-colored glasses, you'd see a lot more clearly. Do you have any idea what might've happened?"

"I can take care of myself. I did take care of myself." When they reached the van, she swung away from him. "I'll look at life any way I like. I don't need you to lecture me, Shade."

"You need something." Grabbing the keys from her, he unlocked the van. "It's brainless to go wandering around alone in the dark in a place like this. Looking for trouble," he muttered as he climbed into the driver's seat.

"You sound remarkably like the idiot I left sprawled on the grass with his hands between his legs."

He shot her a look. Later, when he was calm, he might admire the way she'd dealt with an obnoxious drunk, but now he couldn't see beyond her carelessness. Independence aside, a woman was vulnerable. "I should've known better than to let you go off alone."

"Now just a minute." She whirled around in her seat. "You don't *let* me do anything, Colby. If you've got it in your head that you're my keeper or anything of the sort, then you'd better get it right out again. I answer to myself. Only myself."

"For the next few weeks, you answer to me as well."

She tried to control the temper that pushed at her, but it wasn't possible. "I may work with you," she said, pacing her words. "I may sleep with you. But I don't answer to you. Not now. Not ever."

Shade punched in the van's lighter. "We'll see about that."

"Just remember the contract." Shaking with fury, she turned away again. "We're partners on this job, fifty-fifty."

He gave his opinion of what she could do with the contract. Bryan folded her arms, shut her eyes and willed herself to sleep.

He drove for hours. She might sleep, but there was too much churning inside him to allow him the same release. So he drove, east toward the Atlantic.

She'd been right when she'd said she didn't answer to him. That was one of the first rules they'd laid down. He was damned sick of rules. She was her own woman. His strings weren't on her any more than hers were on him. They were two intelligent, independent people who wanted it that way.

But he'd wanted to protect her. When everything else was stripped away, he'd wanted to protect her. Was she so dense that she couldn't see he'd been furious not with her but with himself for not being there when she'd needed him?

She'd tossed that back in his face, Shade thought grimly as he ran a hand over his gritty eyes. She'd put him very clearly, very concisely, in his place. And his place, he reminded himself, no matter how intimate they'd become, was still at arm's length. It was best for both of them.

With his window open, he could just smell the tang of the ocean. They'd crossed the country. They'd crossed more lines than he'd bargained for. But they were a long way from crossing the final one.

How did he feel about her? He'd asked himself that question time after time, but he'd always managed to block out the answer. Did he really want to hear it? But it was three o'clock in the morning, that hour he knew well. Defenses crumbled easily at three o'clock in the morning. Truth had a way of easing its way in.

He was in love with her. It was too late to take a step back and say no thanks. He was in love with her in a way that was completely foreign to him. Unselfishly. Unlimitedly.

Looking back, he could almost pinpoint the moment when it had happened to him, though he'd called it something else. When he'd stood on the rock island in the Arizona lake, he'd desired her, desired her more intensely than he'd desired anything or anyone. When he'd woken from the nightmare and had found her warm and solid beside him, he'd needed her, again more than anything or anyone.

But when he'd looked across the dusty road on the Oklahoma border and seen her standing in front of a sad little house with a plot of pansies, he'd fallen in love.

They were a long way from Oklahoma now, a long way from that moment. Love had grown, overwhelming him. He hadn't known how to deal with it then. He hadn't a clue what to do about it now.

He drove toward the ocean where the air was moist. When he pulled the van between two low-rising dunes, he could just see the water, a shadow with sound in the distance. Watching it, listening to it, he slept.

Bryan woke when she heard the gulls. Stiff, disoriented, she opened her eyes. She saw the ocean, blue and quiet in the early light that wasn't quite dawn. At the horizon, the sky was pink and serene. Misty. Waking slowly, she watched gulls swoop over the shoreline and soar to sea again.

Shade slept in the seat beside her, turned slightly in his seat, his head resting against the door. He'd driven for hours, she realized. But what had driven him?

She thought of their argument with a kind of weary tolerance. Quietly, she slipped from the van. She wanted the scent of the sea.

Had it only been two months since they'd stood on the shore of the Pacific? Was this really so different? she wondered as she stepped out of her shoes and felt the sand, cool and rough under her feet. He'd driven through the night to get here, she mused. To get here, one step closer to the end. They had only to drive up the coast now, winding their way through New England. A quick stop in New York for pictures and darkroom work, then on to Cape Cod, where summer would end for both of them.

It might be best, she thought, if they broke there completely. Driving back together, touching on some of the places they'd discovered as a team, might be too much to handle. Perhaps when the time came, she'd make some excuse and fly back to L.A. It might be best, she reflected, to start back to those separate lives when summer ended.

They'd come full circle. Through the tension and annoyance of the beginning, into the cautious friendship, the frenzied passion, and right back to the tension again.

Bending, Bryan picked up a shell small enough to fit into the palm of her hand, but whole.

Tension broke things, didn't it? Cracked the whole

until pressure crumbled it into pieces. Then whatever you'd had was lost. She didn't want that for Shade. With a sigh, she looked out over the ocean, where the water was green, then blue. The mist was rising.

No, she didn't want that for him. When they turned from each other, they should do so as they'd turned to each other. As whole, separate people, standing independently.

She kept the shell in her hand as she walked back toward the van. The weariness was gone. When she saw him standing beside the van watching her, with his hair ruffled by the wind, his face shadowed, eyes heavy, her heart turned over.

The break would come soon enough, she told herself. For now, there should be no pressure.

Smiling, she went to him. She took his hand and pressed the shell into it. "You can hear the ocean if you listen for it."

He said nothing, but put his arm around her and held her. Together they watched the sun rise over the east.

Chapter 12

On a street corner in Chelsea, five enterprising kids loosened the bolts on a fire hydrant and sent water swooshing. Bryan liked the way they dived through the stream, soaking their sneakers, plastering their hair. It wasn't necessary to think long about her feelings toward the scene. As she lifted her camera and focused, her one predominant emotion was envy, pure and simple.

Not only were they cool and delightfully wet while she was limp from the heat, but they hadn't a care in the world. They didn't have to worry if their lives were heading in the right direction, or any direction at all. It was their privilege in these last breathless weeks of summer to enjoy—their youth, their freedom and a cool splash in city water.

If she was envious, there were others who felt the same way. As it happened, Bryan's best shot came from incorporating one passerby in the scene. The middle-aged deliveryman in the sweaty blue shirt and dusty work shoes looked over his shoulder as one of the children lifted his arms up to catch a stream. On one face was pleasure, pure and giddy. On the other was amusement, laced with regret for something that couldn't be recaptured.

Bryan walked on, down streets packed with bad-tempered traffic, over sidewalks that tossed up heat like insults. New York didn't always weather summer with a smile and a wave.

Shade was in the darkroom they'd rented, while she'd opted to take the field first. She was putting it off, she admitted, as she skirted around a sidewalk salesman and his array of bright-lensed plastic sunglasses. Putting off coping with the last darkroom session she'd have before they returned to California. After this brief stop in New York, they'd head north for the final weekend of summer in Cape Cod.

And she and Shade had gone back to being almost unbearably careful with each other. Since that morning when they'd woken at the beach, Bryan had taken a step back. Deliberately, she admitted. She'd discovered all too forcibly that he could hurt her. Perhaps it was true that she'd left herself wide open. Bryan wouldn't deny that somewhere along the way she'd lost her determination to maintain a certain distance. But it wasn't too late to pull back just enough to keep from getting battered. She had to accept that the season was nearly over, and when it was, her relationship with Shade ended with it.

With this in mind, she took a slow, meandering route back toward midtown and the rented darkroom.

Shade already had ten rows of proofs. Sliding a strip under the enlarger, he methodically began to select and eliminate. As always, he was more ruthless, more critical with his own work than he'd have been with anyone else's. He knew Bryan would be back shortly, so any printing he did would have to wait until the following day. Still, he wanted to see one now, for himself.

He remembered the little motel room they'd taken that rainy night just outside of Louisville. He remembered the way he'd felt then—involved, a little reckless. That night had been preying on his mind, more and more often, as he and Bryan seemed to put up fences again. There'd been no boundaries between them that night.

Finding the print he was looking for, he brought the magnifier closer. She was sitting on the bed, her dress falling off her shoulders, raindrops clinging to her hair. Soft, passionate, hesitant. All those things were there in the way she held herself, in the way she looked at the camera. But her eyes…

Frustrated, he narrowed his own. What was in her eyes? He wanted to enlarge the proof now, to blow it up so that he could see and study and understand.

She was holding back now. Every day he could feel it, sense it. Just a little bit more distance every day. But what had been in her eyes on that rainy night? He had to know. Until he did, he couldn't take a step, either toward her or away.

When the knock came on the door, he cursed it. He wanted another hour. With another hour, he could have the print, and perhaps his answer. He found it a simple matter to ignore the knock.

"Shade, come on. Time for the next shift."

"Come back in an hour."

"An hour!" On the other side of the door, Bryan pounded again. "Look, I'm melting out there. Besides,

I've already given you twenty minutes more than your share."

The moment he yanked open the door, Bryan felt the waves of impatience. Because she wasn't in the mood to wrestle with it, she merely lifted a brow and skirted around him. If he wanted to be in a foul mood, fine. As long as he took it outside with him. Casually she set down her camera and a paper cup filled with soft drink and ice.

"So how'd it go?"

"I'm not finished."

With a shrug, she began to set out the capsules of undeveloped film she'd stored in her bag. "You've tomorrow for that."

He didn't want to wait until tomorrow, not, he discovered, for another minute. "If you'd give me the rest of the time I want, I wouldn't need tomorrow."

Bryan began to run water in a shallow plastic tub. "Sorry, Shade. I've run out of steam outside. If I don't get started in here, the best I'll do is go back to the hotel and sleep the rest of the afternoon. Then I'll be behind. What's so important?"

He stuffed his hands in his pockets. "Nothing. I just want to finish."

"And I've got to start," she murmured absently as she checked the temperature of the water.

He watched her a moment, the competent way she set up, arranging bottles of chemicals to her preference. Little tendrils of her hair curled damply around her face from the humidity. Even as she set up to work, she slipped out of her shoes. He felt a wave of love, of need, of confusion, and reached out to touch her shoulder. "Bryan—"

"Hmm?"

He started to move closer, then stopped himself. "What time will you be finished?"

There were touches of amusement and annoyance in her voice. "Shade, will you stop trying to push me out?"

"I want to come back for you."

She stopped long enough to look over her shoulder. "Why?"

"Because I don't want you walking around outside after it's dark."

"For heaven's sake." Exasperated, she turned completely around. "Do you have any idea how many times I've been to New York alone? Do I look stupid?"

"No."

Something in the way he said it had her narrowing her eyes. "Look—"

"I want to come back for you," he repeated, and this time touched her cheek. "Humor me."

She let out a long breath, tried to be annoyed and ended by lifting her hand to his. "Eight, eight-thirty."

"Okay. We can grab something to eat on the way back."

"There's something we can agree on." She smiled and lowered her hand before she could give in to the urge to move closer. "Now go take some pictures, will you? I've got to get to work."

He lifted his camera bag and started out. "Any longer than eight-thirty and you buy dinner."

Bryan locked the door behind him with a decisive click.

She didn't lose track of time while she worked. Time was too essential. In the dark she worked briskly. In the amber light, her movements flowed with the same rhythm. As one set of negatives was developed and hung to dry, she went on to the next, then the next. When at length she could switch on the overhead light, Bryan arched her back, stretched her shoulders and relaxed.

An idle glance around showed her that she'd forgotten the carryout drink she'd picked up on the way. Unconcerned, she took a long gulp of lukewarm, watered-down soda.

The work satisfied her—the precision it required. Now her thoughts were skipping ahead to the prints. Only then would the creativity be fully satisfied. She had time, she noticed as she took a quick glance at her watch, to fuss with the negatives a bit before he came back. But then she'd end up putting herself in the same position she'd put him in—leaving something half done. Instead, mildly curious, she walked over to study his proofs.

Impressive, she decided, but then she'd expected no less. She might just be inclined to beg for a blowup of the old man in the baseball cap. Not Shade's usual style, she mused as she bent over the strip. It was so rare that he focused in on one person and let the emotions flow. The man who'd taken it had once told her he had no compassion. Bryan shook her head as she skimmed over other proofs. Did Shade believe that, or did he simply want the rest of the world to?

Then she saw herself and stopped with a kind of dazed wonder. Of course she remembered Shade setting up that picture, amusing, then arousing her while he changed angles and f-stops. The way he'd touched her… It wasn't something she'd forget, so it shouldn't surprise her to see the proof. Yet it did more than surprise her.

Not quite steady, Bryan picked up a magnifying glass and held it over one tiny square. She looked…pliant. She heard her own nervous swallow as she looked deeper.

She looked…soft. It could be her imagination or, more likely, the skill of the photographer. She looked…in love.

Slowly, Bryan set down the glass and straightened. The skill of the photographer, she repeated, fighting to believe it. A trick of the angle, of the light and shadows. What a photographer captured on film wasn't always the truth. It was often illusion, often that vague blur between truth and illusion.

A woman knew when she loved. That's what Bryan told herself. A woman knew when she'd given her heart. It wasn't something that could happen and not be felt.

She closed her eyes a moment and listened to the quiet. Was there anything she hadn't felt when it came to Shade? How much longer was she going to pretend that passion, needs, longings, stood on their own? Love had bound them together. Love had cemented them into something solid and strong and undeniable.

She turned to where her negatives hung. There was one she'd managed to ignore. There was one tiny slice of film she'd taken on impulse and then buried because she'd come to be afraid of the answer she'd find. Now, when she had the answer already, Bryan stared at it.

It was reversed, so that his hair was light, his face dark. The little sliver of river in the corner was white, like the oars in his hands. But she saw him clearly.

His eyes were too intense, though his body seemed relaxed. Would he ever allow his mind true rest? His face was hard, lean, with the only tangible sensitivity around his mouth. He was a man, Bryan knew, who'd have little patience with mistakes—his own or others'. He was a man with a rigid sense of what was important. And he was a man who was capable of harnessing his own emotions and denying them to another. What he gave, when he gave, would be on his terms.

She knew, and understood, and loved regardless.

She'd loved before, and love had made more sense then. At least it had seemed to. Still, in the end, love hadn't been enough. What did she know about making love work? Could she possibly believe that when she'd failed once, she could succeed with a man like Shade?

She loved now, and told herself she was wise enough, strong enough, to let him go.

Rule number one, Bryan reminded herself as she put the darkroom in order. No complications. It was a litany she had running through her head until Shade knocked on the door. When she opened it for him, she nearly believed it.

They'd reached the last stop, the last day. Summer was not, as some would wish it, endless. Perhaps the weather would stay balmy for weeks longer. Flowers might still bloom defiantly, but just as Bryan had considered the last day of school summer's conception, so did she consider the Labor Day weekend its demise.

Clambakes, beach parties, bonfires. Hot beaches and cool water. That was Cape Cod. There were volleyball games in the sand and blasting portable radios. Teenagers perfected the tans they'd show off during those first few weeks of school. Families took to the water in a last, frantic rush before autumn signaled the end. Backyard barbecues smoked. Baseball hung on gamely before football could push its way through. As if it knew its time was limited, summer poured on the heat.

Bryan didn't mind. She wanted this last weekend to be everything summer could be—hot, hazy, torrid. She wanted her last weekend with Shade to reflect it. Love could be disguised with passion. She could let herself flow with it. Long, steamy days led to long, steamy nights, and Bryan held on to them.

If her lovemaking was a little frantic, if her desires were a little desperate, she could blame it on the heat. While Bryan became more aggressive, Shade became more gentle.

He'd noticed the change. Though he'd said nothing, Shade had noticed it the night he'd come back to meet her at the darkroom. Perhaps because she rarely had nerves, Bryan thought she hid them well. Shade could almost see them jump every time he looked at her.

Bryan had made a decision in the darkroom—a decision she felt would be best for both herself and for Shade. Shade had made a decision in the darkroom as well, the day after, when he'd watched the print of Bryan slowly come to life.

On the ride east, they'd become lovers. Now he had to find a way on the ride west to court her, as a man does the woman he wants to spend his life with.

Gentleness came first, though he wasn't an expert at it. Pressure, if it came to that, could be applied later. He was more experienced there.

"What a day." After long hours walking, watching and shooting, Bryan dropped down on the back of the van where the doors were open wide to let in the breeze. "I can't believe how many half-naked people I've seen." Grinning at Shade, she arched her back. She wore nothing but her sleek red bathing suit and a loose white cover-up that drooped over one shoulder.

"You seem to fit right in."

Lazily, she lifted one leg and examined it. "Well, it's nice to know that this assignment hasn't ruined my tan." Yawning, she stretched. "We've got a couple more hours of sun. Why don't you put on something indecent and walk down to the beach with me?" She rose, lifting her arms so they could wind easily around his neck. "We could cool off in the water." She touched her lips to his, teasing, taunting. "Then we could come back and heat up again."

"I like the second part." He turned the kiss into something staggering with an increase of pressure and change of angle. Beneath his hands, he felt her sigh. "Why don't you go ahead down, do the cooling-off? I've got some things to do."

With her head resting against his shoulder, Bryan struggled not to ask again. She wanted him to go with her, be with her every second they had left. Tomorrow she'd have to tell him that she'd made arrangements to fly back to the Coast. This was their last night, but only she knew it.

"All right." She managed to smile as she drew away. "I can't resist the beach when we're camped so close. I'll be back in a couple hours."

"Have fun." He gave her a quick, absent kiss and didn't watch as she walked away. If he had, he might've seen her hesitate and start back once, only to turn around again and walk on.

The air had cooled by the time Bryan started back to the van. It chilled her skin, a sure sign that summer was on its last legs. Bonfires were set and ready to light down on the beach. In the distance, Bryan heard a few hesitant, amateur guitar chords. It wouldn't be a quiet night, she decided as she passed two other campsites on the way to the van.

She paused a moment to look toward the water, tossing her hair back. It was loose from its braid and slightly damp from her dip in the Atlantic. Idly she considered grabbing her shampoo out of the van and taking a quick trip to the showers. She could do that before she threw together a cold sandwich. In an hour or two, when the bonfires were going steadily, and the music was at its peak, she and Shade would go back down and work.

For the last time, she thought as she reached for the door of the van.

At first, she stood blinking, confused by the low, flickering light. Candles, she saw, baffled. Candles and white linen. There on the little collapsible table they sometimes set between the bunks were a fresh, snowy cloth and two red tapers in glass holders. There were red linen napkins folded at angles. A rosebud stood in a narrow, clear glass vase. On the little radio in the back was low, soft music.

At the narrow makeshift counter was Shade, legs spread as he added a sprinkling of alfalfa to a salad.

"Have a nice swim?" he said casually, as if she'd climbed into the van every evening to just such a scene.

"Yeah, I… Shade, where did you get all this?"

"Took a quick trip into town. Hope you like your shrimp spicy. I made it to my taste."

She could smell it. Over the scent of candle wax, under the fragrance of the single rose, was the rich, ripe aroma of spiced shrimp. With a laugh, Bryan moved to the table and ran a finger down one of the tapers. "How did you manage all this?"

"I've been called adept occasionally." She looked up from the candle to him. Her face was lovely, clean-lined. In the soft light, her eyes were dark, mysterious. But above all he saw her lips curve hesitantly as she reached out for him.

"You did this for me."

He touched her, lightly, just a hand to her hair. Both of them felt something shimmer. "I intend to eat, too."

"I don't know what to say." She felt her eyes fill and didn't bother to blink the tears back. "I really don't."

He lifted her hand and, with a simplicity he'd never shown, kissed her fingers, one by one. "Try thanks."

She swallowed and whispered. "Thanks."

"Hungry?"

"Always. But…" In a gesture that always moved him, she lifted her hands to his face. "Some things are more important."

Bryan brought her lips to his. It was a taste he could drown in—a taste he could now admit he wanted to drown in. Moving slowly, gently, he brought her into his arms.

Their bodies fit. Bryan knew it was so, and ached from the knowledge. Even their breathing seemed to merge until she was certain their hearts beat at precisely the same rhythm. He ran his hands under her shirt, along her back, where the skin was still damp from the sea.

Touch me. She drew him closer, as if her body could shout the words to him.

Savor me. Her mouth was suddenly avid, hot and open, as if with lips alone she could draw what she needed from him.

Love me. Her hands moved over him as if she could touch the emotion she wanted. Touch it, hold it, keep it—if only for one night.

He could smell the sea on her, and the summer and the evening. He could feel the passion as her body pressed against his. Needs, demands, desires—they could be tasted as his mouth drew from hers. But tonight he found he needed to hear the words. Too soon, his mind warned as he began to lose himself. It was too soon to ask, too soon to tell. She'd need time, he thought, time and more finesse than he was accustomed to employing.

But even when he drew her away, he wasn't able to let go. Looking down at her, he saw his own beginning. Whatever he'd seen and done in the past, whatever memories he had, were unimportant. There was only one vital thing in his life, and he held it in his arms.

"I want to make love with you."

Her breath was already unsteady, her body trembling. "Yes."

His hands tightened on her as he tried to be logical. "Room's at a premium."

This time she smiled and drew him closer. "We have the floor." She pulled him down with her.

Later, when her mind was clearer and her blood cooler, Bryan would remember only the tumult of feeling, only the flood of sensation. She wouldn't be able to separate the dizzying feel of his mouth on her skin from the heady taste of his under hers.

She'd know that his passion had never been more intense, more relentless, but she wouldn't be able to say how she'd known. Had it been the frantic way he'd said her name? Had it been the desperate way he'd pulled the snug suit down her body, exploiting, ravishing, as he went?

She understood that her own feelings had reached an apex she could never express with words. Words were inadequate. She could only show him. Love, regrets, desires, wishes, had all culminated to whirl inside her until she'd clung to him. And when they'd given each other all they could, she clung still, holding the moment to her as she might a photograph faded after years of looking.

As she lay against him, her head on his chest, she smiled. They had given each other all they could. What more could anyone ask? With her eyes still closed, she pressed her lips against his chest. Nothing would spoil the night. Tonight they'd have candlelight and laughter. She'd never forget it.

"I hope you bought plenty of shrimp," she murmured. "I'm starving."

"I bought enough to feed an average person and a greedy one."

Grinning, she sat up. "Good." With a rare show of energy, she struggled back into the bulky cover-up and sprang up. Bending over the pot of shrimp, she breathed deep. "Wonderful. I didn't know you were so talented."

"I decided it was time I let you in on some of my more admirable qualities."

With a half smile, she looked back to see him slipping on his shorts. "Oh?"

"Yeah. After all, we've got to travel a long way together yet." He sent her a quiet, enigmatic look. "A long way."

"I don't—" She stopped herself and turned to toy with the salad. "This looks good," she began, too brightly.

"Bryan." He stopped her before she could reach in the cupboard above for bowls. "What is it?"

"Nothing." Did he always have to see? she demanded. Couldn't she hide anything from him?

He stepped over, took her arms and held her face to face. "What?"

"Let's talk about it tomorrow, all right?" The brightness was still there, straining. "I'm really hungry. The shrimp's cool by now, so—"

"Now." With a quick shake, he reminded both of them that his patience only stretched so far.

"I've decided to fly back," she blurted out. "I can get a flight out tomorrow afternoon."

He went very still, but she was too busy working out her explanation to notice just how dangerously still. "Why?"

"I've had to reschedule like crazy to fit in this assignment. The extra time I'd get would ease things." It sounded weak. It was weak.

"Why?"

She opened her mouth, prepared to give him a variation on the same theme. One look from him stopped her. "I just want to get back," she managed. "I know you'd like company on the drive, but the assignment's finished. Odds are you'll make better time without me."

He fought back the anger. Anger wasn't the way. If he'd given in to it, he'd have shouted, raged, threatened. That wasn't the way. "No," he said simply, and left it at that.

"No?"

"You're not flying back tomorrow." His voice was calm, but his eyes said a great deal more. "We go together, Bryan."

She braced herself. An argument, she decided, would be easy. "Now look—"

"Sit down."

Haughtiness came to her rarely, but when it did, it was exceptional. "I beg your pardon?"

For an answer, Shade gave her a quick shove onto the bench. Without speaking, he pulled open a drawer and took out the manila envelope that held his most recently developed prints. Tossing them onto the table, he pulled out the one of Bryan.

"What do you see?" he demanded.

"Myself." She cleared her throat. "I see myself, of course."

"Not good enough."

"That's what I see," she tossed back, but she didn't look down at the print again. "That's all there is."

Perhaps fear played a part in his actions. He didn't want to admit it. But it was fear, fear that he'd imagined something that wasn't there. "You see yourself, yes. A beautiful woman, a desirable woman. A woman," he continued slowly, "looking at the man she loves."

He'd stripped her. Bryan felt it as though he'd actually peeled off layer after layer of pretense, defense, disguise. She'd seen the same thing in the image he'd frozen on film. She'd seen it, but what gave him the right to strip her?

"You take too much," she said in a quiet voice. Rising, she turned away from him. "Too damned much."

Relief poured through him. He had to close his eyes on it for a moment. Not imagination, not illusion, but truth. Love was there, and with it, his beginning. "You've already given it."

"No." Bryan turned back, holding on to what she had left. "I haven't given it. What I feel is my responsibility. I haven't asked you for anything, and I won't." She took a deep breath. "We agreed, Shade. No complications."

"Then it looks like we both reneged, doesn't it?" He grabbed her hand before she could move out of reach. "Look at me." His face was close, candlelight flickering over it. Somehow the soft light illuminated what he'd seen, what he'd lived through, what he'd overcome. "Don't you see anything when you look at me? Can you see more in a stranger on the beach, a woman in a crowd, a kid on a street corner, than you do when you look at me?"

"Don't—" she began, only to be cut off.

"What do you see?"

"I see a man," she said, speaking quickly, passionately. "A man who's had to see more than he should. I see a man who's learned to keep his feelings carefully controlled because he isn't quite sure what would happen if he let loose. I see a cynic who hasn't been able to completely stamp out his own sensitivity, his own empathy."

"True enough," he returned evenly, though it was both more and less than he'd wanted to hear. "What else?"

"Nothing," she told him, close to panic. "Nothing."

It wasn't enough. The frustration came through; she could feel it in his hands. "Where's your perception now? Where's the insight that takes you under the glitter of some temperamental leading man to the core? I want you to see into me, Bryan."

"I can't." The words came out on a shudder. "I'm afraid to."

Afraid? He'd never considered it. She took emotions in stride, sought them, dug for them. He loosened his grip on her and said the words that were the most difficult for him to speak. "I love you."

She felt the words slam into her, knocking her breathless. If he said them, he meant them, of that she could be sure. Had she been so caught up in her own feelings that she hadn't seen his? It was tempting, it would be easy, to simply go into his arms and take the risk. But she remembered that they'd both risked before, and failed.

"Shade..." She tried to think calmly, but his words of love still rang in her head. "I don't—you can't—"

"I want to hear you say it." He held her close again. There was no place to go. "I want you to look at me, knowing everything you've said about me is true, and tell me."

"It couldn't work," she began quickly, because her knees were shaking. "It couldn't, don't you see? I'd want it all because I'm just idiot enough to think maybe this time—with you... Marriage, children, that's not what you want, and I understand. I didn't think I wanted them either, until everything got so out of control."

He was calmer now, as she became more frazzled. "You haven't told me yet."

"All right." She nearly shouted it. "All right then, I love you, but I—"

He closed his mouth over hers so there could be no excuses. For now, he could simply drink in the words and all they meant to him. Salvation. He could believe in it.

"You've a hell of a nerve," he said against her mouth, "telling me what I want."

"Shade, please." Giving in to the weakness, she dropped her head on his shoulder. "I didn't want to complicate things. I don't want to now. If I fly back, it'll give us both time to put things back in perspective. My work, your work—"

"Are important," he finished. "But not as important as this." He waited until her eyes slowly lifted to his. Now his voice was calm again. His grip eased, still holding her but without the desperation. "Nothing is, Bryan. You didn't want it, maybe I thought I didn't, but I know better now. Everything started with you. Everything important. You make me clean." He ran a hand through her hair. "God, you make me hope again, believe again. Do you think I'm going to let you take all that away from me?"

The doubts began to fade, quietly, slowly. Second chances? Hadn't she always believed in them? Long shots, she remembered. You only had to want to win badly enough.

"No," she murmured. "But I need a promise. I need the promise, Shade, and then I think we could do anything."

So did he. "I promise to love you, to respect you. To care for you whether you like it or not. And I promise that what I am is yours." Reaching up, he flipped open the cupboard door. Speechless, Bryan watched him draw out a tiny cardboard pot of pansies. Their scent was light and sweet and lasting.

"Plant them with me, Bryan."

Her hands closed over his. Hadn't she always believed life was as simple as you made it? "As soon as we're home."

Epilogue

"Cooperate, will you?"

"No." Amused, but not altogether pleased, Shade watched Bryan adjust the umbrellas beside and behind him. It seemed to him she'd been fiddling with the lighting a great deal longer than necessary.

"You said I could have anything I wanted for Christmas," she reminded him as she held the light meter up to his face. "I want this picture."

"It was a weak moment," he mumbled.

"Tough." Unsympathetic, Bryan stepped back to study the angles. There, the lighting was perfect, the shadows just where they should be. But… A long-suffering sigh came out. "Shade, stop glowering, will you?"

"I said you could take the picture. I didn't say it'd be pretty."

"No chance of that," she said under her breath.

Exasperated, she brushed at her hair, and the thin

gold band on her left hand caught the light. Shade watched it glimmer with the same sort of odd pleasure he always felt when it hit him that they were a team, in every way. With a grin, he joined his left hand with hers, so that the twin rings they wore touched lightly.

"Sure you want this picture for Christmas? I'd thought of buying you ten pounds of French chocolate."

She narrowed her eyes, but her fingers laced with his. "A low blow, Colby. Dead low." Refusing to be distracted, she backed off. "I'll have my picture," she told him. "And if you want to be nasty, I'll buy my own chocolate. Some husbands," she continued as she walked back to the camera set on a tripod, "would cater to their wife's every whim when she's in my delicate condition."

He glanced down at the flat stomach under baggy overalls. It still dazed him that there was life growing there. Their life. When summer came again, they'd hold their first child. It wouldn't do to let her know he had to fight the urge to pamper her, to coddle her every moment. Instead, Shade shrugged and dipped his hands in his pockets.

"Not this one," he said lightly. "You knew what you were getting when you married me."

She looked at him through the viewfinder. His hands were in his pockets, but he wasn't relaxed. As always, his body was ready to move, his mind moving already. But in his eyes she saw the pleasure, the kindness and the love. Together they were making it work. He didn't smile, but Bryan did as she clicked the shutter.

"So I did," she murmured.

* * * * *

LESSONS LEARNED

For Jill Gregory, aka The Baby,
one of my favorite roommates.

Chapter 1

So he was gorgeous. And rich…and talented. And sexy; you shouldn't forget that he was outrageously sexy.

It hardly mattered to Juliet. She was a professional, and to a professional, a job was a job. In this case, great looks and personality were bound to help, but that was business. Strictly business.

No, personally it didn't matter a bit. After all, she'd met a few gorgeous men in her life. She'd met a few rich ones, too, and so forth, though she had to admit she'd never met a man with all those elusive qualities rolled up in one. She'd certainly never had the opportunity to work with one. Now she did.

The fact was, Carlo Franconi's looks, charm, reputation and skill were going to make her job a pleasure. So she was told. Still, with her office door closed, Juliet scowled down at the eight-by-ten glossy black-and-white publicity photo. It looked to her as though he'd be more trouble than pleasure.

Carlo grinned cockily up at her, dark, almond-shaped eyes amused and appreciative. She wondered if the photographer had been a woman. His full thick hair was appealingly disheveled with a bit of curl along the nape of his neck and over his ears. Not too much—just enough to disarm. The strong facial bones, jauntily curved mouth, straight nose and expressive brows combined to create a face destined to sabotage any woman's common sense. Gift or cultivated talent, Juliet wasn't certain, but she'd have to use it to her advantage. Author tours could be murder.

A cookbook. Juliet tried, and failed, not to sigh. Carlo Franconi's *The Italian Way,* was, whether she liked it or not, her biggest assignment to date. Business was business.

She loved her job as publicist and was content for the moment with Trinity Press, the publisher she currently worked for, after a half-dozen job changes and upward jumps since the start of her career. At twenty-eight, the ambition she'd started with as a receptionist nearly ten years before had eased very little. She'd worked, studied, hustled and sweated for her own office and position. She had them, but she wasn't ready to relax.

In two years, by her calculations, she'd be ready to make the next jump: her own public relations firm. Naturally, she'd have to start out small, but it was building the business that was exciting. The contacts and experience she gained in her twenties would help her solidify her ambitions in her thirties. Juliet was content with that.

One of the first things she'd learned in public relations was that an account was an account, whether it was a big blockbuster bestseller already slated to be a big blockbuster film or a slim volume of poetry that would barely earn out its advance. Part of the challenge, and the fun, was finding the right promotional hook.

Now, she had a cookbook and a slick Italian chef. Franconi, she thought wryly, had a track record—with women and in publishing. The first was a matter of hot interest to the society and gossip sections of the international press. It wasn't necessary to cook to be aware of Franconi's name. The second was the reason he was being pampered on the road with a publicist.

His first two cookbooks had been solid bestsellers. For good reason, Juliet admitted. It was true she couldn't fry an egg without creating a gooey inedible glob, but she recognized quality and style. Franconi could make linguini sound like a dish to be prepared while wearing black lace. He turned a simple spaghetti dish into an erotic event.

Sex. Juliet tipped back in her chair and wiggled her stockinged toes. That's what he had. That's just what they'd use. Before the twenty-one-day author tour was finished, she'll have made Carlo Franconi the world's sexiest cook. Any red-blooded American woman would fantasize about him preparing an intimate dinner for two. Candlelight, pasta and romance.

One last study of his publicity shot and the charmingly crooked grin assured her he could handle it.

In the meantime, there was a bit more groundwork to cover. Creating a schedule was a pleasure, adhering to one a challenge. She thrived on both.

Juliet lifted the phone, noticed with resignation that she'd broken another nail, then buzzed her assistant. "Terry, get me Diane Maxwell. She's program coordinator on the *Simpson Show* in L.A."

"Going for the big guns?"

Juliet gave a quick, unprofessional grin. "Yeah." She replaced the phone and started making hurried notes. No reason not to start at the top, she told herself. That way, if you fell on your face, at least the trip would be worth it.

As she waited, she looked around her office. Not the top, but a good ways from the bottom. At least she had a window. Juliet could still shudder thinking of some of the walled-in cubicles she'd worked in. Now, twenty stories below, New York rushed, bumped, pushed and shoved its way through another day. Juliet Trent had learned how to do the same thing after moving from the relatively easygoing suburb of Harrisburg, Pennsylvania.

She might've grown up in a polite little neighborhood where only a stranger drove over twenty-five miles per hour and everyone kept the grass clipped close to their side of the chain-link fences, but Juliet had acclimated easily. The truth was she liked the pace, the energy and the "I dare you" tone of New York. She'd never go back to the bee-humming, hedge-clipping quiet of suburbia where everyone knew who you were, what you did and how you did it. She preferred the anonymity and the individuality of crowds.

Perhaps her mother had molded herself into the perfect suburban wife, but not Juliet. She was an eighties woman, independent, self-sufficient and moving up. There was an apartment in the west Seventies that she'd furnished, slowly, meticulously and, most important, personally. Juliet had enough patience to move step by step as long as the result was perfect. She had a career she could be proud of and an office she was gradually altering to suit her own tastes. Leaving her mark wasn't something she took lightly. It had taken her four months to choose the right plants for her work space, from the four-foot split-leaf philodendron to the delicate white-blossomed African violet.

She'd had to make do with the beige carpet, but the six-foot Dali print on the wall opposite her window added life and energy. The narrow-beveled mirror gave an illusion of space and a touch of elegance. She had her eye on a big, gaudy Oriental urn that would be perfect for a spray of equally gaudy peacock feathers. If she waited a bit longer, the price might come down from exorbitant to ridiculous. Then she'd buy it.

Juliet might put on a very practical front to everyone, including herself, but she couldn't resist a sale. As a result, her bank balance wasn't as hefty as her bedroom closet. She wasn't frivolous. No, she would have been appalled to hear the word applied to her. Her wardrobe was organized, well tended and suitable. Perhaps twenty pairs of shoes could be considered excessive, but Juliet rationalized that she was often on her feet ten hours a day and deserved the luxury. In any case, she'd earned them, from the sturdy sneakers, the practical black pumps to the strappy evening sandals. She'd earned them with innumerable long meetings, countless waits in airports and endless hours on the phone. She'd earned them on author tours, where the luck of the draw could have you dealing with the brilliant, the funny, the inept, the boring or the rude. Whatever she had to deal with, the results had to be the same. Media, media and more media.

She'd learned how to deal with the press, from the *New York Times* reporter to the stringer on the small-town weekly. She knew how to charm the staff of talk shows, from the accepted masters to the nervous imitators. Learning had been an adventure, and since she'd allowed herself very few in her personal life, professional success was all the sweeter.

When the intercom buzzed, she caught her tongue between her teeth. Now, she was going to apply everything she'd learned and land Franconi on the top-rated talk show in the States.

Once she did, she thought as she pressed the button, he'd better make the most of it. Or she'd slit his sexy throat with his own chef's knife.

"Ah, *mi amore. Squisito.*" Carlo's voice was a low purr designed to accelerate the blood pressure. The bedroom voice wasn't something he'd had to develop, but something he'd been born with. Carlo had always thought a man who didn't use God-given gifts was less than a fool. *"Bellisimo,"* he murmured and his eyes were dark and dreamy with anticipation.

It was hot, almost steamy, but he preferred the heat. Cold slowed down the blood. The sun coming through the window had taken on the subtle gold texture with tints of red that spoke of the end of the day and hinted at the pleasures of night. The room was rich with scent so he breathed it in. A man was missing a great deal of life if he didn't use and appreciate all of his senses. Carlo believed in missing nothing.

He watched his love of the moment with a connoisseur's eye. He'd caress, whisper to, flatter—it never mattered to him if it took moments or hours to get what he wanted. As long as he got what he wanted. To Carlo, the process, the anticipation, the moves themselves were equally as satisfying as the result. Like a dance, he'd always thought. Like a song. An aria from *The Marriage of Figaro* played in the background while he seduced.

Carlo believed in setting the scene because life was a play not simply to be enjoyed, but to be relished.

"Bellisimo," he whispered and bent nearer what he adored. The clam sauce simmered erotically as he stirred it. Slowly, savoring the moment, Carlo lifted the spoon to his lips and with his eyes half-closed, tasted. The sound of pleasure came from low in his throat. *"Squisito."*

He moved from the sauce to give the same loving attention to his *zabaglione.* He believed there wasn't a woman alive who could resist the taste of that rich, creamy custard with the zing of wine. As usual, it was a woman he was expecting.

The kitchen was as much a den of pleasure to him as the bedroom. It wasn't an accident that he was one of the most respected and admired chefs in the world, or that he was one of the most engaging lovers. Carlo considered it a matter of destiny. His kitchen was cleverly arranged, as meticulously laid out for the seduction of sauces and spices as his bedroom was for the seduction of women. Yes, Carlo Franconi believed life was to be relished. Every drop of it.

When the knock on the front door reverberated through the high-ceilinged rooms of his home, he murmured to his pasta before he removed his apron. As he went to answer, he rolled down the silk sleeves of his shirt but didn't stop for adjustments in any of the antique mirrors that lined the walls. He wasn't so much vain, as confident.

He opened the door to a tall, stately woman with honey-toned skin and dark glossy eyes. Carlo's heart moved as it did whenever he saw her. *"Mi amore."* Taking her hand, he pressed his mouth to the palm, while his eyes smiled into hers. *"Bella. Molto bella."*

She stood in the evening light for a moment, dark, lovely, with a smile only for him. Only a fool wouldn't have known he'd welcomed dozens of women in just this way. She wasn't a fool. But she loved him.

"You're a scoundrel, Carlo." The woman reached out to touch his hair. It was dark and thick and difficult to resist. "Is this the way you greet your mother?"

"This is the way—" he kissed her hand again "—I greet a beautiful woman." Then he wrapped both arms around her and kissed her cheeks. "This is the way I greet my mother. It's a fortunate man who can do both."

Gina Franconi laughed as she returned her son's hug. "To you, all women are beautiful."

"But only one is my mother." With his arm around her waist, he led her inside.

Gina approved, as always, the fact that his home was spotless, if a bit too exotic for her taste. She often wondered how the poor maid managed to keep the ornately carved archways dusted and polished and the hundreds of windowpanes unstreaked. Because she was a woman who'd spent fifteen years of her life cleaning other people's homes and forty cleaning her own, she thought of such things.

She studied one of his new acquisitions, a three-foot ivory owl with a small rodent captured in one claw. A good wife, Gina mused, would guide her son's tastes toward less eccentric paths.

"An aperitif, Mama?" Carlo walked over to a tall smoked-glass cabinet and drew out a slim black bottle. "You should try this," he told her as he chose two small glasses and poured. "A friend sent it to me."

Gina set aside her red snakeskin bag and accepted the glass. The first sip was hot, potent, smooth as a lover's kiss and just as intoxicating. She lifted a brow as she took the second sip. "Excellent."

"Yes, it is. Anna has excellent taste."

Anna, she thought, with more amusement than exasperation. She'd learned years before that it didn't do any good to be exasperated with a man, especially if you loved him. "Are all your friends women, Carlo?"

"No." He held his glass up, twirling it. "But this one was. She sent me this as a wedding present."

"A—"

"Her wedding," Carlo said with a grin. "She wanted a husband, and though I couldn't accommodate her, we parted friends." He held up the bottle as proof.

"Did you have it analyzed before you drank any?" Gina asked dryly.

He touched the rim of his glass to hers. "A clever man turns all former lovers into friends, Mama."

"You've always been clever." With a small movement of her shoulders she sipped again and sat down. "I hear you're seeing the French actress."

"As always, your hearing's excellent."

As if it interested her, Gina studied the hue of the liqueur in her glass. "She is, of course, beautiful."

"Of course."

"I don't think she'll give me grandchildren."

Carlo laughed and sat beside her. "You have six grandchildren and another coming, Mama. Don't be greedy."

"But none from my son. My only son," she reminded him with a tap of her finger on his shoulder. "Still, I haven't given you up yet."

"Perhaps if I could find a woman like you."

She shot him back arrogant look for arrogant look. "Impossible, *caro*."

His feeling exactly, Carlo thought as he guided her into talk about his four sisters and their families. When he looked at this sleek, lovely woman, it was difficult to think of her as the mother who'd raised him, almost single-handedly. She'd worked, and though she'd been known to storm and rage, she'd never complained. Her clothes had been carefully mended, her floors meticulously scrubbed while his father had spent endless months at sea.

When he concentrated, and he rarely did, Carlo could recall an impression of a dark, wiry man with a black mustache and an easy grin. The impression didn't bring on resentment or even regret. His father had been a seaman before his parents had married, and a seaman he'd remained. Carlo's belief in meeting your destiny was unwavering. But while his feelings for his father were ambivalent, his feelings for his mother were set and strong.

She'd supported each of her children's ambitions, and when Carlo had earned a scholarship to the Sorbonne in Paris and the opportunity to pursue his interest in haute cuisine, she'd let him go. Ultimately, she'd supplemented the meager income he could earn between studies with part of the insurance money she'd received when her husband had been lost in the sea he'd loved.

Six years before, Carlo had been able to pay her back in his own way. The dress shop he'd bought for her birthday had been a lifelong dream for both of them. For him, it was a way of seeing his mother happy at last. For Gina it was a way to begin again.

He'd grown up in a big, boisterous, emotional family. It gave him pleasure to look back and remember. A man who grows up in a family of women learns to understand them, appreciate them, admire them. Carlo knew about women's dreams, their vanities, their insecurities. He never took a lover he didn't have affection for as well as desire. If there was only desire, he knew there'd be no friendship at the end, only resentment. Even now, the comfortable affair he was having with the French actress was ending. She'd be starting a film in a few weeks, and he'd be going on tour in America. That, Carlo thought with some regret, would be that.

"Carlo, you go to America soon?"

"Hmm. Yes." He wondered if she'd read his mind, knowing women were capable of doing so. "Two weeks."

"You'll do me a favor?"

"Of course."

"Then notice for me what the professional American woman is wearing. I'm thinking of adding some things to the shop. The Americans are so clever and practical."

"Not too practical, I hope." He swirled his drink. "My publicist is a Ms. Trent." Tipping back his glass, he accepted the heat and the punch. "I'll promise you to study every aspect of her wardrobe."

She gave his quick grin a steady look. "You're so good to me, Carlo."

"But of course, Mama. Now I'm going to feed you like a queen."

Carlo had no idea what Juliet Trent looked like, but put himself in the hands of fate. What he did know, from the letters he'd received from her, was that Juliet Trent was the type of American his mother had described. Practical and clever. Excellent qualities in a publicist.

Physically was another matter. But again, as his mother had said, Carlo could always find beauty in a woman. Perhaps he did prefer, in his personal life, a woman with a lovely shell, but he knew how to dig beneath to find inner beauty. It was something that made life interesting as well as aesthetically pleasing.

Still, as he stepped off the plane into the terminal in L.A., he had his hand on the elbow of a stunning redhead.

Juliet did know what he looked like, and she first saw him, shoulder to shoulder with a luxuriously built woman in pencil-thin heels. Though he carried a bulky leather case in one hand, and a flight bag over his shoulder, he escorted the redhead through the gate as though they were walking into a ballroom. Or a bedroom.

Juliet took a quick assessment of the well-tailored slacks, the unstructured jacket and open-collared shirt. The well-heeled traveler. There was a chunk of gold and diamond on his finger that should've looked ostentatious and vulgar. Somehow it looked as casual and breezy as the rest of him. She felt formal and sticky.

She'd been in L.A. since the evening before, giving herself time to see personally to all the tiny details. Carlo Franconi would have nothing to do but be charming, answer questions and sign his cookbook.

As she watched him kiss the redhead's knuckles, Juliet thought he'd be signing plenty of them. After all, didn't women do the majority of cookbook buying? Carefully smoothing away a sarcastic smirk, Juliet rose. The redhead was sending one last wistful look over her shoulder as she walked away.

"Mr. Franconi?"

Carlo turned away from the woman who'd proven to be a pleasant traveling companion on the long flight from New York. His first look at Juliet brought a quick flutter of interest and a subtle tug of desire he often felt with a woman. It was a tug he could either control or let loose, as was appropriate. This time, he savored it.

She didn't have merely a lovely face, but an interesting one. Her skin was very pale, which should have made her seem fragile, but the wide, strong cheekbones undid the air of fragility and gave her face an intriguing diamond shape. Her eyes were large, heavily lashed and artfully accented with a smoky shadow that only made the cool green shade of the irises seem cooler. Her mouth was only lightly touched with a peach-colored gloss. It had a full, eye-drawing shape that needed no artifice. He gathered she was wise enough to know it.

Her hair was caught somewhere between brown and blond so that its shade was soft, natural and subtle. She wore it long enough in the back to be pinned up in a chignon when she wished, and short enough on the top and sides so that she could style it from fussy to practical as the occasion, and her whim, demanded. At the moment, it was loose and casual, but not windblown. She'd stopped in the ladies' room for a quick check just after the incoming flight had been announced.

"I'm Juliet Trent," she told him when she felt he'd stared long enough. "Welcome to California." As he took the hand she offered, she realized she should've expected him to kiss it rather than shake. Still, she stiffened, hardly more than an instant, but she saw by the lift of his brow, he'd felt it.

"A beautiful woman makes a man welcome anywhere."

His voice was incredible—the cream that rose to the top and then flowed over something rich. She told herself it only pleased her because it would record well and took his statement literally. Thinking of the redhead, she gave him an easy, not entirely friendly smile. "Then you must have had a pleasant flight."

His native language might have been Italian, but Carlo understood nuances in any tongue. He grinned at her. "Very pleasant."

"And tiring," she said remembering her position. "Your luggage should be in by now." Again, she glanced at the large case he carried. "Can I take that for you?"

His brow lifted at the idea of a man dumping his burden on a woman. Equality, to Carlo, never crossed the border into manners. "No, this is something I always carry myself."

Indicating the way, she fell into step beside him. "It's a half-hour ride to the Beverly Wilshire, but after you've settled in, you can rest all afternoon. I'd like to go over tomorrow's schedule with you this evening."

He liked the way she walked. Though she wasn't tall, she moved in long, unhurried strides that made the red side-pleated skirt she wore shift over her hips. "Over dinner?"

She sent him a quick sidelong look. "If you like."

She'd be at his disposal, Juliet reminded herself, for the next three weeks. Without appearing to think about it, she skirted around a barrel-chested man hefting a bulging garment bag and a briefcase. Yes, he liked the way she walked, Carlo thought again. She was a woman who could take care of herself without a great deal of fuss.

"At seven? You have a talk show in the morning that starts at seven-thirty so we'd best make it an early evening."

Seven-thirty A.M. Carlo thought, only briefly, about jet lag and time changes. "So, you put me to work quickly."

"That's what I'm here for, Mr. Franconi." Juliet said it cheerfully as she stepped up to the slowly moving baggage belt. "You have your stubs?"

An organized woman, he thought as he reached into the inside pocket of his loose-fitting buff-colored jacket. In silence, he handed them to her, then hefted a pullman and a garment bag from the belt himself.

Gucci, she observed. So he had taste as well as money. Juliet handed the stubs to a skycap and waited while Carlo's luggage was loaded onto the pushcart. "I think you'll be pleased with what we have for you, Mr. Franconi." She walked through the automatic doors and signaled for her limo. "I know you've always worked with Jim Collins in the past on your tours in the States; he sends his best."

"Does Jim like his executive position?"

"Apparently."

Though Carlo expected her to climb into the limo first, she stepped back. With a bow to women professionals, Carlo ducked inside and took his seat. "Do you like yours, Ms. Trent?"

She took the seat across from him then sent him a straight-shooting, level look. Juliet could have no idea how much he admired it. "Yes, I do."

Carlo stretched out his legs—legs his mother had once said that had refused to stop growing long after it was necessary. He'd have preferred driving himself, particularly after the long, long flight from Rome where someone else had been at the controls. But if he couldn't, the plush laziness of the limo was the next best thing. Reaching over, he switched on the stereo so that Mozart poured out, quiet but vibrant. If he'd been driving, it would've been rock, loud and rambunctious.

"You've read my book, Ms. Trent?"

"Yes, of course. I couldn't set up publicity and promotion for an unknown product." She sat back. It was easy to do her job when she could speak the simple truth. "I was impressed with the attention to detail and the clear directions. It seemed a very friendly book, rather than simply a kitchen tool."

"Hmm." He noticed her stockings were very pale pink and had a tiny line of dots up one side. It would interest his mother that the practical American businesswoman could enjoy the frivolous. It interested him that Juliet Trent could. "Have you tried any of the recipes?"

"No, I don't cook."

"You don't..." His lazy interest came to attention. "At all?"

She had to smile. He looked so sincerely shocked.

As he watched the perfect mouth curve, he had to put the next tug of desire in check.

"When you're a failure at something, Mr. Franconi, you leave it to someone else."

"I could teach you." The idea intrigued him. He never offered his expertise lightly.

"To cook?" She laughed, relaxing enough to let her heel slip out of her shoe as she swung her foot. "I don't think so."

"I'm an excellent teacher," he said with a slow smile.

Again, she gave him the calm, gunslinger look. "I don't doubt it. I, on the other hand, am a poor student."

"Your age?" When her look narrowed, he smiled charmingly. "A rude question when a woman's reached a certain stage. You haven't."

"Twenty-eight," she said so coolly his smile became a grin.

"You look younger, but your eyes are older. I'd find it a pleasure to give you a few lessons, Ms. Trent."

She believed him. She, too, understood nuances. "A pity our schedule won't permit it."

He shrugged easily and glanced out the window. But the L.A. freeway didn't interest him. "You put Philadelphia in the schedule as I requested?"

"We'll have a full day there before we fly up to Boston. Then we'll finish up in New York."

"Good. I have a friend there. I haven't seen her in nearly a year."

Juliet was certain he had—friends—everywhere.

"You've been to Los Angeles before?" he asked her.

"Yes. Several times on business."

"I've yet to come here for pleasure myself. What do you think of it?"

As he had, she glanced out the window without interest. "I prefer New York."

"Why?"

"More grit, less gloss."

He liked her answer, and her phrasing. Because of it, he studied her more closely. "Have you ever been to Rome?"

"No." He thought he heard just a trace of wistfulness in her voice. "I haven't been to Europe at all."

"When you do, come to Rome. It was built on grit."

Her mind drifted a bit as she thought of it, and her smile remained. "I think of fountains and marble and cathedrals."

"You'll find them—and more." She had a face exquisite enough to be carved in marble, he thought. A voice quiet and smooth enough for cathedrals. "Rome rose and fell and clawed its way back up again. An intelligent woman understands such things. A romantic woman understands the fountains."

She glanced out again as the limo pulled up in front of the hotel. "I'm afraid I'm not very romantic."

"A woman named Juliet hasn't a choice."

"My mother's selection," she pointed out. "Not mine."

"You don't look for Romeo?"

Juliet gathered her briefcase. "No, Mr. Franconi. I don't."

He stepped out ahead of her and offered his hand. When Juliet stood on the curb, he didn't move back to give her room. Instead, he experimented with the sensation of bodies brushing, lightly, even politely on a public street. Her gaze came up to his, not wary but direct.

He felt it, the pull. Not the tug that was impersonal and for any woman, but the pull that went straight to the gut and was for one woman. So he'd have to taste her mouth. After all, he was a man compelled to judge a great deal by taste. But he could also bide his time. Some creations took a long time and had complicated preparations to perfect. Like Juliet, he insisted on perfection.

"Some women," he murmured, "never need to look, only to evade and avoid and select."

"Some women," she said just as quietly, "choose not to select at all." Deliberately, she turned her back on him to pay off the driver. "I've already checked you in, Mr. Franconi," she said over her shoulder as she handed his key to the waiting bellboy. "I'm just across the hall from your suite."

Without looking at him, Juliet followed the bellboy into the hotel and to the elevators. "If it suits you, I'll make reservations here in the hotel for dinner at seven. You can just tap on my door when you're ready." With a quick check of her watch she calculated the time difference and figured she could make three calls to New

York and one to Dallas before office hours were over farther east. "If you need anything, you've only to order it and charge it to the room."

She stepped from the elevator, unzipping her purse and pulling out her own room key as she walked. "I'm sure you'll find your suite suitable."

He watched her brisk, economic movements. "I'm sure I will."

"Seven o'clock then." She was already pushing her key into the lock as the bellboy opened the first door to the suite across the hall. As she did, her mind was already on the calls she'd make the moment she'd shed her jacket and shoes.

"Juliet."

She paused, her hair swinging back as she looked over her shoulder at Carlo. He held her there, a moment longer, in silence. "Don't change your scent," he murmured. "Sex without flowers, femininity without vulnerability. It suits you."

While she continued to stare over her shoulder, he disappeared inside the suite. The bellboy began his polite introductions to the accommodations of the suite. Something Carlo said caused him to break off and laugh.

Juliet turned her key with more strength than necessary, pushed open her door, then closed it again with the length of her body. For a minute, she just leaned there, waiting for her system to level.

Professional training had prevented her from stammering and fumbling and making a fool of herself. Professional training had helped her to keep her nerves just at the border where they could be controlled and concealed. Still, under the training, there was a woman. Control had cost her. Juliet was dead certain there wasn't a woman alive who would be totally unaffected by Carlo Franconi. It wasn't balm for her ego to admit she was simply part of a large, varied group.

He'd never know it, she told herself, but her pulse had been behaving badly since he'd first taken her hand. It was still behaving badly. Stupid, she told herself and threw her bag down on a chair. Then she thought it best if she followed it. Her legs weren't steady yet. Juliet let out a long, deep breath. She'd just have to wait until they were.

So he was gorgeous. And rich…and talented. And outrageously sexy. She'd already known that, hadn't she? The trouble was, she wasn't sure how to handle him. Not nearly as sure as she had to be.

Chapter 2

She was a woman who thrived on tight scheduling, minute details and small crises. These were the things that kept you alert, sharp and interested. If her job had been simple, there wouldn't have been much fun to it.

She was also a woman who liked long, lazy baths in mountains of bubbles and big, big beds. These were the things that kept you sane. Juliet felt she'd earned the second after she'd dealt with the first.

While Carlo amused himself in his own way, Juliet spent an hour and a half on the phone, then another hour revising and fine-tuning the next day's itinerary. A print interview had come through and had to be shuffled in. She shuffled. Another paper was sending a reporter and photographer to the book signing. Their names had to be noted and remembered. Juliet noted, circled and committed to memory. The way things were shaping up, they'd be lucky to manage a two-hour breather the next day. Nothing could've pleased her more.

By the time she'd closed her thick, leather-bound notebook, she was more than ready for the tub. The bed, unfortunately, would have to wait. Ten o'clock, she promised herself. By ten, she'd be in bed, snuggled in, curled up and unconscious.

She soaked, designating precisely forty-five minutes for her personal time. In the bath, she didn't plot or plan or estimate. She clicked off the busy, business end of her brain and enjoyed.

Relaxing—it took the first ten minutes to accomplish that completely. Dreaming—she could pretend the white, standard-size tub was luxurious, large and lush. Black marble perhaps and big enough for two. It was a secret ambition of Juliet's to own one like it eventually. The symbol, she felt, of ultimate success. She'd have bristled if anyone had called her goal romantic. Practical, she'd insist. When you worked hard, you needed a place to unwind. This was hers.

Her robe hung on the back of the door—jade green, teasingly brief and silk. Not a luxury as far as she was concerned, but a necessity. When you often had only short snatches to relax, you needed all the help you could get. She considered the robe as much an aid in keeping pace as the bottles of vitamins that lined the counter by the sink. When she traveled, she always took them.

After she'd relaxed and dreamed a bit, she could appreciate soft, hot water against her skin, silky bubbles hissing, steam rising rich with scent.

He'd told her not to change her scent.

Juliet scowled as she felt the muscles in her shoulders tense. Oh no. Deliberately she picked up the tiny cake of hotel soap and rubbed it up and down her arms. Oh no, she wouldn't let Carlo Franconi intrude on her personal time. That was rule number one.

He'd purposely tried to unravel her. He'd succeeded. Yes, he had succeeded, Juliet admitted with a stubborn nod. But that was over now. She wouldn't let it happen again. Her job was to promote his book, not his ego. To promote, she'd go above and beyond the call of duty with her time, her energy and her skill, but not with her emotions.

Franconi wasn't flying back to Rome in three weeks with a smug smile on his face unless it was professionally generated. That instant knife-sharp attraction would be dealt with. Priorities, Juliet mused, were the order of the day. He could add all the American conquests to his list he chose—as long as she wasn't among them.

In any case, he didn't seriously interest her. It was simply that basic, primal urge. Certainly there wasn't any intellect involved. She preferred a different kind of man—steady rather than flashy, sincere rather than charming. That was the kind of man a woman of common sense looked for when the time was right. Juliet judged the time would be right in about three years. By then, she'd have established the structure for her own firm. She'd be financially independent and creatively content. Yes, in three years she'd be ready to think about a serious relationship. That would fit her schedule nicely.

Settled, she decided, and closed her eyes. It was a nice, comfortable word. But the hot water, bubbles and steam didn't relax her any longer. A bit resentful, she released the plug and stood up to let the water drain off her. The wide mirror above the counter and sink was fogged, but only lightly. Through the mist she could see Juliet Trent.

Odd, she thought, how pale and soft and vulnerable a naked woman could look. In her mind, she was strong, practical, even tough. But she could see, in the damp, misty mirror, the fragility, even the wistfulness.

Erotic? Juliet frowned a bit as she told herself she shouldn't be disappointed that her body had been built on slim, practical lines rather than round and lush ones. She should be grateful that her long legs got her where she was going and her narrow hips helped keep her silhouette in a business suit trim and efficient. Erotic would never be a career plus.

Without makeup, her face looked too young, too trusting. Without careful grooming, her hair looked too wild, too passionate.

Fragile, young, passionate. Juliet shook her head. Not qualities for a professional woman. It was fortunate that clothes and cosmetics could play down or play up certain aspects. Grabbing a towel, she wrapped it around herself, then taking another she wiped the steam from the mirror. No more mists, she thought. To succeed you had to see clearly.

With a glance at the tubes and bottles on the counter she began to create the professional Ms. Trent.

Because she hated quiet hotel rooms, Juliet switched on the television as she started to dress. The old Bogart–Bacall movie pleased her and was more relaxing than a dozen bubble baths. She listened to the well-known dialogue while she drew on her smoke-colored stockings. She watched the shimmering restrained passion as she adjusted the straps of a sheer black teddy. While the plot twisted and turned, she zipped on the narrow black dress and knotted the long strand of pearls under her breasts.

Caught up, she sat on the edge of the bed, running a brush through her hair as she watched. She was smiling, absorbed, distracted, but it would've shocked her if anyone had said she was romantic.

When the knock sounded at her door, she glanced at her watch. 7:05. She'd lost fifteen minutes dawdling. To make up for it, Juliet had her shoes on, her earrings clipped and her bag and notebook at hand in twelve seconds flat. She went to the door ready with a greeting and an apology.

A rose. Just one, the color of a young girl's blush. When Carlo handed it to her, she didn't have anything to say at all. Carlo, however, had no problem.

"Bella." He had her hand to his lips before she'd thought to counter the move. "Some women look severe or cold in black. Others..." His survey was long and male, but his smile made it gallant rather than calculating. "In others it simply enhances their femininity. I'm disturbing you?"

"No, no, of course not. I was just—"

"Ah, I know this movie."

Without waiting for an invitation, he breezed past her into the room. The standard, single hotel room didn't seem so impersonal any longer. How could it? He brought life, energy, passion into the air as if it were his mission.

"Yes, I've seen it many times." The two strong faces dominated the screen. Bogart's, creased, heavy-eyed, weary—Bacall's, smooth, steamy and challenging. *"Passione,"* he murmured and made the word seem like honey to be tasted. Incredibly, Juliet found herself swallowing. "A man and a woman can bring many things to each other, but without passion, everything else is tame. *Sì?*"

Juliet recovered herself. Franconi wasn't a man to discuss passion with. The subject wouldn't remain academic for long. "Perhaps." She adjusted her evening bag and her notebook. But she didn't put the rose down. "We've a lot to discuss over dinner, Mr. Franconi. We'd best get started."

With his thumbs still hooked in the pockets of his taupe slacks, he turned his head. Juliet figured hundreds of women had trusted that smile. She wouldn't. With a careless flick, he turned off the television. "Yes, it's time we started."

What did he think of her? Carlo asked himself the question and let the answer come in snatches, twined through the evening.

Lovely. He didn't consider his affection for beautiful women a weakness. He was grateful that Juliet didn't find the need to play down or turn her natural beauty into severity, nor did she exploit it until it was artificial. She'd found a pleasing balance. He could admire that.

She was ambitious, but he admired that as well. Beautiful women without ambition lost his interest quickly.

She didn't trust him. That amused him. As he drank his second glass of Beaujolais, he decided her wariness was a compliment. In his estimation, a woman like Juliet would only be wary of a man if she were attracted in some way.

If he were honest, and he was, he'd admit that most women were attracted to him. It seemed only fair, as he was attracted to them. Short, tall, plump, thin, old or young, he found women a fascination, a delight, an amusement. He respected them, perhaps only as a man who had grown up surrounded by women could do. But respect didn't mean he couldn't enjoy.

He was going to enjoy Juliet.

"*Hello, L.A.* is on first tomorrow." Juliet ran down her notes while Carlo nibbled on pâté. "It's the top-rated morning talk show on the coast, not just in L.A. Liz Marks hosts. She's very personable—not too bubbly. Los Angeles doesn't want bubbly at 8:00 A.M."

"Thank God."

"In any case, she has a copy of the book. It's important that you get the title in a couple of times if she doesn't. You have the full twenty minutes, so it shouldn't be a problem. You'll be autographing at Books, Incorporated on Wilshire Boulevard between one and three." Hastily, she made herself a note to contact the store in the morning for a last check. "You'll want to plug that, but I'll remind you just before airtime. Of course, you'll want to mention that you're beginning a twenty-one-day tour of the country here in California."

"Mmm-hmm. The pâté is quite passable. Would you like some?"

"No, thanks. Just go ahead." She checked off her list and reached for her wine without looking at him. The restaurant was quiet and elegant, but it didn't matter. If they'd been in a loud crowded bar on the Strip, she'd still have gone on with her notes. "Right after the morning show, we go to a radio spot. Then we'll have brunch with a reporter from the *Times*. You've already had an article in the *Trib*. I've got a clipping for you. You'd want to mention your other two books, but concentrate on the new one. It wouldn't hurt to bring up some of the major cities we'll hit. Denver, Dallas, Chicago, New York. Then there's the autographing, a spot on the evening news and dinner with two book reps. The next day—"

"One day at a time," he said easily. "I'll be less likely to snarl at you."

"All right." She closed her notebook and sipped at her wine again. "After all, it's my job to see to the details, yours to sign books and be charming."

He touched his glass to hers. "Then neither of us should have a problem. Being charming is my life."

Was he laughing at himself, she wondered, or at her? "From what I've seen, you excel at it."

"A gift, *cara*." Those dark, deep-set eyes were amused and exciting. "Unlike a skill that's developed and trained."

So, he was laughing at both of them, she realized. It would be both difficult and wise not to like him for it.

When her steak was served, Juliet glanced at it. Carlo, however, studied his veal as though it were a fine old painting. No, Juliet realized after a moment, he studied it as though it were a young, beautiful woman.

"Appearances," he told her, "in food, as in people, are essential." He was smiling at her when he cut into the veal. "And, as in people, they can be deceiving."

Juliet watched him sample the first bite, slowly, his eyes half-closed. She felt an odd chill at the base of her spine. He'd sample a woman the same way, she was certain. Slowly.

"Pleasant," he said after a moment. "No more, no less."

She couldn't prevent the quick smirk as she cut into her steak. "Yours is better of course."

He moved his shoulders. A statement of arrogance. "Of course. Like comparing a pretty young girl with a beautiful woman." When she glanced up he was holding out his fork. Over it, his eyes studied her. "Taste," he invited and the simple word made her blood shiver. "Nothing should ever go untasted, Juliet."

She shrugged, letting him feed her the tiny bite of veal. It was spicy, just bordering on rich and hot on her tongue. "It's good."

"Good, *sì*. Nothing Franconi prepares is ever merely good. Good, I'd pour into the garbage, feed to the dogs in the alley." She laughed, delighting him. "If something isn't special, then it's ordinary."

"True enough." Without realizing it, she slipped out of her shoes. "But then, I suppose I've always looked at food as a basic necessity."

"Necessity?" Carlo shook his head. Though he'd heard such sentiment before, he still considered it a sacrilege. "Oh, *madonna,* you have much to learn. When one knows how to eat, how to appreciate, it's second only to making love. Scents, textures, tastes. To eat only to fill your stomach? Barbaric."

"Sorry." Juliet took another bite of steak. It was tender and cooked well. But it was only a piece of meat. She'd never have considered it sensual or romantic, but simply filling. "Is that why you became a cook? Because you think food's sexy?"

He winced. "Chef, *cara mia*."

She grinned, showing him for the first time a streak of humor and mischief. "What's the difference?"

"What's the difference between a plow horse and a thoroughbred? Plaster and porcelain?"

Enjoying herself, she touched her tongue to the rim of her glass. "Some might say dollar signs."

"No, no, no, my love. Money is only a result, not a cause. A cook makes hamburgers in a greasy kitchen that smells of onions behind a counter where people squeeze plastic bottles of ketchup. A chef creates…" He gestured, a circle of a hand. "An experience."

She lifted her glass and swept her lashes down, but she didn't hide the smile. "I see."

Though he could be offended by a look when he chose, and be ruthless with the offender, Carlo liked her style. "You're amused. But you haven't tasted Franconi." He waited until her eyes, both wry and wary, lifted to him. "Yet."

He had a talent for turning the simplest statement into something erotic, she observed. It would be a challenge to skirt around him without giving way. "But you haven't told me why you became a chef."

"I can't paint or sculpt. I haven't the patience or the talent to compose sonnets. There are other ways to create, to embrace art."

She saw, with surprise mixed with respect, that he was quite serious. "But paintings, sculpture and poetry remain centuries after they've been created. If you make a soufflé, it's here, then it's gone."

"Then the challenge is to make it again, and again. Art needn't be put behind glass or bronzed, Juliet, merely appreciated. I have a friend…" He thought of Summer Lyndon—no, Summer Cocharan now. "She makes pastries like an angel. When you eat one, you're a king."

"Then is cooking magic or art?"

"Both. Like love. And I think you, Juliet Trent, eat much too little."

She met his look as he'd hoped she would. "I don't believe in overindulgence, Mr. Franconi. It leads to carelessness."

"To indulgence then." He lifted his glass. The smile was back, charming and dangerous. "Carefully."

* * *

Anything and everything could go wrong. You had to expect it, anticipate it and avoid it. Juliet knew just how much could be botched in a twenty-minute, live interview at 7:30 A.M. on a Monday. You hoped for the best and made do with the not too bad. Even she didn't expect perfection on the first day of a tour.

It wasn't easy to explain why she was annoyed when she got it.

The morning spot went beautifully. There was no other way to describe it, Juliet decided as she watched Liz Marks talk and laugh with Carlo after the camera stopped taping. If a shrewd operator could be called a natural, Carlo was indeed a natural. During the interview, he'd subtly and completely dominated the show while charmingly blinding his host to it. Twice he'd made the ten-year veteran of morning talk shows giggle like a girl. Once, once, Juliet remembered with astonishment, she'd seen the woman blush.

Yeah. She shifted the strap of her heavy briefcase on her arm. Franconi was a natural. It was bound to make her job easier. She yawned and cursed him.

Juliet always slept well in hotel rooms. *Always.* Except for last night. She might've been able to convince someone else that too much coffee and first-day jitters had kept her awake. But she knew better. She could drink a pot of coffee at ten and fall asleep on command at eleven. Her system was very disciplined. Except for last night.

She'd nearly dreamed of him. If she hadn't shaken herself awake at 2:00 A.M., she would have dreamed of him. That was no way to begin a very important, very long author tour. She told herself now if she had to choose between some silly fantasies and honest fatigue, she'd take the fatigue.

Stifling another yawn, Juliet checked her watch. Liz had her arm tucked through Carlo's and looked as though she'd keep it there unless someone pried her loose. With a sigh, Juliet decided she'd have to be the crowbar.

"Ms. Marks, it was a wonderful show." As she crossed over, Juliet deliberately held out her hand. With obvious reluctance, Liz disengaged herself from Carlo and accepted it.

"Thank you, Miss..."

"Trent," Juliet supplied without a waver.

"Juliet is my publicist," Carlo told Liz, though the two women had been introduced less than an hour earlier. "She guards my schedule."

"Yes, and I'm afraid I'll have to rush Mr. Franconi along. He has a radio spot in a half hour."

"If you must." Juliet was easily dismissed as Liz turned back to Carlo. "You have a delightful way of starting the morning. A pity you won't be in town longer."

"A pity," Carlo agreed and kissed Liz's fingers. Like an old movie, Juliet thought impatiently. All they needed were violins.

"Thank you again, Ms. Marks." Juliet used her most diplomatic smile as she took Carlo's arm and began to lead him out of the studio. After all, she'd very likely need Liz Marks again. "We're in a bit of a hurry," she muttered as they worked their way back to the reception area. The taping was over and she had other fish to fry. "This radio show's one of the top-rated in the city. Since it leans heavily on top forties and classic rock, its audience, at this time of day, falls mainly in the eighteen to thirty-five range. Excellent buying power. That gives us a nice mix with the audience from this morning's show which is generally in the twenty-five to fifty, primarily female category."

Listening with all apparent respect, Carlo reached the waiting limo first and opened the door himself. "You consider this important?"

"Of course." Because she was distracted by what she thought was a foolish question, Juliet climbed into the limo ahead of him. "We've a solid schedule in L.A." And she didn't see the point in mentioning there were some cities on the tour where they wouldn't be quite so busy. "A morning talk show with a good reputation, a popular radio show, two print interviews, two quick spots on the evening news and the *Simpson Show.*" She said the last with a hint of relish. The *Simpson Show* offset what she was doing to the budget with limos.

"So you're pleased."

"Yes, of course." Digging into her briefcase, she took out her folder to recheck the name of her contact at the radio station.

"Then why do you look so annoyed?"

"I don't know what you're talking about."

"You get a line right…here," he said as he ran a fingertip between her eyebrows. At the touch, Juliet jerked back before she could stop herself. Carlo only cocked his head, watching her. "You may smile and speak in a quiet, polite voice, but that line gives you away."

"I was very pleased with the taping," she said again.

"But?"

All right, she thought, he was asking for it. "Perhaps it annoys me to see a woman making a fool of herself." Juliet stuffed the folder back into her briefcase. "Liz Marks is married, you know."

"Wedding rings are things I try to be immediately aware of," he said with a shrug. "Your instructions were to be charming, weren't they?"

"Perhaps *charm* has a different meaning in Italy."

"As I said, you must come to Rome."

"I suppose you enjoy having women drooling all over you."

He smiled at her, easy, attractive, innocent. "But of course."

A gurgle of laughter bubbled in her throat but she swallowed it. She wouldn't be charmed. "You'll have to deal with some men on this tour as well."

"I promise not to kiss Simpson's fingers."

This time the laughter escaped. For a moment, she relaxed with it, let it come. Carlo saw, too briefly, the youth and energy beneath the discipline. He'd like to have kept her like that longer—laughing, at ease with him, and with herself. It would be a challenge, he mused, to find the right sequence of buttons to push to bring laughter to her eyes more often. He liked challenges—particularly when there was a woman connected to them.

"Juliet." Her name flowed off his tongue in a way only the European male had mastered. "You mustn't worry. Your tidily married Liz only enjoyed a mild flirtation with a man she'll more than likely never see again. Harmless. Perhaps because of it, she'll find more romance with her husband tonight."

Juliet eyed him a moment in her straight-on, no-nonsense manner. "You think quite of lot of yourself, don't you?"

He grinned, not sure if he was relieved or if he regretted the fact that he'd never met anyone like her before. "No more than is warranted, *cara.* Anyone who has character leaves a mark on another. Would you like to leave the world without making a ripple?"

No. No, that was one thing she was determined not to do. She sat back determined to hold her own. "I suppose some of us insist on leaving more ripples than others."

He nodded. "I don't like to do anything in a small way."

"Be careful, Mr. Franconi, or you'll begin to believe your own image."

The limo had stopped, but before Juliet could scoot toward the door, Carlo had her hand. When she looked at him this time, she didn't see the affable, amorous Italian chef, but a man of power. A man, she realized, who was well aware of how far it could take him.

She didn't move, but wondered how many other women had seen the steel beneath the silk.

"I don't need imagery, Juliet." His voice was soft, charming, beautiful. She heard the razor-blade cut beneath it. "Franconi is Franconi. Take me for what you see, or go to the devil."

Smoothly, he climbed from the limo ahead of her, turned and took her hand, drawing her out with him. It was a move that was polite, respectful, even ordinary. It was a move, Juliet realized, that expressed their positions. Man to woman. The moment she stood on the curb, she removed her hand.

With two shows and a business brunch under their belts, Juliet left Carlo in the bookstore, already swamped with women crowded in line for a glimpse at and a few words with Carlo Franconi. They'd handled the reporter and photographer already, and a man like Franconi wouldn't need her help with a crowd of women. Armed with change and her credit card, she went to find a pay phone.

For the first forty-five minutes, she spoke with her assistant in New York, filling her pad with times, dates and names while L.A. traffic whisked by outside the phone booth. As a bead of sweat trickled down her back, she wondered if she'd chosen the hottest corner in the city.

Denver still didn't look as promising as she'd hoped, but Dallas… Juliet caught her bottom lip between her teeth as she wrote. Dallas was going to be fabulous. She might need to double her daily dose of vitamins to get through that twenty-four-hour stretch, but it would be fabulous.

After breaking her connection with New York, Juliet dialed her first contact in San Francisco. Ten minutes later, she was clenching her teeth. No, her contact at the department store couldn't help coming down with a virus. She was sorry, genuinely sorry he was ill. But did he have to get sick without leaving someone behind with a couple of working brain cells?

The young girl with the squeaky voice knew about the cooking demonstration. Yes, she knew all about it and wasn't it going to be fun? Extension cords? Oh my, she really didn't know a thing about that. Maybe she could ask someone in maintenance. A table—chairs? Well golly, she supposed she could get something, if it was really necessary.

Juliet was reaching in her bag for her purse-size container of aspirin before it was over. The way it looked now, she'd have to get to the department store at least two hours before the demonstration to make sure everything was taken care of. That meant juggling the schedule.

After completing her calls, Juliet left the corner phone booth, aspirin in hand, and headed back to the bookstore, hoping they could give her a glass of water and a quiet corner.

No one noticed her. If she'd just crawled in from the desert on her belly, no one would have noticed her. The small, rather elegant bookstore was choked with laughter. No bookseller stood behind the counter. There was a magnet in the left-hand corner of the room. Its name was Franconi.

It wasn't just women this time, Juliet noticed with interest. There were men sprinkled in the crowd. Some of them might have been dragged along by their wives, but they were having a time of it now. It looked like a cocktail party, minus the cigarette smoke and empty glasses.

She couldn't even see him, Juliet realized as she worked her way toward the back of the store. He was surrounded, enveloped. Jingling the aspirin in her hand, she was glad she could find a little corner by herself. Perhaps he got all the glory, she mused. But she wouldn't trade places with him.

Glancing at her watch, she noted he had another hour and wondered whether he could dwindle the crowd down in that amount of time. She wished vaguely for a stool, dropped the aspirin in the pocket of her skirt and began to browse.

"Fabulous, isn't he?" Juliet heard someone murmur on the other side of a book rack.

"God, yes. I'm so glad you talked me into coming."

"What're friends for?"

"I thought I'd be bored to death. I feel like a kid at a rock concert. He's got such..."

"Style," the other voice supplied. "If a man like that ever walked into my life, he wouldn't walk out again."

Curious, Juliet walked around the stacks. She wasn't sure what she expected—young housewives, college students. What she saw were two attractive women in their thirties, both dressed in sleek professional suits.

"I've got to get back to the office." One woman checked a trim little Rolex watch. "I've got a meeting at three."

"I've got to get back to the courthouse."

Both women tucked their autographed books into leather briefcases.

"How come none of the men I date can kiss my hand without making it seem like a staged move in a one-act play?"

"Style. It all has to do with style."

With this observation, or complaint, the two women disappeared into the crowd.

At three-fifteen, he was still signing, but the crowd had thinned enough that Juliet could see him. Style, she was forced to agree, he had. No one who came up to his table, book in hand, was given a quick signature, practiced smile and brush-off. He talked to them. Enjoyed them, Juliet corrected, whether it was a grandmother who smelled of lavender or a young woman with a toddler on her hip. How did he know the right thing to say to each one of them, she wondered, that made them leave the table with a laugh or a smile or a sigh?

First day of the tour, she reminded herself. She wondered if he could manage to keep himself up to this level for three weeks. Time would tell, she decided and calculated she could give him another fifteen minutes before she began to ease him out the door.

Even with the half-hour extension, it wasn't easy. Juliet began to see the pattern she was certain would set the pace of the tour. Carlo would charm and delight, and she would play the less attractive role of drill sergeant. That's what she was paid for, Juliet reminded herself as she began to smile, chat and urge people toward the door. By four there were only a handful of stragglers. With apologies and an iron grip, Juliet disengaged Carlo.

"That went very well," she began, nudging him onto the street. "One of the booksellers told me they'd nearly sold out. Makes you wonder how much pasta's going to be cooked in L.A. tonight. Consider this just one more triumph today."

"Grazie."

"*Prego.* However, we won't always have the leeway to run an hour over," she told him as the door of the limo shut behind her. "It would help if you try to keep an eye on the time and pick up the pace say half an hour before finishing time. You've got an hour and fifteen minutes before airtime—"

"Fine." Pushing a button, Carlo instructed the driver to cruise.

"But—"

"Even I need to unwind," he told her, then opened up a small built-in cabinet to reveal the bar. "Cognac," he decided and poured two glasses without asking. "You've had two hours to window-shop and browse." Leaning back, he stretched out his legs.

Juliet thought of the hour and a half she'd spent on the phone, then the time involved in easing customers along. She'd been on her feet for two and a half hours straight, but she said nothing. The cognac went down smooth and warm.

"The spot on the news should run four, four and a half minutes. It doesn't seem like much time, but you'd be surprised how much you can cram in. Be sure to mention the book title, and the autographing and demonstration at the college tomorrow afternoon. The sensual aspect of food, cooking and eating's a great angle. If you'll—"

"Would you care to do the interview for me?" he asked so politely she glanced up.

So, he could be cranky, she mused. "You handle interviews beautifully, Mr. Franconi, but—"

"Carlo." Before she could open her notebook, he had his hand on her wrist. "It's Carlo, and put the damn notes away for ten minutes. Tell me, my very organized Juliet Trent, why are we here together?"

She started to move her hand but his grip was firmer than she'd thought. For the second time, she got the full impression of power, strength and determination. "To publicize your book."

"Today went well, *sì?*"

"Yes, so far—"

"Today went well," he said again and began to annoy her with the frequency of his interruptions.

"I'll go on this local news show, talk for a few minutes, then have this necessary business dinner when I would much rather have a bottle of wine and a steak in my room. With you. Alone. Then I could see you without your proper little business suit and your proper little business manner."

She wouldn't permit herself to shudder. She wouldn't permit herself to react in any way. "Business is what we're here for. It's all I'm interested in."

"That may be." His agreement was much too easy. In direct contrast, he moved his hand to the back of her neck, gently, but not so gently she could move aside. "But we have an hour before business begins again. Don't lecture me on timetables."

The limo smelled of leather, she realized all at once. Of leather and wealth and Carlo. As casually as possible, she sipped from her glass. "Timetables, as you pointed out yourself this morning, are part of my job."

"You have an hour off," he told her, lifting a brow before she could speak. "So relax. Your feet hurt, so take your shoes off and drink your cognac." He set down his own drink, then moved her briefcase to the floor so there was nothing between them. "Relax," he said again but wasn't displeased that she'd stiffened. "I don't intend to make love with you in the back of a car. This time." He smiled as temper flared in her eyes because he'd seen doubt and excitement as well. "One day, one day soon, I'll find the proper moment for that, the proper place, the proper mood."

He leaned closer, so that he could just feel her breath flutter on his lips. She'd swipe at him now, he knew, if he took the next step. He might enjoy the battle. The color that ran along her cheekbones hadn't come from a tube or pot, but from passion. The look in her eyes was very close to a dare. She expected him to move an inch closer, to press her back against the seat with his mouth firm on hers. She was waiting for him, poised, ready.

He smiled while his lips did no more than hover until he knew the tension in her had built to match the tension in him. He let his gaze shift down to her mouth so that he could imagine the taste, the texture, the sweetness. Her chin stayed lifted even as he brushed a thumb over it.

He didn't care to do the expected. In a long, easy move, he leaned back, crossed his feet at the ankles and closed his eyes.

"Take off your shoes," he said again. "My schedule and yours should merge very well."

Then, to her astonishment, he was asleep. Not feigning it, she realized, but sound asleep, as if he'd just flicked a switch.

With a click, she set her half-full glass down and folded her arms. Angry, she thought. Damn right she was angry because he hadn't kissed her. Not because she wanted him to, she told herself as she stared out the tinted window. But because he'd denied her the opportunity to show her claws.

She was beginning to think she'd love drawing some Italian blood.

Chapter 3

Their bags were packed and in the limo. As a precaution, Juliet had given Carlo's room a quick, last-minute going-over to make sure he hadn't left anything behind. She still remembered being on the road with a mystery writer who'd forgotten his toothbrush eight times on an eight-city tour. A quick look was simpler than a late-night search for a drugstore.

Checkout at the hotel had gone quickly and without any last-minute hitches. To her relief, the charges on Carlo's room bill had been light and reasonable. Her road budget might just hold. With a minimum of confusion, they'd left the Wilshire. Juliet could only hope check-in at the airport, then at the hotel in San Francisco would go as well.

She didn't want to think about the *Simpson Show.*

A list of demographics wasn't necessary here. She knew Carlo had spent enough time in the States off and on to know how important his brief demonstration on the proper way to prepare *biscuit tortoni* and his ten minutes on the air would be. It was the top-rated night-time show in the country and had been for fifteen years. Bob Simpson was an American institution. A few minutes on his show could boost the sale of books even in the most remote areas. Or it could kill it.

And boy, oh boy, she thought, with a fresh gurgle of excitement, did it look impressive to have the *Simpson Show* listed on her itinerary. She offered a last-minute prayer that Carlo wouldn't blow it.

She checked the little freezer backstage to be certain the dessert Carlo had prepared that afternoon was in place and ready. The concoction had to freeze for four hours, so they'd play the before-and-after game for the viewers. He'd make it up on the air, then *voilà,* they'd produce the completed frozen dessert within minutes.

Though Carlo had already gone over the procedure, the tools and ingredients with the production manager and the director, Juliet went over them all again. The whipped cream was chilling and so far none of the crew had pilfered any macaroons. The brand of dry sherry Carlo had insisted on was stored and ready. No one had broken the seal for a quick sample.

Juliet nearly believed she could whip up the fancy frozen dessert herself if necessary and only thanked God she wouldn't have to give a live culinary demonstration in front of millions of television viewers.

He didn't seem to be feeling any pressure, she thought as they settled in the green room. No, he'd already given the little half-dressed blonde on the sofa a big smile and offered her a cup of coffee from the available machine.

Coffee? Even for Hollywood, it took a wild imagination to consider the contents of the pot coffee. Juliet had taken one sip of what tasted like lukewarm mud and set the cup aside.

The little blonde was apparently a new love interest on one of the popular nighttime soaps, and she was jittery with nerves. Carlo sat down on the sofa beside her and began chatting away as though they were old friends. By the time the green room door opened again, she was giggling.

The green room itself was beige—pale, unattractive beige and cramped. The air-conditioning worked, but miserably. Still Juliet knew how many of the famous and near-famous had sat in that dull little room chewing their nails. Or taking quick sips from a flask.

Carlo had exchanged the dubious coffee for plain water and was sprawled on the sofa with one arm tossed over the back. He looked as easy as a man entertaining in his own home. Juliet wondered why she hadn't tossed any antacids in her bag.

She made a pretense of rechecking the schedule while Carlo charmed the rising star and the *Simpson Show* murmured away on the twenty-five-inch color console across the room.

Then the monkey walked in. Juliet glanced up and saw the long-armed, tuxedoed chimpanzee waddle in with his hand caught in that of a tall thin man with harassed eyes and a nervous grin. Feeling a bit nervous herself, Juliet looked over at Carlo. He nodded to both newcomers, then went back to the blonde without missing a beat. Even as Juliet told herself to relax, the chimp grinned, threw back his head and let out a long, loud announcement.

The blonde giggled, but looked as though she'd cut and run if the chimp came one step closer—tux or no tux.

"Behave, Butch." The thin man cleared his throat as he swept his gaze around the room. "Butch just finished a picture last week," he explained to the room in general. "He's feeling a little restless."

With a jiggle of the sequins that covered her, the blonde walked to the door when her name was announced. With some satisfaction, Carlo noted that she wasn't nearly as edgy as she'd been when he'd sat down. She turned and gave him a toothy smile. "Wish me luck, darling."

"The best."

To Juliet's disgust, the blonde blew him a kiss as she sailed out.

The thin man seemed to relax visibly. "That's a relief. Blondes make Butch overexcited."

"I see." Juliet thought of her own hair that could be considered blond or brown depending on the whim. Hopefully Butch would consider it brown and unstimulating.

"But where's the lemonade?" The man's nerves came back in full force. "They know Butch wants lemonade before he goes on the air. Calms him down."

Juliet bit the tip of her tongue to hold back a snicker. Carlo and Butch were eyeing each other with a kind of tolerant understanding. "He seems calm enough," Carlo ventured.

"Bundle of nerves," the man disagreed. "I'll never be able to get him on camera."

"I'm sure it's just an oversight." Because she was used to soothing panic, Juliet smiled. "Maybe you should ask one of the pages."

"I'll do that." The man patted Butch on the head and went back through the door.

"But—" Juliet half rose, then sat again. The chimp stood in the middle of the room, resting his knuckles on the floor. "I'm not sure he should've left Cheetah."

"Butch," Carlo corrected. "I think he's harmless enough." He sent the chimp a quick grin. "He certainly has an excellent tailor."

Juliet looked over to see the chimp grinning and winking. "Is he twitching," she asked Carlo, "or is he flirting with me?"

"Flirting, if he's a male of any taste," he mused. "And, as I said, his tailoring is quite good. What do you say, Butch? You find my Juliet attractive?"

Butch threw back his head and let out a series of sounds Juliet felt could be taken either way.

"See? He appreciates a beautiful woman."

Appreciating the ridiculous, Juliet laughed. Whether he was attracted to the sound or simply felt it was time he made his move, Butch bowlegged his way over to her. Still grinning, he put his hand on Juliet's bare knee. This time, she was certain he winked.

"I never make so obvious a move on first acquaintance," Carlo observed.

"Some women prefer the direct approach." Deciding he was harmless, Juliet smiled down at Butch. "He reminds me of someone." She sent Carlo a mild look. "It must be that ingratiating grin." Before she'd finished speaking, Butch climbed into her lap and wrapped one of his long arms around her. "He's kind of sweet." With another laugh, she looked down into the chimp's face. "I think he has your eyes, Carlo."

"Ah, Juliet, I think you should—"

"Though his might be more intelligent."

"Oh, I think he's smart, all right." Carlo coughed into his hand as he watched the chimp's busy fingers. "Juliet, if you'd—"

"Of course he's smart, he's in movies." Enjoying herself, Juliet watched the chimp grin up at her. "Have I seen any of your films, Butch?"

"I wouldn't be surprised if they're blue."

She tickled Butch under the chin. "Really, Carlo, how crude."

"Just a guess." He let his gaze run over her. "Tell me, Juliet, do you feel a draft?"

"No. I'd say it's entirely too warm in here. This poor thing is all wrapped up in a tux." She clucked at Butch and he clacked his teeth at her.

"Juliet, do you believe people can reveal their personalities by the clothes they wear? Send signals, if you understand what I mean."

"Hmm?" Distracted, she shrugged and helped Butch straighten his tie. "I suppose so."

"I find it interesting that you wear pink silk under such a prim blouse."

"I beg your pardon?"

"An observation, *mi amore*." He let his gaze wander down again. "Just an observation."

Sitting very still, Juliet moved only her head. In a moment, her mouth was as open as her blouse. The monkey with the cute face and excellent tailor had nimbly undone every one of the buttons.

Carlo gave Butch a look of admiration. "I must ask him how he perfected that technique."

"Why you son of a—"

"Not me." Carlo put a hand to his heart. "I'm an innocent bystander."

Juliet rose abruptly, dumping the chimp onto the

floor. As she ducked into the adjoining rest room, she heard the laughter of two males—one a chimp, the other a rat.

Juliet took the ride to the airport where they would leave for San Diego in excruciatingly polite silence.

"Come now, *cara,* the show went well. Not only was the title mentioned three times, but there was that nice close-up of the book. My *tortoni* was a triumph, and they liked my anecdote on cooking the long, sensual Italian meal."

"You're a real prince with anecdotes," she murmured.

"*Amore,* it was the monkey who tried to undress you, not I." He gave a long, self-satisfied sigh. He couldn't remember when he'd enjoyed a…demonstration quite so much. "If I had, we'd have missed the show altogether."

"You just had to tell that story on the air, didn't you?" She sent him a cool, killing look. "Do you know how many millions of people watch that show?"

"It was a good story." In the dim light of the limo, she saw the gleam in his eyes. "Most millions of people like good stories."

"Everyone I work with will have seen that show." She found her jaw was clenched and deliberately relaxed it. "Not only did you just—just *sit* there and let that happy-fingered little creature half strip me, but then you broadcast it on national television."

"*Madonna,* you'll remember I did try to warn you."

"I remember nothing of the kind."

"But you were so enchanted with Butch," he continued. "I confess, it was difficult not to be enchanted myself." He let his gaze roam down to her tidily buttoned blouse. "You've lovely skin, Juliet; perhaps I was momentarily distracted. I throw myself, a simple, weak man, on your mercy."

"Oh, shut up." She folded her arms and stared straight ahead, not speaking again until the driver pulled to the curb at their airline.

Juliet pulled her carry-on bag out of the trunk. She knew the chance was always there that the bags could be lost—sent to San Jose while she went to San Diego—so she always carried her absolute essentials with her. She handed over both her ticket and Carlo's so the check-in could get underway while she paid off the driver. It made her think of her budget. She'd managed to justify limo service in L.A., but it would be cabs and rented cars from here on. Goodbye glamour, she thought as she pocketed her receipt. Hello reality.

"No, this I'll carry."

She turned to see Carlo indicate his leather-bound box of about two feet in length, eight inches in width. "You're better off checking something that bulky."

"I never check my tools." He slung a flight bag over his shoulder and picked up the box by its handle.

"Suit yourself," she said with a shrug and moved through the automatic doors with him. Fatigue was creeping in, she realized, and she hadn't had to prepare any intricate desserts. If he were human, he'd be every bit as weary as she. He might annoy her in a dozen ways, but he didn't gripe. Juliet bit back a sigh. "We've a half hour before they'll begin boarding. Would you like a drink?"

He gave her an easy smile. "A truce?"

She returned it despite herself. "No, a drink."

"Okay."

They found a dark, crowded lounge and worked their way through to a table. She watched Carlo maneuver his box, with some difficulty, around people, over chairs and ultimately under their table. "What's in there?"

"Tools," he said again. "Knives, properly weighted, stainless steel spatulas of the correct size and balance. My own cooking oil and vinegar. Other essentials."

"You're going to lug oil and vinegar through airport terminals from coast to coast?" With a shake of her head, she glanced up at a waitress. "Vodka and grapefruit juice."

"Brandy. Yes," he said, giving his attention back to Juliet after he'd dazzled the waitress with a quick smile. "Because there's no brand on the American market to compare with my own." He picked up a peanut from the bowl on the table. "There's no brand on any market to compare with my own."

"You could still check it," she pointed out. "After all, you check your shirts and ties."

"I don't trust my tools to the hands of baggage carriers." He popped the peanut into his mouth. "A tie is a simple thing to replace, even a thing to become bored with. But an excellent whisk is entirely different. Once I teach you to cook, you'll understand."

"You've got as much chance teaching me to cook as you do flying to San Diego without the plane. Now, you know you'll be giving a demonstration of preparing linguini and clam sauce on *A.M. San Diego.* The show airs at eight, so we'll have to be at the studio at six to get things started."

As far as he could see, the only civilized cooking to be done at that hour would be a champagne breakfast for two. "Why do Americans insist on rising at dawn to watch television?"

"I'll take a poll and find out," she said absently. "In the meantime, you'll make up one dish that we'll set aside, exactly as we did tonight. On the air you'll be going through each stage of preparation, but of course we don't have enough time to finish; that's why we need the first dish. Now, for the good news." She sent a quick smile to the waitress as their drinks were served. "There's been a bit of a mix-up at the studio, so we'll have to bring the ingredients along ourselves. I need you to give me a list of what you'll need. Once I see you settled into the hotel, I'll run out and pick them up. There's bound to be an all-night market."

In his head, he went over the ingredients for his *linguini con vongole biance.* True, the American market would have some of the necessities, but he considered himself fortunate that he had a few of his own in the case at his feet. The clam sauce was his specialty, not to be taken lightly.

"Is shopping for groceries at midnight part of a publicist's job?"

She smiled at him. Carlo thought it was not only lovely, but perhaps the first time she'd smiled at him and meant it. "On the road, anything that needs to be done is the publicist's job. So, if you'll run through the ingredients, I'll write them down."

"Not necessary." He swirled and sipped his brandy. "I'll go with you."

"You need your sleep." She was already rummaging for a pencil. "Even with a quick nap on the plane you're only going to get about five hours."

"So are you," he pointed out. When she started to speak again, he lifted his brow in that strange silent way he had of interrupting. "Perhaps I don't trust an amateur to pick out my clams."

Juliet watched him as she drank. Or perhaps he was a gentleman, she mused. Despite his reputation with women, and a healthy dose of vanity, he was one of that rare breed of men who knew how to be considerate of women without patronizing them. She decided to forgive him for Butch after all.

"Drink up, Franconi." And she toasted him, perhaps in friendship. "We've a plane to catch."

"Salute." He lifted his glass to her.

They didn't argue again until they were on the plane.

Grumbling only a little, Juliet helped him stow his fancy box of tools under the seat. "It's a short flight." She checked her watch and calculated the shopping would indeed go beyond midnight. She'd have to take some of the vile tasting brewer's yeast in the morning. "I'll see you when we land."

He took her wrist when she would have gone past him. "Where are you going?"

"To my seat."

"You don't sit here?" He pointed to the seat beside him.

"No, I'm in coach." Impatient, she had to shift to let another oncoming passenger by.

"Why?"

"Carlo, I'm blocking the aisle."

"Why are you in coach?"

She let out a sigh of a parent instructing a stubborn child. "Because the publisher is more than happy to spring for a first-class ticket for a bestselling author and celebrity. There's a different style for publicists. It's called coach." Someone bumped a briefcase against her hip. Damn if she wouldn't have a bruise. "Now if you'd let me go, I could stop being battered and go sit down."

"First class is almost empty," he pointed out. "It's a simple matter to upgrade your ticket."

She managed to pull her arm away. "Don't buck the system, Franconi."

"I always buck the system," he told her as she walked down the aisle to her seat. Yes, he did like the way she moved.

"Mr. Franconi." A flight attendant beamed at him. "May I get you a drink after take-off?"

"What's your white wine?"

When she told him he settled into his seat. A bit pedestrian, he thought, but not entirely revolting. "You noticed the young woman I was speaking with. The honey-colored hair and the stubborn chin."

Her smile remained bright and helpful though she thought it was a shame that he had his mind on another woman. "Of course, Mr. Franconi."

"She'll have a glass of wine, with my compliments."

Juliet would have considered herself fortunate to have an aisle seat if the man beside her hadn't already been sprawled out and snoring. Travel was so glamorous, she thought wryly as she slipped her toes out of her shoes. Wasn't she lucky to have another flight to look forward to the very next night?

Don't complain, Juliet, she warned herself. When you have your own agency, you can send someone else on the down-and-dirty tours.

The man beside her snored through take-off. On the other side of the aisle a woman held a cigarette in one hand and a lighter in the other in anticipation of the No Smoking sign blinking off. Juliet took out her pad and began to work.

"Miss?"

Stifling a yawn, Juliet glanced up at the flight attendant. "I'm sorry, I didn't order a drink."

"With Mr. Franconi's compliments."

Juliet accepted the wine as she looked up toward first class. He was sneaky, she told herself. Trying to get under her defenses by being nice. She let her notebook close as she sighed and sat back.

It was working.

She barely finished the wine before touchdown, but it had relaxed her. Relaxed her enough, she realized, that all she wanted to do was find a soft bed and a dark room. In an hour—or two, she promised herself and gathered up her flight bag and briefcase.

She found Carlo was waiting for her in first class with a very young, very attractive flight attendant. Neither of them seemed the least bit travel weary.

"Ah, Juliet, Deborah knows of a marvelous twenty-four-hour market where we can find everything we need."

Juliet looked at the willowy brunette and managed a smile. "How convenient."

He took the flight attendant's hand and, inevitably Juliet thought, kissed it. *"Arrivederci."*

"Don't waste time, do you?" Juliet commented the moment they deplaned.

"Every moment lived is a moment to be enjoyed."

"What a quaint little sentiment." She shifted her bag and aimed for baggage claim. "You should have it tattooed."

"Where?"

She didn't bother to look at his grin. "Where it would be most attractive, naturally."

They had to wait longer than she liked for their luggage, and by then the relaxing effects of the wine had worn off. There was business to be seen to. Because he enjoyed watching her in action, Carlo let her see to it.

She secured a cab, tipped the skycap and gave the driver the name of the hotel. Scooting in beside Carlo, she caught his grin. "Something funny?"

"You're so efficient, Juliet."

"Is that a compliment or an insult?"

"I never insult women." He said it so simply, she was absolutely certain it was true. Unlike Juliet, he was completely relaxed and not particularly sleepy. "If this was Rome, we'd go to a dark little café, drink heavy red wine and listen to American music."

She closed her window because the air was damp and chilly. "The tour interfering with your night life?"

"So far I find myself enjoying the stimulating company."

"Tomorrow you're going to find yourself worked to a frazzle."

Carlo thought of his background and smiled. At nine, he'd spent the hours between school and supper washing dishes and mopping up kitchens. At fifteen he'd waited tables and spent his free time learning of spices and sauces. In Paris he'd combined long, hard study with work as an assistant chef. Even now, his restaurant and clients had him keeping twelve-hour days. Not all of his background was in the neatly typed bio Juliet had in her briefcase.

"I don't mind work, as long as it interests me. I think you're the same."

"I have to work," she corrected. "But it's easier when you enjoy it."

"You're more successful when you enjoy it. It shows with you. Ambition, Juliet, without a certain joy, is cold, and when achieved leaves a flat taste."

"But I am ambitious."

"Oh, yes." He turned to look at her, starting off flutters she'd thought herself too wise to experience. "But you're not cold."

For a moment, she thought she'd be better off if he

were wrong. "Here's the hotel." She turned from him, relieved to deal with details. "We need you to wait," she instructed the driver. "We'll be going out again as soon as we check in. The hotel has a lovely view of the bay, I'm told." She walked into the lobby with Carlo as the bellboy dealt with their luggage. "It's a shame we won't have time to enjoy it. Franconi and Trent," she told the desk clerk.

The lobby was quiet and empty. Oh, the lucky people who were sleeping in their beds, she thought and pushed at a strand of hair that had come loose.

"We'll be checking out first thing tomorrow, and we won't be able to come back, so be sure you don't leave anything behind in your room."

"But of course you'll check anyway."

She sent him a sidelong look as she signed the form. "Just part of the service." She pocketed her key. "The luggage can be taken straight up." Discreetly, she handed the bellboy a folded bill. "Mr. Franconi and I have an errand."

"Yes, ma'am."

"I like that about you." To Juliet's surprise, Carlo linked arms with her as they walked back outside.

"What?"

"Your generosity. Many people would've slipped out without tipping the bellboy."

She shrugged. "Maybe it's easier to be generous when it's not your money."

"Juliet." He opened the door to the waiting cab and gestured her in. "You're intelligent enough. Couldn't you—how is it—stiff the bellboy then write the tip down on your expense account?"

"Five dollars isn't worth being dishonest."

"Nothing's worth being dishonest." He gave the

driver the name of the market and settled back. "Instinct tells me if you tried to tell a lie—a true lie—your tongue would fall out."

"Mr. Franconi." She planted the tongue in question in her cheek. "You forget, I'm in public relations. If I didn't lie, I'd be out of a job."

"A true lie," he corrected.

"Isn't that a contradiction in terms?"

"Perhaps you're too young to know the variety of truths and lies. Ah, you see? This is why I'm so fond of your country." Carlo leaned out the window as they approached the big, lighted all-night market. "In America, you want cookies at midnight, you can buy cookies at midnight. Such practicality."

"Glad to oblige. Wait here," she instructed the driver, then climbed out opposite Carlo. "I hope you know what you need. I'd hate to get into the studio at dawn and find I had to run out and buy whole peppercorns or something."

"Franconi knows linguini." He swung an arm around her shoulder and drew her close as they walked inside. "Your first lesson, my love."

He led her first to the seafood section where he clucked and muttered and rejected and chose until he had the proper number of clams for two dishes. She'd seen women give as much time and attention to choosing an engagement ring.

Juliet obliged him by pushing the cart as he walked along beside her, looking at everything. And touching. Cans, boxes, bottles—she waited as he picked up, examined and ran his long artist's fingers over the labels as he read every ingredient. Somewhat amused, she watched his diamond wink in the fluorescent light.

"Amazing what they put in this prepackaged garbage," he commented as he dropped a box back on the shelf.

"Careful, Franconi, you're talking about my staple diet."

"You should be sick."

"Prepackaged food's freed the American woman from the kitchen."

"And destroyed a generation of taste buds." He chose his spices carefully and without haste. He opened three brands of oregano and sniffed before he settled on one. "I tell you, Juliet, I admire your American convenience, its practicality, but I would rather shop in Rome where I can walk along the stalls and choose vegetables just out of the ground, fish fresh from the sea. Everything isn't in a can, like the music."

He didn't miss an aisle, but Juliet forgot her fatigue in fascination. She'd never seen anyone shop like Carlo Franconi. It was like strolling through a museum with an art student. He breezed by the flour, scowling at each sack. She was afraid for a moment, he'd rip one open and test the contents. "This is a good brand?"

Juliet figured she bought a two-pound bag of flour about once a year. "Well, my mother always used this, but—"

"Good. Always trust a mother."

"She's a dreadful cook."

Carlo set the flour firmly in the basket. "She's a mother."

"An odd sentiment from a man no mother can trust."

"For mothers, I have the greatest respect. I have one myself. Now, we need garlic, mushrooms, peppers. Fresh."

Carlo walked along the stalls of vegetables, touching, squeezing and sniffing. Cautious, Juliet looked around for clerks, grateful they'd come at midnight rather than midday. "Carlo, you really aren't supposed to handle everything quite so much."

"If I don't handle, how do I know what's good and what's just pretty?" He sent her a quick grin over his shoulder. "I told you, food was much like a woman. They put mushrooms in this box with wrap over it." Disgusted, he tore the wrapping off before Juliet could stop him.

"Carlo! You can't open it."

"I want only what I want. You can see, some are too small, too skimpy." Patiently, he began to pick out the mushrooms that didn't suit him.

"Then we'll throw out what you don't want when we get back to the hotel." Keeping an eye out for the night manager, she began to put the discarded mushrooms back in the box. "Buy two boxes if you need them."

"It's a waste. You'd waste your money?"

"The publisher's money," she said quickly, as she put the broken box into the basket. "He's glad to waste it. Thrilled."

He paused for a moment, then shook his head. "No, no, I can't do it." But when he started to reach into the basket, Juliet moved and blocked his way.

"Carlo, if you break open another package, we're going to be arrested."

"Better to go to jail than to buy mushrooms that will do me no good in the morning."

She grinned at him and stood firm. "No, it's not."

He ran a fingertip over her lips before she could react. "For you then, but against my better judgment."

"*Grazie.* Do you have everything now?"

His gaze followed the path his finger had traced just as slowly. "No."

"Well, what next?"

He stepped closer and because she hadn't expected it, she found herself trapped between him and the grocery cart. "Tonight is for first lessons," he murmured then ran his hands along either side of her face.

She should laugh. Juliet told herself it was ludicrous that he'd make a pass at her under the bright lights of the vegetable section of an all-night market. Carlo Franconi, a man who'd made seduction as much an art as his cooking wouldn't choose such a foolish setting.

But she saw what was in his eyes, and she didn't laugh.

Some women, he thought as he felt her skin soft and warm under his hands, were made to be taught slowly. Very slowly. Some women were born knowing; others were born wondering.

With Juliet, he would take time and care because he understood. Or thought he did.

She didn't resist, but her lips had parted in surprise. He touched his to hers gently, not in question, but with patience. Her eyes had already given him the answer.

He didn't hurry. It didn't matter to him where they were, that the lights were bright and the music manufactured. It only mattered that he explore the tastes that waited for him. So he tasted again, without pressure. And again.

She found she was bracing herself against the cart with her fingers wrapped around the metal. Why didn't she walk away? Why didn't she just brush him aside and stalk out of the store? He wasn't holding her there. On her face his hands were light, clever but not insistent. She could move. She could go. She should.

She didn't.

His thumbs trailed under her chin, tracing there. He

felt the pulse, rapid and jerky, and kept his hold easy. He meant to keep it so, but even he hadn't guessed her taste would be so unique.

Neither of them knew who took the next step. Perhaps they took it together. His mouth wasn't so light on hers any longer, nor was hers so passive. They met, triumphantly, and clung.

Her fingers weren't wrapped around the cart now, but gripping his shoulders, holding him closer. Their bodies fit. Perfectly. It should have warned her. Giving without thought was something she never did, until now. In giving, she took, but she never thought to balance the ledger.

His mouth was warm, full. His hands never left her face, but they were firm now. She couldn't have walked away so easily. She wouldn't have walked away at all.

He'd thought he had known everything there was to expect from a woman—fire, ice, temptation. But a lesson was being taught to both. Had he ever felt this warmth before? This kind of sweetness? No, because if he had, he'd remember. No tastes, no sensations ever experienced were forgotten.

He knew what it was to desire a woman—many women—but he hadn't known what it was to crave. For a moment, he filled himself with the sensation. He wouldn't forget.

But he knew that a cautious man takes a step back and a second breath before he steps off a cliff. With a murmur in his own language, he did.

Shaken, Juliet gripped the cart again for balance. Cursing herself for an idiot, she waited for her breath to even out.

"Very nice," Carlo said quietly and ran a finger along her cheek. "Very nice, Juliet."

An eighties woman, she reminded herself as her heart thudded. Strong, independent, sophisticated. "I'm so glad you approve."

He took her hand before she could slam the cart down the aisle. Her skin was still warm, he noted, her pulse still unsteady. If they'd been alone… Perhaps it was best this way. For now. "It isn't a matter of approval, *cara mia,* but of appreciation."

"From now on, just appreciate me for my work, okay?" A jerk, and she freed herself of him and shoved the cart away. Without regard for the care he'd taken in selecting them, Juliet began to drop the contents of the cart on the conveyor belt at checkout.

"You didn't object," he reminded her. He'd needed to find his balance as well, he realized. Now he leaned against the cart and gave her a cocky grin.

"I didn't want a scene."

He took the peppers from the basket himself before she could wound them. "Ah, you're learning about lies."

When her head came up, he was surprised her eyes didn't bore right through him. "You wouldn't know truth if you fell into it."

"Darling, mind the mushrooms," he warned her as she swung the package onto the belt. "We don't want them bruised. I've a special affection for them now."

She swore at him, loudly enough that the checker's eyes widened. Carlo continued to grin and thought about lesson two.

He thought they should have it soon. Very soon.

Chapter 4

There were times when you knew everything could go wrong, should go wrong, and probably would go wrong, but somehow it didn't. Then there were the other times.

Perhaps Juliet was grouchy because she'd spent another restless night when she couldn't afford to lose any sleep. That little annoyance she could lay smack at Carlo's door, even though it didn't bring any satisfaction. But even if she'd been rested and cheerful, the ordeal at Gallegher's Department Store would have had her steaming. With a good eight hours' sleep, she might have kept things from boiling over.

First, Carlo insisted on coming with her two hours before he was needed. Or wanted. Juliet didn't care to spend the first two hours of what was bound to be a long, hectic day with a smug, self-assured, egocentric chef who looked as though he'd just come back from two sun-washed weeks on the Riviera.

Obviously, *he* didn't need any sleep, she mused as they took the quick, damp cab ride from hotel to mall.

Whatever the tourist bureau had to say about sunny California, it was raining—big, steady drops of it that immediately made the few minutes she'd taken to fuss with her hair worthless.

Prepared to enjoy the ride, Carlo looked out the window. He liked the way the rain plopped in puddles. It didn't matter to him that he'd heard it start that morning, just past four. "It's a nice sound," he decided. "It makes things more quiet, more…subtle, don't you think?"

Breaking away from her own gloomy view of the rain, Juliet turned to him. "What?"

"The rain." Carlo noted she looked a bit hollow-eyed. Good. She hadn't been unaffected. "Rain changes the look of things."

Normally, she would have agreed. Juliet never minded dashing for the subway in a storm or strolling along Fifth Avenue in a drizzle. Today, she considered it her right to look on the dark side. "This one might lower the attendance in your little demonstration by ten percent."

"So?" He gave an easy shrug as the driver swung into the parking lot of the mall.

What she didn't need at that moment was careless acceptance. "Carlo, the purpose of all this is exposure."

He patted her hand. "You're only thinking of numbers. You should think instead of my *pasta con pesto*. In a few hours, everyone else will."

"I don't think about food the way you do," she muttered. It still amazed her that he'd lovingly prepared the first linguini at 6:00 A.M., then the second two hours later for the camera. Both dishes had been an exquisite example of Italian cooking at its finest. He'd looked more like a film star on holiday than a working chef, which was precisely the image Juliet had wanted to project. His spot on the morning show had been perfect. That only made Juliet more pessimistic about the rest of the day. "It's hard to think about food at all on this kind of a schedule."

"That's because you didn't eat anything this morning."

"Linguini for breakfast doesn't suit me."

"My linguini is always suitable."

Juliet gave a mild snort as she stepped from the cab into the rain. Though she made a dash for the doors, Carlo was there ahead of her, opening one. "Thanks." Inside, she ran a hand through her hair and wondered how soon she could come by another cup of coffee. "You don't need to do anything for another two hours." And he'd definitely be in the way while things were being set up on the third floor.

"So, I'll wander." With his hands in his pockets, he looked around. As luck would have it, they'd entered straight into the lingerie department. "I find your American malls fascinating."

"I'm sure." Her voice was dry as he fingered the border of lace on a slinky camisole. "You can come upstairs with me first, if you like."

"No, no." A saleswoman with a face that demanded a second look adjusted two negligees and beamed at him. "I think I'll just roam around and see what your shops have to offer." He beamed back. "So far, I'm charmed."

She watched the exchange and tried not to clench her teeth. "All right, then, if you'll just be sure to—"

"Be in Special Events on the third floor at eleven-forty-five," he finished. In his friendly, casual way, he kissed her forehead. She wondered why he could touch her like a cousin and make her think of a lover. "Believe me, Juliet, nothing you say to me is forgotten." He took her hand, running his thumb over her knuckles. That was definitely not the touch of a cousin. "I'll buy you a present."

"It isn't necessary."

"A pleasure. Things that are necessary are rarely a pleasure."

Juliet disengaged her hand while trying not to dwell on the pleasure he could offer. "Please, don't be later than eleven-forty-five, Carlo."

"Timing, *mi amore,* is something I excel in."

I'll bet, she thought as she started toward the escalator. She'd have bet a week's pay he was already flirting with the lingerie clerk.

It only took ten minutes in Special Events for Juliet to forget Carlo's penchant for romancing anything feminine.

The little assistant with the squeaky voice was still in charge as her boss continued his battle with the flu. She was young, cheerleader pretty and just as pert. She was also in completely over her head.

"Elise," Juliet began because it was still early on enough for her to have some optimism. "Mr. Franconi's going to need a working area in the kitchen department. Is everything set?"

"Oh, yes." Elise gave Juliet a toothy, amiable grin. "I'm getting a nice folding table from Sporting Goods."

Diplomacy, Juliet reminded herself, was one of the primary rules of PR. "I'm afraid we'll need something a bit sturdier. Perhaps one of the islands where Mr. Franconi could prepare the dish and still face the audience. Your supervisor and I had discussed it."

"Oh, is that what he meant?" Elise looked blank for

a moment, then brightened. Juliet began to think dark thoughts about mellow California. "Well, why not?"

"Why not," Juliet agreed. "We've kept the dish Mr. Franconi is to prepare as simple as possible. You do have all the ingredients listed?"

"Oh, yes. It sounds just delicious. I'm a vegetarian, you know."

Of course she was, Juliet thought. Yogurt was probably the high point of her day. "Elise, I'm sorry if it seems I'm rushing you along, but I really need to work out the setup as soon as possible."

"Oh, sure." All cooperation, Elise flashed her straight-toothed smile. "What do you want to know?"

Juliet offered up a prayer. "How sick is Mr. Francis?" she asked, thinking of the levelheaded, business-like man she had dealt with before.

"Just miserable." Elise swung back her straight California-blond hair. "He'll be out the rest of the week."

No help there. Accepting the inevitable, Juliet gave Elise her straight, no-nonsense look. "All right, what have you got so far?"

"Well, we've taken a new blender and some really lovely bowls from Housewares."

Juliet nearly relaxed. "That's fine. And the range?"

Elise smiled. "Range?"

"The range Mr. Franconi needs to cook the spaghetti for this dish. It's on the list."

"Oh. We'd need elecricity for that, wouldn't we?"

"Yes." Juliet folded her hands to keep them from clenching. "We would. For the blender, too."

"I guess I'd better check with maintenance."

"I guess you'd better." Diplomacy, tact, Juliet reminded herself as her fingers itched for Elise's neck.

"Maybe I'll just go over to the kitchen layouts and see which one would suit Mr. Franconi best."

"Terrific. He might want to do his interview right there."

Juliet had taken two steps before she stopped and turned back. "Interview?"

"With the food editor of the *Sun.* She'll be here at eleven-thirty."

Calm, controlled, Juliet pulled out her itinerary of the San Diego stop. She skimmed it, though she knew every word by heart. "I don't seem to have anything listed here."

"It came up at the last minute. I called your hotel at nine, but you'd already checked out."

"I see." Should she have expected Elise to phone the television studio and leave a message? Juliet looked into the personality-plus smile. No, she supposed not. Resigned, she checked her watch. The setup could be dealt with in time if she started immediately. Carlo would just have to be paged. "How do I call mall management?"

"Oh, you can call from my office. Can I do anything?"

Juliet thought of and rejected several things, none of which were kind. "I'd like some coffee, two sugars."

She rolled up her sleeves and went to work.

By eleven, Juliet had the range, the island and the ingredients Carlo had specified neatly arranged. It had taken only one call, and some finesse, to acquire two vivid flower arrangements from a shop in the mall.

She was on her third coffee and considering a fourth when Carlo wandered over. "Thank God." She drained the last from the foam cup. "I thought I was going to have to send out a search party."

"Search party?" Idly he began looking around the kitchen set. "I came when I heard the page."

"You've been paged five times in the last hour."

"Yes?" He smiled as he looked back at her. Her hair was beginning to stray out of her neat bun. He might have stepped off the cover of *Gentlemen's Quarterly.* "I only just heard. But then, I spent some time in the most fantastic record store. Such speakers. Quadraphonic."

"That's nice." Juliet dragged a hand through her already frazzled hair.

"There's a problem?"

"Her name's Elise. I've come very close to murdering her half a dozen times. If she smiles at me again, I just might." Juliet gestured with her hand to brush it off. This was no time for fantasies, no matter how satisfying. "It seems things were a bit disorganized here."

"But you've seen to that." He bent over to examine the range as a driver might a car before Le Mans. "Excellent."

"You can be glad you've got electricity rather than your imagination," she muttered. "You have an interview at eleven-thirty with a food editor, Marjorie Ballister, from the *Sun.*"

He only moved his shoulders and examined the blender. "All right."

"If I'd known it was coming up, I'd have bought a paper so we could have seen her column and gauged her style. As it is—"

"*Non importante.* You worry too much, Juliet."

She could have kissed him. Strictly in gratitude, but she could have kissed him. Considering that unwise, she smiled instead. "I appreciate your attitude, Carlo. After the last hour of dealing with the inept, the insane and the unbearable, it's a relief to have someone take things in stride."

"Franconi always takes things in stride." Juliet started to sink into a chair for a five-minute break.

"*Dio!* What joke is this?" She was standing again and looking down at the little can he held in his hand. "Who would sabotage my pasta?"

"Sabotage?" Had he found a bomb in the can? "What are you talking about?"

"This!" He shook the can at her. "What do you call this?"

"It's basil," she began, a bit unsteady when she lifted her gaze and caught the dark, furious look in his eyes. "It's on your list."

"Basil!" He went off in a stream of Italian. "You dare call this basil?"

Soothe, Juliet reminded herself. It was part of the job. "Carlo, it says basil right on the can."

"On the can." He said something short and rude as he dropped it into her hand. "Where in your clever notes does it say Franconi uses basil from a can?"

"It just says basil," she said between clenched teeth. "B-a-s-i-l."

"Fresh. On your famous list you'll see fresh. *Accidenti!* Only a philistine uses basil from a can for *pasta con pesto.* Do I look like a philistine?"

She wouldn't tell him what he looked like. Later, she might privately admit that temper was spectacular on him. Dark and unreasonable, but spectacular. "Carlo, I realize things aren't quite as perfect here as both of us would like, but—"

"I don't need perfect," he tossed at her. "I can cook in a sewer if I have to, but not without the proper ingredients."

She swallowed—though it went down hard—pride, temper and opinion. She only had fifteen minutes left until the interview. "I'm sorry, Carlo. If we could just compromise on this—"

"Compromise?" When the word came out like an obscenity, she knew she'd lost the battle. "Would you ask Picasso to compromise on a painting?"

Juliet stuck the can into her pocket. "How much fresh basil do you need?"

"Three ounces."

"You'll have it. Anything else?"

"A mortar and pestle, marble."

Juliet checked her watch. She had forty-five minutes to handle it. "Okay. If you'll do the interview right here, I'll take care of this and we'll be ready for the demonstration at noon." She sent up a quick prayer that there was a gourmet shop within ten miles. "Remember to get in the book title and the next stop on the tour. We'll be hitting another Gallegher's in Portland, so it's a good tie-in. Here." Digging into her bag she brought out an eight-by-ten glossy. "Take the extra publicity shot for her in case I don't get back. Elise didn't mention a photographer."

"You'd like to chop and dice that bouncy little woman," Carlo observed, noting that Juliet was swearing very unprofessionally under her breath.

"You bet I would." She dug in again. "Take a copy of the book. The reporter can keep it if necessary."

"I can handle the reporter," he told her calmly enough. "You handle the basil."

It seemed luck was with her when Juliet only had to make three calls before she found a shop that carried what she needed. The frenzied trip in the rain didn't improve her disposition, nor did the price of a marble pestle. Another glance at her watch reminded her she didn't have time for temperament. Carrying what she considered Carlo's eccentricities, she ran back to the waiting cab.

At exactly ten minutes to twelve, dripping wet, Juliet rode up to the third floor of Gallegher's. The first thing she saw was Carlo, leaning back in a cozy wicker dinette chair laughing with a plump, pretty middle-aged woman with a pad and pencil. He looked dashing, amiable and most of all, dry. She wondered how it would feel to grind the pestle into his ear.

"Ah, Juliet." All good humor, Carlo rose as she walked up to the table. "You must meet Marjorie. She tells me she's eaten my pasta in my restaurant in Rome."

"Loved every sinful bite. How do you do? You must be the Juliet Trent Carlo bragged about."

Bragged about? No, she wouldn't be pleased. But Juliet set her bag on the table and offered her hand. "It's nice to meet you. I hope you can stay for the demonstration."

"Wouldn't miss it." She twinkled at Carlo. "Or a sample of Franconi's pasta."

Juliet felt a little wave of relief. Something would be salvaged out of the disaster. Unless she was way off the mark, Carlo was about to be given a glowing write-up.

Carlo was already taking the little sack of basil out of the bag. "Perfect," he said after one sniff. "Yes, yes, this is excellent." He tested the pestle weight and size. "You'll see over at our little stage a crowd is gathering," he said easily to Juliet. "So we moved here to talk, knowing you'd see us as soon as you stepped off the escalator."

"Very good." They'd both handled things well, she decided. It was best to take satisfaction from that. A quick glance showed her that Elise was busy chatting away with a small group of people. Not a worry in the world, Juliet thought nastily. Well, she'd already resigned herself to that. Five minutes in the rest room for some quick repairs, she calculated, and she could keep everything on schedule.

"You have everything you need now, Carlo?"

He caught the edge of annoyance, and her hand, smiling brilliantly. "*Grazie, cara mia.* You're wonderful."

Perhaps she'd rather have snarled, but she returned the smile. "Just doing my job. You have a few more minutes before we should begin. If you'll excuse me, I'll just take care of some things and be right back."

Juliet kept up a brisk, dignified walk until she was out of sight, then made a mad dash for the rest room, pulling out her brush as she went in.

"What did I tell you?" Carlo held the bag of basil in his palm to judge the weight. "She's fantastic."

"And quite lovely," Marjorie agreed. "Even when she's damp and annoyed."

With a laugh, Carlo leaned forward to grasp both of Marjorie's hands. He was a man who touched, always. "A woman of perception. I knew I liked you."

She gave a quick dry chuckle, and for a moment felt twenty years younger. And twenty pounds lighter. It was a talent of his that he was generous with. "One last question, Carlo, before your fantastic Ms. Trent rushes you off. Are you still likely to fly off to Cairo or Cannes to prepare one of your dishes for an appreciative client and a stunning fee?"

"There was a time this was routine." He was silent a moment, thinking of the early years of his success. There'd been mad, glamorous trips to this country and to that, preparing fettuccine for a prince or cannelloni for a tycoon. It had been a heady, spectacular time.

Then he'd opened his restaurant and had learned that the solid continuity of his own place was so much more fulfilling than the flash of the single dish.

"From time to time I would still make such trips. Two months ago there was Count Lequine's birthday. He's an old client, an old friend, and he's fond of my spaghetti. But my restaurant is more rewarding to me." He gave her a quizzical look as a thought occurred to him. "Perhaps I'm settling down?"

"A pity you didn't decide to settle in the States." She closed her pad. "I guarantee if you opened a Franconi's right here in San Diego, you'd have clientele flying in from all over the country."

He took the idea, weighed it in much the same way he had the basil, and put it in a corner of his mind. "An interesting thought."

"And a fascinating interview. Thank you." It pleased her that he rose as she did and took her hand. She was a tough outspoken feminist who appreciated genuine manners and genuine charm. "I'm looking forward to a taste of your pasta. I'll just ease over and try to get a good seat. Here comes your Ms. Trent."

Marjorie had never considered herself particularly romantic, but she'd always believed where there was smoke, there was fire. She watched the way Carlo turned his head, saw the change in his eyes and the slight tilt of his mouth. There was fire all right, she mused. You only had to be within five feet to feel the heat.

Between the hand dryer and her brush, Juliet had managed to do something with her hair. A touch here, a dab there, and her makeup was back in shape. Carrying her raincoat over her arm, she looked competent and collected. She was ready to admit she'd had one too many cups of coffee.

"Your interview went well?"

"Yes." He noticed, and approved, that she'd taken the time to dab on her scent. "Perfectly."

"Good. You can fill me in later. We'd better get started."

"In a moment." He reached in his pocket. "I told you I'd buy you a present."

There was a flutter of surprised pleasure she tried to ignore. Just wired from the coffee, she told herself. "Carlo, I told you not to. We don't have time—"

"There's always time." He opened the little box himself and drew out a small gold heart with an arrow of diamonds running through it. She'd been expecting something along the line of a box of chocolates.

"Oh, I—" Words were her business, but she'd lost them. "Carlo, really, you can't—"

"Never say can't to Franconi," he murmured and began to fasten the pin to her lapel. He did so smoothly, with no fumbling. After all, he was a man accustomed to such feminine habits. "It's very delicate, I thought, very elegant. So it suits you." Narrowing his eyes, he stood back, then nodded. "Yes, I was sure it would."

It wasn't possible to remember her crazed search for fresh basil when he was smiling at her in just that way. It was barely possible to remember how furious she was over the lackadaisical setup for the demonstration. Instinctively, she put up her hand and ran a finger over the pin. "It's lovely." Her lips curved, easily, sweetly, as he thought they didn't do often enough. "Thank you."

He couldn't count or even remember the number of presents he'd given, or the different styles of gratitude he'd received. Somehow, he was already sure this would be one he wouldn't forget.

"Prego."

"Ah, Ms. Trent?"

Juliet glanced over to see Elise watching her. Present or no present, it tightened her jaw. "Yes, Elise. You haven't met Mr. Franconi yet."

"Elise directed me from the office to you when I answered the page," Carlo said easily, more than appreciating Juliet's aggravation.

"Yes." She flashed her touchdown smile. "I thought your cookbook looked just super, Mr. Franconi. Everyone's dying to watch you cook something." She opened a little pad of paper with daisies on the cover. "I thought you could spell what it is so I could tell them when I announce you."

"Elise, I have everything." Juliet managed charm and diplomacy to cover a firm nudge out the door. "Why don't I just announce Mr. Franconi?"

"Great." She beamed. Juliet could think of no other word for it. "That'll be a lot easier."

"We'll get started now, Carlo, if you'd just step over there behind those counters, I'll go give the announcements." Without waiting for an assent, she gathered up the basil, mortar and pestle and walked over to the area that she'd prepared. In the most natural of moves, she set everything down and turned to the audience. Three hundred, she judged. Maybe even over. Not bad for a rainy day in a department store.

"Good afternoon." Her voice was pleasant and well pitched. There'd be no need for a microphone in the relatively small space. Thank God, because Elise had botched that minor detail as well. "I want to thank you all for coming here today, and to thank Gallegher's for providing such a lovely setting for the demonstration."

From a few feet away, Carlo leaned on a counter and watched her. She was, as he'd told the reporter, fantastic. No one would guess she'd been up and on her feet since dawn.

"We all like to eat." This drew the murmured laughter she'd expected. "But I've been told by an expert that eating is more than a basic necessity, it's an experience. Not all of us like to cook, but the same expert told me that cooking is both art and magic. This afternoon, the expert, Carlo Franconi, will share with you the art, the magic and the experience with his own *pasta con pesto*."

Juliet started the applause herself, but it was picked up instantly. As Carlo stepped out, she melted back. Center stage was his the moment he stepped on it.

"It's a fortunate man," he began, "who has the opportunity to cook for so many beautiful women. Some of you have husbands?" At the question there was a smatter of chuckles and the lifting of hands. "Ah, well." He gave a very European shrug. "Then I must be content to cook."

She knew Carlo had chosen that particular dish because it took little time in preparation. After the first five minutes, Juliet was certain not one member of the audience would have budged if he'd chosen something that took hours. She wasn't yet convinced cooking was magic, but she was certain he was.

His hands were as skilled and certain as a surgeon's, his tongue as glib as a politician's. She watched him measure, grate, chop and blend and found herself just as entertained as she might have been with a well produced one-act play.

One woman was bold enough to ask a question. It opened the door and dozens of others followed. Juliet needn't have worried that the noise and conversations would disturb him. Obviously he thrived on the interaction. He wasn't, she decided, simply doing his job or fulfilling an obligation. He was enjoying himself.

Calling one woman up with him, Carlo joked about all truly great chefs requiring both inspiration and assistance. He told her to stir the spaghetti, made a fuss out of showing her the proper way to stir by putting his hand over hers and undoubtedly sold another ten books then and there.

Juliet had to grin. He'd done it for fun, not for sales. He was fun, Juliet realized, even if he did take his basil too seriously. He was sweet. Unconsciously, she began to toy with the gold and diamonds on her lapel. Uncommonly considerate and uncommonly demanding. Simply uncommon.

As she watched him laugh with his audience, something began to melt inside of her. She sighed with it, dreaming. There were certain men that prompted a woman, even a practical woman, to dream.

One of the women seated closer to her leaned toward a companion. "Good God, he's the sexiest man I've ever seen. He could keep a dozen lovers patiently waiting."

Juliet caught herself and dropped her hand. Yes, he could keep a dozen lovers patiently waiting. She was sure he did. Deliberately she tucked her hands in the pockets of her skirt. She'd be better off remembering she was encouraging this public image, even exploiting it. She'd be better off remembering that Carlo himself had told her he needed no imagery.

If she started believing half the things he said to her, she might just find herself patiently waiting. The thought of that was enough to stop the melting. Waiting didn't fit into her schedule.

When every last bite of pasta had been consumed, and every last fan had been spoken with, Carlo allowed himself to think of the pleasures of sitting down with a cool glass of wine.

Juliet already had his jacket.

"Well done, Carlo." As she spoke, she began to help him into it. "You can leave California with the satisfaction of knowing you were a smashing success."

He took her raincoat from her when she would've shrugged into it herself. "The airport."

She smiled at his tone, understanding. "We'll pick up our bags in the holding room at the hotel on the way. Look at it this way. You can sit back and sleep all the way to Portland if you like."

Because the thought had a certain appeal, he cooperated. They rode down to the first floor and went out the west entrance where Juliet had told the cab to wait. She let out a quick sigh of relief when it was actually there.

"We get into Portland early?"

"Seven." Rain splattered against the cab's windshield. Juliet told herself to relax. Planes took off safely in the rain every day. "You have a spot on *People of Interest,* but not until nine-thirty. That means we can have breakfast at a civilized hour and go over the scheduling."

Quickly, efficiently, she checked off her San Diego list and noted everything had been accomplished. She had time for a quick, preliminary glance at her Portland schedule before the cab pulled up to the hotel.

"Just wait here," she ordered both the driver and Carlo. She was up and out of the cab and, because they were running it close, managed to have the bags installed in the trunk within seven minutes. Carlo knew because it amused him to time her.

"You, too, can sleep all the way to Portland."

She settled in beside him again. "No, I've got some work to do. The nice thing about planes is that I can pretend I'm in my office and forget I'm thousands of feet off the ground."

"I didn't realize flying bothered you."

"Only when I'm in the air." Juliet sat back and closed her eyes, thinking to relax for a moment. The next thing she knew, she was being kissed awake.

Disoriented, she sighed and wrapped her arms around Carlo's neck. It was soothing, so sweet. And then the heat began to rise.

"Cara." She'd surprised him, but that had brought its own kind of pleasure. "Such a pity to wake you."

"Hmm?" When she opened her eyes, his face was close, her mouth still warm, her heart still thudding. She jerked back and fumbled with the door handle. "That was uncalled for."

"True enough." Leisurely, Carlo stepped out into the rain. "But it was illuminating. I've already paid the driver, Juliet," he continued when she started to dig into her purse. "The baggage is checked. We board from gate five." Taking her arm, and his big leather case, he led her into the terminal.

"You didn't have to take care of all that." She'd have pulled her arm away if she'd had the energy. Or so she told herself. "The reason I'm here is to—"

"Promote my book," he finished easily. "If it makes you feel better, I've been known to do the same when I traveled with your predecessor."

The very fact that it did, made her feel foolish as well. "I appreciate it, Carlo. It's not that I mind you lending a hand, it's that I'm not used to it. You'd be surprised how many authors are either helpless or careless on the road."

"You'd be surprised how many chefs are temperamental and rude."

She thought of the basil and grinned. "No!"

"Oh, yes." And though he'd read her thoughts perfectly, his tone remained grave. "Always flying off the handle, swearing, throwing things. It leads to a bad reputation for all of us. Here, they're boarding. If only they have a decent Bordeaux."

Juliet stifled a yawn as she followed him through. "I'll need my boarding pass, Carlo."

"I have it." He flashed them both for the flight attendant and nudged Juliet ahead. "Do you want the window or the aisle?"

"I need my pass to see which I've got."

"We have 2A and B. Take your pick."

Someone pushed past her and bumped her solidly. It brought a sinking sensation of déjà vu. "Carlo, I'm in coach, so—"

"No, your tickets are changed. Take the window."

Before she could object, he'd maneuvered her over and slipped in beside her. "What do you mean my ticket's been changed? Carlo, I have to get in the back before I cause a scene."

"Your seat's here." After handing Juliet her boarding pass he stretched out his legs. "*Dio,* what a relief."

Frowning, Juliet studied her stub—2A. "I don't know how they could've made a mistake like this. I'd better see to it right away."

"There's no mistake. You should fasten your belt," he advised, then did so himself. "I changed your tickets for the remaining flights on the tour."

Juliet reached to undo the clasp he'd just secured. "You—but you can't."

"I told you, don't say can't to Franconi." Satisfied with her belt, he dealt with his own. "You work as hard as I do—why should you travel in tourist?"

"Because I'm paid to work. Carlo, let me out so I can fix this before we take off."

"No." For the first time, his voice was blunt and final. "I prefer your company to that of a stranger or an empty seat." When he turned his head, his eyes were like his voice. "I want you here. Leave it."

Juliet opened her mouth and closed it again. Professionally, she was on shaky ground either direction she went. She was supposed to see to his needs and wants within reason. Personally, she'd counted on the distance, at least during flight time, to keep her balanced. With Carlo, even a little distance could help.

He was being kind, she knew. Considerate. But he was also being stubborn. There was always a diplomatic way to handle such things.

She gave him a patient smile. "Carlo—"

He stopped her by simply closing his mouth over hers, quietly, completely and irresistibly. He held her there a moment, one hand on her cheek, the other over the fingers which had frozen in her lap. Juliet felt the floor tilt and her head go light.

We're taking off, she thought dimly, but knew the plane hadn't left the ground.

His tongue touched hers briefly, teasingly; then it was only his lips again. After brushing a hand through her hair, he leaned back. "Now, go back to sleep awhile," he advised. "This isn't the place I'd choose to seduce you."

Sometimes, Juliet decided, silence was the best diplomacy. Without another word, she closed her eyes and slept.

Chapter 5

Colorado. The Rockies, Pike's Peak, Indian ruins, aspens and fast-running streams. It sounded beautiful, exciting. But a hotel room was a hotel room after all.

They'd been busy in Washington State. For most of their three-day stay, Juliet had had to work and think on her feet. But the media had been outstanding. Their schedule had been so full her boss back in New York had probably done handstands. Her report on their run on the coast would be a publicist's dream. Then there was Denver.

What coverage she'd managed to hustle there would barely justify the plane fare. One talk show at the ungodly hour of 7:00 A.M. and one miserly article in the food section of a local paper. No network or local news coverage of the autographing, no print reporter who'd confirm an appearance. Lousy.

It was 6:00 A.M. when Juliet dragged herself out of

the shower and began to search through her unpacked garment bag for a suit and a fresh blouse. The cleaners was definitely a priority the minute they moved on to Dallas.

At least Carlo wasn't cooking this morning. She didn't think she could bear to look at food in any form for at least two hours.

With any luck she could come back to the hotel after the show, catch another hour's sleep and then have breakfast in her room while she made her morning calls. The autographing wasn't until noon, and their flight out wasn't until early the next morning.

That was something to hold on to, Juliet told herself as she looked for the right shade of stockings. For the first time in a week, they had an evening free with no one to entertain, no one to be entertained by. A nice, quiet meal somewhere close by and a full night's sleep. With that at the end of the tunnel, she could get through the morning.

With a grimace, she gulped down her daily dose of brewer's yeast.

It wasn't until she was fully dressed that she woke up enough to remember she hadn't dealt with her makeup. With a shrug Juliet slipped out of her little green jacket and headed for the bathroom. She stared at the front door with a combination of suspicion and bad temper when she heard the knock. Peeking through the peephole, she focused on Carlo. He grinned at her, then crossed his eyes. She only swore a little as she pulled open the door.

"You're early," she began, then caught the stirring aroma of coffee. Looking down, she saw that he carried a tray with a small pot, cups and spoons. "Coffee," she murmured, almost like a prayer.

"Yes." He nodded as he stepped into the room. "I thought you'd be ready, though room service isn't." He walked over to a table, saw that her room could fit into one section of his suite and set down the tray. "So, we deliver."

"Bless you." It was so sincere he grinned again as she crossed the room. "How did you manage it? Room service doesn't open for half an hour."

"There's a small kitchen in my suite. A bit primitive, but adequate to brew coffee."

She took the first sip, black and hot, and she closed her eyes. "It's wonderful. Really wonderful."

"Of course. I fixed it."

She opened her eyes again. No, she decided, she wouldn't spoil gratitude with sarcasm. After all, they'd very nearly gotten along for three days running. With the help of her shower, the yeast and the coffee, she was feeling almost human again.

"Relax," she suggested. "I'll finish getting ready." Expecting him to sit, Juliet took her cup and went into the bathroom to deal with her face and hair. She was dotting on foundation when Carlo leaned on the doorjamb.

"*Mi amore,* doesn't this arrangement strike you as impractical?"

She tried not to feel self-conscious as she smoothed on the thin, translucent base. "Which arrangement is that?"

"You have this—broom closet," he decided as he gestured toward her room. Yes, it was small enough that the subtle, feminine scent from her shower reached all the corners. "While I have a big suite with two baths, a bed big enough for three friends and one of those sofas that unfold."

"You're the star," she murmured as she brushed color over the slant of her cheeks.

"It would save the publisher money if we shared the suite."

She shifted her eyes in the mirror until they met his. She'd have sworn, absolutely sworn, he meant no more than that. That is, if she hadn't known him. "He can afford it," she said lightly. "It just thrills the accounting department at tax time."

Carlo moved his shoulders then sipped from his cup again. He'd known what her answer would be. Of course, he'd enjoy sharing his rooms with her for the obvious reason, but neither did it sit well with him that her accommodations were so far inferior to his.

"You need a touch more blusher on your left cheek," he said idly, not noticing her surprised look. What he'd noticed was the green silk robe that reflected in the mirror from the back of the door. Just how would she look in that? Carlo wondered. How would she look out of it?

After a narrowed-eyed study, Juliet discovered he'd been right. She picked up her brush again and evened the color. "You're a very observant man."

"Hmm?" He was looking at her again, but mentally, he'd changed her neat, high-collared blouse and slim skirt for the provocative little robe.

"Most men wouldn't notice unbalanced blusher." She picked up a grease pencil to shadow her eyes.

"I notice everything when it comes to a woman." There was still a light fog near the top of the mirror from the steam of her shower. Seeing it gave Carlo other, rather pleasant mental images. "What you're doing now gives you a much different look."

Relaxed again, she laughed. "That's the idea."

"But, no." He stepped in closer so he could watch

over her shoulder. The small, casual intimacy was as natural for him as it was uncomfortable for her. "Without the pots of paint, your face is younger, more vulnerable, but no less attractive than it is with them. Different..." Easily, he picked up her brush and ran it through her hair. "It's not more, not less, simply different. I like both of your looks."

It wasn't easy to keep her hand steady. Juliet set down the eye-shadow and tried the coffee instead. Better to be cynical than be moved, she reminded herself and gave him a cool smile. "You seem right at home in the bathroom with a woman fixing her face."

He liked the way her hair flowed as he brushed it. "I've done it so often."

Her smile became cooler. "I'm sure."

He caught the tone, but continued to brush as he met her eyes in the glass. "Take it as you like, *cara,* but remember, I grew up in a house with five women. Your powders and bottles hold no secrets from me."

She'd forgotten that, perhaps because she'd chosen to forget anything about him that didn't connect directly with the book. Yet now it made her wonder. Just what sort of insight did a man get into women when he'd been surrounded by them since childhood? Frowning a bit, she picked up her mascara.

"Were you a close family?"

"We are a close family," he corrected. "My mother's a widow who runs a successful dress shop in Rome." It was typical of him not to mention that he'd bought it for her. "My four sisters all live within thirty kilometers. Perhaps I no longer share the bathroom with them, but little else changes."

She thought about it. It sounded cozy and easy and

rather sweet. Juliet didn't believe she could relate at all. "Your mother must be proud of you."

"She'd be prouder if I added to her growing horde of grandchildren."

She smiled at that. It sounded more familiar. "I know what you mean."

"You should leave your hair just like this," he told her as he set down the brush. "You have a family?"

"My parents live in Pennsylvania."

He struggled with geography a moment. "Ah, then you'll visit them when we go to Philadelphia."

"No." The word was flat as she recapped the tube of mascara. "There won't be time for that."

"I see." And he thought he was beginning to. "You have brothers, sisters?"

"A sister." Because he was right about her hair, Juliet let it be and slipped out for her jacket. "She married a doctor and produced two children, one of each gender, before she was twenty-five."

Oh yes, he was beginning to see well enough. Though the words had been easy, the muscles in her shoulders had been tight. "She makes an excellent doctor's wife?"

"Carrie makes a perfect doctor's wife."

"Not all of us are meant for the same things."

"I wasn't." She picked up her briefcase and her purse. "We'd better get going. They said it would take about fifteen minutes to drive to the studio."

Strange, he thought, how people always believed their tender spots could go undetected. For now, he'd leave her with the illusion that hers had.

Because the directions were good and the traffic was light, Juliet drove the late model Chevy she'd rented with confidence. Carlo obliged by navigating because he enjoyed the poised, skilled way she handled the wheel.

"You haven't lectured me on today's schedule," he pointed out. "Turn right here at this light."

Juliet glanced in the mirror, switched lanes, then made the turn. She wasn't yet sure what his reaction would be to the fact that there barely was one. "I've decided to give you a break," she said brightly, knowing how some authors snarled and ranted when they had a dip in exposure. "You have this morning spot, then the autographing at World of Books downtown."

He waited, expecting the list to go on. When he turned to her, his brow was lifted. "And?"

"That's all." She heard the apology in her voice as she stopped at a red light. "It happens sometimes, Carlo. Things just don't come through. I knew it was going to be light here, but as it happens they've just started shooting a major film using Denver locations. Every reporter, every news team, every camera crew is covering it this afternoon. The bottom line is we got bumped."

"Bumped? Do you mean there is no radio show, no lunch with a reporter, no dinner engagement?"

"No, I'm sorry. It's just—"

"Fantastico!" Grabbing her face with both hands he kissed her hard. "I'll find out the name of this movie and go to its premiere."

The little knot of tension and guilt vanished. "Don't take it so hard, Carlo."

He felt as though he'd just been paroled. "Juliet, did you think I'd be upset? *Dio,* for a week it's been nothing but go here, rush there."

She spotted the TV tower and turned left. "You've been wonderful," she told him. The best time to admit it, she decided, was when they only had two minutes to spare. “Not everyone I’ve toured with has been as considerate.”

She surprised him. He preferred it when a woman could do so. He twined a lock of the hair he’d brushed around his finger. “So, you’ve forgiven me for the basil?”

She smiled and had to stop herself from reaching up to touch the heart on her lapel. “I’d forgotten all about it.”

He kissed her cheek in a move so casual and friendly she didn’t object. “I believe you have. You’ve a kind heart, Juliet. Such things are beauty in themselves.”

He could soften her so effortlessly. She felt it, fought it and, for the moment, surrendered to it. In an impulsive, uncharacteristic move, she brushed the hair on his forehead. “Let’s go in. You’ve got to wake up Denver.”

Professionally, Juliet should’ve been cranky at the lack of obligations and exposure in Denver. It was going to leave a few very obvious blanks on her overall report. Personally, she was thrilled.

According to schedule, she was back in her room by eight. By 8:03, she’d stripped out of her suit and had crawled, naked and happy, into her still-rumpled bed. For exactly an hour she slept deeply, and without any dreams she could remember. By ten-thirty, she’d gone through her list of phone calls and an enormous breakfast. After freshening her makeup, she dressed in her suit then went downstairs to meet Carlo in the lobby.

It shouldn’t have surprised her that he was huddled in one of the cozy lounging areas with three women. It shouldn’t have irked her. Pretending it did neither, Juliet strolled over. It was then she noticed that all three women were built stupendously. That shouldn't have surprised her, either.

"Ah, Juliet." He smiled, all grace, all charm. She didn't stop to wonder why she'd like to deck him. "Always prompt. Ladies." He turned to bow to all three of them. "It's been a pleasure."

"Bye-bye, Carlo." One of them sent him a look that could have melted lead. "Remember, if you're ever in Tucson…"

"How could I forget?" Hooking his arm with Juliet's, he strolled outside. "Juliet," he murmured, "where is Tucson?"

"Don't you ever quit?" she demanded.

"Quit what?"

"Collecting women."

He lifted a brow as he pulled open the door on the driver's side. "Juliet, one collects matchbooks, not women."

"It would seem there are some who consider them on the same level."

He blocked her way before she could slip inside. "Any who do are too stupid to matter." He walked around the side of the car and opened his own door before she spoke again.

"Who were they anyhow?"

Soberly, Carlo adjusted the brim of the buff-colored fedora he wore. "Female bodybuilders. It seems they're having a convention."

A muffled laugh escaped before she could prevent it. "Figures."

"Indeed yes, but such muscular ones." His expression was still grave as he lowered himself into the car.

Juliet remained quiet a moment, then gave up and laughed out loud. Damn, she'd never had as much fun on tour with anyone. She might as well accept it. "Tucson's in Arizona," she told him with another laugh. "And it's not on the itinerary."

They would have been on time for the autographing if they hadn't run into the detour. Traffic was clogged, rerouted and bad tempered as roads were blocked off for the film being shot. Juliet spent twenty minutes weaving, negotiating and cursing until she found she'd done no more than make a nice big circle.

"We've been here before," Carlo said idly and received a glowering look.

"Oh, really?" Her sweet tone had an undertone of arsenic.

He merely shifted his legs into a less cramped position. "It's an interesting city," he commented. "I think perhaps if you turn right at the next corner, then left two corners beyond, we'll find ourselves on the right track."

Juliet meticulously smoothed her carefully written directions when she'd have preferred to crumple them into a ball. "The book clerk specifically said—"

"I'm sure she's a lovely woman, but things seem a bit confused today." It didn't particularly bother him. The blast of a horn made her jolt. Amused, Carlo merely looked over. "As someone from New York City, you should be used to such things."

Juliet set her teeth. "I never drive in the city."

"I do. Trust me, *innamorata*."

Not on your life, Juliet thought, but turned right. It took nearly ten minutes in the crawling traffic to manage the next two blocks, but when she turned left she found herself, as Carlo had said, on the right track. She waited, resigned, for him to gloat.

"Rome moves faster" was all he said.

How could she anticipate him? she wondered. He

didn't rage when you expected, didn't gloat when it was natural. With a sigh, she gave up. "Anything moves faster." She found herself in the right block, but parking space was at a premium. Weighing the ins and outs, Juliet swung over beside a car at the curb. "Look, Carlo, I'm going to have to drop you off. We're already running behind. I'll find a place to park and be back as soon as I can."

"You're the boss," he said, still cheerful after forty-five minutes of teeth-grinding traffic.

"If I'm not there in an hour, send up a flare."

"My money's on you."

Still cautious, she waited until she saw him swing into the bookstore before she fought her way into traffic again.

Twenty frustrating minutes later, Juliet walked into the dignified little bookstore herself. It was, she noted with a sinking stomach, too quiet and too empty. A clerk with a thin-striped tie and shined shoes greeted her.

"Good morning. May I help you?"

"I'm Juliet Trent, Mr. Franconi's publicist."

"Ah yes, right this way." He glided across the carpet to a set of wide steps. "Mr. Franconi's on the second level. It's unfortunate that the traffic and confusion have discouraged people from coming out. Of course, we rarely do these things." He gave her a smile and brushed a piece of lint from the sleeve of his dark blue jacket. "The last time was…let me see, in the fall. J. Jonathan Cooper was on tour. I'm sure you've heard of him. He wrote *Metaphysical Force and You.*"

Juliet bit back a sigh. When you hit dry ground, you just had to wait for the tide.

She spotted Carlo in a lovely little alcove on a curvy love seat. Beside him was a woman of about forty with a neat suit and pretty legs. Such things didn't warrant even a raised brow. But to Juliet's surprise, Carlo wasn't busy charming her. Instead, he was listening intently to a young boy who sat across from him.

"I've worked in the kitchens there for the last three summers. I'm not allowed to actually prepare anything, but I can watch. At home, I cook whenever I can, but with school and the job, it's mostly on weekends."

"Why?"

The boy stopped in midstream and looked blank. "Why?"

"Why do you cook?" Carlo asked. He acknowledged Juliet with a nod, then gave his attention back to the boy.

"Because..." The boy looked at his mother, then back at Carlo. "Well, it's important. I like to take things and put them together. You have to concentrate, you know, and be careful. But you can make something really terrific. It looks good and it smells good. It's... I don't know." His voice lowered in embarrassment. "Satisfying, I guess."

"Yes." Pleased, Carlo smiled at him. "That's a good answer."

"I have both your other books," the boy blurted out. "I've tried all your recipes. I even made your *pasta al tre formaggi* for this dinner party at my aunt's."

"And?"

"They liked it." The boy grinned. "I mean they really liked it."

"You want to study."

"Oh yeah." But the boy dropped his gaze to where his hands rubbed nervously over his knees. "Thing is we can't really afford college right now, so I'm hoping to get some restaurant work."

"In Denver?"

"Any place where I could start cooking instead of wiping up."

"We've taken up enough of Mr. Franconi's time." The boy's mother rose, noting there was now a handful of people milling around on the second level with Carlo's books in hand. "I want to thank you." She offered her hand to Carlo as he rose with her. "It meant a great deal to Steven to talk with you."

"My pleasure." Though he was gracious as always, he turned back to the boy. "Perhaps you'd give me your address. I know of some restaurant owners here in the States. Perhaps one of them needs an apprentice chef."

Stunned, Steven could do nothing but stare. "You're very kind." His mother took out a small pad and wrote on it. Her hand was steady, but when she handed the paper to Carlo and looked at him, he saw the emotion. He thought of his own mother. He took the paper, then her hand.

"You have a fortunate son, Mrs. Hardesty."

Thoughtful, Juliet watched them walk away, noting that Steven looked over his shoulder with the same, blank, baffled expression.

So he has a heart, Juliet decided, touched. A heart that wasn't altogether reserved for *amore*. But she saw Carlo slip the paper into his pocket and wondered if that would be the end of it.

The autographing wasn't a smashing success. Six books by Juliet's count. That had been bad enough, but then there'd been The Incident.

Looking at the all but empty store, Juliet had considered hitting the streets with a sign on her back, then the homey little woman had come along bearing all three of Carlo's books. Good for the ego, Juliet thought. That was before the woman had said something that caused

Carlo's eyes to chill and his voice to freeze. All Juliet heard was the name LaBare.

"I beg your pardon, Madame?" Carlo said in a tone Juliet had never heard from him. It could've sliced through steel.

"I said I keep all your books on a shelf in my kitchen, right next to André LaBare's. I love to cook."

"LaBare?" Carlo put his hand over his stack of books as a protective parent might over a threatened child. "You would dare put my work next to that—that peasant's?"

Thinking fast, Juliet stepped up and broke into the conversation. If ever she'd seen a man ready to murder, it was Carlo. "Oh, I see you have all of Mr. Franconi's books. You must love to cook."

"Well, yes I—"

"Wait until you try some of his new recipes. I had the *pasta con pesto* myself. It's wonderful." Juliet started to take the woman's books from under Carlo's hand and met with resistance and a stubborn look. She gave him one of her own and jerked the books away. "Your family's going to be just thrilled when you serve it," Juliet went on, keeping her voice pleasant as she led the woman out of the line of fire. "And the fettuccine..."

"LaBare is a swine." Carlo's voice was very clear and reached the stairs. The woman glanced back nervously.

"Men." Juliet made her voice a conspiratorial whisper. "Such egos."

"Yes." Gathering up her books, the woman hurried down the stairs and out of the store. Juliet waited until she was out of earshot before she pounced on Carlo.

"How could you?"

"How could I?" He rose, and though he skimmed just under six feet, he looked enormous. "She would *dare* speak that name to me? She would *dare* associate the work of an artist with the work of a jackass? LaBare—"

"At the moment, I don't give a damn who or what this LaBare is." Juliet put a hand on his shoulder and shoved him back onto the love seat. "What I do care about is you scaring off the few customers we have. Now behave yourself."

He sat where he was only because he admired the way she'd ordered him to. Fascinating woman, Carlo decided, finding it wiser to think of her than LaBare. It was wiser to think of flood and famine than of LaBare.

The afternoon had dragged on and on, except for the young boy, Carlo thought and touched the paper in his pocket. He'd call Summer in Philadelphia about young Steven Hardesty.

But other than Steven and the woman who upped his blood pressure by speaking of LaBare, Carlo had found himself perilously close to boredom. Something he considered worse than illness.

He needed some activity, a challenge—even a small one. He glanced over at Juliet as she spoke with a clerk. That was no small challenge. The one thing he'd yet to be in Juliet's company was bored. She kept him interested. Sexually? Yes, that went without saying. Intellectually. That was a plus, a big one.

He understood women. It wasn't a matter of pride, but to Carlo's thinking, a matter of circumstance. He enjoyed women. As lovers, of course, but he also enjoyed them as companions, as friends, as associates. It was a rare thing when a man could find a woman to be all of those things. That's what he wanted from Juliet. He hadn't resolved it yet, only felt it. Convincing her to be his friend would be as challenging, and as rewarding, as it would be to convince her to be his lover.

No, he realized as he studied her profile. With this woman, a lover would come easier than a friend. He had two weeks left to accomplish both. With a smile, he decided to start the campaign in earnest.

Half an hour later, they were walking the three blocks to the parking garage Juliet had found.

"This time I drive," he told Juliet as they stepped inside the echoing gray building. When she started to object, he held out his hand for the keys. "Come, my love, I've just survived two hours of boredom. Why should you have all the fun?"

"Since you put it that way." She dropped the keys in his hand, relieved that whatever had set him off before was forgotten.

"So now we have a free evening."

"That's right." With a sigh she leaned back in her seat and waited for him to start the engine.

"We'll have dinner at seven. Tonight, I make the arrangements."

A hamburger in her room, an old movie and bed. Juliet let the wish come and go. Her job was to pamper and entertain as much as possible. "Whatever you like."

Carlo pulled out of the parking space with a squeal of tires that had Juliet bolting up. "I'll hold you to that, *cara*."

He zoomed out of the garage and turned right with hardly a pause. "Carlo—"

"We should have champagne to celebrate the end of our first week. You like champagne?"

"Yes, I—Carlo, the light's changing."

He breezed through the amber light, skimmed by the bumper of a battered compact and kept going. "Italian food. You have no objection?"

"No." She gripped the door handle until her knuckles turned white. "That truck!"

"Yes, I see it." He swerved around it, zipped through another light and cut a sharp right. "You have plans for the afternoon?"

Juliet pressed a hand to her throat, thinking she might be able to push out her voice. "I was thinking of making use of the hotel spa. If I live."

"Good. Me, I think I'll go shopping."

Juliet's teeth snapped together as he changed lanes in bumper-to-bumper traffic. "How do I notify next of kin?"

With a laugh, Carlo swung in front of their hotel. "Don't worry, Juliet. Have your whirlpool and your sauna. Knock on my door at seven."

She looked back toward the street. Pamper and entertain, she remembered. Did that include risking your life? Her supervisor would think so. "Maybe I should go with you."

"No, I insist." He leaned over, cupping her neck before she'd recovered enough to evade. "Enjoy," he murmured lightly against her lips. "And think of me as your skin grows warm and your muscles grow lax."

In self-defense, Juliet hurried out of the car. Before she could tell him to drive carefully, he was barreling back out into the street. She offered a prayer for Italian maniacs, then went inside.

By seven, she felt reborn. She'd sweated out fatigue in the sauna, shocked herself awake in the pool and splurged on a massage. Life, she thought as she splashed on her scent, had its good points after all. Tomorrow's flight to Dallas would be soon enough to draft her Denver report. Such as it was. Tonight, all she had to worry about was eating. After pressing a hand to her stomach, Juliet admitted she was more than ready for that.

With a quick check, she approved the simple ivory dress with the high collar and tiny pearly buttons. Unless Carlo had picked a hot dog stand it would suit. Grabbing her evening bag, she slipped across the hall to knock on Carlo's door. She only hoped he'd chosen some place close by. The last thing she wanted to do was fight Denver's downtown traffic again.

The first thing she noticed when Carlo opened his door were the rolled-up sleeves of his shirt. It was cotton, oversized and chic, but her eyes were drawn to the surprising cord of muscles in his forearms. The man did more than lift spoons and spatulas. The next thing she noticed was the erotic scents of spices and sauce.

"Lovely." Carlo took both hands and drew her inside. She pleased him, the smooth, creamy skin, the light, subtle scent, but more, the confused hesitation in her eyes as she glanced over to where the aroma of food was strongest.

"An interesting cologne," she managed after a moment. "But don't you think you've gotten a bit carried away?"

"*Innamorata,* you don't wear Franconi's spaghetti sauce, you absorb it." He kissed the back of her hand. "Anticipate it." Then the other. "Savor it." This time her palm.

A smart woman wasn't aroused by a man who used such flamboyant tactics. Juliet told herself that as the chills raced up her arms and down again. "Spaghetti sauce?" Slipping her hands from his, she linked them behind her back.

"I found a wonderful shop. The spices pleased me

very much. The burgundy was excellent. Italian, of course."

"Of course." Cautious, she stepped farther into the suite. "You spent the day cooking?"

"Yes. Though you should remind me to speak to the hotel owner about the quality of this stove. All in all, it went quite well."

She told herself it wasn't wise to encourage him when she had no intention of eating alone with him in his suite. Perhaps if she'd been made out of rock she could have resisted wandering toward the little kitchenette. Her mouth watered. "Oh, God."

Delighted, Carlo slipped an arm around her waist and led her to the stove. The little kitchen itself was in shambles. She'd never seen so many pots and bowls and spoons jammed into a sink before. Counters were splattered and streaked. But the smells. It was heaven, pure and simple.

"The senses, Juliet. There's not one of us who isn't ruled by them. First, you smell, and you begin to imagine." His fingers moved lightly over her waist. "Imagine. You can almost taste it on your tongue from that alone."

"Hmm." Knowing she was making a mistake, she watched him take the lid off the pot on the stove. The tang made her close her eyes and just breathe. "Oh, Carlo."

"Then we look, and the imagination goes one step further." His fingers squeezed lightly at her waist until she opened her eyes and looked into the pot. Thick, red, simmering, the sauce was chunky with meat, peppers and spice. Her stomach growled.

"Beautiful, yes?"

"Yes." She wasn't aware that her tongue slid out over her lips in anticipation. He was.

"And we hear." Beside the sauce a pot of water began to boil. In an expert move, he measured pasta by sight and slid it in. "Some things are destined to be mated." With a slotted spoon, he stirred gently. "Without each other, they are incomplete. But when merged…" he adjusted the flame, "a treasure. Pasta and the sauce. A man and a woman. Come, you'll have some burgundy. The champagne's for later."

It was time to take a stand, even though she took it by the stove. "Carlo, I had no idea this was what you intended. I think—"

"I like surprises." He handed her a glass half filled with dark, red wine. "And I wanted to cook for you."

She wished he hadn't put it quite that way. She wished his voice wasn't so warm, so deep, like his eyes. Like the feelings he could urge out of her. "I appreciate that, Carlo, it's just that—"

"You had your sauna?"

"Yes, I did. Now—"

"It relaxed you. It shows."

She sighed, sipping at the wine without thinking. "Yes."

"This relaxes me. We eat together tonight." He tapped his glass to hers. "Men and women have done so for centuries. It has become civilized."

Her chin tilted. "You're making fun of me."

"Yes." Ducking into the refrigerator, he pulled out a small tray. "First you'll try my antipasto. Your palate should be prepared."

Juliet chose a little chunk of zucchini. "I'd think you'd prefer being served in a restaurant."

"Now and then. There are times I prefer privacy." He set down the tray. As he did, she took a small step back. Interested, he lifted a brow. "Juliet, do I make you nervous?"

She swallowed the zucchini. "Don't be absurd."

"Am I?" On impulse, he set his wine down as well and took another step toward her. Juliet found her back pressed into the refrigerator.

"Carlo—"

"No, shh. We experiment." Gently, watching her, he brushed his lips over one cheek, then the other. He heard her breath catch then shudder out. Nerves—these he accepted. When a man and woman were attracted and close, there had to be nerves. Without them, passion was bland, like a sauce without spice.

But fear? Wasn't that what he saw in her eyes? Just a trace of it, only briefly. Nerves he'd use, play on, exploit. Fear was something different. It disturbed him, blocked him and, at the same time, moved him.

"I won't hurt you, Juliet."

Her eyes were direct again, level, though her hand was balled into a fist. "Won't you?"

He took her hand, slowly working it open. "No." In that moment, he promised both of them. "I won't. Now we'll eat."

Juliet held off the shudder until he'd turned around to stir and drain his pasta. Perhaps he wouldn't hurt her, she thought and recklessly tossed back her wine. But she might hurt herself.

He didn't fuss. He merely perfected. It occurred to Juliet, as she watched him put the last touches on the meal, that he was no different here in the little hotel kitchen than he'd been before the camera. Juliet added her help in the only way she'd have dared. She set the table.

Yes, it was a mistake, she told herself as she arranged plates. But no one but a fool would walk away from anything that smelled like that sauce. She wasn't a fool. She could handle herself. The moment of weak fear she'd felt in the kitchen was past. She'd enjoy a take-your-shoes-off meal, drink two glasses of really excellent burgundy, then go across the hall and catch eight hours' sleep. The merry-go-round would continue the next day.

She selected a marinated mushroom as Carlo brought in the platter of spaghetti. "Better," he said when she smiled at him. "You're ready to enjoy yourself."

With a shrug, Juliet sat. "If one of the top chefs in the world wants to cook me dinner, why should I complain?"

"*The* top," he corrected and gestured for her to serve herself. She did, barely conquering greed.

"Does it really relax you to stand in a kitchen?"

"It depends. Sometimes it relaxes, sometimes it excites. Always it pleases. No, don't cut." With a shake of his head, he reached over. "Americans. You roll it onto the fork."

"It falls off when I do."

"Like this." With his hands on her wrists, he guided her. Her pulse was steady, he noted, but not slow. "Now." Still holding her hand, he lifted the fork toward her mouth. "Taste."

As she did, he had the satisfaction of watching her face. Spices exploded on her tongue. Heat seeped through, mellowing to warmth. She savored it, even as she thought of the next bite. "Oh, this is no little sin."

Nothing could have delighted him more. With a laugh, he sat back and started on his own plate. "Small sins are only small pleasures. When Franconi cooks for you, food is not a basic necessity."

She was already rolling the next forkful. "You win that one. Why aren't you fat?"

"Prego?"

"If I could cook like this..." She tasted again and sighed. "I'd look like one of your meatballs."

With a chuckle, he watched her dig in. It pleased him to see someone he cared for enjoying what he'd created. After years of cooking, he'd never tired of it. "So, your mother didn't teach you to cook?"

"She tried." Juliet accepted a piece of the crusty bread he offered but set it aside as she rolled more spaghetti. First things first. "I never seemed to be very good at the things she wanted me to be good at. My sister plays the piano beautifully; I can barely remember the scales."

"So, what did you want to do instead of taking piano lessons?"

"Play third base." It came out so easily, it stunned her. Juliet had thought she'd buried that along with a dozen other childhood frustrations. "It just wasn't done," she said with a shrug. "My mother was determined to raise two well-rounded ladies who would become two well-rounded, successful wives. Win some, lose some."

"You think she's not proud of you?"

The question hit a target she hadn't known was exposed. Juliet reached for her wine. "It's not a matter of pride, but of disappointment, I suppose. I disappointed her; I confused my father. They still wonder what they did wrong."

"What they did wrong was not to accept what you are."

"Maybe," she murmured. "Or maybe I was determined to be something they couldn't accept. I've never worked it out."

"Are you unhappy with your life?"

Surprised, she glanced up. Unhappy? Sometimes frustrated, harassed and pressured. But unhappy? "No. No, I'm not."

"Then perhaps that's your answer."

Juliet took a moment to study him. He was more than gorgeous, more than sexy, more than all those qualities she'd once cynically attributed to him. "Carlo." For the first time she reached out to touch him, just his hand, but he thought it a giant step. "You're a very nice man."

"But of course I am." His fingers curled over hers because he couldn't resist. "I could give you references."

With a laugh, Juliet backed off. "I'm sure you could." With concentration, dedication and just plain greed, she cleared off her plate.

"Time for dessert."

"Carlo!" Moaning, Juliet pressed a hand to her stomach. "Please, don't be cruel."

"You'll like it." He was up and in the kitchen before she found the strength to refuse again. "It's an old, old, Italian tradition. Back to the empire. American cheesecake is sometimes excellent, but this…" He brought out a small, lovely cake with cherries dripping lavishly over it.

"Carlo, I'll die."

"Just a taste with the champagne." He popped the cork with an expert twist and poured two fresh glasses. "Go, sit on the sofa, be comfortable."

As she did, Juliet realized why the Romans traditionally slept after a meal. She could've curled up in a happy little ball and been unconscious in moments. But the champagne was lively, insistent.

"Here." He brought over one plate with a small slice. "We'll share."

"One bite," she told him, prepared to stand firm. Then she tasted. Creamy, smooth, not quite sweet, more nutty. Exquisite. With a sigh of surrender, Juliet took another. "Carlo, you're a magician."

"Artist," he corrected.

"Whatever you want." Using all the willpower she had left, Juliet exchanged the cake for champagne. "I really can't eat another bite."

"Yes, I remember. You don't believe in overindulgence." But he filled her glass again.

"Maybe not." She sipped, enjoying that rich, luxurious aura only champagne could give. "But now I've gotten a different perspective on indulgence." Slipping out of her shoes, she laughed over the rim of her glass. "I'm converted."

"You're lovely." The lights were low, the music soft, the scents lingering and rich. He thought of resisting. The fear that had been in her eyes demanded he think of it. But just now, she was relaxed, smiling. The desire he'd felt tug the moment he'd seen her had never completely gone away.

Senses were aroused, heightened, by a meal. That was something he understood perfectly. He also understood that a man and a woman should never ignore whatever pleasure they could give to each other.

So he didn't resist, but took her face in his hands. There he could watch her eyes, feel her skin, nearly taste her. This time he saw desire, not fear but wariness. Perhaps she was ready for lesson two.

She could have refused. The need to do so went through her mind. But his hands were so strong, so gentle on her skin. She'd never been touched like that before. She knew how he'd kiss her and the sense of anticipation mixed with nerves. She knew, and wanted.

Wasn't she a woman who knew her own mind? She took her hands to his wrists, but didn't push away. Her fingers curled around and held as she touched her mouth to his. For a moment they stayed just so, allowing themselves to savor that first taste, that first sensation. Then slowly, mutually, they asked for more.

She seemed so small when he held her that a man could forget how strong and competent she was. He found himself wanting to treasure. Desire might burn, but when she was so pliant, so vulnerable, he found himself compelled to show only gentleness.

Had any man ever shown her such care? Juliet's head began to swim as his hands moved into her hair. Was there another man so patient? His heart was pounding against hers. She could feel it, like something wild and desperate. But his mouth was so soft, his hands so gentle. As though they'd been lovers for years, she thought dimly. And had all the time left in the world to continue to love.

No hurry, no rush, no frenzy. Just pleasure. Her heart opened reluctantly, but it opened. He began to pour through. When the phone shrilled, he swore and she sighed. They'd both been prepared to take all the chances.

"Only a moment," he murmured.

Still dreaming, she touched his cheek. "All right."

As he went to answer, she leaned back, determined not to think.

"Cara!" The enthusiasm in his voice, and the endearment had her opening her eyes again. With a warm laugh, Carlo went into a stream of Italian. Juliet had no choice but to think.

Affection. Yes, it was in his voice. She didn't have to understand the words. She looked around to see him smiling as he spoke to the woman on the other end. Resigned, Juliet picked up her champagne. It wasn't easy for her to admit she'd been a fool. Or for her to admit she'd been hurt.

She knew who he was. What he was. She knew how many women he'd seduced. Perhaps she was a woman who knew her own mind, and perhaps she wanted him. But she would never be eased into a long line of *others*. Setting down the champagne, she rose.

"*Sì, sì*. I love you."

Juliet turned away at the phrase I love you. How well it slid off his tongue, in any language. How little it meant, in any language.

"Interruptions. I'm sorry."

Juliet turned back and gave him her uncompromising look. "Don't be. The dinner was marvelous, Carlo, thank you. You should be ready to check out by eight."

"A moment," he murmured. Crossing over, he took her by the arms. "What's this? You're angry."

"Of course not." She tried to back away and failed. It was easy to forget just how strong he was. "Why should I be?"

"Reasons aren't always necessary for a woman."

Though he'd said it in a simple tone that offered no insult, her eyes narrowed. "The expert. Well, let me tell you something about *this* woman, Franconi. She doesn't think much of a man who makes love to her one minute then pushes another lover in her face the next."

He held up his hand as he struggled to follow her drift. "I'm not following you. Maybe my English is failing."

"Your English is perfect," she spit at him. "From what I just heard, so's your Italian."

"My..." His grin broke out. "The phone."

"Yes. The phone. Now, if you'll excuse me."

He let her get as far as the door. "Juliet, I admit I'm hopelessly enamored of the woman I was speaking to. She's beautiful, intelligent, interesting and I've never met anyone quite like her."

Furious, Juliet whirled around. "How marvelous."

"I think so. It was my mother."

She walked back to snatch up the purse she'd nearly forgotten. "I'd think a man of your experience and imagination could do better."

"So I could." He held her again, not so gently, not so patiently. "If it was necessary. I don't make a habit to explain myself, and when I do, I don't lie."

She took a deep breath because she was abruptly certain she was hearing the truth. Either way, she'd been a fool. "I'm sorry. It's none of my business in any case."

"No, it's not." He took her chin in his hand and held it. "I saw fear in your eyes before. It concerned me. Now I think it wasn't me you were afraid of, but yourself."

"That's none of your business."

"No, it's not," he said again. "You appeal to me, Juliet, in many ways, and I intend to take you to bed. But we'll wait until you aren't afraid."

She wanted to rage at him. She wanted to weep. He saw both things clearly. "We have an early flight in the morning, Carlo."

He let her go, but stood where he was for a long time after he'd heard her door shut across the hall.

Chapter 6

Dallas was different. Dallas was Dallas without apology. Texas rich, Texas big and Texas arrogant. If it was the city that epitomized the state, then it did so with flair. Futuristic architecture and mind-twisting freeways abounded in a strange kind of harmony with the more sedate buildings downtown. The air was hot and carried the scents of oil, expensive perfumes and prairie dust. Dallas was Dallas, but it had never forgotten its roots.

Dallas held the excitement of a boomtown that was determined not to stop booming. It was full of down-home American energy that wasn't about to lag. As far as Juliet was concerned they could have been in downtown Timbuktu.

He acted as though nothing had happened—no intimate dinner, no arousal, no surrender, no cross words. Juliet wondered if he did it to drive her crazy.

Carlo was amiable, cooperative and charming. She knew better now. Under the amiability was a shaft of steel that wouldn't bend an inch. She'd seen it. One could say she'd felt it. It would have been a lie to say she didn't admire it.

Cooperative, sure. In his favor, Juliet had to admit that she'd never been on tour with anyone as willing to work without complaint. And touring was hard work, no matter how glamorous it looked on paper. Once you were into your second full week, it became difficult to smile unless you were cued. Carlo never broke his rhythm.

But he expected perfection—spelled his way—and wouldn't budge an inch until he got it.

Charming. No one could enchant a group of people with more style than Franconi. That alone made her job easier. No one would deny his charm unless they'd seen how cold his eyes could become. She had.

He had flaws like any other man, Juliet thought. Remembering that might help her keep an emotional distance. It always helped her to list the pros and cons of a situation, even if the situation was a man. The trouble was, though flawed, he was damn near irresistible.

And he knew it. That was something else she had to remind herself of.

His ego was no small matter. That was something she'd be wise to balance against his unrestricted generosity. Vanity about himself and his work went over the border into arrogance. It didn't hurt her sense of perspective to weigh that against his innate consideration for others.

But then, there was the way he smiled, the way he said her name. Even the practical, professional Juliet

Trent had a difficult time finding a flaw to balance those little details.

The two days in Dallas were busy enough to keep her driving along on six hours' sleep, plenty of vitamins and oceans of coffee. They were making up for Denver all right. She had the leg cramps to prove it.

Four minutes on the national news, an interview with one of the top magazines in the country, three write-ups in the Dallas press and two autograph sessions that sold clean out. There was more, but those headed up her report. When she went back to New York, she'd go back in triumph.

She didn't want to think of the dinners with department store executives that started at 10:00 P.M. and lasted until she was falling asleep in her bananas flambé. She couldn't bear to count the lunches of poached salmon or shrimp salad. She'd had to refill her pocket aspirin bottles and stock up on antacids. But it was worth it. She should have been thrilled.

She was miserable.

She was driving him mad. Polite, Carlo thought as they prepared to sit through another luncheon interview. Yes, she was polite. Her mother had taught her perfect manners even if she hadn't taught her to cook.

Competent? As far as he was concerned, he'd never known anyone, male or female, who was as scrupulously competent as Juliet Trent. He'd always admired that particular quality in a companion, insisted on it in an associate. Of course, Juliet was both. Precise, prompt, cool in a crisis and unflaggingly energetic. Admirable qualities all.

For the first time in his life he gave serious thought to strangling a woman.

Indifferent. That's what he couldn't abide. She acted

as though there was nothing more between them than the next interview, the next television spot, the next plane. She acted as though there'd been no flare of need, of passion, of understanding between them. One would think she didn't want him with the same intensity that he wanted her.

He knew better. Didn't he?

He could remember her ripe, unhesitating response to him. Mouth to mouth, body to body. There'd been no indifference in the way her arms had held him. No, there'd been strength, pliancy, need, demand, but no indifference. Yet now…

They'd spent nearly two days exclusively in each other's company, but he'd seen nothing in her eyes, heard nothing in her voice that indicated more than a polite business association. They ate together, drove together, worked together. They did everything but sleep together.

He'd had his fill of polite. But he hadn't had his fill of Juliet.

He thought of her. It didn't bruise Carlo's pride to admit he thought of her a great deal. He often thought of women, and why not? When a man didn't think of a woman, he was better off dead.

He wanted her. It didn't worry him to admit that he wanted her more every time he thought of her. He'd wanted many women. He'd never believed in self-denial. When a man didn't want a woman, he *was* dead.

But… Carlo found it odd that "buts" so often followed any thoughts he had on Juliet. But he found himself dwelling on her more often than he'd have once considered healthy. Though he didn't mind wanting a woman until he ached, he found Juliet could make him ache more than he'd have once considered comfortable.

He might have been able to rationalize the threat to his health and comfort. But…she was so damn indifferent.

If he did nothing else in the short time they had left in Dallas, he was going to change that.

Lunch was white linen, heavy silver flatware and thin crystal. The room was done in tones of dusty rose and pastel greens. The murmur of conversation was just as quiet.

Carlo thought it a pity they couldn't have met the reporter at one of the little Tex-Mex restaurants over Mexican beer with chili and nachos. Briefly, he promised himself he'd rectify that in Houston.

He barely noticed the reporter was young and running on nerves as they took their seats. He'd decided, no matter what it took, he'd break through Juliet's inflexible shield of politeness before they stood up again. Even if he had to play dirty.

"I'm so happy you included Dallas on your tour, Mr. Franconi," the reporter began, already reaching for her water glass to clear her throat. "Mr. Van Ness sends his apologies. He was looking forward to meeting you."

Carlo smiled at her, but his mind was on Juliet. "Yes?"

"Mr. Van Ness is the food editor for the *Tribune*." Juliet spread her napkin over her lap as she gave Carlo information she'd related less than fifteen minutes before. She sent him the friendliest of smiles and hoped he felt the barbs in it. "Ms. Tribly is filling in for him."

"Of course." Carlo smoothed over the gap of attention. "Charmingly, I'm sure."

As a woman she wasn't immune to that top-cream voice. As a reporter, she was well aware of the importance of her assignment. "It's all pretty confused." Ms.

Tribly wiped damp hands on her napkin. "Mr. Van Ness is having a baby. That is, what I mean is, his wife went into labor just a couple of hours ago."

"So, we should drink to them." Carlo signaled a waiter. "Margaritas?" He phrased the question as a statement, earned a cool nod from Juliet and a grateful smile from the reporter.

Determined to pull off her first really big assignment, Ms. Tribly balanced a pad discreetly on her lap. "Have you been enjoying your tour through America, Mr. Franconi?"

"I always enjoy America." Lightly he ran a finger over the back of Juliet's hand before she could move it out of reach. "Especially in the company of a beautiful woman." She started to slide her hand away then felt it pinned under his. For a man who could whip up the most delicate of soufflés, his hands were as strong as a boxer's.

Wills sparked, clashed and fumed. Carlo's voice remained mild, soft and romantic. "I must tell you, Ms. Tribly, Juliet is an extraordinary woman. I couldn't manage without her."

"Mr. Franconi's very kind." Though Juliet's voice was as mild and quiet as his, the nudge she gave him under the table wasn't. "I handle the details; Mr. Franconi's the artist."

"We make an admirable team, wouldn't you say, Ms. Tribly?"

"Yes." Not quite sure how to handle that particular line, she veered off to safer ground. "Mr. Franconi, besides writing cookbooks, you own and run a successful restaurant in Rome and occasionally travel to prepare a special dish. A few months ago, you flew to a yacht in the Aegean to cook minestrone for Dimitri Azares, the shipping magnate."

"His birthday," Carlo recalled. "His daughter arranged a surprise." Again, his gaze skimmed over the woman whose hand he held. "Juliet will tell you, I'm fond of surprises."

"Yes, well." Ms. Tribly reached for her water glass again. "Your schedule's so full and exciting. I wonder if you still enjoy the basics as far as cooking."

"Most people think of cooking as anything from a chore to a hobby. But as I've told Juliet—" His fingers twined possessively with hers "—food is a basic need. Like making love, it should appeal to all the senses. It should excite, arouse, satisfy." He slipped his thumb around to skim over her palm. "You remember, Juliet?"

She'd tried to forget, had told herself she could. Now with that light, insistent brush of thumb, he was bringing it all back. "Mr. Franconi is a strong believer in the sensuality of food. His unusual flair for bringing this out has made him one of the top chefs in the world."

"Grazie, mi amore," he murmured and brought her stiff hand to his lips.

She pressed her shoe down on the soft leather of his loafers and hoped she ground bones. "I think you, and your readers, will find that Mr. Franconi's book, *The Italian Way,* is a really stunning example of his technique, his style and his opinions, written in such a way that the average person following one of his recipes step-by-step can create something very special."

When their drinks were served, Juliet gave another tug on her hand thinking she might catch him off guard. She should have known better.

"To the new baby." He smiled over at Juliet. "It's always a pleasure to drink to life in all its stages."

Ms. Tribly sipped lightly at her margarita in a glass the size of a small birdbath. "Mr. Franconi, have you actually cooked and tasted every recipe that's in your book?"

"Of course." Carlo enjoyed the quick tang of his drink. There was a time for the sweet, and a time for the tart. His laugh came low and smooth as he looked at Juliet. "When something's mine, there's nothing I don't learn about it. A meal, Ms. Tribly, is like a love affair."

She broke the tip of her pencil and hurriedly dug out another. "A love affair?"

"Yes. It begins slowly, almost experimentally. Just a taste, to whet the appetite, to stir the anticipation. Then the flavor changes, perhaps something light, something cool to keep the senses stirred, but not overwhelmed. Then there's the spice, the meat, the variety. The senses are aroused; the mind is focused on the pleasure. It should be lingered over. But finally, there's dessert, the time of indulgence." When he smiled at Juliet, there was no mistaking his meaning. "It should be enjoyed slowly, savored, until the palate is satisfied and the body sated."

Ms. Tribly swallowed. "I'm going to buy a copy of your book for myself."

With a laugh, Carlo picked up his menu. "Suddenly, I have a huge appetite."

Juliet ordered a small fruit salad and picked at it for thirty minutes.

"I've really got to get back." After polishing off her meal and an apricot tart, Ms. Tribly gathered up her pad. "I can't tell you how much I've enjoyed this, Mr. Franconi. I'm never going to sit down to pot roast with the same attitude again."

Amused, Carlo rose. "It was a pleasure."

"I'll be glad to send a clipping of the article to your office, Ms. Trent."

"I'd appreciate that." Juliet offered her hand, surprised when the reporter held it an extra moment.

"You're a lucky woman. Enjoy the rest of your tour, Mr. Franconi."

"Arrivederci." He was still smiling when he sat down to finish his coffee.

"You put on a hell of a show, Franconi."

He'd been expecting the storm. Anticipating it. "Yes, I think I did my—what was it you called it? Ah yes, my spiel very well."

"It was more like a three-act play." With calm, deliberate movements, she signed the check. "But the next time, don't cast me unless you ask first."

"Cast you?"

His innocence was calculated to infuriate. He never missed his mark. "You gave that woman the very clear impression that we were lovers."

"Juliet, I merely gave her the very correct impression that I respect and admire you. What she takes from that isn't my responsibility."

Juliet rose, placed her napkin very carefully on the table and picked up her briefcase. "Swine."

Carlo watched her walk out of the restaurant. No endearment could have pleased him more. When a woman called a man a swine, she wasn't indifferent. He was whistling when he walked out to join her. It pleased him even more to see her fumbling with the keys of the rented car parked at the curb. When a woman was indifferent, she didn't swear at inanimate objects.

"Would you like me to drive to the airport?"

"No." Swearing again, she jabbed the key into the lock. She'd control her temper. She would control it.

Like hell. Slamming both hands down on the roof of the car, she stared at him. "Just what was the point of that little charade?"

Squisito, he thought briefly. Her eyes were a dangerous blade-sharp green. He'd discovered he preferred a woman with temper. "Charade?"

"All that hand-holding, those intimate looks you were giving me?"

"It's not a charade that I enjoy holding your hand, and that I find it impossible not to look at you."

She refused to argue with the car between them. In a few quick steps she was around the hood and toe-to-toe with him. "It was completely unprofessional."

"Yes. It was completely personal."

It was going to be difficult to argue at all if he turned everything she said to his own advantage.

"Don't ever do it again."

"Madonna." His voice was very mild, his move very calculated. Juliet found herself boxed in between him and the car. "Orders I'll take from you when they have to do with schedules and plane flights. When it comes to more personal things, I do as I choose."

It wasn't something she'd expected; that's why she lost her advantage. Juliet would tell herself that again and again—later. He had her by both shoulders and his eyes never left hers as he gave her a quick jerk. It wasn't the smooth, calculated seduction she'd have anticipated from him. It was rough, impulsive and enervating.

His mouth was on hers, all demand. His hands held her still, all power. She had no time to stiffen, to struggle or to think. He took her with him quickly, through a journey of heat and light. She didn't resist. Later, when she would tell herself she had, it would be a lie.

There were people on the sidewalk, cars in the street.

Juliet and Carlo were unaware of everything. The heat of a Dallas afternoon soaked into the concrete beneath them. It blasted the air until it hummed. They were concerned with a fire of their own.

Her hands were at his waist, holding on, letting go. A car streaked by, country rock blasting through open windows. She never heard it. Though she'd refused wine at lunch, she tasted it on his tongue and was intoxicated.

Later, much later, he'd take time to think about what was happening. It wasn't the same. Part of him already knew and feared because it wasn't the same. Touching her was different than touching other women. Tasting her—lightly, deeply, teasingly—just tasting her was different than tasting other women. The feelings were new, though he'd have sworn he'd experienced all the feelings that any man was capable of.

He knew about sensations. He incorporated them in his work and in his life. But they'd never had this depth before. A man who found more and didn't reach for it was a fool.

He knew about intimacy. He expected, demanded it in everything he did. But it had never had this strength before.

New experiences were not to be refused, but explored and exploited. If he felt a small, nagging fear, he could ignore it. For now.

Later. They clung to each other and told themselves they'd think later. Time was unimportant after all. Now held all the meaning necessary.

He took his mouth from hers, but his hands held her still. It shocked him to realize they weren't quite steady. Women had made him ache. Women had made him burn. But no woman had ever made him tremble.

"We need a place," he murmured. "Quiet, private. It's time to stop pretending this isn't real."

She wanted to nod, to simply put herself completely in his hands. Wasn't that the first step in losing control over your own life? "No, Carlo." Her voice wasn't as strong as she would have liked but she didn't back away. "We've got to stop mixing personal feelings with business. We've got just under two weeks to go on the road."

"I don't give a damn if it's two days or two years. I want to spend it making love with you."

She brought herself back enough to remember they were standing on a public street in the middle of afternoon traffic. "Carlo, this isn't the time to discuss it."

"Now is always the time. Juliet—" He cupped her face in his hand. "It's not me you're fighting."

He didn't have to finish the thought. She was all too aware that the war was within herself. What she wanted, what was wise. What she needed, what was safe. The tug-of-war threatened to split her apart, and the two halves, put back together, would never equal the whole she understood.

"Carlo, we have a plane to catch."

He said something soft and pungent in Italian. "You'll talk to me."

"No." She lifted her hands to grip his forearms. "Not about this."

"Then we'll stay right here until you change your mind."

They could both be stubborn, and with stubbornness, they could both get nowhere. "We have a schedule."

"We have a great deal more than that."

"No, we don't." His brow lifted. "All right then, we can't. We have a plane to catch."

"We'll catch your plane, Juliet. But we'll talk in Houston."

"Carlo, don't push me into a corner."

"Who pushes?" he murmured. "Me or you?"

She didn't have an easy answer. "What I'll do is arrange for someone else to come out and finish the tour with you."

He only shook his head. "No, you won't. You're too ambitious. Leaving a tour in the middle wouldn't look good for you."

She set her teeth. He knew her too well already. "I'll get sick."

This time he smiled. "You're too proud. Running away isn't possible for you."

"It's not a matter of running." But of survival, she thought and quickly changed the phrase. "It's a matter of priorities."

He kissed her again, lightly. "Whose?"

"Carlo, we have business."

"Yes, of different sorts. One has nothing to do with the other."

"To me they do. Unlike you, I don't go to bed with everyone I'm attracted to."

Unoffended, he grinned. "You flatter me, *cara*."

She could have sighed. How like him to make her want to laugh while she was still furious. "Purely unintentional."

"I like you when you bare your teeth."

"Then you're going to enjoy the next couple of weeks." She pushed his hands away. "It's a long ride to the airport, Carlo. Let's get going."

Amiable as ever, he pulled his door open. "You're the boss."

A foolish woman might've thought she'd won a victory.

Chapter 7

Juliet was an expert on budgeting time. It was her business every bit as much as promotion. So, if she could budget time, she could just as easily overbudget it when the circumstances warranted. If she did her job well enough, hustled fast enough, she could create a schedule so tight that there could be no time for talk that didn't directly deal with business. She counted on Houston to cooperate.

Juliet had worked with Big Bill Bowers before. He was a brash, warmhearted braggart who handled special events for Books, Etc., one of the biggest chains in the country. Big Bill had Texas sewed up and wasn't ashamed to say so. He was partial to long, exaggerated stories, ornate boots and cold beer.

Juliet liked him because he was sharp and tough and invariably made her job easier. On this trip, she blessed him because he was also long-winded and gregarious. He wouldn't give her or Carlo many private moments.

From the minute they arrived at Houston International, the six-foot-five, two-hundred-and-sixty-pound Texan made it his business to entertain. There was a crowd of people waiting at the end of the breezeway, some already packed together and chatting, but there was no overlooking Big Bill. You only had to look for a Brahma bull in a Stetson.

"Well now, there's little Juliet. Pretty as ever."

Juliet found herself caught in a good-natured, rib-cracking bear hug. "Bill." She tested her lungs gingerly as she drew away. "It's always good to be back in Houston. You look great."

"Just clean living, honey." He let out a boom of a laugh that turned heads. Juliet found her mood lifting automatically.

"Carlo Franconi, Bill Bowers. Be nice to him," she added with a grin. "He's not only big, he's the man who'll promote your books for the largest chain in the state."

"Then I'll be very nice." Carlo offered his hand and met an enormous, meaty paw.

"Glad you could make it." The same meaty hand gave Carlo a friendly pat on the back that could have felled a good-sized sapling. Juliet gave Carlo points for not taking a nosedive.

"It's good to be here" was all he said.

"Never been to Italy myself, but I'm partial to Eye-talian cooking. The wife makes a hell of a pot of spaghetti. Let me take that for you." Before Carlo could object, Bill had hefted his big leather case. Juliet couldn't prevent the smirk when Carlo glanced down at the case as though it were a small child boarding a school bus for the first time.

"Car's outside. We'll just pick up your bags and get

going. Airports and hospitals, can't stand 'em." Bill started toward the terminal in his big, yard-long strides. "Hotel's all ready for you; I checked this morning."

Juliet managed to keep up though she still wore three-inch heels. "I knew I could depend on you, Bill. How's Betty?"

"Mean as ever," he said proudly of his wife. "With the kids up and gone, she's only got me to order around."

"But you're still crazy about her."

"A man gets used to mean after a while." He grinned, showing one prominent gold tooth. "No need to go by the hotel straight off. We'll show Carlo here what Houston's all about." As he walked he swung Carlo's case at his side.

"I'd like that." Diplomatically, Carlo moved closer to his side. "I could take that case..."

"No need for that. What you got in here, boy? Weighs like a steer."

"Tools," Juliet put in with an innocent smile. "Carlo's very temperamental."

"Man can't be too temperamental about his tools," Bill said with a nod. He tipped his hat at a young woman with a short skirt and lots of leg. "I've still got the same hammer my old man gave me when I was eight."

"I'm just as sentimental about my spatulas," Carlo murmured. But he hadn't, Juliet noted, missed the legs, either.

"You got a right." A look passed between the two men that was essential male and pleased. Juliet decided it had more to do with long smooth thighs than tools. "Now, I figured you two must've had your fill of fancy restaurants and creamed chicken by now. Having a little barbecue over at my place. You can take off your shoes, let down your hair and eat real food."

Juliet had been to one of Bill's *little* barbecues before. It meant grilling a whole steer along with several chickens and the better part of a pig, then washing it all down with a couple hundred gallons of beer. It also meant she wouldn't see her hotel room for a good five hours. "Sounds great. Carlo, you haven't lived until you've tasted one of Bill's steaks grilled over mesquite."

Carlo slipped a hand over her elbow. "Then we should live first." The tone made her turn her head and meet the look. "Before we attend to business."

"That's the ticket." Bill stopped in front of the conveyor belt. "Just point 'em out and we'll haul 'em in."

They lived, mingling at Bill's little barbecue with another hundred guests. Music came from a seven-piece band that never seemed to tire. Laughter and splashing rose up from a pool separated from the patio by a spread of red flowering bushes that smelled of spice and heat. Above all was the scent of grilled meat, sauce and smoke. Juliet ate twice as much as she would normally have considered because her host filled her plate then kept an eagle eye on her.

It should have pleased her that Carlo was surrounded by a dozen or so Texas ladies in bathing suits and sundresses who had suddenly developed an avid interest in cooking. But, she thought nastily, most of them wouldn't know a stove from a can opener.

It should have pleased her that she had several men dancing attendance on her. She was barely able to keep the names and faces separate as she watched Carlo laugh with a six-foot brunette in two minuscule ribbons of cloth.

The music was loud, the air heavy and warm. Giving into necessity, Juliet had dug a pair of pleated shorts and a crop top out of her bag and changed. It occurred to her that it was the first time since the start of the tour that she'd been able to sit out in the sun, soak up rays and not have a pad and pencil in her hand.

Though the blond beside her with the gleaming biceps was in danger of becoming both a bore and a nuisance, she willed herself to enjoy the moment.

It was the first time Carlo had seen her in anything other than her very proper suits. He'd already concluded, by the way she walked, that her legs were longer than one might think from her height. He hadn't been wrong. They seemed to start at her waist and continued down, smooth, slim and New York pale. The statuesque brunette beside him might not have existed for all the attention he paid her.

It wasn't like him to focus on a woman yards away when there was one right beside him. Carlo knew it, but not what to do about it. The woman beside him smelled of heat and musk—heavy and seductive. It made him think that Juliet's scent was lighter, but held just as much punch.

She had no trouble relaxing with other men. Carlo tipped back a beer as he watched her fold those long legs under her and laugh with the two men sitting on either side of her. She didn't stiffen when the young, muscle-bound hunk on her left put his hand on her shoulder and leaned closer.

It wasn't like him to be jealous. As emotional as he was, Carlo had never experienced that particular sensation. He'd also felt that a woman had just as much right to flirt and experiment as he did. He found that particular rule didn't apply to Juliet. If she let that slick-skinned, weight-lifting *buffone* put his hand on her again…

He didn't have time to finish the thought. Juliet laughed again, set aside her plate and rose. Carlo couldn't hear whatever she'd said to the man beside her, but she strolled into the sprawling ranch house. Moments later, the burnished, bare-chested man rose and followed her.

"Maledetto!"

"What?" The brunette stopped in the middle of what she'd thought was an intimate conversation.

Carlo barely spared her a glance. *"Scusi."* Muttering, he strode off in the direction Juliet had taken. There was murder in his eye.

Fed up with fending off the attentions of Big Bill's hotshot young neighbor, Juliet slipped into the house through the kitchen. Her mood might have been foul, but she congratulated herself on keeping her head. She hadn't taken a chunk out of the free-handed, self-appointed Adonis. She hadn't snarled out loud even once in Carlo's direction.

Attending to business always helped steady her temper. With a check of her watch, Juliet decided she could get one collect call through to her assistant at home. She'd no more than picked up the receiver from the kitchen wall phone than she was lifted off her feet.

"Ain't much to you. But it sure is a pleasure to look at what there is."

She barely suppressed the urge to come back with her elbow. "Tim." She managed to keep her voice pleasant while she thought how unfortunate it was that most of his muscle was from the neck up. "You're going to have to put me down so I can make my call."

"It's a party, sweetheart." Shifting her around with a flex of muscle, he set her on the counter. "No need to go calling anybody when you've got me around."

"You know what I think?" Juliet gauged that she

could give him a quick kick below the belt, but tapped his shoulder instead. After all, he was Bill's neighbor. "I think you should get back out to the party before all the ladies miss you."

"Got a better idea." He leaned forward, boxing her in with a hand on each side. His teeth gleamed in the style of the best toothpaste ads. "Why don't you and I go have a little party of our own? I imagine you New York ladies know how to have fun."

If she hadn't considered him such a jerk, she'd have been insulted for women in general and New York in particular. Patiently, Juliet considered the source. "We New York ladies," she said calmly, "know how to say no. Now back off, Tim."

"Come on, Juliet." He hooked a finger in the neck of her top. "I've got a nice big water bed down the street."

She put a hand on his wrist. Neighbor or not, she was going to belt him. "Why don't you go take a dive."

He only grinned as his hand slid up her leg. "Just what I had in mind."

"Excuse me." Carlo's voice was soft as a snake from the doorway. "If you don't find something else to do with your hands quickly, you might lose the use of them."

"Carlo." Her voice was sharp, but not with relief. She wasn't in the mood for a knight-in-armor rescue.

"The lady and I're having a private conversation." Tim flexed his pectorals. "Take off."

With his thumbs hooked in his pockets, Carlo strolled over. Juliet noted he looked as furious as he had over the canned basil. In that mood, there was no telling what he'd do. She swore, let out a breath and tried to avoid a scene. "Why don't we all go outside?"

"Excellent." Carlo held out a hand to help her down. Before she could reach for it, Tim blocked her way.

"You go outside, buddy. Juliet and I haven't finished talking."

Carlo inclined his head then shifted his gaze to Juliet. "Have you finished talking?"

"Yes." She'd have slid off the counter, but that would have put her on top of Tim's shoulders. Frustrated, she sat where she was.

"Apparently Juliet is finished." Carlo's smile was all amiability, but his eyes were flat and cold. "You seem to be blocking her way."

"I told you to take off." Big and annoyed, he grabbed Carlo by the lapels.

"Cut it out, both of you." With a vivid picture of Carlo bleeding from the nose and mouth, Juliet grabbed a cookie jar shaped like a ten-gallon hat. Before she could use it, Tim grunted and bent over from the waist. As he gasped, clutching his stomach, Juliet only stared.

"You can put that down now," Carlo said mildly. "It's time we left." When she didn't move, he took the jar himself, set it aside, then lifted her from the counter. "You'll excuse us," he said pleasantly to the groaning Tim, then led Juliet outside.

"What did you do?"

"What was necessary."

Juliet looked back toward the kitchen door. If she hadn't seen it for herself… "You hit him."

"Not very hard." Carlo nodded to a group of sunbathers. "All his muscle is in his chest and his brain."

"But—" She looked down at Carlo's hands. They were lean-fingered and elegant with the flash of a diamond on the pinky. Not hands one associated with self-defense. "He was awfully big."

Carlo lifted a brow as he took his sunglasses back out of his pocket. "Big isn't always an advantage. The neighborhood where I grew up was an education. Are you ready to leave?"

No, his voice wasn't pleasant, she realized. It was cold. Ice cold. Instinctively hers mirrored it. "I suppose I should thank you."

"Unless of course you enjoyed being pawed. Perhaps Tim was just acting on the signals you were sending out."

Juliet stopped in her tracks. "What signals?"

"The ones women send out when they want to be pursued."

Thinking she could bring her temper to order, she gave herself a moment. It didn't work. "He might have been bigger than you," she said between her teeth. "But I think you're just as much of an ass. You're very much alike."

The lenses of his glasses were smoky, but she saw his eyes narrow. "You compare what's between us with what happened in there?"

"I'm saying some men don't take no for an answer graciously. You might have a smoother style, Carlo, but you're after the same thing, whether it's a roll in the hay or a cruise on a water bed."

He dropped his hand from her arm, then very deliberately tucked both in his pockets. "If I've mistaken your feelings, Juliet, I apologize. I'm not a man who finds it necessary or pleasurable to pressure a woman. Do you wish to leave or stay?"

She felt a great deal of pressure—in her throat, behind her eyes. She couldn't afford the luxury of giving into it. "I'd like to get to the hotel. I still have some work to do tonight."

"Fine." He left her there to find their host.

* * *

Three hours later, Juliet admitted working was impossible. She'd tried all the tricks she knew to relax. A half hour in a hot tub, quiet music on the radio while she watched the sun set from her hotel window. When relaxing failed, she went over the Houston schedule twice. They'd be running from 7:00 A.M. to 5:00 P.M., almost nonstop. Their flight to Chicago took off at 6:00.

There'd be no time to discuss, think or worry about anything that had happened within the last twenty-four hours. That's what she wanted. Yet when she tried to work on the two-day Chicago stand, she couldn't. All she could do was think about the man a few steps across the hall.

She hadn't realized he could be so cold. He was always so full of warmth, of life. True, he was often infuriating, but he infuriated with verve. Now, he'd left her in a vacuum.

No. Tossing her notebook aside, Juliet dropped her chin in her hand. No, she'd put herself there. Maybe she could have stood it if she'd been right. She'd been dead wrong. She hadn't sent any signals to the idiot Tim, and Carlo's opinion on that still made her steam, but… But she hadn't even thanked him for helping her when, whether she liked to admit it or not, she'd needed help. It didn't sit well with her to be in debt.

With a shrug, she rose from the table and began to pace the room. It might be better all around if they finished off the tour with him cold and distant. There'd certainly be fewer personal problems that way because there'd be nothing personal between them. There'd be no edge to their relationship because they wouldn't have a relationship. Logically, this little incident was probably the best thing that could have happened. It hardly mattered if she'd been right or wrong as long as the result was workable.

She took a glimpse around the small, tidy, impersonal room where she'd spend little more than eight hours, most of it asleep.

No, she couldn't stand it.

Giving in, Juliet stuck her room key in the pocket of her robe.

Women had made him furious before. Carlo counted on it to keep life from becoming too tame. Women had frustrated him before. Without frustrations, how could you fully appreciate success?

But hurt. That was something no woman had ever done to him before. He'd never considered the possibility. Frustration, fury, passion, laughter, shouting. No man who'd known so many women—mother, sisters, lovers—expected a relationship without them. Pain was a different matter.

Pain was an intimate emotion. More personal than passion, more elemental than anger. When it went deep, it found places inside you that should have been left alone.

It had never mattered to him to be considered a rogue, a rake, a playboy—whatever term was being used for a man who appreciated women. Affairs came and went, as affairs were supposed to. They lasted no longer than the passion that conceived them. He was a careful man, a caring man. A lover became a friend as desire waned. There might be spats and hard words during the storm of an affair, but he'd never ended one that way.

It occurred to him that he'd had more spats, more hard words with Juliet than with any other woman.

Yet they'd never been lovers. Nor would they be. After pouring a glass of wine, he sat back in a deep chair and closed his eyes. He wanted no woman who compared him with a muscle-bound idiot, who confused passion for lust. He wanted no woman who compared the beauty of lovemaking to—what was it?—a cruise on a water bed. *Dio!*

He wanted no woman who could make him ache so—in the middle of the night, in the middle of the day. He wanted no woman who could bring him pain with a few harsh words.

God, he wanted Juliet.

He heard the knock on the door and frowned. By the time he'd set his glass aside and stood, it came again.

If Juliet hadn't been so nervous, she might have thought of something witty to say about the short black robe Carlo wore with two pink flamingos twining up one side. As it was, she stood in her own robe and bare feet with her fingers linked together.

"I'm sorry," she said when he opened the door.

He stepped back. "Come in, Juliet."

"I had to apologize." She let out a deep breath as she walked into the room. "I was awful to you this afternoon, and you'd helped me out of a very tricky situation with a minimum of fuss. I was angry when you insinuated that I'd led that—that idiot on in some way. I had a right to be." She folded her arms under her chest and paced the room. "It was an uncalled for remark, and insulting. Even if by the remotest possibility it had been true, you had no right to talk. After all, you were basking in your own harem."

"Harem?" Carlo poured another glass of wine and offered it.

"With that amazon of a brunette leading the pack."

She sipped, gestured with the glass and sipped again. “Everywhere we go, you’ve got half a dozen women nipping at your ankles, but do I say a word?”

“Well, you—”

“And once, just once, I have a problem with some creep with an overactive libido, and you assume I asked for it. I thought that kind of double standard was outdated even in Italy.”

Had he ever known a woman who could change his moods so quickly? Thinking it over, and finding it to his taste, Carlo studied his wine. “Juliet, did you come here to apologize, or demand that I do so?”

She scowled at him. “I don’t know why I came, but obviously it was a mistake.”

“Wait.” He held up a hand before she could storm out again. “Perhaps it would be wise if I simply accepted the apology you came in with.”

Juliet sent him a killing look. “You can take the apology I came in with and—”

“And offer you one of my own,” he finished. “Then we’ll be even.”

“I didn’t encourage him,” she murmured. And pouted. He’d never seen that sulky, utterly feminine look on her face before. It did several interesting things to his system.

“And I’m not looking for the same thing he was.” He came to her then, close enough to touch. “But very much more.”

“Maybe I know that,” she whispered, but took a step away. “Maybe I’d like to believe it. I don’t understand affairs, Carlo.” With a little laugh, she dragged her hand through her hair and turned away. “I should; my father had plenty of them. Discreet,” she added with a lingering taste of bitterness. “My mother could always turn a blind eye as long as they were discreet.”

He understood such things, had seen them among both friends and relatives, so he understood the scars and disillusionments that could be left. “Juliet, you’re not your mother.”

“No.” She turned back, head up. “No, I’ve worked long and hard to be certain I’m not. She’s a lovely, intelligent woman who gave up her career, her self-esteem, her independence to be no more than a glorified housekeeper because my father wanted it. He didn’t want a wife of his to work. A wife of his,” she repeated. “What a phrase. Her job was to take care of him. That meant having dinner on the table at six o’clock every night, and his shirts folded in his drawer. He—damn, he’s a good father, attentive, considerate. He simply doesn’t believe a man should shout at a woman or a girl. As a husband, he’d never forget a birthday, an anniversary. He’s always seen to it that she was provided for in the best material fashion, but he dictated my mother’s lifestyle. While he was about it, he enjoyed a very discreet string of women.”

“Why does your mother stay his wife?”

“I asked her that a few years ago, before I moved away to New York. She loves him.” Juliet stared into her wine. “That’s reason enough for her.”

“Would you rather she’d have left him?”

“I’d rather she’d have been what she could be. What she might’ve been.”

“The choice was hers, Juliet. Just as your life is yours.”

“I don’t want to ever be bound to anyone, *anyone* who could humiliate me that way.” She lifted her head again. "I won't put myself in my mother's position. Not for anyone."

"Do you see all relationships as being so imbalanced?"

With a shrug, she drank again. "I suppose I haven't seen so many of them."

For a moment he was silent. Carlo understood fidelity, the need for it, and the lack of it. "Perhaps we have something in common. I don't remember my father well, I saw him little. He, too, was unfaithful to my mother."

She looked over at him, but he didn't see any surprise in her face. It was as though she expected such things. "But he committed his adultery with the sea. For months he'd be gone, while she raised us, worked, waited. When he'd come home, she'd welcome him. Then he'd go again, unable to resist. When he died, she mourned. She loved him, and made her choice."

"It's not fair, is it?"

"No. Did you think love was?"

"It's not something I want."

He remembered once another woman, a friend, telling him the same thing when she was in turmoil. "We all want love, Juliet."

"No." She shook her head with the confidence born of desperation. "No, affection, respect, admiration, but not love. It steals something from you."

He looked at her as she stood in the path of the lamplight. "Perhaps it does," he murmured. "But until we love, we can't be sure we needed what was lost."

"Maybe it's easier for you to say that, to think that. You've had many lovers."

It should have amused him. Instead, it seemed to accent a void he hadn't been aware of. "Yes. But I've never been in love. I have a friend—" again he thought of Summer

"—once she told me love was a merry-go-round. Maybe she knew best."

Juliet pressed her lips together. "And an affair?"

Something in her voice had him looking over. For the second time he went to her, but slowly. "Perhaps it's just one ride on the carousel."

Because her fingers weren't steady, Juliet set down the glass. "We understand each other."

"In some ways."

"Carlo—" She hesitated, then admitted the decision had already been made before she crossed the hall. "Carlo, I've never taken much time for carousels, but I do want you."

How should he handle her? Odd, he'd never had to think things through so carefully before. With some women, he'd have been flamboyant, sweeping her up, carrying her off. With another he might have been impulsive, tumbling with her to the carpet. But nothing he'd ever done seemed as important as the first time with Juliet.

Words for a woman had always come easily to him. The right phrase, the right tone had always come as naturally as breathing. He could think of nothing. Even a murmur might spoil the simplicity of what she'd said to him and how she'd said it. So he didn't speak.

He kissed her where they stood, not with the raging passion he knew she could draw from him, not with the hesitation she sometimes made him feel. He kissed her with the truth and the knowledge that longtime lovers often experience. They came to each other with separate needs, separate attitudes, but with this, they locked out the past. Tonight was for the new, and for renewing.

She'd expected the words, the flash and style that seemed so much a part of him. Perhaps she'd even expected something of triumph. Again, he gave her the different and the fresh with no more than the touch of mouth to mouth.

The thought came to her, then was discounted, that he was no more certain of his ground than she. Then he held out his hand. Juliet put hers in it. Together they walked to the bedroom.

If he'd set the scene for a night of romance, Carlo would've added flowers with a touch of spice, music with the throb of passion. He'd have given her the warmth of candlelight and the fun of champagne. Tonight, with Juliet, there was only silence and moonlight. The maid had turned down the bed and left the drapes wide. White light filtered through shadows and onto white sheets.

Standing by the bed, he kissed her palms, one by one. They were cool and carried a hint of her scent. At her wrist her pulse throbbed. Slowly, watching her, he loosened the tie of her robe. With his eyes still on hers, he brought his hands to her shoulders and slipped the material aside. It fell silently to pool at her feet.

He didn't touch her, nor did he yet look at anything but her face. Through nerves, through needs, something like comfort began to move through her. Her lips curved, just slightly, as she reached for the tie of his robe and drew the knot. With her hands light and sure on his shoulders, she pushed the silk aside.

They were both vulnerable, to their needs, to each other. The light was thin and white and washed with shadows. No other illumination was needed this first time that they looked at each other.

He was lean but not thin. She was slender but soft. Her skin seemed only more pale when he touched her. Her hand seemed only more delicate when she touched him.

They came together slowly. There was no need to rush.

The mattress gave, the sheets rustled. Quietly. Side by side they lay, giving themselves time—all the time needed to discover what pleasures could come from the taste of mouth to mouth, the touch of flesh to flesh.

Should she have known it would be like this? So easy. Inevitable. Her skin was warm, so warm wherever he brushed it. His lips demanded, they took, but with such patience. He loved her gently, slowly, as though it were her first time. As she drifted deeper, Juliet thought dimly that perhaps it was.

Innocence. He felt it from her, not physical, but emotional. Somehow, incredibly, he discovered it was the same for himself. No matter how many had come before, for either of them, they came to each other now in innocence.

Her hands didn't hesitate as they moved over him, but stroked as though she were blind and could only gain her own picture through other senses. He smelled of a shower, water and soap, but he tasted richer, of wine. Then he spoke for the first time, only her name. It was to her more moving, more poetic than any endearment.

Her body moved with his, in rhythm, keeping pace. She seemed to know, somehow, where he would touch her just before she felt his fingers trace, his palms press. Then his lips began a long, luxurious journey she hoped would never end.

She was so small. Why had he never noticed before how small she was? It was easy to forget her strength, her control, her stamina. He could give her tenderness and wait for the passion.

The line of her neck was slender and so white in the moonlight. Her scent was trapped there, at her throat.

Intensified. Arousing. He could linger there while blood heated. His and hers.

He slid his tongue over the subtle curve of her breast to find the peak. When he drew it into his mouth, she moaned his name, giving them both a long, slow nudge to the edge.

But there was more to taste, more to touch. Passion, when heated, makes a mockery of control. Sounds slipped into the room—a catch of breath, a sigh, a moan—all pleasure. Their scents began to mix together—a lover's fragrance. In the moonlight, they were one form. The sheets were hot, twisted. When with tongue and fingertips he drove her over the first peak, Juliet gripped the tousled sheets as her body arched and shuddered with a torrent of sensations.

While she was still weak, still gasping, he slipped into her.

His head was spinning—a deliciously foreign sensation to him. He wanted to bury himself in her, but he wanted to see her. Her eyes were shut; her lips just parted as the breath hurried in and out. She moved with him, slowly, then faster, still faster until her fingers dug into his shoulders.

On a cry of pleasure, her eyes flew open. Looking into them, he saw the dark, astonished excitement he'd wanted to give her.

At last, giving in to the rushing need of his own body, he closed his mouth over hers and let himself go.

Chapter 8

Were there others who understood true passion? Wrapped in Carlo, absorbing and absorbed by Carlo, Juliet knew she hadn't until moments ago. Should it make you weak? She felt weak, but not empty.

Should she feel regret? Yes, logically she should. She'd given more of herself than she'd intended, shared more than she'd imagined, risked more than she should have dared. But she had no regrets. Perhaps later she'd make her list of the whys and why nots. For now, she wanted only to enjoy the soft afterglow of loving.

"You're quiet." His breath whispered across her temple, followed by his lips.

She smiled a little, content to let her eyes close. "So are you."

Nuzzling his cheek against her hair, he looked over to the slant of moonlight through the window. He wasn't sure which words to use. He'd never felt quite like this before with any woman. He'd never expected to. How could he tell her that and expect to be believed? He was having a hard time believing it himself. And yet… perhaps truth was the hardest thing to put into words.

"You feel very small when I hold you like this," he murmured. "It makes me want to hold you like this for a long, long time."

"I like having you hold me." The admission was much easier to make than she'd thought. With a little laugh, she turned her head so that she could see his face. "I like it very much."

"Then you won't object if I go on holding you for the next few hours."

She kissed his chin. "The next few minutes," she corrected. "I have to get back to my room."

"You don't like my bed?"

She stretched and cuddled and thought how wonderful it would be never to move from that one spot. "I think I'm crazy about it, but I've got a little work to do before I call it a night, then I have to be up by six-thirty, and—"

"You work too much." He cut her off, then leaned over her to pick up the phone. "You can get up in the morning just as easily from my bed as yours."

Finding she liked the way his body pressed into hers, she prepared to be convinced. "Maybe. What're you doing?"

"Shh. Yes, this is Franconi in 922. I'd like a wake-up call for six." He replaced the phone and rolled, pulling her on top of him. "There now, everything is taken care of. The phone will ring at dawn and wake us up."

"It certainly will." Juliet folded her hands over his chest and rested her chin on them. "But you told them to call at six. We don't have to get up until six-thirty."

"Yes." He slid his hands down low over her back. "So we have a half hour to—ah—wake up."

With a laugh, she pressed her lips to his shoulder. This once, she told herself, just this once, she'd let someone else do the planning. "Very practical. Do you think we might take a half hour or so to—ah—go to sleep?"

"My thoughts exactly."

When the phone did ring, Juliet merely groaned and slid down under the sheets. For the second time, she found herself buried under Carlo as he rolled over to answer it. Without complaint, she lay still, hoping the ringing of the phone had been part of a dream.

"Come now, Juliet." Shifting most of his weight from her, Carlo began to nibble on her shoulder. "You're playing mole."

She murmured in drowsy excitement as he slid his hand down to her hip. "Mole? I don't have a mole."

"Playing mole." She was so warm and soft and pliant. He'd known she would be. Mornings were made for lazy delights and waking her was a pleasure just begun.

Juliet stretched under the stroke and caress of his hands. Mornings were for a quick shower and a hasty cup of coffee. She'd never known they could be luxurious. "Playing mole?"

"An American expression." The skin over her rib cage was soft as butter. He thought there was no better time to taste it. "You pretend to be dead."

Because her mind was clouded with sleep, her system already churning with passion, it took a moment. "Possum."

"Prego?"

"Playing possum," she repeated and, guided by his hands, shifted. "A mole's different."

"So, they're both little animals."

She opened one eye. His hair was rumpled around his face, his chin darkened with a night's growth of beard. But when he smiled he looked as though he'd been awake for hours. He looked, she admitted, absolutely wonderful.

"You want an animal?" With a sudden burst of energy, she rolled on top of him. Her hands were quick, her mouth avid. In seconds, she'd taken his breath away.

She'd never been aggressive, but found the low, surprised moan and the fast pump of his heart to her liking. Her body reacted like lightning. She didn't mind that his hands weren't as gentle, as patient as they'd been the night before. This new desperation thrilled her.

He was Franconi, known for his wide range of expertise in the kitchen and the bedroom. But she was making him wild and helpless at the same time. With a laugh, she pressed her mouth to his, letting her tongue find all the dark, lavish tastes. When he tried to shift her, to take her because the need had grown too quickly to control, she evaded. His breathless curse whispered into her mouth.

He never lost finesse with a woman. Passion, his passion, had always been melded with style. Now, as she took her frenzied journey over him, he had no style, only needs. He'd never been a man to rush. When he cooked, he went slowly, step-by-step. Enjoy, experience, experiment. He made love the same way. Such things were meant to be savored, to be appreciated by each of the five senses.

It wasn't possible to savor when you were driven beyond the civilized. When your senses were whirling and tangled, it wasn't possible to separate them. Being driven was something new for him, something intoxicating. No, he wouldn't fight it, but pull her with him.

Rough and urgent, he grabbed her hips. Within moments, they were both beyond thought, beyond reason…

His breath was still unsteady, but he held her close and tight. Whatever she'd done, or was doing to him, he didn't want to lose it. The thought flickered briefly that he didn't want to lose her. Carlo pushed it aside. It was a dangerous thought. They had now. It was much wiser to concentrate on that.

"I have to go." Though she wanted nothing more than to curl up against him, Juliet made herself shift away. "We have to be downstairs at checkout in forty minutes."

"To meet Big Bill."

"That's right." Juliet reached onto the floor for her robe, slipping it onto her arms before she stood up. Carlo's lips trembled at the way she turned her back to him to tie it. It was rather endearing to see the unconscious modesty from a woman who'd just exploited every inch of his body. "You don't know how grateful I am that Bill volunteered to play chauffeur. The last thing I want to do is fight the freeway system in this town. I've had to do it before, and it's not a pretty sight."

"I could drive," he murmured, enjoying the way the rich green silk reached the top of her thighs.

"Staying alive is another reason I'm grateful for Bill. I'll call and have a bellman come up for the bags in—thirty-five minutes. Be sure—"

"You check everything because we won't be coming back," he finished. "Juliet, haven't I proven my competency yet?"

"Just a friendly reminder." She checked her watch before she remembered she wasn't wearing it. "The TV spot should be a breeze. Jacky Torrence hosts. It's a jovial sort of show that goes after the fast, funny story rather than nuts and bolts."

"Hmm." He rose, stretching. The publicist was back, he noted with a half smile, but as he reached down for his own robe, he noticed that she'd broken off. Lifting his head, he looked up at her.

Good God, he was beautiful. It was all she could think. Schedules, planning, points of information all went out of her head. In the early morning sun, his skin was more gold than brown, smooth and tight over his rib cage, nipped in at the waist to a narrow line of hip. Letting out a shaky breath, she took a step back.

"I'd better go," she managed. "We can run through today's schedule on the way to the studio."

It pleased him enormously to understand what had broken her concentration. He held the robe loosely in one hand as he took a step closer. "Perhaps we'll get bumped."

"Bite your tongue." Aiming for a light tone, she succeeded with a whisper. "That's an interesting robe."

The tone of her voice was a springboard to an arousal already begun. "You like the flamingos? My mother has a sense of humor." But he didn't put it on as he stepped closer.

"Carlo, stay right where you are. I mean it." She held up a hand as she walked backward to the doorway.

He grinned, and kept on grinning after he heard the click of the hallway door.

Between Juliet cracking the whip and Bill piloting, their Houston business went like clockwork. TV, radio and print, the media was responsive and energetic. The midafternoon autograph party turned out to be a party in the true sense of the word and was a smashing success. Juliet found herself a spot in a storeroom and ripped open the oversized envelope from her office that had been delivered to the hotel. Settling back, she began to go through the clippings her assistant had air expressed.

L.A. was excellent, as she'd expected. Upbeat and enthusiastic. San Diego might've tried for a little more depth, but they'd given him page one of the *Food* section in one spread and a below-the-fold in the *Style* section in another. No complaints. Portland and Seattle listed a recipe apiece and raved shamelessly. Juliet could've rubbed her hands together with glee if she hadn't been drinking coffee. Then she hit Denver.

Coffee sloshed out of the cup and onto her hand.

"Damn!" Fumbling in her briefcase, she found three crumpled tissues and began to mop up. A gossip column. Who'd have thought it? She gave herself a moment to think then relaxed. Publicity was publicity, after all. And the truth of the matter was, Franconi was gossip. Looking at it logically, the more times his name was in print, the more successful the tour. Resolved, Juliet began to read.

She nodded absently as she skimmed the first paragraph. Chatty, shallow, but certainly not offensive. A lot of people who might not glance at the food or cooking sections would give the gossip columns a working over. All in all, it was probably an excellent break. Then she read the second paragraph.

Juliet was up out of her folding chair. This time the coffee that dripped onto the floor went unnoticed. Her expression changed from surprised astonishment to fury in a matter of seconds. In the same amount of time, she stuffed the clippings back into their envelope. It wasn't easy, but she gave herself five minutes for control before she walked back into the main store.

The schedule called for another fifteen minutes, but Carlo had more than twenty people in line, and that many again just milling around. Fifteen minutes would have to be stretched to thirty. Grinding her teeth, Juliet stalked over to Bill.

"There you are." Friendly as always, he threw his arm over her shoulder and squeezed. "Going great guns out here. Old Carlo knows how to twinkle to the ladies without setting the men off. Damn clever sonofabitch."

"I couldn't have said it better myself." Her knuckles were white on the strap of her briefcase. "Bill, is there a phone I can use? I have to call the office."

"No problem at all. Y'all just come on back with me." He led her through Psychology, into Westerns and around Romances to a door marked Private. "You just help yourself," he invited and showed her into a room with a cluttered metal desk, a goosenecked lamp and stacks upon stacks of books. Juliet headed straight for the phone.

"Thanks, Bill." She didn't even wait until the door closed before she started dialing. "Deborah Mortimor, please," she said to the answering switchboard. Tapping her foot, Juliet waited.

"Ms. Mortimor."

"Deb, it's Juliet."

"Hi. I've been waiting for you to call in. Looks like we've got a strong nibble with the *Times* when you come back to New York. I just—"

"Later." Juliet reached into her briefcase for a roll of antacids. "I got the clippings today."

"Great, aren't they?"

"Oh sure. They're just dandy."

"Uh-huh." Deb waited only a beat. "It's the little number in Denver, isn't it?"

She gave the rolling chair a quick kick. "Of course it is."

"Sit down, Juliet." Deb didn't have to see to know her boss was pacing.

"Sit down? I'm tempted to fly back to Denver and ring Chatty Cathy's neck."

"Killing columnists isn't good for PR, Juliet."

"It was garbage."

"No, no, it wasn't that bad. Trash maybe, but not garbage."

She struggled for control and managed to get a very slippery rein on her temper. Popping the first antacid into her mouth, she crunched down. "Don't be cute, Deb. I didn't like the insinuations about Carlo and me. *Carlo Franconi's lovely American traveling companion,*" she quoted between her teeth. "Traveling companion. It makes me sound as though I'm just along for the ride. And then—"

"I read it," Deb interrupted. "So did Hal," she added, referring to the head of publicity.

Juliet closed her eyes a moment. "And?"

"Well, he went through about six different reactions. In the end, he decided a few comments like that were bound to come up and only added to Franconi's—well, mystique might be the best term."

"I see." Her jaw clenched, her fingers tight around the little roll of stomach pills. "That's fine then, isn't it? I'm just thrilled to add to a client's mystique."

"Now, Juliet—"

"Look, just tell dear old Hal that Houston went perfectly." She was definitely going to need two pills. Juliet popped another out of the roll with her thumb. "I don't even want you to mention to him that I called about this—this tripe in Denver."

"Whatever you say."

Taking a pen, she sat down and made space on the desk. "Now, give me what you have with the *Times*."

A half hour later, Juliet was just finishing up her last call when Carlo poked his head in the office. Seeing she was on the phone, he rolled his eyes, closed the door and leaned against it. His brow lifted when he spotted the half-eaten roll of antacids.

"Yes, thank you, Ed, Mr. Franconi will bring all the necessary ingredients and be in the studio at 8:00. Yes." She laughed, though her foot was tapping out a rhythm on the floor. "It's absolutely delicious. Guaranteed. See you in two days."

When she hung up the receiver, Carlo stepped forward. "You didn't come to save me."

She gave him a long, slow look. "You seemed to be handling the situation without me."

He knew the tone, and the expression. Now all he had to do was find the reason for them. Strolling over, he picked up the roll of pills. "You're much too young to need these."

"I've never heard that ulcers had an age barrier."

His brows drew together as he sat on the edge of the desk. "Juliet, if I believed you had an ulcer, I'd pack you off to my home in Rome and keep you in bed on bland foods for the next month. Now..." He slipped the roll into his pocket. "What problem is there?"

"Several," she said briskly as she began to gather up her notes. "But they're fairly well smoothed out now. We'll need to go shopping again in Chicago for that chicken dish you'd planned to cook. So, if you've finished up here, we can just—"

"No." He put a hand on her shoulder and held her in the chair. "We're not finished. Shopping for chicken in Chicago isn't what had you reaching for pills. What?"

The best defense was always ice. Her voice chilled. "Carlo, I've been very busy."

"You think after two weeks I don't know you?" Impatient, he gave her a little shake. "You dig in that briefcase for your aspirin or your little mints only when you feel too much pressure. I don't like to see it."

"It comes with the territory." She tried to shrug off his hand and failed. "Carlo, we've got to get to the airport."

"We have more than enough time. Tell me what's wrong."

"All right then." In two sharp moves, she pulled the clipping out of her case and pushed it into his hands.

"What's this?" He skimmed it first without really reading it. "One of those little columns about who is seen with whom and what they wear while they're seen?"

"More or less."

"Ah." As he began to read from the top, he nodded. "And you were seen with me."

Closing her notebook, she slipped it neatly into her briefcase. Twice she reminded herself that losing her temper would accomplish nothing. "As your publicist, that could hardly be avoided."

Because he'd come to expect logic from her, he only nodded again. "But you feel this intimates something else."

"It *says* something else," she tossed back. "Something that isn't true."

"It calls you my traveling companion." He glanced up, knowing that wouldn't sit well with her. "It's perhaps not the full story, but not untrue. Does it upset you to be known as my companion?"

She didn't want him to be reasonable. She had no intention of emulating him. "When companion takes on this shade of meaning, it isn't professional or innocent. I'm not here to have my name linked with you this way, Carlo."

"In what way, Juliet?"

"It gives my name and goes on to say that I'm never out of arm's length, that I guard you as though you were my own personal property. And that you—"

"That I kiss your hand in public restaurants as though I couldn't wait for privacy," Carlo read at a glance. "So? What difference does it make what it says here?"

She dragged both hands through her hair. "Carlo, I'm here, with you, to do a job. This clipping came through my office, through my supervisor. Don't you know something like this could ruin my credibility?"

"No," he said simply enough. "This is no more than gossip. Your supervisor, he's upset by this?"

She laughed, but it had little to do with humor. "No, actually, it seems he's decided it's just fine. Good for your image."

"Well, then?"

"I don't want to be good for your image," she threw back with such passion, it shocked both of them. "I won't be one of the dozens of names and faces linked with you."

"So," he murmured. "Now, we push away to the truth. You're angry with me, for this." He set the clipping down. "You're angry because there's more truth in it now than there was when it was written."

"I don't want to be on anyone's list, Carlo." Her voice had lowered, calmed. She dug balled fists into the pockets of her skirt. “Not yours, not anyone’s. I haven’t come this far in my life to let that happen now.”

He stood, wondering if she understood how insulting her words were. No, she’d see them as facts, not as darts. “I haven’t put you on a list. If you have one in your own mind, it has nothing to do with me.”

“A few weeks ago it was the French actress, a month before that a widowed countess.”

He didn’t shout, but it was only force of will that kept his voice even. “I never pretended you were the first woman in my bed. I never expected I was the first man in yours.”

“That’s entirely different.”

“Ah, now you find the double standard convenient.” He picked up the clipping, balled it in his fist then dropped it into the wastebasket. “I’ve no patience for this, Juliet.”

He was to the door again before she spoke. “Carlo, wait.” With a polite veneer stretched thinly over fury he turned. “Damn.” Hands still in her pockets, she paced from one stack of books to the other. “I never intended to take this out on you. It’s totally out of line and I’m sorry, really. You might guess I’m not thinking very clearly right now.”

“So it would seem.”

Juliet let out a sigh, knowing she observed the cutting edge of his voice. “I don’t know how to explain, except to say that my career’s very important to me.”

“I understand that.”

“But it’s no more important to me than my privacy. I don’t want my personal life discussed around the office water cooler.”

“People talk, Juliet. It’s natural and it’s meaningless.”

“I can’t brush it off the way you do.” She picked up

her briefcase by the strap then set it down again. "I'm used to staying in the background. I set things up, handle the details, do the legwork, and someone else's picture gets in the paper. That's the way I want it."

"You don't always get what you want." With his thumbs hooked in his pockets, he leaned back against the door and watched her. "Your anger goes deeper than a few lines in a paper people will have forgotten tomorrow."

She closed her eyes a moment, then turned back to him. "All right, yes, but it's not a matter of being angry. Carlo, I've put myself in a delicate position with you."

Carefully, he weighed the phrase, tested it, judged it. "Delicate position?"

"Please, don't misunderstand. I'm here, with you, because of my job. It's very important to me that that's handled in the best, the most professional manner I can manage. What's happened between us…"

"What has happened between us?" he prompted when she trailed off.

"Don't make it difficult."

"All right, we'll make it easy. We're lovers."

She let out a long, unsteady breath, wondering if he really believed that was easy. For him it might be just another stroll through the moonlight. For her, it was a race through a hurricane. "I want to keep that aspect of our relationship completely separate from the professional area."

It surprised him he could find such a statement endearing. Perhaps the fact that she was half romanticist and half businesswoman was part of her appeal to him. "Juliet, my love, you sound as though you're negotiating a contract."

"Maybe I do." Nerves were beginning to run through her too quickly again. "Maybe I am, in a way."

His own anger had disappeared. Her eyes weren't nearly as certain as her voice. Her hands, he noted, were twisting together. Slowly, he walked toward her, pleased that though she didn't back away, the wariness was back. "Juliet…" He lifted a hand to brush through her hair. "You can negotiate terms and times, but not emotion."

"You can—regulate it."

He took both her hands, kissing them. "No."

"Carlo, please—"

"You like me to touch you," he murmured. "Whether we stand here alone, or we stand in a group of strangers. If I touch your hand, like this, you know what's in my mind. It's not always passion. There are times, I see you, I touch you, and I think only of being with you—talking, or sitting silently. Will you negotiate now how I am to touch your hand, how many times a day it's permitted?"

"Don't make me sound like a fool."

His fingers tightened on hers. "Don't make what I feel for you sound foolish."

"I—" No, she couldn't touch that. She didn't dare. "Carlo, I just want to keep things simple."

"Impossible."

"No, it's not."

"Then tell me, is this simple?" With just his fingertips on her shoulder, he leaned down to kiss her. So softly, so lightly, it was hardly a kiss at all. She felt her legs dissolve from the knees down.

"Carlo, we're not staying on the point."

He slipped his arms around her. "I like this point much better. When we get to Chicago…" His fingers slipped up and down her spine as he began to brush his lips over her face. "I want to spend the evening alone with you."

"We—have an appointment for drinks at ten with—"

"Cancel it."

"Carlo, you know I can't."

"Very well." He caught the lobe of her ear between his teeth. "I'll plead fatigue and make certain we have a very quick, very early evening. Then, I'll spend the rest of the night doing little things, like this."

His tongue darted inside her ear, then retreated to the vulnerable spot just below. The shudder that went through her was enough to arouse both of them. "Carlo, you don't understand."

"I understand that I want you." In a swift mood swing, he had her by the shoulders. "If I told you now that I want you more than I've wanted any other woman, you wouldn't believe me."

She backed away from that, but was caught close again. "No, I wouldn't. It isn't necessary to say so."

"You're afraid to hear it, afraid to believe it. You won't get simple with me, Juliet. But you'll get a lover you'll never forget."

She steadied a bit, meeting his look levelly. "I've already resigned myself to that, Carlo. I don't apologize to myself, and I don't pretend to have any regrets about coming to you last night."

"Then resign yourself to this." The temper was back in his eyes, hot and volatile. "I don't care what's written in the paper, what's whispered about in offices in New York. You, this moment, are all I care about."

Something shattered quietly inside her. A defense built instinctively through years. She knew she shouldn't take him literally. He was Franconi after all. If he cared about her, it was only in his way, and in his time. But something had shattered, and she couldn't rebuild it so quickly. Instead, she chose to be blunt.

"Carlo, I don't know how to handle you. I haven't the experience."

"Then don't handle me." Again, he took her by the shoulders. "Trust me."

She put her hands on his, held them a moment, then drew them away. "It's too soon, and too much."

There were times, in his work, where he had to be very, very patient. As a man, it happened much more rarely. Yet he knew if he pushed now, as for some inexplicable reason he wanted to, he'd only create more distance between them. "Then, for now, we just enjoy each other."

That's what she wanted. Juliet told herself that was exactly what she wanted—no more, no less. But she felt like weeping.

"We'll enjoy each other," she agreed. Letting out a sigh, she framed his face with her hands as he so often did with her. "Very much."

He wondered, when he lowered his brow to hers, why it didn't quite satisfy.

Chapter 9

Burned out from traveling, ready for a drink and elevated feet, Juliet walked up to the front desk of their Chicago hotel. Taking a quick glimpse around the lobby, she was pleased with the marble floors, sculpture and elegant potted palms. Such places usually lent themselves to big, stylish bathrooms. She intended to spend her first hour in Chicago with everything from the neck down submerged.

"May I help you?"

"You have a reservation for Franconi and Trent."

With a few punches on the keyboard, the clerk brought up their reservations on the screen. "You'll both be staying for two nights, Miss Trent?"

"Yes, that's right."

"It's direct bill. Everything's set. If you and Mr. Franconi will just fill out these forms, I'll ring for a bellman."

As he scrawled the information on the form, Carlo

glanced over. From the profile, she looked lovely, though perhaps a bit tired. Her hair was pinned up in the back, fluffed out on the sides and barely mussed from traveling. She looked as though she could head a three-hour business meeting without a whimper. But then she arched her back, closing her eyes briefly as she stretched her shoulders. He wanted to take care of her.

"Juliet, there's no need for two rooms."

She shifted her shoulder bag and signed her name. "Carlo, don't start. Arrangements have already been made."

"But it's absurd. You'll be staying in my suite, so the extra room is simply extra."

The desk clerk stood at a discreet distance and listened to every word.

Juliet pulled her credit card out of her wallet and set it down on the counter with a snap. Carlo noted, with some amusement, that she no longer looked the least bit tired. He wanted to make love with her for hours.

"You'll need the imprint on this for my incidentals," she told the clerk calmly enough. "All Mr. Franconi's charges will be picked up."

Carlo pushed his form toward the clerk then leaned on the counter. "Juliet, won't you feel foolish running back and forth across the hall? It's ridiculous, even for a publisher, to pay for a bed that won't be slept in."

With her jaw clenched, she picked up her credit card again. "I'll tell you what's ridiculous," she said under her breath. "It's ridiculous for you to be standing here deliberately embarrassing me."

"You have rooms 1102 and 1108." The clerk pushed the keys toward them. "I'm afraid they're just down the hall from each other rather than across."

"That's fine." Juliet turned to find the bellman had their luggage packed on the cart and his ears open. Without a word, she strode toward the bank of elevators.

Strolling along beside her, Carlo noted that the cashier had a stunning smile. "Juliet, I find it odd that you'd be embarrassed over something so simple."

"I don't think it's simple." She jabbed the up button on the elevator.

"Forgive me." Carlo put his tongue in his cheek. "It's only that I recall you specifically saying you wanted our relationship to be simple."

"Don't tell me what I said. What I said has nothing to do with what I meant."

"Of course not," he murmured and waited for her to step inside the car.

Seeing the look on Juliet's face, the bellman began to worry about his tip. He put on a hospitality-plus smile. "So, you in Chicago long?"

"Two days," Carlo said genially enough.

"You can see a lot in a couple of days. You'll want to get down to the lake—"

"We're here on business," Juliet interrupted. "Only business."

"Yes, ma'am." With a smile, the bellman pushed his cart into the hall. "1108's the first stop."

"That's mine." Juliet dug out her wallet again and pulled out bills as the bellman unlocked her door. "Those two bags," she pointed out then turned to Carlo. "We'll meet Dave Lockwell in the bar for drinks at 10:00. You can do as you like until then."

"I have some ideas on that," he began but Juliet moved past him. After stuffing the bills in the bellman's hand, she shut the door with a quick click.

* * *

Thirty minutes, to Carlo's thinking, was long enough for anyone to cool down. Juliet's stiff-backed attitude toward their room situation had caused him more exasperation than annoyance. But then, he expected to be exasperated by women. On one hand, he found her reaction rather sweet and naive. Did she really think the fact that they were lovers would make the desk clerk or a bellman blink twice?

The fact that she did, and probably always would, was just another aspect of her nature that appealed to him. In whatever she did, Juliet Trent would always remain proper. Simmering passion beneath a tidy, clean-lined business suit. Carlo found her irresistible.

He'd known so many kinds of women—the bright young ingenue greedy to her fingertips, the wealthy aristocrat bored both by wealth and tradition, the successful career woman who both looked for and was wary of marriage. He'd known so many—the happy, the secure, the desperate and seeking, the fulfilled and the grasping. Juliet Trent with the cool green eyes and quiet voice left him uncertain as to what pigeonhole she'd fit into. It seemed she had all and none of the feminine qualities he understood. The only thing he was certain of was that he wanted her to fit, somehow, into his life.

The best way, the only way, he knew to accomplish that was to distract her with charm until she was already caught. After that, they'd negotiate the next step.

Carlo lifted the rose he'd had sent up from the hotel florist out of its bud vase, sniffed its petals once, then walked down the hall to Juliet's room.

She was just drying off from a hot, steamy bath. If she'd heard the knock five minutes before, she'd have growled. As it was, she pulled on her robe and went to answer.

She'd been expecting him. Juliet wasn't foolish enough to believe a man like Carlo would take a door in the face as final. It had given her satisfaction to close it, just as it gave her satisfaction to open it again. When she was ready.

She hadn't been expecting the rose. Though she knew it wasn't wise to be moved by a single long-stemmed flower with a bud the color of sunshine, she was moved nonetheless. Her plans to have a calm, serious discussion with him faltered.

"You look rested." Rather than giving her the rose, he took her hand. Before she could decide whether or not to let him in, he was there.

A stand, Juliet reminded herself even as she closed the door behind him. If she didn't take a stand now, she'd never find her footing. "Since you're here, we'll talk. We have an hour."

"Of course." As was his habit, he took a survey of her room. Her suitcase sat on a stand, still packed, but with its top thrown open. It wasn't practical to unpack and repack when you were bouncing around from city to city. Though they were starting their third week on the road, the contents of the case were still neat and organized. He'd have expected no less from her. Her notebook and two pens were already beside the phone. The only things remotely out of place in the tidy, impersonal room were the Italian heels that sat in the middle of the rug where she'd stepped out of them. The inconsistency suited her perfectly.

"I can discuss things better," she began, "if you weren't wandering around."

"Yes?" All cooperation, Carlo sat and waved the rose

under his nose. "You want to talk about our schedule here in Chicago?"

"No—yes." She had at least a dozen things to go over with him. For once she let business take a back seat. "Later." Deciding to take any advantage, Juliet remained standing. "First, I want to talk about that business down at the desk."

"Ah." The sound was distinctly European and as friendly as a smile. She could have murdered him.

"It was totally uncalled for."

"Was it?" He'd learned that strategy was best plotted with friendly questions or simple agreement. That way, you could swing the final result to your own ends without too much blood being shed.

"Of course it was." Forgetting her own strategy, Juliet dropped down on the edge of the bed. "Carlo, you had no right discussing our personal business in public."

"You're quite right."

"I—" His calm agreement threw her off. The firm, moderately angry speech she'd prepared in the tub went out the window.

"I must apologize," he continued before she could balance herself. "It was thoughtless of me."

"Well, no." As he'd planned, she came to his defense. "It wasn't thoughtless, just inappropriate."

With the rose, he waved her defense away. "You're too kind, Juliet. You see, I was thinking only of how practical you are. It's one of the things I most admire about you." In getting his way, Carlo had always felt it best to use as much truth as possible. "You see, besides my own family, I've known very few truly practical women. This trait in you appeals to me, as much as the color of your eyes, the texture of your skin."

Because she sensed she was losing ground, Juliet sat

up straighter. "You don't have to flatter me, Carlo. It's simply a matter of establishing ground rules."

"You see." As if she'd made his point, he sat forward to touch her fingertips. "You're too practical to expect flattery or to be swayed by it. Is it any wonder I'm enchanted by you?"

"Carlo—"

"I haven't made my point." He retreated just enough to keep his attack in full gear. "You see, knowing you, I thought you would agree that it was foolish and impractical to book separate rooms when we want to be together. You do want to be with me, don't you, Juliet?"

Frustrated, she stared at him. He was turning the entire situation around. Certain of it, Juliet groped for a handhold. "Carlo, it has nothing to do with my wanting to be with you."

His brow lifted. "No?"

"No. It has to do with the line that separates our business and our personal lives."

"A line that's difficult to draw. Perhaps impossible for me." The truth came out again, though this time unplanned. "I want to be with you, Juliet, every moment we have. I find myself resenting even the hour that you're here and I'm there. A few hours at night isn't enough for me. I want more, much more for us."

Saying it left him stunned. It hadn't been one of his clever moves, one of his easy catch-phrases. That little jewel had come from somewhere inside where it had quietly hidden until it could take him by surprise.

He rose, and to give himself a moment, stood by the window to watch a stream of Chicago traffic. It rushed, then came to fitful stops, wound and swung then sped on again. Life was like this, he realized. You could speed right along but you never knew when something was going to stop you dead in your tracks.

Juliet was silent behind him, torn between what he'd said, what he'd meant and what she felt about it. From the very beginning, she'd kept Carlo's definition of an affair in the front of her mind. Just one ride on the carousel. When the music stopped, you got off and knew you'd gotten your money's worth. Now, with a few words he was changing the scope. She wondered if either of them was ready.

"Carlo, since you say I am, I'll be practical." Drawing together her resources, she rose. "We have a week left on tour. During that time, we've got Chicago and four other cities to deal with. To be honest, I'd rather if our only business right now was with each other."

He turned, and though she thought the smile was a bit odd, at least he smiled. "That's the nicest thing you've said to me in all these days and all these cities, Juliet."

She took a step toward him. It seemed foolish to think about risks when they had such little time. "Being with you isn't something I'll ever forget, no matter how much I might want to in years to come."

"Juliet—"

"No, wait. I want to be with you, and part of me hates the time we lose with other people, in separate rooms, in all the demands that brought us to each other in the first place. But another part of me knows that all of those things are completely necessary. Those things will still be around after we're each back in our separate places."

No, don't think about that now, she warned herself. If she did, her voice wouldn't be steady.

"No matter how much time I spend with you in your suite, I need a room of my own if for no other reason than to know it's there. Maybe that's the practical side of me, Carlo."

Or the vulnerable one, he mused. But hadn't he just discovered he had a vulnerability of his own? Her name was Juliet. "So, it will be as you want in this." And for the best perhaps. He might just need a bit of time to himself to think things through.

"No arguing?"

"Do we argue ever, *cara?*"

Her lips curved. "Never." Giving in to herself as much as him, she stepped forward and linked her arms around his neck. "Did I ever tell you that when I first started setting up this tour I looked at your publicity shot and thought you were gorgeous?"

"No." He brushed his lips over hers. "Why don't you tell me now?"

"And sexy," she murmured as she drew him closer to the bed. "Very, very sexy."

"Is that so?" He allowed himself to be persuaded onto the bed. "So you decided in your office in New York that we'd be lovers?"

"I decided in my office in New York that we'd never be lovers." Slowly, she began to unbutton his shirt. "I decided that the last thing I wanted was to be romanced and seduced by some gorgeous, sexy Italian chef who had a string of women longer than a trail of his own pasta, but—"

"Yes." He nuzzled at her neck. "I think I'll prefer the 'but.'"

"But it seems to me that you can't make definitive decisions without all the facts being in."

"Have I ever told you that your practicality arouses me to the point of madness?"

She sighed as he slipped undone the knot in her robe.

"Have I ever told you that I'm a sucker for a man who brings me flowers?"

"Flowers." He lifted his head then picked up the rosebud he'd dropped on the pillow beside them. "Darling, did you want one, too?"

With a laugh, she pulled him back to her.

Juliet decided she'd seen more of Chicago in the flight into O'Hare than during the day and a half she'd been there. Cab drives from hotel to television station, from television station to department store, from department store to bookstore and back to the hotel again weren't exactly leisurely sight-seeing tours. Then and there she decided that when she took her vacation at the end of the month, she'd go somewhere steamy with sun and do nothing more energetic than laze by a pool from dawn to dusk.

The only hour remotely resembling fun was another shopping expedition where she watched Carlo select a plump three-pound chicken for his cacciatore.

He was to prepare his *pollastro alla cacciatora* from simmer to serve during a live broadcast of one of the country's top-rated morning shows. Next to the *Simpson Show* in L.A., Juliet considered this her biggest coup for the tour. *Let's Discuss It* was the hottest hour on daytime TV, and remained both popular and controversial after five consecutive seasons.

Despite the fact that she knew Carlo's showmanship abilities, Juliet was nervous as a cat. The show would air live in New York. She had no doubt that everyone in her department would be watching. If Carlo was a smash, it would be his triumph. If he bombed, the bomb was all hers. Such was the rationale in public relations.

It never occurred to Carlo to be nervous. He could

make cacciatore in the dark, from memory with the use of only one hand. After watching Juliet pace the little green room for the fifth time, he shook his head. “Relax, my love, it’s only chicken.”

“Don’t forget to bring up the dates we’ll be in the rest of the cities. This show reaches all of them.”

“You’ve already told me.”

“And the title of the book.”

“I won’t forget.”

“You should remember to mention you prepared this dish for the President when he visited Rome last year.”

“I’ll try to keep it in mind. Juliet, wouldn’t you like some coffee?”

She shook her head and kept pacing. What else?

“I could use some,” he decided on the spot.

She glanced toward the pot on a hot plate. “Help yourself.”

He knew if she had something to do, she’d stop worrying, even for a few moments. And she’d stop pacing up and down in front of him. “Juliet, no one with a heart would ask a man to drink that poison that’s been simmering since dawn.”

“Oh.” Without hesitation, she assumed the role of pamperer. “I’ll see about it.”

“Grazie.”

At the door, she hesitated. “The reporter for the *Sun* might drop back before the show.”

“Yes, you told me. I’ll be charming.”

Muttering to herself, she went to find a page.

Carlo leaned back and stretched his legs. He’d have to drink the coffee when she brought it back, though he didn’t want any. He didn’t want to board the plane for Detroit that afternoon, but such things were inevitable.

In any case, he and Juliet would have the evening free in Detroit—what American state was that in?

They wouldn't be there long enough to worry about it.

In any case, he would soon be in Philadelphia and there, see Summer. He needed to. Though he'd always had friends and was close to many of them, he'd never needed one as he felt he needed one now. He could talk to Summer and know what he said would be listened to carefully and not be repeated. Gossip had never bothered him in the past, but when it came to Juliet… When it came to Juliet, nothing was as it had been in the past.

None of his previous relationships with women had ever become a habit. Waking up in the morning beside a woman had always been pleasant, but never necessary. Every day, Juliet was changing that. He couldn't imagine his bedroom back in Rome without her, yet she'd never been there. He'd long since stopped imagining other women in his bed.

Rising, he began to pace as Juliet had.

When the door opened, he turned, expecting her. The tall, willowy blonde who entered wasn't Juliet, but she was familiar.

"Carlo! How wonderful to see you again."

"Lydia." He smiled, cursing himself for not putting the name of the *Sun*'s reporter with the face of the woman he'd spent two interesting days in Chicago with only eighteen months before. "You look lovely."

Of course she did. Lydia Dickerson refused to look anything less. She was sharp, sexy and uninhibited. She was also, in his memory, an excellent cook and critic of gourmet foods.

"Carlo, I was just thrilled when I heard you were coming into town. We'll do the interview after the show, but I just had to drop back and see you." She swirled toward him with the scent of spring lilacs and the swish of a wide-flared skirt. "You don't mind?"

"Of course not." Smiling, he took her outstretched hand. "It's always good to see an old friend."

With a laugh, she put her hands on his shoulders. "I should be angry with you, *caro.* You do have my number, and my phone didn't ring last night."

"Ah." He put his hands to her wrists, wondering just how to untangle himself. "You'll have to forgive us, Lydia. The schedule is brutal. And there's a…complication." He winced, thinking how Juliet would take being labeled a complication.

"Carlo." She edged closer. "You can't tell me you haven't got a few free hours for…an old friend. I've a tremendous recipe for *vitèllo tonnato.*" She murmured the words and made the dish sound like something to be eaten in the moonlight. "Who else should I cook it for but the best chef in Italy?"

"I'm honored." He put his hands on her hips hoping to draw her away with the least amount of insult. It wouldn't occur to him until later that he'd felt none, absolutely none, of the casual desire he should have. "I haven't forgotten what a superb cook you are, Lydia."

Her laugh was low and full of memories. "I hope you haven't forgotten more than that."

"No." He let out a breath and opted to be blunt. "But you see I'm—"

Before he could finish being honest, the door opened again. With a cup of coffee in her hand, Juliet walked in, then came to a dead stop. She looked at the blonde wound around Carlo like an exotic vine. Her brow lifted as she took her gaze to Carlo's face. If only she had a camera.

Her voice was as cool and dry as her eyes. "I see you've met."

"Juliet, I—"

"I'll give you a few moments for the…pre-interview," she said blandly. "Try to wrap it up by eight-fifty, Carlo. You'll want to check the kitchen set." Without another word, she shut the door behind her.

Though her arms were still around Carlo's neck, Lydia looked toward the closed door. "Oops," she said lightly.

Carlo let out a long breath as they separated. "You couldn't have put it better."

At nine o'clock, Juliet had a comfortable seat midway back in the audience. When Lydia slipped into the seat beside her, she gave the reporter an easy nod, then looked back to the set. As far as she could tell, and she'd gone over every inch of it, it was perfect.

When Carlo was introduced to cheerful applause she began to relax, just a little. But when he began preparations on the chicken, moving like a surgeon and talking to his host, his studio and television audience like a seasoned performer, her relaxation was complete. He was going to be fantastic.

"He's really something, isn't he?" Lydia murmured during the first break.

"Something," Juliet agreed.

"Carlo and I met the last time he was in Chicago."

"Yes, I gathered. I'm glad you could make it by this morning. You did get the press kit I sent in?"

She's a cool one, Lydia thought and shifted in her seat. "Yes. The feature should be out by the end of the week. I'll send you a clipping."

"I'd appreciate it."

"Miss Trent—"

"Juliet, please." For the first time, Juliet turned and smiled at her fully. "No need for formality."

"All right, Juliet, I feel like a fool."

"I'm sorry. You shouldn't."

"I'm very fond of Carlo, but I don't poach."

"Lydia, I'm sure there isn't a woman alive who wouldn't be fond of Carlo." She crossed her legs as the countdown for taping began again. "If I thought you'd even consider poaching, you wouldn't be able to pick up your pencil."

Lydia sat still for a moment, then leaned back with a laugh. Carlo had picked himself quite a handful. Served him right. "Is it all right to wish you luck?"

Juliet shot her another smile. "I'd appreciate it."

The two women might've come to amicable terms, but it wasn't easy for Carlo to concentrate on his job while they sat cozily together in the audience. His experience with Lydia had been a quick and energetic two days. He knew little more of her than her preference for peanut oil for cooking and blue bed linen. He understood how easy it was for a man to be executed without trial. He thought he could almost feel the prickle of the noose around his throat.

But he was innocent. Carlo poured the mixture of tomatoes, sauce and spices over the browned chicken and set the cover. If he had to bind and gag her, Juliet would listen to him.

He cooked his dish with the finesse of an artist completing a royal portrait. He performed for the audience like a veteran thespian. He thought the dark thoughts of a man already at the dock.

When the show was over, he spent a few obligatory moments with his host, then left the crew to devour one of his best cacciatores.

But when he went back to the green room, Juliet was nowhere in sight. Lydia was waiting. He had no choice but to deal with her, and the interview, first.

She didn't make it easy for him. But then, to his knowledge, women seldom did. Lydia chatted away as though nothing had happened. She asked her questions, noted down his answers, all the while with mischief gleaming in her eyes. At length, he'd had enough.

"All right, Lydia, what did you say to her?"

"To whom?" All innocence, Lydia blinked at him. "Oh, your publicist. A lovely woman. But then I'd hardly be one to fault your taste, darling."

He rose, swore and wondered what a desperate man should do with his hands. "Lydia, we had a few enjoyable hours together. No more."

"I know." Something in her tone made him pause and glance back. "I don't imagine either of us could count the number of few enjoyable hours we've had." With a shrug, she rose. Perhaps she understood him, even envied what she thought she'd read in his eyes, but it wasn't any reason to let him off the hook. "Your Juliet and I just chatted, darling." She dropped her pad and pencil in her bag. "Girl talk, you know. Just girl talk. Thanks for the interview, Carlo." At the door, she paused and turned back. "If you're ever back in town without a…complication, give me a ring. *Ciao*."

When she left he considered breaking something. Before he could decide what would be the most satisfying and destructive, Juliet bustled in. "Let's get moving, Carlo. The cab's waiting. It looks like we'll have enough time to get back to the hotel, check out and catch the earlier plane."

"I want to speak with you."

"Yes, fine. We'll talk in the cab." Because she was

already heading down the winding corridor he had no choice but to follow.

"When you told me the name of the reporter, I simply didn't put it together."

"Put what together?" Juliet pulled open the heavy metal door and stepped out on the back lot. If it had been much hotter, she noted, Carlo could've browned his chicken on the asphalt. "Oh, that you'd known her. Well, it's so hard to remember everyone we've met, isn't it?" She slipped into the cab and gave the driver the name of the hotel.

"We've come halfway across the country." Annoyed, he climbed in beside her. "Things begin to blur."

"They certainly do." Sympathetic, she patted his hand. "Detroit and Boston'll be down and dirty. You'll be lucky to remember your own name." She pulled out her compact to give her makeup a quick check. "But then I can help out in Philadelphia. You've already told me you have a…friend there."

"Summer's different." He took the compact from her. "I've known her for years. We were students together. We never— Friends, we're only friends," he ended on a mutter. "I don't enjoy explaining myself."

"I can see that." She pulled out bills and calculated the tip as the cab drew up to the hotel. As she started to slide out, she gave Carlo a long look. "No one asked you to."

"Ridiculous." He had her by the arm before she'd reached the revolving doors. "You ask. It isn't necessary to ask with words to ask."

"Guilt makes you imagine all sorts of things." She swung through the doors and into the lobby.

"Guilt?" Incensed, he caught up with her at the elevators. "I've nothing to be guilty for. A man has to commit some crime, some sin, for guilt."

She listened calmly as she stepped into the elevator car and pushed the button for their floor. "That's true, Carlo. You seem to me to be a man bent on making a confession."

He went off on a fiery stream of Italian that had the other two occupants of the car edging into the corners. Juliet folded her hands serenely and decided she'd never enjoyed herself more. The other passengers gave Carlo a wide berth as the elevator stopped on their floor.

"Did you want to grab something quick to eat at the airport or wait until we land?"

"I'm not interested in food."

"An odd statement from a chef." She breezed into the hall. "Take ten minutes to pack and I'll call for a bellman." The key was in her hand and into the lock before his fingers circled her wrist. When she looked up at him, she thought she'd never seen him truly frustrated before. Good. It was about time.

"I pack nothing until this is settled."

"Until what's settled?" she countered.

"When I commit a crime or a sin, I do so with complete honesty." It was the closest he'd come to an explosion. Juliet lifted a brow and listened attentively. "It was Lydia who had her arms around me."

Juliet smiled. "Yes, I saw quite clearly how you were struggling. A woman should be locked up for taking advantage of a man that way."

His eyes, already dark, went nearly black. "You're sarcastic. But you don't understand the circumstances."

"On the contrary." She leaned against the door. "Carlo, I believe I understood the circumstances perfectly. I don't believe I've asked you to explain anything. Now, you'd better pack if we're going to catch that early plane." For the second time, she shut the door in his face.

He stood where he was for a moment, torn. A man expected a certain amount of jealousy from a woman he was involved with. He even, well, enjoyed it to a point. What he didn't expect was a smile, a pat on the head and breezy understanding when he'd been caught in another woman's arms. However innocently.

No, he didn't expect it, Carlo decided. He wouldn't tolerate it.

When the sharp knock came on the door, Juliet was still standing with a hand on the knob. Wisely, she counted to ten before she opened it.

"Did you need something?"

Carefully, he studied her face for a trap. "You're not angry."

She lifted her brows. "No, why?"

"Lydia's very beautiful."

"She certainly is."

He stepped inside. "You're not jealous?"

"Don't be absurd." She brushed a speck of lint from her sleeve. "If you found me with another man, under similar circumstances, you'd understand, I'm sure."

"No." He closed the door behind him. "I'd break his face."

"Oh?" Rather pleased, she turned away to gather a few things from her dresser. "That's the Italian temperament, I suppose. Most of my ancestors were rather staid. Hand me that brush, will you?"

Carlo picked it up and dropped it into her hand. "Staid—this means?"

"Calm and sturdy, I suppose. Though there was one—my great-great-grandmother, I think. She found her husband tickling the scullery maid. In her staid sort of way, she knocked him flat with a cast-iron skillet. I don't think he ever tickled any of the other servants." Securing the brush in a plastic case, she arranged it in the bag. "I'm said to take after her."

Taking her by the shoulders, he turned her to face him. "There were no skillets available."

"True enough, but I'm inventive. Carlo..." Still smiling, she slipped her arms around his neck. "If I hadn't understood exactly what was going on, the coffee I'd fetched for you would've been dumped over your head. *Capice?*"

"Sì." He grinned as he rubbed his nose against hers. But he didn't really understand her. Perhaps that was why he was enchanted by her. Lowering his mouth to hers, he let the enchantment grow. "Juliet," he murmured. "There's a later plane for Detroit, yes?"

She had wondered if he would ever think of it. "Yes, this afternoon."

"Did you know it's unhealthy for the system to rush." As he spoke, he slipped the jacket from her arms so that it slid to the floor.

"I've heard something about that."

"Very true. It's much better, medically speaking, to take one's time. To keep a steady pace, but not a fast one. And, of course, to give the system time to relax at regular intervals. It could be very unhealthy for us to pack now and race to the airport." He unhooked her skirt so that it followed her jacket.

"You're probably right."

"Of course I'm right," he murmured in her ear. "It would never do for either of us to be ill on the tour."

"Disastrous," she agreed. "In fact, it might be best if we both just lay down for a little while."

"The very best. One must guard one's health."

"I couldn't agree more," she told him as his shirt joined her skirt and jacket.

She was laughing as they tumbled onto the bed.

He liked her this way. Free, easy, enthusiastic. Just as he liked her cooler, more enigmatic moods. He could enjoy her in a hundred different ways because she wasn't always the same woman. Yet she was always the same.

Soft, as she was now. Warm wherever he touched, luxurious wherever he tasted. She might be submissive one moment, aggressive the next, and he never tired of the swings.

They made love in laughter now, something he knew more than most was precious and rare. Even when the passion began to dominate, there was an underlying sense of enjoyment that didn't cloud the fire. She gave him more in a moment than he'd thought he'd ever find with a woman in a lifetime.

She'd never known she could be this way—laughing, churning, happy, desperate. There were so many things she hadn't known. Every time he touched her it was something new, though it was somehow as if his touch was all she'd ever known. He made her feel fresh and desirable, wild and weepy all at once. In the space of minutes, he could bring her a sense of contentment and a frantic range of excitements.

The more he brought, the more he gave, and the easier it became for her to give. She wasn't aware yet, nor was he, that every time they made love, the intimacy grew and spread. It was gaining a strength and weight that wouldn't break with simply walking away. Perhaps if they'd known, they would have fought it.

Instead, they loved each other through the morning with the verve of youth and the depth of familiarity.

Chapter 10

Juliet hung up the phone, dragged a hand through her hair and swore. Rising, she swore again then moved toward the wide spread of window in Carlo's suite. For a few moments she muttered at nothing and no one in particular. Across the room, Carlo lay sprawled on the sofa. Wisely, he waited until she'd lapsed into silence.

"Problems?"

"We're fogged in." Swearing again, she stared out the window. She could see the mist, thick and still hanging outside the glass. Detroit was obliterated. "All flights are cancelled. The only way we're going to get to Boston is to stick out our thumbs."

"Thumbs?"

"Never mind." She turned and paced around the suite.

Detroit had been a solid round of media and events, and the Renaissance Center a beautiful place to stay, but now it was time to move on. Boston was just a hop away by air, so that the evening could be devoted to drafting out reports and a good night's sleep. Except for the fact that fog had driven in from the lake and put the whole city under wraps.

Stuck, Juliet thought as she glared out the window again. Stuck when they had an 8:00 A.M. live demonstration on a well-established morning show in Boston.

He shifted a bit, but didn't sit up. If it hadn't been too much trouble, he could've counted off the number of times he'd been grounded for one reason or another. One, he recalled, had been a flamenco dancer in Madrid who'd distracted him into missing the last flight out. Better not to mention it. Still, when such things happened, Carlo reflected, it was best to relax and enjoy the moment. He knew Juliet better.

"You're worried about the TV in the morning."

"Of course I am." As she paced, she went over every possibility. Rent a car and drive—no, even in clear weather it was simply too far. They could charter a plane and hope the fog cleared by dawn. She took another glance outside. They were sixty-five floors up, but they might as well have been sixty-five feet under. No, she decided, no television spot was worth the risk. They'd have to cancel. That was that.

She dropped down on a chair and stuck her stockinged feet up by Carlo's. "I'm sorry, Carlo, there's no way around it. We'll have to scrub Boston."

"Scrub Boston?" Lazily he folded his arms behind his head. "Juliet, Franconi scrubs nothing. Cook, yes, scrub, no."

It took her a moment to realize he was serious. "I mean cancel."

"You didn't say cancel."

She heaved out a long breath. "I'm saying it now." She wiggled her toes, finding them a bit stiff after a ten-hour day. "There's no way we can make the television spot, and that's the biggest thing we have going in Boston. There're a couple of print interviews and an autographing. We didn't expect much to move there, and we were depending on the TV spot for that. Without it..." She shrugged and resigned herself. "It's a wash."

Letting his eyes half close, Carlo decided the sofa was an excellent place to spend an hour or so. "I don't wash."

She shot him a level look. "You're not going to have to do anything but lie on your—back," she decided after a moment, "for the next twenty-four hours."

"Nothing?"

"Nothing."

He grinned. Moving faster than he looked capable of, he sat up, grabbed her by the arms and pulled her down with him. "Good, you lie with me. Two backs, *madonna,* are better than one."

"Carlo." She couldn't avoid the first kiss. Or perhaps she didn't put her best effort into it, but she knew it was essential to avoid the second. "Wait a minute."

"Only twenty-four hours," he reminded her as he moved to her ear. "No time to waste."

"I've got to— Stop that," she ordered when her thoughts started to cloud. "There're arrangements to be made."

"What arrangements?"

She made a quick mental sketch. True, she'd already checked out of her room. They'd only kept the suite for convenience, and until six. She could book another separate room for the night, but—she might as well admit in this case it was foolish. Moving her shoulders, she gave in to innate practicality. "Like keeping the suite overnight."

"That's important." He lifted his head a moment. Her face was already flushed, her eyes already soft. Almost as if she'd spoken aloud, he followed the train of thought. He couldn't help but admire the way her mind worked from one point to the next in such straight lines.

"I have to call New York and let them know our status. I have to call Boston and cancel, then the airport and change our flight. Then I—"

"I think you have a love affair with the phone. It's difficult for a man to be jealous of an inanimate object."

"Phones are my life." She tried to slip out from under him, but got nowhere. "Carlo."

"I like it when you say my name with just a touch of exasperation."

"It's going to be more than a touch in a minute."

He'd thought he'd enjoy that as well. "But you haven't told me yet how fantastic I was today."

"You were fantastic." It was so easy to relax when he held her like this. The phone calls could wait, just a bit. After all, they weren't going anywhere. "You mesmerized them with your linguini."

"My linguini is hypnotic," he agreed. "I charmed the reporter from the *Free Press*."

"You left him stupefied. Detroit'll never be the same."

"That's true." He kissed her nose. "Boston won't know what it's missing."

"Don't remind me," she began, then broke off. Carlo could almost hear the wheels turning.

"An idea." Resigned, he rolled her on top of him and watched her think.

"It might work," she murmured. "If everyone cooperates, it might work very well. In fact, it might just be terrific."

"What?"

"You claim to be a magician as well as an artist."

"Modesty prevents me from—"

"Save it." She scrambled up until she stradled him. "You told me once you could cook in a sewer."

Frowning, he toyed with the little gold hoop she wore in her ear. "Yes, perhaps I did. But this is only an expression—"

"How about cooking by remote control?"

His brows drew together, but he ran his hand idly to the hem of her skirt that had ridden high on her thigh. "You have extraordinary legs," he said in passing, then gave her his attention. "What do you mean by remote control?"

"Just that." Wound up with the idea, Juliet rose and grabbed her pad and pencil. "You give me all the ingredients—it's linguini again tomorrow, right?"

"Yes, my specialty."

"Good, I have all that in the file anyway. We can set up a phone session between Detroit and the studio in Boston. You can be on the air there while we're here."

"Juliet, you ask for a lot of magic."

"No, it's just basic electronics. The host of the show—Paul O'Hara—can put the dish together on the air while you talk him through it. It's like talking a plane in, you know. Forty degrees to the left—a cup of flour."

"No."

"Carlo."

Taking his time, he pried off his shoes. "You want him, this O'Hara who smiles for the camera, to cook my linguini?"

"Don't get temperamental on me," she warned, while

her mind leaped ahead to possibilities. "Look, you write cookbooks so the average person can cook one of your dishes."

"Cook them, yes." He examined his nails. "Not like Franconi."

She opened her mouth, then closed it again. Tread softly on the ego, Juliet reminded herself. At least until you get your way. "Of course not, Carlo. No one expects that. But we could turn this inconvenience into a real event. Using your cookbook on the air, and some personal coaching from you via phone, O'Hara can prepare the linguini. He's not a chef or a gourmet, but an average person. Therefore, he'll be giving the audience the average person's reactions. He'll make the average person's mistakes that you can correct. If we pull it off, the sales of your cookbook are going to soar. You know you can do it." She smiled winningly. "Why you even said you could teach me to cook, and I'm helpless in the kitchen. Certainly you can talk O'Hara through one dish."

"Of course I can." Folding his arms again, he stared up at the ceiling. Her logic was infallible, her idea creative. To be truthful, he liked it—almost as much as he liked the idea of not having to fly to Boston. Still, it hardly seemed fair to give without getting. "I'll do it—on one condition."

"Which is?"

"Tomorrow morning, I talk this O'Hara through linguini. Tonight…" And he smiled at her. "We have a dress rehearsal. I talk you through it."

Juliet stopped tapping the end of her pencil on the pad. "You want me to cook linguini?"

"With my guidance, *cara mia,* you could cook anything."

Juliet thought it over and decided it didn't matter. The suite didn't have a kitchen this time, so he'd be counting on using the hotel's. That may or may not work. If it did, once she'd botched it, they could order room service. The bottom line was saving what she could of Boston. "I'd love to. Now, I've got to make those calls."

Carlo closed his eyes and opted for a nap. If he was going to teach two amateurs the secrets of linguini within twelve hours, he'd need his strength. "Wake me when you've finished," he told her. "We have to inspect the kitchen of the hotel."

It took her the best part of two hours, and when she hung up for the last time, Juliet's neck was stiff and her fingers numb. But she had what she wanted. Hal told her she was a genius and O'Hara said it sounded like fun. Arrangements were already in the works.

This time Juliet grinned at the stubborn fog swirling outside the window. Neither rain nor storm nor dark of night, she thought, pleased with herself. Nothing was going to stop Juliet Trent.

Then she looked over at Carlo. Something tilted inside her that had both her confidence and self-satisfaction wavering. Emotion, she reflected. It was something she hadn't written into the itinerary.

Well, maybe there was one catastrophe that wasn't in the books. Maybe it was one she couldn't work her way through with a creative idea and hustle. She simply had to take her feelings for Carlo one step at a time.

Four more days, she mused, and the ride would be over. The music would stop and it would be time to get off the carousel.

It wasn't any use trying to see beyond that yet; it was all blank pages. She had to hold on to the belief that life was built one day at a time. Carlo would go, then she would pick up the pieces and begin her life again from that point.

She wasn't fool enough to tell herself she wouldn't cry. Tears would be shed over him, but they'd be shed quietly and privately. Schedule in a day for mourning, she thought then tossed her pad away.

It wasn't healthy to think of it now. There were only four days left. For a moment, she looked down at her empty hands and wondered if she'd have taken the steps she'd taken if she'd known where they would lead her. Then she looked over at him and simply watched him sleep.

Even with his eyes closed and that irrepressible inner life he had on hold, he could draw her. It wasn't simply a matter of his looks, she realized. She wasn't a woman who'd turn her life sideways for simple physical attraction. It was a matter of style. Smiling, she rose and walked closer to him as he slept. No matter how practical she was, how much common sense she possessed, she couldn't have resisted his style.

There'd be no regrets, she reaffirmed. Not now, nor in five days' time when an ocean and priorities separated them. As years passed, and their lives flowed and altered, she'd remember a handful of days when she'd had something special.

No time to waste, he'd said. Catching her tongue in her teeth Juliet decided she couldn't agree more. Reaching up, she began to unbutton her blouse. As a matter of habit, she draped it carefully over the back of a chair before she unhooked her skirt. When that fell, she lifted it, smoothed it out and folded it. The pins were drawn out of her hair, one by one, then set aside.

Dressed in a very impractical lace camisole and string bikini she moved closer.

Carlo awoke with his blood pumping and his head whirling. He could smell her scent lightly in her hair, more heady on her skin as her mouth took command of his. Her body was already heated as she lay full length on him. Before he could draw his first thoughts together, his own body followed suit.

She was all lace and flesh and passion. There wasn't time to steady his control or polish his style. Urgent and desperate, he reached for her and found silk and delicacy, strength and demand wherever he touched.

She unbuttoned his shirt and drew it aside so that their skin could meet and arouse. Beneath hers, she felt his heartbeat race and pound until power made her dizzy. Capturing his lips once again, she thought only of driving him to madness. She could feel it spread through him, growing, building, so that it would dominate both of them.

When he rolled so that she was trapped between the back of the sofa and his body, she was ready to relinquish control. With a moan, dark and liquid, she let herself enjoy what she'd begun.

No woman had ever done this to him. He understood that as his only thoughts were to devour everything she had. His fingers, so clever, so skilled, so gentle, pulled at the lace until the thin strap tore with hardly a sound.

He found her—small soft breasts that fit so perfectly in his hands, the strong narrow rib cage and slender waist. His. The word nearly drove him mad. She was his now, as she'd been in the dream she'd woken him from. Perhaps he was still dreaming.

She smelled of secrets, small, feminine secrets no man ever fully understood. She tasted of passion, ripe, shivering passion every man craved. With his tongue he tasted that sweet subtle valley between her breasts and felt her tremble. She was strong; he'd never doubted it. In her strength, she was surrendering completely to him, for the pleasure of each.

The lace smelled of her. He could have wallowed in it, but her skin was irresistible. He drew the camisole down to her waist and feasted on her.

With her hands tangled in his hair, her body on fire, she thought only of him. No tomorrows, no yesterdays. However much she might deny it in an hour, they'd become a single unit. One depended on the other for pleasure, for comfort, for excitement. For so much more she didn't dare think of it. She yearned for him; nothing would ever stop it. But now, he was taking her, fast and furious, through doors they'd opened together. Neither of them had gone there before with another, nor would again.

Juliet gave herself over to the dark, the heat, and to Carlo.

He drew the thin strings riding on her hips, craving the essence of her. When he'd driven her over the first peak, he knew and reveled in it. With endless waves of desire, he whipped her up again, and yet again, until they were both trembling. She called out his name as he ran his lips down her leg. All of her was the thought paramount in his mind. He'd have all of her until she was willing, ready to have all of him.

"Juliet, I want you." His face was above hers again, his breath straining. "Look at me."

She was staggering on that razor's edge between reason and madness. When she opened her eyes, his face filled her vision. It was all she wanted.

"I want you," he repeated while the blood raged in his head. "Only you."

She was wrapped around him, her head arched back.

For an instant, their eyes met and held. What coursed through them wasn't something they could try to explain. It was both danger and security.

"Only," she murmured and took him into her.

They were both stunned, both shaken, both content. Naked, damp and warm, they lay tangled together in silence. Words had been spoken, Juliet thought. Words that were part of the madness of the moment. She would have to take care not to repeat them when passion was spent. They didn't need words; they had four days. Yet she ached to hear them again, to say them again.

She could set the tone between them, she thought. She had only to begin now and continue. No pressure. She kept her eyes closed a moment longer. No regrets. The extra moment she took to draw back her strength went unnoticed.

"I could stay just like this for a week," she murmured. Though she meant it, the words were said lazily. Turning her head, she looked at him, smiled. "Are you ready for another nap?"

There was so much he wanted to say. So much, he thought, she didn't want to hear. They'd set the rules; he had only to follow them. Nothing was as easy as it should've been.

"No." He kissed her forehead. "Though I've never found waking from a nap more delightful. Now, I think it's time for your next lesson."

"Really?" She caught her bottom lip between her teeth. "I thought I'd graduated."

"Cooking," he told her, giving her a quick pinch where Italian males were prone to.

Juliet tossed back her hair and pinched him back. "I thought you'd forget about that."

"Franconi never forgets. A quick shower, a change of clothes and down to the kitchen."

Agreeable, Juliet shrugged. She didn't think for one minute the management would allow him to give a cooking lesson in their kitchen.

Thirty minutes later, she was proven wrong.

Carlo merely bypassed management. He saw no reason to go through a chain of command. With very little fuss, he steered her through the hotel's elegant dining room and into the big, lofty kitchen. It smelled exotic and sounded like a subway station.

They'd stop him here, Juliet decided, still certain they'd be dining outside or through room service within the hour. Though she'd changed into comfortable jeans, she had no plans to cook. After one look at the big room with its oversized appliances and acres of counter, she was positive she wouldn't.

It shouldn't have surprised her to be proven wrong again.

"Franconi!" The name boomed out and echoed off the walls. Juliet jumped back three inches.

"Carlo, I think we should—" But as she spoke, she looked up at his face. He was grinning from ear to ear.

"Pierre!"

As she looked on, Carlo was enveloped by a wide, white-aproned man with a drooping mustache and a face as big and round as a frying pan. His skin glistened with sweat, but he smelt inoffensively of tomatoes.

"You Italian lecher, what do you do in my kitchen?"

"Honor it," Carlo said as they drew apart. "I thought you were in Montreal, poisoning the tourists."

"They beg me to take the kitchen here." The big man with the heavy French accent shrugged tanklike shoulders. "I feel sorry for them. Americans have so little finesse in the kitchen."

"They offered to pay you by the pound," Carlo said dryly. "Your pounds."

Pierre held both hands to his abundant middle and laughed. "We understand each other, old friend. Still, I find America to my liking. You, why aren't you in Rome pinching ladies?"

"I'm finishing up a tour for my book."

"But yes, you and your cookbooks." A noise behind him had him glancing around and bellowing in French. Juliet was certain the walls trembled. With a smile, he adjusted his hat and turned back to them. "That goes well?"

"Well enough." Carlo drew Juliet up. "This is Juliet Trent, my publicist."

"So it goes very well," Pierre murmured as he took Juliet's hand and brushed his lips over it. "Perhaps I will write a cookbook. Welcome to my kitchen, *mademoiselle.* I'm at your service."

Charmed, Juliet smiled. "Thank you, Pierre."

"Don't let this one fool you," Carlo warned. "He has a daughter your age."

"Bah!" Pierre gave him a lowered brow look. "She's but sixteen. If she were a day older I'd call my wife and tell her to lock the doors while Franconi is in town."

Carlo grinned. "Such flattery, Pierre." With his hands hooked in his back pockets, he looked around the room. "Very nice," he mused. Lifting his head, he scented the air. "Duck. Is that duck I smell?"

Pierre preened. "The specialty. *Canard au Pierre.*"

"Fantastico." Carlo swung an arm around Juliet as he led her closer to the scent. "No one, absolutely no one, does to duck what Pierre can do."

The black eyes in the frying-pan face gleamed. “No, you flatter me, *mon ami.*”

“There’s no flattery in truth.” Carlo looked on while an assistant carved Pierre’s duck. With the ease of experience, he took a small sliver and popped it into Juliet’s mouth. It dissolved there, leaving behind an elusive flavor that begged for more. Carlo merely laid his tongue on his thumb to test. “Exquisite, as always. Do you remember, Pierre, when we prepared the Shah’s engagement feast? Five, six years ago.”

“Seven,” Pierre corrected and sighed.

“Your duck and my cannelloni.”

“Magnificent. Not so much paprika on that fish,” he boomed out. “We are not in Budapest. Those were the days,” he continued easily. “But…” The shrug was essentially Gallic. “When a man has his third child, he has to settle down, *oui?*”

Carlo gave another look at the kitchen, and with an expert’s eye approved. “You’ve picked an excellent spot. Perhaps you’d let me have a corner of it for a short time.”

“A corner?”

“A favor,” Carlo said with a smile that would have charmed the pearls from oysters. “I’ve promised my Juliet to teach her how to prepare linguini.”

“Linguini con vongole biance?” Pierre’s eyes glittered.

“Naturally. It is my specialty.”

“You can have a corner of my kitchen, *mon ami,* in exchange for a plate.”

Carlo laughed and patted Pierre’s stomach. “For you, *amico,* two plates.”

Pierre clasped him by the shoulders and kissed both cheeks. “I feel my youth coming back to me. Tell me what you need.”

In no time at all, Juliet found herself covered in a white apron with her hair tucked into a chef's hat. She might have felt ridiculous if she'd been given the chance.

"First you mince the clams."

Juliet looked at Carlo, then down at the mess of clams on the cutting board. "Mince them?"

"Like so." Carlo took the knife and with a few quick moves had half of the clams in small, perfect pieces. "Try."

Feeling a bit like an executioner, Juliet brought the knife down. "They're not…well, alive, are they?"

"*Madonna,* any clam considers himself honored to be part of Franconi's linguini. A bit smaller there. Yes." Satisfied, he passed her an onion. "Chopped, not too fine." Again, he demonstrated, but this time Juliet felt more at home. Accepting the knife, she hacked again until the onion was in pieces and her eyes were streaming.

"I hate to cook," she muttered but Carlo only pushed a clove of garlic at her.

"This is chopped very fine. Its essence is what we need, not so much texture." He stood over her shoulder, watching until he approved. "You've good hands, Juliet. Now here, melt the butter."

Following instructions, she cooked the onion and garlic in the simmering butter, stirring until Carlo pronounced it ready.

"Now, it's tender, you see. We add just a bit of flour." He held her hand to direct it as she stirred it in. "So it thickens. We add the clams. Gently," he warned before she could dump them in. "We don't want them bruised. Ah…" He nodded with approval. "Spice," he told her. "It's the secret and the strength."

Bending over her, he showed her how to take a pinch

of this, a touch of that and create. As the scent became more pleasing, her confidence grew. She'd never remember the amounts or the ingredients, but found it didn't matter.

"How about that?" she asked, pointing to a few sprigs of parsley.

"No, that comes just at the end. We don't want to drown it. Turn the heat down, just a little more. There." Satisfied, he nodded. "The cover goes on snug, then you let it simmer while the spices wake up."

Juliet wiped the back of her hand over her damp brow. "Carlo, you talk about the sauce as though it lived and breathed."

"My sauces do," he said simply. "While this simmers, you grate the cheese." He picked up a hunk and with his eyes closed, sniffed. *"Squisito."*

He had her grate and stir while the rest of the kitchen staff worked around them. Juliet thought of her mother's kitchen with its tidy counters and homey smells. She'd never seen anything like this. It certainly wasn't quiet. Pans were dropped, people and dishes were cursed, and fast was the order of the day. Busboys hustled in and out, weighed down with trays, waiters and waitresses breezed through demanding their orders. While she watched wide-eyed, Carlo ignored. It was time to create his pasta.

Unless it was already cooked and in a meal, Juliet thought of pasta as something you got off the shelf in a cardboard box. She learned differently, after her hands were white to the wrists with flour. He had her measure and knead and roll and spread until her elbows creaked. It was nothing like the five-minute throw-it-together kind she was used to.

As she worked, she began to realize why he had such

stamina. He had to. In cooking for a living the way Franconi cooked for a living, he used as much energy as any athlete did. By the time the pasta had passed his inspection, her shoulder muscles ached the way they did after a brisk set of tennis.

Blowing the hair out of her eyes and mopping away sweat, Juliet turned to him. "What now?"

"Now you cook the pasta."

She tried not to grumble as she poured water into a Dutch oven and set it on to boil.

"One tablespoon salt," Carlo instructed.

"One tablespoon salt," she muttered and poured it in. When she turned around, he handed her a glass of wine.

"Until it boils, you relax."

"Can I turn down the heat?"

He laughed and kissed her, then decided it was only right to kiss her again. She smelled like heaven. "I like you in white." He dusted flour from her nose. "You're a messy cook, my love, but a stunning one."

It was easy to forget the noisy, bustling kitchen. "Cook?" A bit primly, she adjusted her hat. "Isn't it chef?"

He kissed her again. "Don't get cocky. One linguini doesn't make a chef."

She barely finished her wine when he put her back to work. "Put one end of the linguini in the water. Yes, just so. Now, as it softens coil them in. Careful. Yes, yes, you have a nice touch. A bit more patience and I might take you on in my restaurant."

"No, thanks," Juliet said definitely as the steam rose in her face. She was almost certain she felt each separate pore opening.

"Stir easily. Seven minutes only, not a moment more." He refilled her glass and kissed her cheek.

She stirred, and drained, measured parsley, poured and sprinkled cheese. By the time she was finished, Juliet didn't think she could eat a thing. Nerves, she discovered with astonishment. She was as nervous as a new bride on her first day in the kitchen.

With her hands clasped together, she watched Carlo take a fork and dip in. Eyes closed, he breathed in the aroma. She swallowed. His eyes remained closed as he took the first sample. Juliet bit her lip. Until then, she hadn't noticed that the kitchen had become as quiet as a cathedral. A quick glimpse around showed her all activity had stopped and all eyes were on Carlo. She felt as though she were waiting to be sentenced or acquitted.

"Well?" she demanded when she couldn't stand it any longer.

"Patience," Carlo reminded her without opening his eyes. A busboy rushed in and was immediately shushed. Carlo opened his eyes and carefully set down the fork. *"Fantastico!"* He took Juliet by the shoulders and gave her the ceremonial kiss on each cheek as applause broke out.

Laughing, she pulled off her hat with a flourish. "I feel like I won a Gold Medal in the decathlon."

"You've created." As Pierre boomed orders for plates, Carlo took both her hands. "We make a good team, Juliet Trent."

She felt something creeping too close to the heart. It just didn't seem possible to stop it. "Yes, we make a good team, Franconi."

Chapter 11

By twelve the next day, there was absolutely nothing left to be done. Carlo's remote control demonstration on the proper way to prepare linguini had gone far beyond Juliet's hopes for success. She'd stayed glued to the television, listening to Carlo's voice beside her and through the speakers. When her supervisor called personally to congratulate her, Juliet knew she had a winner. Relaxed and satisfied, she lay back on the bed.

"Wonderful." She folded her arms, crossed her ankles and grinned. "Absolutely wonderful."

"Did you ever doubt it?"

Still grinning, she shot a look at Carlo as he finished off the last of both shares of the late breakfast they'd ordered. "Let's just say I'm glad it's over."

"You worry too much, *mi amore.*" But he hadn't seen her dig for her little roll of pills in three days. It pleased him enormously to know that he relaxed her so that she didn't need them. "When it comes to Franconi's linguini, you have always a success."

"After this I'll never doubt it. Now we have five hours before flight time. Five full, completely unscheduled hours."

Rising he sat on the end of the bed and ran his fingers along the arch of her foot. She looked so lovely when she smiled, so lovely when she let her mind rest. "Such a bonus," he murmured.

"It's like a vacation." With a sigh, she let herself enjoy the little tingles of pleasure.

"What would you like to do with our vacation of five full, unscheduled hours?"

She lifted a brow at him. "You really want to know?"

Slowly, he kissed each one of her toes. "Of course. The day is yours." He brushed his lips over her ankle. "I'm at your service."

Springing up, she threw her arms around his neck and kissed him, hard. "Let's go shopping."

Fifteen minutes later, Juliet strolled with Carlo through the first tower of the enormous circular shopping center attached to the hotel. People huddled around the maps of the complex, but she breezed around the curve and bypassed one. No maps, no schedules, no routes. Today, it didn't matter where they went.

"Do you know," she began, "with all the department stores, malls and cities we've been through, I haven't had a chance to shop?"

"You don't give yourself time."

"Same thing. Oh, look." She stopped at a window display and studied a long evening dress covered with tiny silver bangles.

"Very dashing," Carlo decided.

"Dashing," Juliet agreed. "If I were six inches taller

it might not make me look like a scaled-down pillar. Shoes." She pulled him along to the next shop.

In short order, Carlo discovered Juliet's biggest weakness. The way to her heart wasn't through food, nor was it paved with furs and diamonds. Jewelry displays barely earned her glance. Evening clothes brought a brief survey while day wear and sports clothes won mild interest. But shoes were something different. Within an hour, she'd studied, fondled and critiqued at least fifty pairs. She found a pair of sneakers at 30 percent off and bought them to add to an already substantial collection. Then with a careful maneuver to pick and choose, she weeded her selection down to three pair of heels, all Italian.

"You show excellent taste." With the patience of a man accustomed to shopping expeditions, Carlo lounged in a chair and watched her vacillate between one pair then the other. Idly, he picked up one shoe and glanced at the signature inside. "He makes an elegant shoe and prefers my lasagna."

Wide-eyed, Juliet pivoted on the thin heels. "You know him?"

"Of course. Once a week he eats in Franconi's."

"He's my hero." When Carlo gave her his lifted brow look, she laughed. "I know I can put on a pair of his shoes and go eight hours without needing emergency surgery. I'll take all three," she said on impulse, then sat down to exchange the heels for her newly bought sneakers.

"You make me surprised," he commented. "So many shoes when you have only two feet. This is not my practical Juliet."

"I'm entitled to a vice." Juliet pushed the Velcro closed. "Besides, I've always known Italians make the best shoes." She leaned closer to kiss his cheek. "Now I know they make the best…pasta." Without a blink at the total, she charged the shoes and pocketed the receipt.

Swinging the bag between them, they wandered from tower to tower. A group of women strolled by, earning Carlo's appreciation. Shopping during lunch hour, he gauged as he tossed an extra look over his shoulder. One had to admire the American workforce.

"You'll strain your neck that way," Juliet commented easily. She couldn't help but be amused by his blatant pleasure in anything female. He merely grinned.

"It's simply a matter of knowing just how far to go."

Comfortable, Juliet enjoyed the feel of his fingers laced with hers. "I'd never argue with the expert."

Carlo stopped once, intrigued by a choker in amethysts and diamonds. "This is lovely," he decided. "My sister, Teresa, always preferred purple."

Juliet leaned closer to the glass. The small, delicate jewels glimmered, hot and cold. "Who wouldn't? It's fabulous."

"She has a baby in a few weeks," he murmured, then nodded to the discreetly anxious clerk. "I'll see this."

"Of course, a lovely piece, isn't it?" After taking it out of the locked case, he placed it reverently in Carlo's hand. "The diamonds are all superior grade, naturally, and consist of one point three carat. The amethyst—"

"I'll have it."

Thrown off in the middle of his pitch, the clerk blinked. "Yes, sir, an excellent choice." Trying not to show surprise, he took the credit card Carlo handed him along with the choker and moved farther down the counter.

"Carlo." Juliet edged closer and lowered her voice. "You didn't even ask the price."

He merely patted her hand as he skimmed the other contents in the case. "My sister's about to make me an uncle again," he said simply. "The choker suits her. Now emeralds," he began, "would be your stone."

She glanced down at a pair of earrings with stones the color of dark, wet summer grass. The momentary longing was purely feminine and easily controlled. Shoes she could justify; emeralds, no. She shook her head and laughed at him. "I'll just stick with pampering my feet."

When Carlo had his present nicely boxed and his receipt in hand they wandered back out. "I love to shop," Juliet confessed. "Sometimes I'll spend an entire Saturday just roaming. It's one of the things I like best about New York."

"Then you'd love Rome." He'd like to see her there, he discovered. By the fountains, laughing, strolling through the markets and cathedrals, dancing in the clubs that smelled of wine and humanity. He wanted to have her there, with him. Going back alone was going back to nothing. He brought her hand to his lips as he thought of it, holding it there until she paused, uncertain.

"Carlo?" People brushed by them, and as his look became more intense, she swallowed and repeated his name. This wasn't the mild masculine appreciation she'd seen him send passing women, but something deep and dangerous. When a man looked at a woman this way, the woman was wise to run. But Juliet didn't know if it were toward him or away.

He shook off the mood, warning himself to tread carefully with her, and himself. "If you came," he said lightly, "I could introduce you to your hero. Enough of my lasagna and you'd have your shoes at cost."

Relieved, she tucked her arm through his again. "You

tempt me to start saving for the airfare immediately. Oh, Carlo, look at this!" Delighted, she stopped in front of a window and pointed. In the midst of the ornate display was a three-foot Indian elephant done in high-gloss ceramic. Its blanket was a kaleidoscope of gilt and glitter and color. Opulent and regal, its head was lifted, its trunk curled high. Juliet fell in love. "It's wonderful, so unnecessarily ornate and totally useless."

He could see it easily in his living room along with the other ornate and useless pieces he'd collected over the years. But he'd never have imagined Juliet's taste running along the same path. "You surprise me again."

A bit embarrassed, she moved her shoulders. "Oh, I know it's awful, really, but I love things that don't belong anywhere at all."

"Then you must come to Rome and see my house." At her puzzled look, he laughed. "The last piece I acquired is an owl, this high." He demonstrated by holding out a palm. "It's caught a small, unfortunate rodent in its talons."

"Dreadful." With something close to a giggle, she kissed him. "I'm sure I'd love it."

"Perhaps you would at that," he murmured. "In any case, I believe the elephant should have a good home."

"You're going to buy it?" Thrilled, she clasped his hand as they went inside. The shop smelled of sandalwood and carried the tinkle of glass from wind chimes set swaying by a fan. She left him to make arrangements for shipping while she poked around, toying with long strings of brass bells, alabaster lions and ornamental tea services.

All in all, Juliet mused, it had been the easiest, most relaxing day she'd had in weeks, maybe longer. She'd remember it, that she promised herself, when she was alone again and life wound down to schedules and the next demand.

Turning, she looked at Carlo as he said something to make the clerk laugh. She hadn't thought there were men like him—secure, utterly masculine and yet sensitive to female moods and needs. Arrogant, he was certainly that, but generous as well. Passionate but gentle, vain but intelligent.

If she could have conjured up a man to fall in love with…oh no, Juliet warned herself with something like desperation. It wouldn't be Carlo Franconi. Couldn't be. He wasn't a man for one woman, and she wasn't a woman for any man. They both needed their freedom. To forget that would be to forget the plans she'd made and had been working toward for ten years. It was best to remember that Carlo was a ride on a carousel, and that the music only played so long.

She took a deep breath and waited for her own advice to sink in. It took longer than it should have. Determined, she smiled and walked to him. "Finished?"

"Our friend will be home soon, very soon after we are."

"Then we'll wish him bon voyage. We'd better start thinking airport ourselves."

With his arm around her shoulders, they walked out. "You'll give me our Philadelphia schedule on the plane."

"You're going to be a smash," she told him. "Though you might want to try my brewer's yeast before it's done."

"I can't believe it." At eight o'clock, Juliet dropped down into a chair outside customer service. Behind her, the conveyor belt of baggage was stopped. "The luggage went to Atlanta."

"Not so hard to believe," Carlo returned. He'd lost his luggage more times than he cared to remember. He gave his leather case a pat. His spatulas were safe. "So, when do we expect our underwear?"

"Maybe by ten tomorrow morning." Disgusted, Juliet looked down at the jeans and T-shirt she'd worn on the flight. She carried her toiletries and a few odds and ends in her shoulder bag, but nothing remotely resembling a business suit. No matter, she decided. She'd be in the background. Then she took a look at Carlo.

He wore a short-sleeved sweatshirt with the word *Sorbonne* dashed across it, jeans white at the stress points and a pair of sneakers that weren't nearly as new as hers. How the hell, she wondered, was he supposed to go on the air at 8:00 A.M. dressed like that?

"Carlo, we've got to get you some clothes."

"I have clothes," he reminded her, "in my bags."

"You're on *Hello, Philadelphia* in the morning at eight, from there we go directly to breakfast with reporters from the *Herald* and the *Inquirer.* At ten, when our bags may or may not be back, you're on *Midmorning Report.* After that—"

"You've already given me the schedule, my love. What's wrong with this?"

When he gestured toward what he wore, Juliet stood up. "Don't be cute, Carlo. We're heading for the closest department store."

"Department store?" Carlo allowed himself to be pulled outside. "Franconi doesn't wear department store."

"This time you do. No time to be choosey. What's in Philadelphia?" she muttered as she hailed a cab. "Wanamaker's." Holding the door open for him, she checked her watch. "We might just make it."

They arrived a half hour before closing. Though he grumbled, Carlo let her drag him through the old, respected Philadelphia institution. Knowing time was against them, Juliet pushed through a rack of slacks. "What size?"

"Thirty-one, thirty-three," he told her with his brow lifted. "Do I choose my own clothes?"

"Try this." Juliet held out a pair of dun-colored pleated slacks.

"I prefer the buff," he began.

"This is better for the camera. Now shirts." Leaving him holding the hanger, she pounced on the next rack. "Size?"

"What do I know from American sizes?" he grumbled.

"This should be right." She chose an elegant shade of salmon in a thin silk that Carlo was forced to admit he'd have looked twice at himself. "Go put these on while I look at the jackets."

"It's like shopping with your mother," he said under his breath as he headed for the dressing rooms.

She found a belt, thin and supple with a fancy little buckle she knew he wouldn't object to. After rejecting a half dozen jackets she came across one in linen with a casual, unstructured fit in a shade between cream and brown.

When Carlo stepped out, she thrust them at him, then stood back to take in the entire view. "It's good," she decided as he shrugged the jacket on. "Yes, it's really good. The color of the shirt keeps the rest from being drab and the jacket keeps it just casual enough without being careless."

"The day Franconi wears clothes off the rack—"

"Only Franconi could wear clothes off the rack and make them look custom-tailored."

He stopped, meeting the laughter in her eyes. "You flatter me."

"Whatever it takes." Turning him around, she gave him a quick push toward the dressing room. "Strip it off, Franconi. I'll get you some shorts."

The look he sent her was cool, with very little patience. "There's a limit, Juliet."

"Don't worry about a thing," she said breezily. "The publisher'll pick up the tab. Make it fast; we've got just enough time to buy your shoes."

She signed the last receipt five minutes after the PA system announced closing. "You're set." Before he could do so himself, she bundled up his packages. "Now, if we can just get a cab to the hotel, we're in business."

"I wear your American shoes in protest."

"I don't blame you," she said sincerely. "Emergency measures, *caro*."

Foolishly, he was moved by the endearment. She'd never lowered her guard enough to use one before. Because of it, Carlo decided to be generous and forgive her for cracking the whip. "My mother would admire you."

"Oh?" Distracted, Juliet stood at the curb and held out her hand for a cab. "Why?"

"She's the only one who's ever poked and prodded me through a store and picked out my clothes. She hasn't done so in twenty years."

"All publicists are mothers," she told him and switched to her other arm. "We have to be."

He leaned closer and caught her earlobe between his teeth. "I prefer you as a lover."

A cab screeched to a halt at the curb. Juliet wondered if it was that which had stolen her breath. Steadying, she bundled Carlo and the packages inside. "For the next few days, I'll be both."

It was nearly ten before they checked into the Cocharan House. Carlo managed to say nothing about the separate rooms, but he made up his mind on the spot that she'd spend no time in her own. They had three days and most of that time would be eaten up with business. Not a moment that was left would be wasted.

He said nothing as they got into the elevator ahead of the bellman. As they rode up, he hummed to himself as Juliet chatted idly. At the door of his suite, he took her arm.

"Put all the bags in here, please," he instructed the bellman. "Ms. Trent and I have some business to see to immediately. We'll sort them out." Before she could say a word, he took out several bills and tipped the bellman himself. She remained silent only until they were alone again.

"Carlo, just what do you think you're doing? I told you before—"

"That you wanted a room of your own. You still have it," he pointed out. "Two doors down. But you're staying here, with me. Now, we'll order a bottle of wine and relax." He took the packages she still carried out of her hands and tossed them on a long, low sofa. "Would you prefer something light?"

"I'd prefer not to be hustled around."

"So would I." With a grin, he glanced over at his new clothes. "Emergency measures."

Hopeless, she thought. He was hopeless. "Carlo, if you'd just try to understand—"

The knock on the door stopped her. She only muttered a little as he went to answer.

"Summer!" She heard the delight in his voice and turned to see him wrapped close with a stunning brunette.

"Carlo, I thought you'd be here an hour ago."

The voice was exotic, hints of France, a slight touch of British discipline. As she stepped away from Carlo, Juliet saw elegance, flash and style all at once. She saw Carlo take the exquisite face in his hands, as he had so often with hers, and kiss the woman long and hard.

"Ah, my little puff pastry, you're as beautiful as ever."

"And you, Franconi, are as full of..." Summer broke off as she spotted the woman standing in the center of the room. She smiled, and though it was friendly enough, she didn't attempt to hide the survey. "Hello. You must be Carlo's publicist."

"Juliet Trent." Odd, Carlo felt as nervous as a boy introducing his first heartthrob to his mother. "This is Summer Cocharan, the finest pastry chef on either side of the Atlantic."

Summer held out a hand as she crossed into the room. "He's flattering me because he hopes I'll fix him an éclair."

"A dozen of them," Carlo corrected. "Beautiful, isn't she, Summer?"

While Juliet struggled for the proper thing to say, Summer smiled again. She'd heard something in Carlo's voice she'd never expected to. "Yes, she is. Horrid to work with, isn't he, Juliet?"

Juliet felt the laugh come easily. "Yes, he is."

"But never dull." Angling her head, she gave Carlo a quick, intimate look. Yes, there was something here other than business. About time, too. "By the way, Carlo, I should thank you for sending young Steven to me."

Interested, Carlo set down his leather case. "He's working out then?"

"Wonderfully."

"The young boy who wanted to be a chef," Juliet murmured and found herself incredibly moved. He hadn't forgotten.

"Yes, did you meet him? He's very dedicated," Summer went on when Juliet nodded. "I think your idea of sending him to Paris for training will pay off. He's going to be excellent."

"Good." Satisfied, Carlo patted her hand. "I'll speak with his mother and make the arrangements."

Brows knit, Juliet stared at him. "You're going to send him to Paris?"

"It's the only place to study cordon bleu properly." Carlo gave a shrug as though the matter were everyday. "Then, when he's fully trained, I'll simply steal him away from Summer for my own restaurant."

"Perhaps you will," Summer smiled. "Then again, perhaps you won't."

He was going to pay for the education and training of a boy he'd met only once, Juliet thought, baffled. What sort of a man was it who could fuss for twenty minutes over the knot of his tie and give with such total generosity to a stranger? How foolish she'd been to think, even for a minute, that she really knew him.

"It's very kind of you, Carlo," she murmured after a moment.

He gave her an odd look, then shrugged it off. "Dues are meant to be paid, Juliet. I was young once and had only a mother to provide for me. Speaking of mothers," he went on smoothly, changing the topic. "How is Monique?"

"Gloriously happy still," Summer told him, and

smiled thinking of her mother. "Keil was obviously the man she'd been looking for." With a laugh, she turned back to Juliet. "I'm sorry, Carlo and I go back a long way."

"Don't be. Carlo tells me you and he were students together."

"A hundred years ago, in Paris."

"Now Summer's married her big American. Where's Blake, *cara?* Does he trust you with me?"

"Not for long." Blake came through the open doorway, still elegant after a twelve-hour day. He was taller than Carlo, broader, but Juliet thought she recognized a similarity. Power, both sexual and intellectual.

"This is Juliet Trent," Summer began. "She's keeping Carlo in line on his American tour."

"Not an easy job." A waiter rolled in a bucket of champagne and glasses. Blake dismissed him with a nod. "Summer tells me your schedule in Philadelphia's very tight."

"She holds the whip," Carlo told him with a gesture toward Juliet. But when his hand came down, it brushed her shoulder in a gesture of casual and unmistakable intimacy.

"I thought I might run over to the studio in the morning and watch your demonstration." Summer accepted the glass of champagne from her husband. "It's been a long time since I've seen you cook."

"Good." Carlo relaxed with the first sip of frosty wine. "Perhaps I'll have time to give your kitchen an inspection. Summer came here to remodel and expand Blake's kitchen, then stayed on because she'd grown attached to it."

"Quite right." Summer sent her husband an amused

look. "In fact, I've grown so attached I've decided to expand again."

"Yes?" Interested, Carlo lifted his brow. "Another Cocharan House?"

"Another Cocharan," Summer corrected.

It took him a moment, but Juliet saw the moment the words had sunk in. Emotion she'd always expected from him, and it was there now, in his eyes as he set down his glass. "You're having a child."

"In the winter." Summer smiled and stretched out her hand. "I haven't figured out how I'm going to reach the stove for Christmas dinner."

He took her hand and kissed it, then kissed her cheeks, one by one. "We've come a long way, *cara mia*."

"A very long way."

"Do you remember the merry-go-round?"

She remembered well her desperate flight to Rome to flee from Blake and her feelings. "You told me I was afraid to grab the brass ring, and so you made me try. I won't forget it."

He murmured something in Italian that made Summer's eyes fill. "And I've always loved you. Now make a toast or something before I disgrace myself."

"A toast." Carlo picked up his glass and slipped his free arm around Juliet. "To the carousel that doesn't end."

Juliet lifted her glass and, sipping, let the champagne wash away the ache.

Cooking before the camera was something Summer understood well. She spent several hours a year doing just that while handling the management of the kitchen in the Philadelphia Cocharan House, satisfying her own select clients with a few trips a year if the price and the occasion were important enough, and, most important of all, learning to enjoy her marriage.

Though she'd often cooked with Carlo, in the kitchen of a palace, in the less expensive area of the flat she still kept in Paris and dozens of other places, she never tired of watching him in action. While she was said to create with the intensity of a brain surgeon, Carlo had the flair of an artist. She'd always admired his expansiveness, his ease of manner, and especially his theatrics.

When he'd put the finishing touches on the pasta dish he'd named, not immodestly, after himself, she applauded with the rest of the audience. But she'd hitched a ride to the studio with him and Juliet for more reason than to feed an old friend's ego. If Summer knew anyone in the world as well as she did herself, it was Carlo. She'd often thought, in many ways, they'd risen from the same dough.

"*Bravo,* Franconi." As the crew began to serve his dish to the audience, Summer went up to give him a formal kiss on the cheek.

"Yes." He kissed her back. "I was magnificent."

"Where's Juliet?"

"On the phone." Carlo rolled his eyes to the ceiling. "*Dio,* that woman spends more time on the phone than a new bride spends in bed."

Summer checked her watch. She'd noted Carlo's schedule herself. "I don't imagine she'll be long. I know you're having a late breakfast at the hotel with reporters."

"You promised to make crêpes," he reminded her, thinking unapologetically of his own pleasure.

"So I did. In return, do you think you could find a small, quiet room for the two of us?"

He grinned and wiggled his brows. "My love, when

Franconi can't oblige a lady with a quiet room, the world stops."

"My thoughts exactly." She hooked her arm through his and let him lead her down a corridor and into what turned out to be a storage room with an overhead light. "You've never lacked class, *caro*."

"So." He made himself comfortable on a stack of boxes. "Since I know you don't want my body, superb as it is, what's on your mind?"

"You, of course, *chérie*."

"Of course."

"I love you, Carlo."

Her abrupt seriousness made him smile and take her hands. "And I you, always."

"You remember, not so long ago when you came through Philadelphia on tour for another book?"

"You were wondering how to take the job redoing the American's kitchen when you were attracted to him and determined not to be."

"In love with him and determined not to be," she corrected. "You gave me some good advice here, and when I visited you in Rome. I want to return the favor."

"Advice?"

"Grab the brass ring, Carlo, and hold on to it."

"Summer—"

"Who knows you better?" she interrupted.

He moved his shoulders. "No one."

"I saw you were in love with her the moment I stepped into the room, the moment you said her name. We understand each other too well to pretend."

He sat a moment, saying nothing. He'd been skirting around the word, and its consequences, very carefully for days. "Juliet is special," he said slowly. "I've thought perhaps what I feel for her is different."

"Thought?"

He let out a small sound and gave up. "Known. But the kind of love we're speaking of leads to commitment, marriage, children."

Instinctively Summer touched a hand to her stomach. Carlo would understand that she still had small fears. She didn't have to speak of them. "Yes. You told me once, when I asked you why you'd never married, that no woman had made your heart tremble. Do you remember what you told me you'd do if you met her?"

"Run for a license and a priest." Rising, he slipped his hands into the pockets of the slacks Juliet had selected for him. "Easy words *before* the heart trembles. I don't want to lose her." Once said, he sighed. "It's never mattered before, but now it matters too much to make the wrong move. She's elusive, Summer. There are times I hold her and feel part of her pull away. I understand her independence, her ambition, and even admire them."

"I have Blake, but I still have my independence and my ambition."

"Yes." He smiled at her. "Do you know, she's so like you. Stubborn." When Summer lifted a brow, he grinned. "Hard in the head and so determined to be the best. Qualities I've always found strangely appealing in a beautiful woman."

"Merci, mon cher ami," Summer said dryly. "Then where's your problem?"

"You'd trust me."

She looked surprised, then moved her shoulders as though he'd said something foolish. "Of course."

"She can't—won't," Carlo corrected. "Juliet would find it easier to give me her body, even part of her heart than her trust. I need it, Summer, as much as I need what she's already given me."

Thoughtful, Summer leaned against a crate. "Does she love you?"

"I don't know." A difficult admission for a man who'd always thought he understood women so well. He smiled a little as he realized a man never fully understood the woman most important to him. With any other woman he'd have been confident he could guide and mold the emotions to his own preference. With Juliet, he was confident of nothing.

"There are times she seems very close and times she seems very detached. Until yesterday I hadn't fully begun to know my own mind."

"Which is?"

"I want her with me," he said simply. "When I'm an old man sitting by the fountains watching the young girls, I'll still want her with me."

Summer moved over to put her hands on his shoulders. "Frightening, isn't it?"

"Terrifying." Yet somehow, he thought, easier now that he'd admitted it. "I'd always thought it would be easy. There'd be love, romance, marriage and children. How could I know the woman would be a stubborn American?"

Summer laughed and dropped her forehead to his. "No more than I could know the man would be a stubborn American. But he was right for me. Your Juliet is right for you."

"So." He kissed Summer's temple. "How do I convince her?"

Summer frowned a moment, thinking. With a quick smile, she walked over to a corner. Picking up a broom, she held it out to him. "Sweep her off her feet."

* * *

Juliet was close to panic when she spotted Carlo strolling down the corridor with Summer on his arm. They might've been taking in the afternoon sun on the Left Bank. The first wave of relief evaporated into annoyance. "Carlo, I've turned this place upside down looking for you."

He merely smiled and touched a finger to her cheek. "You were on the phone."

Telling herself not to swear, she dragged a hand through her hair. "Next time you wander off, leave a trail of bread crumbs. In the meantime, I've got a very cranky cab driver waiting outside." As she pulled him along, she struggled to remember her manners. "Did you enjoy the show?" she asked Summer.

"I always enjoy watching Carlo cook. I only wish the two of you had more time in town. As it is, your timing's very wise."

"Yes?" Carlo pushed open the door and held it for both women.

"The French swine comes through next week."

The door shut with the punch of a bullet. "LaBare?"

Juliet turned back. She'd heard him snarl that name before. "Carlo—"

He held up a hand, silencing any interruption. "What does the Gallic slug do here?"

"Precisely what you've done," Summer returned. Tossing back her hair, she scowled at nothing. "He's written another book."

"Peasant. He's fit to cook only for hyenas."

"For rabid hyenas," Summer corrected.

Seeing that both of her charges were firing up, Juliet took an arm of each. "I think we can talk in the cab."

"He will not speak to you," Carlo announced, ignoring Juliet. "I will dice him into very small pieces."

Though she relished the image, Summer shook her head. "Don't worry. I can handle him. Besides, Blake finds it amusing."

Carlo made a sound like a snake. Juliet felt her nerves fraying. "Americans. Perhaps I'll come back to Philadelphia and murder him."

Trying her best, Juliet nudged him toward the cab. "Come now, Carlo, you know you don't want to murder Blake."

"LaBare," he corrected with something close to an explosion.

"Who is LaBare?" Juliet demanded in exasperation.

"Swine," Carlo answered.

"Pig," Summer confirmed. "But I have plans of my own for him. He's going to stay at the Cocharan House." Summer spread her hands and examined her nails. "I'm going to prepare his meals personally."

With a laugh, Carlo lifted her from the ground and kissed her. "Revenge, my love, is sweeter than even your meringue." Satisfied, he set her down again. "We were students with this slug," Carlo explained to Juliet. "His crimes are too numerous to mention." With a snap, Carlo adjusted his jacket. "I refuse to be on the same continent as he."

Running out of patience, Juliet glanced at the scowling cab driver. "You won't be," she reminded him. "You'll be back in Italy when he's here."

Carlo brightened and nodded. "You're right. Summer, you'll call me and tell me how he fell on his face?"

"Naturally."

"Then it's settled." His mood altered completely, he smiled and picked up the conversation as it ended before the mention of the Frenchman's name. "Next time we come to Philadelphia," Carlo promised. "You and I will make a meal for Blake and Juliet. My veal, your bombe. You haven't sinned, Juliet, until you've tasted Summer's bombe."

There wouldn't be a next time, Juliet knew, but she managed to smile. "I'll look forward to it."

Carlo paused as Juliet opened the door of the cab. "But tonight, we leave for New York."

Summer smiled as she stepped inside. "Don't forget to pack your broom."

Juliet started to climb into the front seat. "Broom?"

Carlo took Summer's hand in his and smiled. "An old French expression."

Chapter 12

New York hadn't changed. Perhaps it was hotter than when Juliet had left it, but the traffic still pushed, the people still rushed and the noise still rang. As she stood at her window at the Harley, she absorbed it.

No, New York hadn't changed, but she had.

Three weeks before, she'd looked out her office window at not so different a view. Her primary thought then had been the tour, to make a success of it. For herself, she admitted. She'd wanted the splash.

She realized she'd gotten it. At that moment, Carlo was in his suite, giving an interview to a reporter for the *Times*. She'd made a half-dozen excuses why she didn't have time to sit in on it. He'd accepted her usual list of phone calls and details, but the truth had been, she'd needed to be alone.

Later, there'd be another reporter and a photographer from one of the top magazines on the stands.

They had network coverage of his demonstration at Bloomingdale's. *The Italian Way* had just climbed to number five on the bestsellers list. Her boss was ready to canonize her.

Juliet tried to remember when she'd ever been more miserable.

Time was running out. The next evening, Carlo would board a plane and she'd take the short cab ride back to her apartment. While she unpacked, he'd be thousands of miles above the Atlantic. She'd be thinking of him while he flirted with a flight attendant or a pretty seat companion. That was his way; she'd always known it.

It wasn't possible to bask in success, to begin plans on her next assignment when she couldn't see beyond the next twenty-four hours.

Wasn't this exactly what she'd always promised herself wouldn't happen? Hadn't she always picked her way carefully through life so that she could keep everything in perfect focus? She'd made a career for herself from the ground up, and everything she had, she'd earned. She'd never considered it ungenerous not to share it, but simply practical. After all, Juliet had what she considered the perfect example before her of what happened when you let go of the reins long enough to let someone else pick them up.

Her mother had blindly handed over control and had never guided her own life again. Her promising career in nursing had dwindled down to doctoring the scraped knees of her children. She'd sacrificed hunks of herself for a man who'd cared for her but could never be faithful. How close had she come to doing precisely the same thing?

If she was still certain of anything, Juliet was certain she couldn't live that way. Exist, she thought, but not live.

So whether she wanted to or not, whether she thought she could or not, she had to think beyond the next twenty-four hours. Picking up her pad, she went to the phone. There were always calls to be made.

Before she could push the first button, Carlo strolled in. "I took your key," he said before she could ask. "So I wouldn't disturb you if you were napping. But I should've known." He nodded toward the phone, then dropped into a chair. He looked so pleased with himself she had to smile.

"How'd the interview go?"

"Perfectly." With a sigh, Carlo stretched out his legs. "The reporter had prepared my ravioli only last night. He thinks, correctly, that I'm a genius."

She checked her watch. "Very good. You've another reporter on the way. If you can convince him you're a genius—"

"He has only to be perceptive."

She grinned, then on impulse rose and went to kneel in front of him. "Don't change, Carlo."

Leaning down, he caught her face in his hands. "What I am now, I'll be tomorrow."

Tomorrow he'd be gone. But she wouldn't think of it. Juliet kissed him quickly then made herself draw away. "Is that what you're wearing?"

Carlo glanced down at his casual linen shirt and trim black jeans. "Of course it's what I'm wearing. If I wasn't wearing this, I'd be wearing something else."

"Hmm." She studied him, trying to judge him with a camera's eye. "Actually, I think it might be just right for this article. Something informal and relaxed for a magazine that's generally starched collars and ties. It should be a unique angle."

"Grazie," he said dryly as he rose. "Now when do we talk about something other than reporters?"

"After you've earned it."

"You're a hard woman, Juliet."

"Solid steel." But she couldn't resist putting her arms around him and proving otherwise. "After you've finished being a hit across the hall, we'll head down to Bloomingdale's."

He nudged her closer, until their bodies fit. "And then?"

"Then you have drinks with your editor."

He ran the tip of his tongue down her neck. "Then?"

"Then you have the evening free."

"A late supper in my suite." Their lips met, clung, then parted.

"It could be arranged."

"Champagne?"

"You're the star. Whatever you want."

"You?"

She pressed her cheek against his. Tonight, this last night, there'd be no restriction. "Me."

It was ten before they walked down the hall to his suite again. Juliet had long since lost the urge to eat, but her enthusiasm in the evening hadn't waned.

"Carlo, it never ceases to amaze me how you perform. If you'd chosen show business, you'd have a wall full of Oscars."

"Timing, *innamorata.* It all has to do with timing."

"You had them eating your pasta out of your hand."

"I found it difficult," he confessed and stopped at the door to take her into his arms. "When I could think of nothing but coming back here tonight with you."

"Then you do deserve an Oscar. Every woman in the audience was certain you were thinking only of her."

"I did receive two interesting offers."

Her brow lifted. "Oh, really?"

Hopeful, he nuzzled her chin. "Are you jealous?"

She linked her fingers behind his neck. "I'm here and they're not."

"Such arrogance. I believe I still have one of the phone numbers in my pocket."

"Reach for it, Franconi, and I'll break your wrist."

He grinned at her. He liked the flare of aggression in a woman with skin the texture of rose petals. "Perhaps I'll just get my key then."

"A better idea." Amused, Juliet stood back as he opened the door. She stepped inside and stared.

The room was filled with roses. Hundreds of them in every color she'd ever imagined flowed out of baskets, tangled out of vases, spilled out of bowls. The room smelled like an English garden on a summer afternoon.

"Carlo, where did you get all these?"

"I ordered them."

She stopped as she leaned over to sniff at a bud. "Ordered them, for yourself?"

He plucked the bud out of its vase and handed it to her. "For you."

Overwhelmed, she stared around the room. "For me?"

"You should always have flowers." He kissed her wrist. "Roses suit Juliet best."

A single rose, a hundred roses, there was no in between with Carlo. Again, he moved her unbearably. "I don't know what to say."

"You like them."

"Like them? Yes, of course, I love them, but—"

"Then you have to say nothing. You promised to share a late supper and champagne." Taking her hand, he led her across the room to the table already set by the wide uncurtained window. A magnum of champagne was chilling in a silver bucket, white tapers were waiting to be lit. Carlo lifted a cover to show delicately broiled lobster tails. It was, Juliet thought, the most beautiful spot in the world.

"How did you manage to have all this here, waiting?"

"I told room service to have it here at ten." He pulled out her chair. "I, too, can keep a schedule, my love." When he'd seated her, Carlo lit the candles, then dimmed the lights so that the silver glinted. At another touch, music flowed out toward her.

Juliet ran her fingertip down the slim white column of a candle then looked at him when he joined her. He drew the cork on the champagne. As it frothed to the lip, he filled two glasses.

He'd make their last night special, she thought. It was so like him. Sweet, generous, romantic. When they parted ways, they'd each have something memorable to take with them. No regrets, Juliet thought again and smiled at him.

"Thank you."

"To happiness, Juliet. Yours and mine."

She touched her glass to his, watching him as she sipped. "You know, some women might suspect a seduction when they're dined with champagne and candlelight."

"Yes. Do you?"

She laughed and sipped again. "I'm counting on it."

God, she excited him, just watching her laugh, hearing her speak. He wondered if such a thing would mellow and settle after years of being together. How would it feel, he wondered, to wake comfortably every morning beside the woman you loved?

Sometimes, he thought, you would come together at dawn with mutual need and sleepy passion. Other times you would simply lie together, secure in the night's warmth. He'd always considered marriage sacred, almost mysterious. Now he thought it would be an adventure—one he intended to share with no one but Juliet.

"This is wonderful." Juliet let the buttery lobster dissolve on her tongue. "I've been completely spoiled."

Carlo filled her glass again. "Spoiled. How?"

"This champagne's a far cry from the little Riesling I splurge on from time to time. And the food." She took another bite of lobster and closed her eyes. "In three weeks my entire attitude toward food has changed. I'm going to end up fat and penniless supporting my habit."

"So, you've learned to relax and enjoy. Is it so bad?"

"If I continue to relax and enjoy I'm going to have to learn how to cook."

"I said I'd teach you."

"I managed the linguini," she reminded him as she drew out the last bite.

"One lesson only. It takes many years to learn properly."

"Then I guess I'll have to make do with the little boxes that say complete meal inside."

"Sacrilege, *cara,* now that your palate is educated." He touched her fingers across the table. "Juliet, I still want to teach you."

She felt her pulse skid, and though she concentrated, she couldn't level it. She tried to smile. "You'll have to write another cookbook. Next time you tour, you can show me how to make spaghetti." Ramble, she told herself. When you rambled, you couldn't think. "If you write one book a year, I should be able to handle it. When you come around this time next year, I could manage the next lesson. By then, maybe I'll have my own firm and you can hire me. After three bestsellers, you should think about a personal publicist."

"A personal publicist?" His fingers tightened on hers then released. "Perhaps you're right." He reached in his pocket and drew out an envelope. "I have something for you."

Juliet recognized the airline folder and took it with a frown. "Is there trouble on your return flight? I thought I'd..." She trailed off when she saw her own name on a departing flight for Rome.

"Come with me, Juliet." He waited until her gaze lifted to his. "Come home with me."

More time, she thought as she gripped the ticket. He was offering her more time. And more pain. It was time she accepted there'd be pain. She waited until she was certain she could control her voice, and her words. "I can't, Carlo. We both knew the tour would end."

"The tour, yes. But not us." He'd thought he'd feel confident, assured, even cheerful. He hadn't counted on desperation. "I want you with me, Juliet."

Very carefully, she set the ticket aside. It hurt, she discovered, to take her hand from it. "It's impossible."

"Nothing's impossible. We belong with each other."

She had to deflect the words, somehow. She had to pretend they didn't run deep inside her and swell until her heart was ready to burst. "Carlo, we both have obligations, and they're thousands of miles apart. On Monday, we'll both be back at work."

"That isn't something that must be," he corrected. "It's you and I who must be. If you need a few days to tidy your business here in New York, we'll wait. Next week, the week after, we fly to Rome."

"Tidy my business?" She rose and found her knees were shaking. "Do you hear what you're saying?"

He did, and didn't know what had happened to the words he'd planned. Demands were coming from him where he'd wanted to show her need and emotion. He was stumbling over himself where he'd always been surefooted. Even now, cursing himself, he couldn't find solid ground.

"I'm saying I want you with me." He stood and grabbed her arms. The candlelight flickered over two confused faces. "Schedules and plans mean nothing, don't you see? I love you."

She went stiff and cold, as though he'd slapped her. A hundred aches, a multitude of needs moved through her, and with them the knowledge that he'd said those words too many times to count to women he couldn't even remember.

"You won't use that on me, Carlo." Her voice wasn't strong, but he saw fury in her eyes. "I've stayed with you until now because you never insulted me with that."

"Insult?" Astonished, then enraged, he shook her. "Insult you by loving you?"

"By using a phrase that comes much too easily to a man like you and doesn't mean any more than the breath it takes to say it."

His fingers loosened slowly until he'd dropped her arms. "After this, after what we've had together, you'd throw yesterdays at me? You didn't come to me untouched, Juliet."

"We both know there's a difference. I hadn't made my success as a lover a career." She knew it was a filthy thing to say but thought only of defense. "I told you before how I felt about love, Carlo. I won't have it churning up my life and pulling me away from every goal I've ever set. You—you hand me a ticket and say come to Rome, then expect me to run off with you for a fling, leaving my work and my life behind until we've had our fill."

His eyes frosted. "I have knowledge of flings, Juliet, of where they begin and where they end. I was asking you to be my wife."

Stunned, she took a step back, again as if he'd struck her. His wife? She felt panic bubble hot in her throat. "No." It came out in a whisper, terrified. Juliet ran to the door and across the hall without looking back.

It took her three days before she'd gathered enough strength to go back to her office. It hadn't been difficult to convince her supervisor she was ill and needed a replacement for the last day of Carlo's tour. As it was, the first thing he told her when she returned to the office days later was that she belonged in bed.

She knew how she looked—pale, hollow-eyed. But she was determined to do as she'd once promised herself. Pick up the pieces and go on. She'd never do it huddled in her apartment staring at the walls.

"Deb, I want to start cleaning up the schedule for Lia Barrister's tour in August."

"You look like hell."

Juliet glanced up from her desk, already cluttered with schedules to be photocopied. "Thanks."

"If you want my advice, you'll move your vacation by a few weeks and get out of town. You need some sun, Juliet."

"I need a list of approved hotels in Albuquerque for the Barrister tour."

With a shrug, Deb gave up. "You'll have them. In the meantime, look over these clippings that just came in on Franconi." Looking up, she noted that Juliet had knocked her container of paperclips on the floor. "Co-ordination's the first thing to go."

"Let's have the clippings."

"Well, there's one I'm not sure how to deal with." Deb slipped a clipping out of the folder and frowned at it. "It's not one of ours, actually, but some French chef who's just starting a tour."

"LaBare?"

Impressed, Deb looked up. "Yeah. How'd you know?"

"Just a sick feeling."

"Anyway, Franconi's name was brought up in the interview because the reporter had done a feature on him. This LaBare made some—well, unpleasant comments."

Taking the clipping, Juliet read what her assistant had highlighted. "Cooking for peasants by a peasant," she read in a mumble. "Oil, starch and no substance…" There was more, but Juliet just lifted a brow. She hoped Summer's plan of revenge went perfectly. "We're better off ignoring this," she decided, and dropped the clipping in the trash. "If we passed it on to Carlo, he might challenge LaBare to a duel."

"Skewers at ten paces?"

Juliet merely sent her a cool look. "What else have you got?"

"There might be a problem with the Dallas feature," she said as she gave Juliet a folder. "The reporter got carried away and listed ten of the recipes straight out of the book."

Juliet's head flew back. "Did you say ten?"

"Count 'em. I imagine Franconi's going to blow when he sees them."

Juliet flipped through the clippings until she came to it. The feature was enthusiastic and flattering. The timid Ms. Tribly had used the angle of preparing an entire meal from antipasto to dessert. Carlo's recipes from *The Italian Way* were quoted verbatim. "What was she thinking of?" Juliet muttered. "She could've used one or two without making a ripple. But this…"

"Think Franconi's going to kick up a storm?"

"I think our Ms. Tribly's lucky she's a few thousand miles away. You'd better get me legal. If he wants to sue, we'll be better off having all the facts."

After nearly two hours on the phone, Juliet felt almost normal. If there was a hollowness, she told herself it was a skipped lunch—and breakfast. If she tended to miss whole phrases that were recited to her, she told herself it was hard to keep up with legalese.

They could sue, or put Ms. Tribly's neck in a sling, both of which would create a miserable mess when she had two other authors scheduled for Dallas that summer.

Carlo would have to be told, she reflected as she hung up. It wouldn't be possible, or at least ethical, to crumple up the clipping and pretend it didn't exist as she had with the one from LaBare. The problem was whether to let legal inform him, pass it off through his editor or bite the bullet and write him herself.

It wouldn't hurt to write him, she told herself as she toyed with her pen. She'd made her decision, said her piece and stepped off the carousel. They were both adults, both professionals. Dictating his name on a letter couldn't cause her any pain.

Thinking his name caused her pain.

Swearing, Juliet rose and paced to the window. He hadn't meant it. As she had consistently for days, Juliet went over and over their last evening together.

It was all romance to him. Just flowers and candlelight. He could get carried away with the moment and not suffer any consequences. I love you—such a simple phrase. Careless and calculating. He hadn't meant it the way it had to be meant.

Marriage? It was absurd. He'd slipped and slid his way out of marriage all of his adult life. He'd known exactly how she'd felt about it. That's why he'd said it, Juliet decided. He'd known it was safe and she'd never agree. She couldn't even think about marriage for years. There was her firm to think of. Her goals, her obligations.

Why couldn't she forget the way he'd made her laugh, the way he'd made her burn? Memories, sensations didn't fade even a little with the days that had passed. Somehow they gained in intensity, haunted her. Taunted her. Sometimes—too often—she'd remember just the way he'd looked as he'd taken her face in his hands.

She touched the little heart of gold and diamonds she hadn't been able to make herself put away. More time, she told herself. She just needed more time. Perhaps she'd have legal contact him after all.

"Juliet?"

Turning from the window, Juliet saw her assistant at the door. "Yes?"

"I rang you twice."

"I'm sorry."

"There's a delivery for you. Do you want them to bring it in here?"

An odd question, Juliet thought and returned to her desk. "Of course."

Deb opened the door wider. "In here."

A uniformed man wheeled a dolly into the room.

Confused, Juliet stared at the wooden crate nearly as big as her desk. "Where do you want this, Miss?"

"Ah—there. There's fine."

With an expert move, he drew the dolly free. "Just sign here." He held out a clipboard as Juliet continued to stare at the crate. "Have a nice day."

"Oh—yes, thank you." She was still staring at it when Deb came back in with a small crowbar.

"What'd you order?"

"Nothing."

"Come on, open it." Impatient, Deb handed her the crowbar. "I'm dying."

"I can't think what it might be." Slipping the crowbar under the lid, Juliet began to pry. "Unless my mother sent on my grandmother's china like she's been threatening for the last couple of years."

"This is big enough to hold a set for an army."

"Probably all packing," Juliet muttered as she put her back into it. When the lid came off, she began to push at the heaps of packing peanuts.

"Does your grandmother's china have a trunk?"

"A what?"

"A trunk." Unable to wait, Deb shoved through the foam herself. "Good God, Juliet, it looks like an elephant."

Juliet saw the first foolish glitter and stopped thinking. "Help me get it out."

Between the two of them, they managed to lift the big, bulky piece of ceramic out of the crate and onto her desk. "That's the most ridiculous thing I've ever seen," Deb said when she caught her breath. "It's ugly, ostentatious and ridiculous."

"Yes," Juliet murmured, "I know."

"What kind of madman would send you an elephant?"

"Only one kind," Juliet said to herself and ran her hand lovingly down the trunk.

"My two-year-old could ride on it," Deb commented and spotted the card that had come out with the packing. "Here you are. Now you'll know who to press charges against."

She wouldn't take the card. Juliet told herself she wouldn't look at it. She'd simply pack the elephant back up and ship it away. No sensible woman became emotional about a useless piece of glass three feet high.

She took the card and ripped it open.

Don't forget.

She started to laugh. As the first tears fell, Deb stood beside her without a clue. "Juliet—are you all right?"

"No." She pressed her cheek against the elephant and kept laughing. "I've just lost my mind."

When she arrived in Rome, Juliet knew it was too late for sanity. She carried one bag which she'd packed in a frenzy. If it'd been lost en route, she wouldn't have been able to identify the contents. Practicality? She'd left it behind in New York. What happened next would determine whether she returned for it.

She gave the cab driver Carlo's address and settled back for her first whirlwind ride through Rome. Perhaps she'd see it all before she went home. Perhaps she was home. Decisions had to be made, but she hoped she wouldn't make them alone.

She saw the fountains Carlo had spoken of. They rose and fell, never ending and full of dreams. On impulse she made the driver stop and wait while she dashed over to one she couldn't even name. With a wish, she flung in a coin. She watched it hit and fall to join thousands of other wishes. Some came true, she told herself. That gave her hope.

When the driver barreled up to the curb and jerked to a halt she began to fumble with bills. He took pity on her and counted out the fare himself. Because she was young and in love, he added only a moderate tip.

Not daring to let herself stop her forward progress, Juliet ran up to the door and knocked. The dozens of things she wanted to say, had planned to say, jumbled in her mind until she knew she'd never be able to guarantee what would come out first. But when the door opened, she was ready.

The woman was lovely, dark, curvy and young. Juliet felt the impetus slip away from her as she stared. So soon, was all she could think. He already had another woman in his home. For a moment, she thought only to turn and walk away as quickly as she could. Then her shoulders straightened and she met the other woman's eyes straight on.

"I've come to see Carlo."

The other woman hesitated only a moment, then smiled beautifully. "You're English."

Juliet inclined her head. She hadn't come so far, risked so much to turn tail and run. "American."

"Come in. I'm Angelina Tuchina."

"Juliet Trent."

The moment she offered her hand, it was gripped. "Ah, yes, Carlo spoke of you."

Juliet nearly laughed. "How like him."

"But he never said you would visit. Come this way. We're just having some tea. I missed him when he was in America, you see, so I've kept him home from the restaurant today to catch up."

It amazed her that she could find it amusing. It ran through her mind that Angelina, and many others, were going to be disappointed from now on. The only woman who was going to catch up with Carlo was herself.

When she stepped into the salon, amusement became surprise. Carlo sat in a high-backed satin chair, having an intense conversation with another female. This one sat on his lap and was no more than five.

"Carlo, you have company."

He glanced up, and the smile he'd used to charm the child on his lap vanished. So did every coherent thought in his mind. "Juliet."

"Here, let me take this." Angelina slipped Juliet's bag from her hand while she gave Carlo a speculative look. She'd never seen him dazed by a woman before. "Rosa, come say good morning to Signorina Trent. Rosa is my daughter."

Rosa slipped off Carlo's lap and, staring all the way, came to Juliet. "Good morning, Signorina Trent." Pleased with her English, she turned to her mother with a spate of Italian.

With a laugh, Angelina picked her up. "She says you have green eyes like the princess Carlo told her of. Carlo, aren't you going to ask Miss Trent to sit down?" With a sigh, Angelina indicated a chair. "Please, be comfortable. You must forgive my brother, Miss Trent. Sometimes he loses himself in the stories he tells Rosa."

Brother? Juliet looked at Angelina and saw Carlo's warm, dark eyes. Over the quick elation, she wondered how many different ways you could feel like a fool.

"We must be on our way." Angelina walked over to kiss her still silent brother's cheek. As she did, she was already planning to drop by her mother's shop and relate the story of the American who'd made Carlo lose his voice. "I hope we meet again while you're in Rome, Miss Trent."

"Thank you." Juliet took her hand and met the smile, and all its implications, with an acknowledging nod. "I'm sure we will."

"We'll let ourselves out, Carlo. *Ciao.*"

He was still silent as Juliet began to wander around the room, stopping here to admire this, there to study that. Art of every culture was represented at its most opulent. It should've been overwhelming, museumlike. Instead it was friendly and lighthearted, just a bit vain and utterly suited to him.

"You told me I'd like your home," she said at length. "I do."

He managed to rise but not to go to her. He'd left part of himself back in New York, but he still had his pride. "You said you wouldn't come."

She moved one shoulder and decided it was best not to throw herself at his feet as she'd intended. "You know women, Franconi. They change their minds. You know me." She turned then and managed to face him. "I like to keep business in order."

"Business?"

Grateful she'd had the foresight, Juliet reached in her purse and drew out the Dallas clipping. "This is something you'll want to look over."

When she came no farther, he was forced to go over and take it from her. Her scent was there, as always. It reminded him of too much, too quickly. His voice was flat and brisk as he looked at her. "You came to Rome to bring me a piece of paper?"

"Perhaps you'd better look at it before we discuss anything else."

He kept his eyes on hers for a long, silent minute before he lowered them to the paper. "So, more clippings," he began, then stopped. "What's this?"

She felt her lips curve at the change of tone. "What I thought you'd want to see."

She thought she understood the names he called the unfortunate Ms. Tribly though they were all in fast, furious Italian. He said something about a knife in the back, balled the clipping up and heaved it in a scrubbed hearth across the room. Juliet noted, as a matter of interest, that his aim was perfect.

"What does she try to do?" he demanded.

"Her job. A bit too enthusiastically."

"Job? Is it her job to quote all my recipes? And wrong!" Incensed, he whirled around the room. "She has too much oregano in my veal."

"I'm afraid I didn't notice," Juliet murmured. "In any case, you're entitled to retribution."

"Retribution." He relished the word and made a circle of his hands. "I'll fly to Dallas and squeeze my retribution from her skinny throat."

"There's that, of course." Juliet pressed her lips together to keep the laughter in. How had she ever thought she'd convince herself she could do without him? "Or a legal suit. I've given it a lot of thought, however, and feel the best way might be a very firm letter of disapproval."

"Disapproval?" He spun back to her. "Do you simply disapprove of murder in your country? She overspiced my veal."

After clearing her throat, Juliet managed to soothe. "I understand, Carlo, but I believe it was an honest mistake all around. If you remember the interview, she was nervous and insecure. It appears to be you just overwhelmed her."

Muttering something nasty, he stuck his hands in his pockets. "I'll write to her myself."

"That might be just the right touch—if you let legal take a look at it first."

He scowled, then looked at her carefully from head to foot. She hadn't changed. He'd known she wouldn't. Somehow that fact comforted and distressed all at once. "You came to Rome to discuss lawsuits with me?"

She took her life in her hands. "I came to Rome," she said simply.

He wasn't sure he could go any closer without having to touch, and touching, take. The hurt hadn't faded. He wasn't certain it ever would. "Why?"

"Because I didn't forget." Since he wouldn't come to her, she went to him. "Because I couldn't forget, Carlo. You asked me to come and I was afraid. You said you loved me and I didn't believe you."

He curled his fingers to keep them still. "And now?"

"Now I'm still afraid. The moment I was alone, the moment I knew you'd gone, I had to stop pretending. Even when I had to admit I was in love with you, I thought I could work around it. I thought I had to work around it."

"Juliet." He reached for her, but she stepped back quickly.

"I think you'd better wait until I finish. Please," she added when he only came closer.

"Then finish quickly. I need to hold you."

"Oh, Carlo." She closed her eyes and tried to hang on. "I want to believe I can have a life with you without giving up what I am, what I need to be. But you see, I love you so much I'm afraid I'd give up everything the moment you asked me."

"*Dio,* what a woman!" Because she wasn't certain if it was a compliment or an insult, Juliet remained silent as he took a quick turn around the room. "Don't you understand that I love you too much to ask? If you weren't who you are, I wouldn't be in love with you? If I love Juliet Trent, why would I want to change her into that Juliet Trent?"

"I don't know, Carlo. I just—"

"I was clumsy." When she lifted her hands, he caught them in his to quiet her. "The night I asked you to marry me, I was clumsy. There were things I wanted to say, ways I'd wanted to say them, but it was too important. What comes easily with every woman becomes impossible with the only woman."

"I didn't think you'd meant—"

"No." Before she could resist, he'd brought her hands to his lips. "I've thought back on what I said to you. You thought I was asking you to give up your job, your home, and come to Rome to live with me. I was asking less, and much more. I should have said—Juliet, you've become my life and without you, I'm only half of what I was. Share with me."

"Carlo, I want to." She shook her head and went into his arms. "I want to. I can start over, learn Italian. There must be a publisher in Rome who could use an American."

Drawing her back by the shoulders, he stared at her. "What are you talking about, starting over? You're starting your own firm. You told me."

"It doesn't matter. I can—"

"No." He took her more firmly. "It matters a great deal, to both of us. So you'll have your own firm one day in New York. Who knows better than I how successful you'll be? I can have a wife to brag about as much as I brag about myself."

"But you have your restaurant here."

"Yes. I think perhaps you'd consider having a branch of your public relations company in Rome. Learning Italian is an excellent decision. I'll teach you myself. Who better?"

"I don't understand you. How can we share our lives if I'm in New York and you're in Rome?"

He kissed her because it had been much too long. He drew her closer because she was willing to give something he'd never have asked. "I never told you my plans that night. I've been considering opening another restaurant. Franconi's in Rome is, of course, the best. Incomparable."

She found his mouth again, dismissing any plans but that. "Of course."

"So, a Franconi's in New York would be twice the best."

"In New York?" She tilted her head back just enough to see him. "You're thinking of opening a restaurant in New York?"

"My lawyers are already looking for the right property. You see, Juliet, you wouldn't have escaped me for long."

"You were coming back."

"Once I could be certain I wouldn't murder you. We have our roots in two countries. We have our business in two countries. We'll have our lives in two countries."

Things were so simple. She'd forgotten his unending generosity. Now she remembered everything they'd already shared, thought of everything they'd yet to share. She blinked at tears. "I should've trusted you."

"And yourself, Juliet." He framed her face until his fingers slid into her hair. *"Dio,* how I've missed you. I want my ring on your finger, and yours on mine."

"How long does it take to get a license in Rome?"

Grinning, he whirled her in his arms. "I have connections. By the end of the week you'll be—what is it?—stuck with me."

"And you with me. Take me to bed, Carlo." She pressed against him, knowing she had to get still closer. "I want you to show me again what the rest of our lives will be like."

"I've thought of you, here, with me." He pressed his lips against her temple as he remembered the words she'd hurled at him on that last night. "Juliet." Troubled, he drew away, touching only her hands. "You know what I am, how I've lived. I can't take it back, nor would I if I could. There've been other women in my bed."

"Carlo." Her fingers tightened on his. "Perhaps I said foolish things once, but I'm not a fool. I don't want to be the first woman in your bed. I want to be the last. The only."

"Juliet, *mi amore,* from this moment there is only you."

She pressed his hand to her cheek. "Can you hear it?"

"What?"

"The carousel." Smiling, she held out her arms. "It's never stopped."

* * * * *